SHAKESPEARE

GREAT CLASSIC LIBRARY

SHAKESPEARE

HAMLET

MACBETH

KING LEAR

OTHELLO

LONGMEADOW
PRESS

Hamlet was first produced c. 1602
Macbeth was first produced c. 1606
King Lear was first produced c. 1606
Othello was first produced c. 1604

This collected volume published in 1995 by Longmeadow Press, 201 High Ridge Road, Stamford, CT 06904

Cover design by Les Needham
Interior design by Gwyn Lewis
ISBN 0-681-10347-7
Printed in Great Britain
First Longmeadow Press Edition
0 9 8 7 6 5 4 3 2 1

Contents

HAMLET
PRINCE OF DENMARK

DRAMATIS PERSONAE

Claudius – *King of Denmark*
Hamlet – *Son to the former, and Nephew to the present King*
Horatio – *Friend to Hamlet*
Polonius – *Lord Chamberlain*
Laertes – *his Son*
Voltimand, Cornelius, Rosencrantz, Guildenstern, Osrick – *Courtiers*
A Gentleman
A Priest
Marcellus, Bernardo – *Officers*
Francisco – *a Soldier*
Reynaldo – *Servant to Polonius*
A Captain
English Ambassadors
Ghost of Hamlet's Father
Fortinbras – *Prince of Norway*
Players
Two Clowns, Grave-diggers
Gertrude – *Queen of Denmark and Mother to Hamlet*
Ophelia – *Daughter to Polonius*
Lords, Ladies, Officers, Soldiers, Sailors, Messengers, and Attendants

SCENE

DENMARK

ACT ONE

SCENE 1 – ELSINORE. A PLATFORM BEFORE THE CASTLE.

Francisco on his post. Enter to him Bernardo.

BERNARDO Who's there?
FRANCISCO Nay, answer me: stand, and unfold yourself.
BERNARDO Long live the king!
FRANCISCO Bernardo?
BERNARDO He.
FRANCISCO You come most carefully upon your hour.
BERNARDO 'T is now struck twelve: get thee to bed, Francisco.
FRANCISCO For this relief much thanks: 't is bitter cold,
And I am sick at heart.
BERNARDO Have you had quiet guard?
FRANCISCO Not a mouse stirring.
BERNARDO Well, good night.
If you do meet Horatio and Marcellus,
The rivals of my watch, bid them make haste.
FRANCISCO I think I hear them. – Stand! Who's there?

Enter Horatio and Marcellus.

HORATIO Friends to this ground.
MARCELLUS And liegemen to the Dane.
FRANCISCO Give you good night.
MARCELLUS O! farewell, honest soldier:
Who hath reliev'd you?

FRANCISCO Bernardo has my place.
Give you good night. *[Exit.*
MARCELLUS Holla! Bernardo!
BERNARDO Say.
What! is Horatio there?
HORATIO A piece of him.
BERNARDO Welcome, Horatio: welcome, good Marcellus.
MARCELLUS What, has this thing appear'd again to-night?
BERNARDO I have seen nothing.
MARCELLUS Horatio says, 't is but our fantasy,
And will not let belief take hold of him,
Touching this dreaded sight twice seen of us.
Therefore, I have entreated him along
With us to watch the minutes of this night,
That, if again this apparition come,
He may approve our eyes, and speak to it.
HORATIO Tush, tush! 't will not appear.
BERNARDO Sit down awhile,
And let us once again assail your ears,
That are so fortified against our story,
What we two nights have seen.
HORATIO Well, sit we down,
And let us hear Bernardo speak of this.
BERNARDO Last night of all,
When yond same star, that's westward from the pole,
Had made his course to illume that part of heaven
Where now it burns, Marcellus, and myself,
The bell then beating one, –
MARCELLUS Peace! break thee off: look, where it comes again!

Enter Ghost.

BERNARDO In the same figure, like the king that's dead.
MARCELLUS Thou art a scholar; speak to it, Horatio.
BERNARDO Looks it not like the king? mark it, Horatio.
HORATIO Most like: – it harrows me with fear and wonder.
BERNARDO It would be spoke to.
MARCELLUS Question it, Horatio.
HORATIO What art thou, that usurp'st this time of night,
Together with that fair and warlike form,
In which the majesty of buried Denmark
Did sometimes march? by Heaven, I charge thee, speak!
MARCELLUS It is offended.
BERNARDO See! it stalks away.
HORATIO Stay! speak: speak, I charge thee, speak! *[Exit Ghost.*
MARCELLUS 'T is gone, and will not answer.
BERNARDO How now. Horatio? you tremble, and look pale:
Is not this something more than fantasy?
What think you on 't?
HORATIO Before my God, I might not this believe,
Without the sensible and true avouch
Of mine own eyes.
MARCELLUS Is it not like the king?
HORATIO As thou art to thyself.
Such was the very armour he had on,
When he the ambitious Norway combated.
So frown'd he once, when, in an angry parle,
He smote the sledded Polacks on the ice.
'T is strange.
MARCELLUS Thus, twice before, and just at this dead hour,
With martial stalk hath he gone by our watch.
HORATIO In what particular thought to work, I know not;

But in the gross and scope of my opinion,
This bodes some strange eruption to our state.

MARCELLUS Good now, sit down, and tell me, he that knows,
Why this same strict and most observant watch
So nightly toils the subject of the land?
And why such daily cast of brazen cannon,
And foreign mart for implements of war?
Why such impress of shipwrights, whose sore task
Does not divide the Sunday from the week?
What might be toward, that this sweaty haste
Doth make the night joint-labourer with the day,
Who is 't, that can inform me?

HORATIO That can I;
At least, the whisper goes so. Our last king,
Whose image even but now appear'd to us,
Was, as you know, by Fortinbras of Norway,
Thereto prick'd on by a most emulate pride,
Dar'd to the combat; in which our valiant Hamlet
(For so this side of our known world esteem'd him)
Did slay this Fortinbras; who, by a seal'd compact,
Well ratified by law and heraldry,
Did forfeit with his life all those his lands,
Which he stood seiz'd of, to the conqueror:
Against the which, a moiety competent
Was gaged by our king; which had return'd
To the inheritance of Fortinbras,
Had he been vanquisher; as, by the same cov'nant,
And carriage of the article design'd,
His fell to Hamlet. Now, sir, young Fortinbras,
Of unimproved mettle hot and full,
Hath in the skirts of Norway, here and there,

Shark'd up a list of landless resolutes,
For food and diet, to some enterprise
That hath a stomach in 't: which is no other
(As it doth well appear unto our state)
But to recover of us, by strong hand
And terms compulsative, those 'foresaid lands.
So by his father lost. And this, I take it,
Is the main motive of our preparations,
The source of this our watch, and the chief head
Of this post-haste and romage in the land.
BERNARDO I think, it be no other, but e'en so:
Well may it sort, that this portentous figure
Comes armed through our watch, so like the king
That was, and is, the question of these wars.
HORATIO A moth it is to trouble the mind's eye.
In the most high and palmy state of Rome,
A little ere the mightiest Julius fell,
The graves stood tenantless, and the sheeted dead
Did squeak and gibber in the Roman streets:
As stars with trains of fire and dews of blood,
Disasters in the sun; and the moist star,
Upon whose influence Neptune's empire stands,
Was sick almost to doomsday with eclipse:
And even the like precurse of fierce events –
As harbingers preceding still the fates,
And prologue to the omen coming on –
Have heaven and earth together demonstrated
Unto our climatures and countrymen. –
But, soft! behold! lo, where it comes again!

Re-enter Ghost.

I'll cross it, though it blast me. – Stay, illusion!
If thou hast any sound, or use of voice,
Speak to me:
If there be any good thing to be done,
That may to thee do ease, and grace to me,
Speak to me:
If thou art privy to thy country's fate,
Which happily foreknowing may avoid,
O, speak!
Or if thou hast uphoarded in thy life
Extorted treasure in the womb of earth,
For which, they say, you spirits oft walk in death.
[Cock crows.
Speak of it: – stay, and speak! – Stop it, Marcellus.

MARCELLUS Shall I strike at it with my partisan?

HORATIO Do, if it will not stand.

BERNARDO 'T is here!

HORATIO 'T is here!

MARCELLUS 'T is gone! *[Exit Ghost.*
We do it wrong, being so majestical,
To offer it the show of violence;
For it is, as the air, invulnerable,
And our vain blows malicious mockery.

BERNARDO It was about to speak, when the cock crew.

HORATIO And then it started, like a guilty thing
Upon a fearful summons. I have heard,
The cock, that is the trumpet to the morn,
Doth with his lofty and shrill-sounding throat
Awake the god of day; and, at his warning,
Whether in sea or fire, in earth or air,

The extravagant and erring spirit hies
To his confine; and of the truth herein
This present object made probation.

MARCELLUS It faded on the crowing of the cock.
Some say, that ever 'gainst that season comes
Wherein our Saviour's birth is celebrated,
The bird of dawning singeth all night long:
And then, they say, no spirit can walk abroad:
The nights are wholesome; then no planets strike,
No fairy takes, nor witch hath power to charm,
So hallow'd and so gracious is the time.

HORATIO So have I heard, and do in part believe it.
But, look, the morn, in russet mantle clad,
Walks o'er the dew of yon high eastern hill.
Break we our watch up; and, by my advice,
Let us impart what we have seen to-night
Unto young Hamlet; for, upon my life,
This spirit, dumb to us, will speak to him.
Do you consent we shall acquaint him with it,
As needful in our loves, fitting our duty?

MARCELLUS Let's do 't, I pray; and I this morning know
Where we shall find him most conveniently. *[Exeunt.*

SCENE II – THE SAME. A ROOM OF STATE.

Enter the King, Queen, Hamlet, Polonius, Laertes, Voltimand, Cornelius, Lords and Attendants.

KING Though yet of Hamlet our dear brother's death
The memory be green, and that it us befitted

To bear our hearts in grief, and our whole kingdom
To be contracted in one brow of woe;
Yet so far hath discretion fought with nature,
That we with wisest sorrow think on him,
Together with remembrance of ourselves.
Therefore, our sometime sister, now our queen,
The imperial jointress of this warlike state,
Have we, as 't were, with a defeated joy, –
With one auspicious, and one dropping eye,
With mirth in funeral, and with dirge in marriage,
In equal scale weighing delight and dole, –
Taken to wife: nor have we herein barr'd
Your better wisdoms, which have freely gone
With this affair along: for all, our thanks.
Now follows, that you know, young Fortinbras,
Holding a weak supposal of our worth,
Or thinking, by our late dear brother's death,
Our state to be disjoint and out of frame,
Colleagued with the dream of his advantage,
He hath not fail'd to pester us with message,
Importing the surrender of those lands
Lost by his father, with all bonds of law,
To our most valiant brother. – So much for him.
Now for ourself, and for this time of meeting.
Thus much the business is. We have here writ
To Norway, uncle of young Fortinbras, –
Who, impotent and bed-rid, scarcely hears
Of this his nephew's purpose, – to suppress
His further gait herein, in that the levies,
The lists, and full proportions, are all made
Out of his subject: and we here despatch

You, good Cornelius, and you, Voltimand,
For bearers of this greeting to old Norway;
Giving to you no further personal power
To business with the king, more than the scope
Of these dilated articles allow.
Farewell; and let your haste commend your duty.

CORNELIUS, VOLTIMAND In that, and all things, will we show our duty.

KING We doubt it nothing: heartily farewell.

[Exeunt Voltimand and Cornelius.

And now, Laertes, what's the news with you?
You told us of some suit; what is 't, Laertes?
You cannot speak of reason to the Dane,
And lose your voice: what wouldst thou beg, Laertes,
That shall not be my offer, not thy asking?
The head is not more native to the heart,
The hand more instrumental to the mouth,
Than is the throne of Denmark to thy father.
What wouldst thou have, Laertes?

LAERTES Dread my lord,
Your leave and favour to return to France;
From whence though willingly I came to Denmark,
To show my duty in your coronation,
Yet now, I must confess, that duty done,
My thoughts and wishes bend again toward France,
And bow them to your gracious leave and pardon.

KING Have you your father's leave? What says Polonius?

POLONIUS He hath, my lord, wrung from me my slow leave,
By laboursome petition; and, at last,
Upon his will I seal'd my hard consent:
I do beseech you, give him leave to go.

KING Take thy fair hour, Laertes; time be thine,
And thy best graces spend it at thy will. –
But now my cousin Hamlet, and my son, –
HAMLET *[Aside.]* A little more than kin, and less than kind.
KING How is it that the clouds still hang on you?
HAMLET Not so, my lord; I am too much i' the sun.
QUEEN Good Hamlet, cast thy nighted colour off,
And let thine eye look like a friend on Denmark.
Do not, for ever, with thy vailed lids
Seek for thy noble father in the dust:
Thou know'st, 't is common; all that lives must die,
Passing through nature to eternity.
HAMLET Ay, madam, it is common.
QUEEN If it be,
Why seems it so particular with thee?
HAMLET Seems, madam! nay, it is; I know not seems.
'T is not alone my inky cloak, good mother,
Nor customary suits of solemn black,
Nor windy suspiration of forc'd breath,
No, nor the fruitful river in the eye,
Nor the dejected behaviour of the visage,
Together with all forms, modes, shows of grief,
That can denote me truly: these, indeed, seem,
For they are actions that a man might play;
But I have that within, which passeth show,
These but the trappings and the suits of woe.
KING 'T is sweet and commendable in your nature, Hamlet,
To give these mourning duties to your father:
But, you must know, your father lost a father;
That father lost, lost his; and the survivor bound
In filial obligation, for some term,

To do obsequious sorrow: but to persever
In obstinate condolement, is a course
Of impious stubbornness; 't is unmanly grief;
It shows a will most incorrect to Heaven,
A heart unfortified, a mind impatient,
An understanding simple and unschool'd:
For what, we know, must be, and is as common
As any the most vulgar thing to sense,
Why should we, in our peevish opposition,
Take it to heart? Fie! 't is a fault to Heaven,
A fault against the dead, a fault to nature,
To reason most absurd, whose common theme
Is death of fathers, and who still hath cried,
From the first corse till he that died to-day,
'This must be so.' We pray you, throw to earth
This unprevailing woe, and think of us
As of a father; for let the world take note,
You are the most immediate to our throne;
And, with no less nobility of love,
Than that which dearest father bears his son,
Do I impart toward you. For your intent
In going back to school in Wittenberg,
It is most retrograde to our desire;
And we beseech you, bend you to remain
Here, in the cheer and comfort of our eye,
Our chiefest courtier, cousin, and our son.

QUEEN Let not thy mother lose her prayers, Hamlet:
I pray thee, stay with us; go not to Wittenberg.

HAMLET I shall in all my best obey you, madam.

KING Why, 't is a loving and a fair reply:
Be as ourself in Denmark. – Madam, come;

This gentle and unforc'd accord of Hamlet
Sits smiling to my heart: in grace whereof,
No jocund health that Denmark drinks to-day,
But the great cannon to the clouds shall tell,
And the king's rouse the heavens shall bruit again,
Re-speaking earthly thunder. Come away.

[Flourish. Exeunt King, Queen, Lords, &c., Polonius, and Laertes.

HAMLET O! that this too too solid flesh would melt,
Thaw, and resolve itself into a dew;
Or that the Everlasting had not fix'd
His canon 'gainst self-slaughter! O God! O God!
How weary, stale, flat, and unprofitable,
Seem to me all the uses of this world!
Fie on 't! O fie! 't is an unweeded garden,
That grows to seed; things rank, and gross in nature,
Possess it merely. That it should come to this!
But two months dead! – nay, not so much, not two:
So excellent a king; that was, to this,
Hyperion to a satyr; so loving to my mother,
That he might not beteem the winds of heaven
Visit her face too roughly. Heaven and earth!
Must I remember? why, she would hang on him,
As if increase of appetite had grown
By what it fed on; and yet, within a month, –
Let me not think on 't: – Frailty, thy name is woman! –
A little month; or ere those shoes were old,
With which she follow'd my poor father's body,
Like Niobe, all tears; – why she, even she,
(O God! a beast, that wants discourse of reason,
Would have mourn'd longer,) – married with my uncle,

My father's brother, but no more like my father
Than I to Hercules: within a month;
Ere yet the salt of most unrighteous tears
Had left the flushing in her galled eyes,
She married. – O most wicked speed, to post
With such dexterity to incestuous sheets!
It is not, nor it cannot come to, good;
But break, my heart, for I must hold my tongue!

Enter Horatio, Bernardo, and Marcellus.

HORATIO Hail to your lordship!
HAMLET I am glad to see you well:
Horatio, – or I do forget myself.
HORATIO The same, my lord, and your poor servant ever.
HAMLET Sir, my good friend; I'll change that name with you.
And what make you from Wittenberg, Horatio? –
Marcellus?
MARCELLUS My good lord, –
HAMLET I am very glad to see you. – Good even, sir. –
But what, in faith, make you from Wittenberg?
HORATIO A truant disposition, good my lord.
HAMLET I would not hear your enemy say so;
Nor shall you do mine ear that violence,
To make it truster of your own report
Against yourself: I know, you are no truant,
But what is your affair in Elsinore?
We'll teach you to drink deep, ere you depart.
HORATIO My lord, I came to see your father's funeral.
HAMLET I pray thee, do not mock me, fellow-student;
I think, it was to see my mother's wedding.
HORATIO Indeed, my lord, it follow'd hard upon.

HAMLET Thrift, thrift, Horatio! the funeral bak'd meats
Did coldly furnish forth the marriage tables.
'Would I had met my dearest foe in heaven
Ere I had ever seen that day, Horatio! –
My father, – methinks, I see my father.

HORATIO O! where, my lord?

HAMLET In my mind's eye, Horatio.

HORATIO I saw him once: he was a goodly king.

HAMLET He was a man, take him for all in all,
I shall not look upon his like again.

HORATIO My lord, I think I saw him yesternight.

HAMLET Saw who?

HORATIO My lord, the king your father.

HAMLET The king my father!

HORATIO Season your admiration for a while
With an attent ear, till I may deliver,
Upon the witness of these gentlemen,
This marvel to you.

HAMLET For God's love, let me hear.

HORATIO Two nights together had these gentlemen,
Marcellus and Bernardo, on their watch,
In the dead waste and middle of the night,
Been thus encounter'd: a figure like your father,
Armed at point, exactly, cap-a-pe,
Appears before them, and with solemn march
Goes slow and stately by them: thrice he walk'd,
By their oppress'd and fear-surprised eyes,
Within his truncheon's length; whilst they, distill'd
Almost to jelly with the act of fear,
Stand dumb, and speak not to him. This to me
In dreadful secrecy impart they did,

And I with them the third night kept the watch;
Where, as they had deliver'd, both in time,
Form of the thing, each word made true and good,
The apparition comes. I knew your father:
These hands are not more like.

HAMLET But where was this?

MARCELLUS My lord, upon the platform where we watched.

HAMLET Did you not speak to it?

HORATIO My lord, I did;
But answer made it none; yet once, methought,
It lifted up its head, and did address
Itself to motion, like as it would speak;
But, even then, the morning cock crew loud,
And at the sound it shrunk in haste away,
And vanish'd from our sight.

HAMLET 'T is very strange.

HORATIO As I do live, my honour'd lord, 't is true;
And we did think it writ down in our duty,
To let you know it.

HAMLET Indeed, indeed, sirs, but this troubles me.
Hold you the watch to-night?

MARCELLUS, BERNARDO We do, my lord.

HAMLET Arm'd, say you?

MARCELLUS, BERNARDO Arm'd, my lord.

HAMLET From top to toe?

MARCELLUS, BERNARDO My lord, from head to foot.

HAMLET Then, saw you not his face?

HORATIO O! yes, my lord; he wore his beaver up.

HAMLET What, look'd he frowningly?

HORATIO A countenance more in sorrow than in anger.

HAMLET Pale, or red?

HORATIO Nay, very pale.

HAMLET And fix'd his eyes upon you?

HORATIO Most constantly.

HAMLET I would I had been there.

HORATIO It would have much amaz'd you.

HAMLET Very like, very like. Stay'd it long?

HORATIO While one with moderate haste might tell a hundred.

MARCELLUS, BERNARDO Longer, longer.

HORATIO Not when I saw 't.

HAMLET His beard was grizzled? no?

HORATIO It was, as I have seen it in his life,
A sable silver'd.

HAMLET I will watch to-night:
Perchance, 't will walk again.

HORATIO I warrant it will.

HAMLET If it assume my noble father's person,
I'll speak to it, though hell itself should gape,
And bid me hold my peace. I pray you all,
If you have hitherto conceal'd this sight,
Let it be tenable in your silence still;
And whatsoever else shall hap to-night,
Give it an understanding, but no tongue:
I will requite your loves. So, fare you well.
Upon the platform, 'twixt eleven and twelve,
I'll visit you.

ALL Our duty to your honour.

HAMLET Your loves, as mine to you. Farewell.

[Exeunt Horatio, Marcellus, and Bernardo.

My father's spirit in arms! all is not well;
I doubt some foul play: 'would, the night were come!
Till then sit still, my soul. Foul deeds will rise,
Though all the earth o'erwhelm them, to men's eyes. *[Exit.*

SCENE III – A ROOM IN POLONIUS' HOUSE.

Enter Laertes and Ophelia.

LAERTES My necessaries are embark'd: farewell;
And, sister, as the winds give benefit,
And convoy is assistant, do not sleep,
But let me hear from you.
OPHELIA Do you doubt that?
LAERTES For Hamlet, and the trifling of his favour,
Hold it a fashion, and a toy in blood;
A violet in the youth of primy nature,
Forward, not permanent, sweet, not lasting,
The perfume and suppliance of a minute;
No more.
OPHELIA No more but so?
LAERTES Think it no more:
For nature, crescent, does not grow alone
In thews, and bulk; but, as this temple waxes,
The inward service of the mind and soul
Grows wide withal. Perhaps, he loves you now;
And now no soil, nor cautel, doth besmirch
The virtue of his will: but you must fear,
His greatness weigh'd, his will is not his own,
For he himself is subject to his birth:
He may not, as unvalu'd persons do,
Carve for himself; for on his choice depends
The safety and the health of the whole state;
And therefore must his choice be circumscrib'd
Unto the voice and yielding of that body,
Whereof he is the head. Then, if he says he loves you,

It fits your wisdom so far to believe it,
As he in his particular act and place
May give his saying deed; which is no further,
Than the main voice of Denmark goes withal.
Then weigh what loss your honour may sustain,
If with too credent ear you list his songs,
Or lose your heart, or your chaste treasure open
To his unmaster'd importunity.
Fear it, Ophelia, fear it, my dear sister;
And keep within the rear of your affection,
Out of the shot and danger of desire.
The chariest maid is prodigal enough,
If she unmask her beauty to the moon.
Virtue itself 'scapes not calumnious strokes:
The canker galls the infants of the spring,
Too oft before their buttons be disclos'd;
And in the morn and liquid dew of youth
Contagious blastments are most imminent.
Be wary then; best safety lies in fear:
Youth to itself rebels, though none else near.

OPHELIA I shall the effect of this good lesson keep,
As watchman to my heart. But, good my brother,
Do not, as some ungracious pastors do,
Show me the steep and thorny way to heaven,
Whilst like a puff'd and reckless libertine,
Himself the primrose path of dalliance treads,
And recks not his own read.

LAERTES O! fear me not.
I stay too long; – but here my father comes.

Enter Polonius

A double blessing is a double grace;
Occasion smiles upon a second leave.

POLONIUS Yet here, Laertes? aboard, aboard, for shame!
The wind sits in the shoulder of your sail,
And you are stay'd for. There, – my blessing with you;
[Laying his hand on Laertes' head.
And these few precepts in thy memory
See thou character. Give thy thoughts no tongue,
Nor any unproportion'd thought his act.
Be thou familiar, but by no means vulgar:
The friends thou hast, and their adoption tried,
Grapple them to thy soul with hoops of steel;
But do not dull thy palm with entertainment
Of each new-hatch'd, unfledg'd comrade. Beware
Of entrance to a quarrel; but, being in,
Bear 't, that the opposed may beware of thee.
Give every man thine ear, but few thy voice;
Take each man's censure, but reserve thy judgment.
Costly thy habit as thy purse can buy,
But not express'd in fancy; rich, not gaudy:
For the apparel oft proclaims the man;
And they in France, of the best rank and station,
Are most select and generous, chief in that.
Neither a borrower, nor a lender be;
For loan oft loses both itself and friend,
And borrowing dulls the edge of husbandry.
This above all, – to thine own self be true;
And it must follow, as the night the day,
Thou canst not then be false to any man.
Farewell; my blessing season this in thee!

LAERTES Most humbly do I take my leave, my lord.

POLONIUS The time invites you: go, your servants tend.

LAERTES Farewell, Ophelia; and remember well
What I have said to you.

OPHELIA 'T is in my memory lock'd,
And you yourself shall keep the key of it.

LAERTES Farewell. *[Exit.*

POLONIUS What is 't, Ophelia, he hath said to you?

OPHELIA So please you, something touching the Lord Hamlet.

POLONIUS Marry, well bethought:
'T is told me, he hath very oft of late
Given private time to you; and you yourself
Have of your audience been most free and bounteous.
If it be so, (as so 't is put on me,
And that in way of caution,) I must tell you,
You do not understand yourself so clearly,
As it behoves my daughter, and your honour.
What is between you? give me up the truth.

OPHELIA He hath, my lord, of late made many tenders
Of his affection to me.

POLONIUS Affection? pooh! you speak like a green girl,
Unsifted in such perilous circumstance.
Do you believe his tenders, as you call them?

OPHELIA I do not know, my lord, what I should think.

POLONIUS Marry, I'll teach you: think yourself a baby;
That you have ta'en these tenders for true pay,
Which are not sterling. Tender yourself more dearly;
Or, not to crack the wind of the poor phrase,
Running it thus, you'll tender me a fool.

OPHELIA My lord, he hath importun'd me with love,
In honourable fashion.

POLONIUS Ay, fashion you may call it; go to, go to.

OPHELIA And hath given countenance to his speech, my lord.
With almost all the holy vows of heaven.

POLONIUS Ay, springes to catch woodcocks. I do know,
When the blood burns, how prodigal the soul
Lends the tongue vows: these blazes, daughter,
Giving more light than heat, – extinct in both,
Even in their promise, as it is a-making, –
You must not take for fire. From this time,
Be somewhat scanter of your maiden presence:
Set your entreatments at a higher rate,
Than a command to parley. For Lord Hamlet,
Believe so much in him, that he is young;
And with a larger tether may he walk,
Than may be given you. In few, Ophelia,
Do not believe his vows, for they are brokers
Not of that dye which their investments show,
But mere implorators of unholy suits,
Breathing like sanctified and pious bawds,
The better to beguile. This is for all, –
I would not, in plain terms, from this time forth,
Have you so slander any moment leisure,
As to give words or talk with the Lord Hamlet.
Look to 't, I charge you; come your ways.

OPHELIA I shall obey, my lord. *[Exeunt.*

SCENE IV – THE PLATFORM.

Enter Hamlet, Horatio, and Marcellus.

HAMLET The air bites shrewdly; it is very cold.
HORATIO It is a nipping and an eager air.
HAMLET What hour now?
HORATIO I think, it lacks of twelve.
MARCELLUS No, it is struck.
HORATIO Indeed? I heard it not: it then draws near the season,
Wherein the spirit held his wont to walk.
[A flourish of trumpets, and ordnance shot off, within.
What does this mean, my lord?
HAMLET The king doth wake to-night, and takes his rouse.
Keeps wassail, and the swaggering up-spring reels;
And as he drains his draughts of Rhenish down,
The kettle-drum and trumpet thus bray out
The triumph of his pledge.
HORATIO Is it a custom?
HAMLET Ay, marry, is 't:
But to my mind, – though I am native here,
And to the manner born, – it is a custom
More honour'd in the breach than the observance.
This heavy-headed revel, east and west,
Makes us traduc'd and tax'd of other nations:
They clepe us drunkards, and with swinish phrase
Soil our addition; and, indeed, it takes
From our achievements, though perform'd at height,
The pith and marrow of our attribute.
So, oft it chances in particular men,
That for some vicious mole of nature in them,

As, in their birth, (wherein they are not guilty,
Since nature cannot choose his origin,)
By their o'ergrowth of some complexion,
Oft breaking down the pales and forts of reason;
Or by some habit, that too much o'er-leavens
The form of plausive manners; – that these men, –
Carrying, I say, the stamp of one defect,
Being nature's livery, or fortune's star, –
Their virtues else, be they as pure as grace,
As infinite as man may undergo,
Shall in the general censure take corruption
From that particular fault: the dram of bale
Doth all the noble substance off and out
To his own scandal.

Enter Ghost.

HORATIO Look, my lord! It comes.

HAMLET Angels and ministers of grace defend us!
Be thou a spirit of health, or globin damn'd,
Bring with thee airs from heaven, or blasts from hell,
Be thy intents wicked, or charitable,
Thou com'st in such a questionable shape,
That I will speak to thee. I'll call thee Hamlet,
King, father, royal Dane: O! answer me:
Let me not burst in ignorance; but tell,
Why thy canonis'd bones, hearsed in death,
Have burst their cerements; why the sepulchre,
Wherein we saw thee quietly in-urn'd,
Hath op'd his ponderous and marble jaws,
To cast thee up again. What may this mean,
That thou, dead corse, again, in complete steel,

Revisit'st thus the glimpses of the moon,
Making night hideous; and we fools of nature,
So horridly to shake our disposition,
With thoughts beyond the reaches of our souls?
Say, why is this? wherefore? what should we do?
[The Ghost beckons Hamlet.

HORATIO It beckons you to go away with it,
As if it some impartment did desire
To you alone.

MARCELLUS Look, with what courteous action
It waves you to a more removed ground:
But do not go with it.

HORATIO No, by no means.

HAMLET It will not speak; then will I follow it.

HORATIO Do not, my lord.

HAMLET Why, what should be the fear?
I do not set my life at a pin's fee;
And, for my soul, what can it do to that,
Being a thing immortal as itself?
It waves me forth again: – I'll follow it.

HORATIO What, if it tempt you toward the flood, my lord.
Or to the dreadful summit of the cliff,
That beetles o'er his base into the sea,
And there assume some other horrible form,
Which might deprive your sovereignty of reason
And draw you into madness? think of it:
The very place puts toys of desperation,
Without more motive, into every brain
That looks so many fathoms to the sea,
And hears it roar beneath.

HAMLET It waves me still: – go on, I'll follow thee.

MARCELLUS You shall not go, my lord.

HAMLET Hold off your hands.

HORATIO Be rul'd: you shall not go.

HAMLET My fate cries out,
And makes each petty artery in this body
As hardy as the Nemean lion's nerve. – *[Ghost beckons.*
Still am I call'd. – Unhand me, gentlemen, –
[Breaking from them.
By Heaven, I'll make a ghost of him that lets me: –
I say, away! – Go on, I'll follow thee.
[Exeunt Ghost and Hamlet.

HORATIO He waxes desperate with imagination.

MARCELLUS Let's follow; 't is not fit thus to obey him.

HORATIO Have after. – To what issue will this come?

MARCELLUS Something is rotten in the state of Denmark.

HORATIO Heaven will direct it.

MARCELLUS Nay, let's follow him. *[Exeunt.*

SCENE V – A MORE REMOTE PART OF THE PLATFORM.

Enter Ghost and Hamlet.

HAMLET Where wilt thou lead me? speak, I'll go no further.

GHOST Mark me.

HAMLET I will.

GHOST My hour is almost come,
When I to sulphurous and tormenting flames
Must render up myself.

HAMLET Alas, poor ghost!

GHOST Pity me not; but lend thy serious hearing
To what I shall unfold.

HAMLET Speak, I am bound to hear.
GHOST So art thou to revenge, when thou shalt hear.
HAMLET What?
GHOST I am thy father's spirit;
Doom'd for a certain term to walk the night,
And for the day confin'd to fast in fires,
Till the foul crimes, done in my days of nature,
Are burnt and purg'd away. But that I am forbid
To tell the secrets of my prison-house,
I could a tale unfold, whose lightest word
Would harrow up thy soul, freeze thy young blood,
Make thy two eyes, like stars, start from their spheres,
Thy knotted and combined locks to part,
And each particular hair to stand an-end,
Like quills upon the fretful porpentine;
But this eternal blazon must not be
To ears of flesh and blood. – List, Hamlet. O list!
If thou didst ever thy dear father love, –
HAMLET O God!
GHOST Revenge his foul and most unnatural murder.
HAMLET Murder?
GHOST Murder most foul, as in the best it is;
But this most foul, strange, and unnatural.
HAMLET Haste me to know't, that I, with wings as swift
As meditation, or the thoughts of love,
May sweep to my revenge.
GHOST I find thee apt;
And duller shouldst thou be than the fat weed
That rots itself in ease on Lethe wharf,
Wouldst thou not stir in this. Now, Hamlet, hear.
'T is given out, that, sleeping in mine orchard,

A serpent stung me; so the whole ear of Denmark
Is by a forged process of my death
Rankly abus'd; but know, thou noble youth,
The serpent that did sting thy father's life
Now wears his crown.

HAMLET O my prophetic soul!
Mine uncle!

GHOST Ay, that incestuous, that adulterate beast,
With witchcraft of his wit, with traitorous gifts,
(O wicked wit, and gifts, that have the power
So to seduce!) won to his shameful lust
The will of my most seeming-virtuous queen.
O Hamlet, what a falling-off was there!
From me, whose love was of that dignity,
That it went hand in hand even with the vow
I made to her in marriage; and to decline
Upon a wretch, whose natural gifts were poor
To those of mine!
But virtue, as it never will be mov'd,
Though lewdness court it in a shape of heaven,
So lust, though to a radiant angel link'd,
Will sate itself in a celestial bed,
And prey on garbage.
But, soft! methinks, I scent the morning air:
Brief let me be. – Sleeping within mine orchard,
My custom always in the afternoon,
Upon my secure hour thy uncle stole,
With juice of cursed hebenon in a vial,
And in the porches of mine ears did pour
The leperous distilment; whose effect
Holds such an enmity with blood of man,

That, swift as quicksilver, it courses through
The natural gates and alleys of the body;
And with a sudden vigour it doth posset
And curd, like eager droppings into milk,
The thin and wholesome blood: so did it mine;
And a most instant tetter bark'd about,
Most lazar-like, with vile and loathsome crust,
All my smooth body.
Thus was I, sleeping, by a brother's hand,
Of life, of crown, and queen, at once despatch'd;
Cut off even in the blossoms of my sin,
Unhousel'd, disappointed, unanel'd;
No reckoning made, but sent to my account
With all my imperfections on my head:
O, horrible! O, horrible! most horrible!
If thou hast nature in thee, bear it not;
Let not the royal bed of Denmark be
A couch for luxury and damned incest.
But, howsoever thou pursu'st this act,
Taint not thy mind, nor let thy soul contrive
Against thy mother aught: leave her to Heaven,
And to those thorns that in her bosom lodge,
To prick and sting her. Fare thee well at once.
The glow-worm shows the matin to be near,
And 'gins to pale his uneffectual fire:
Adieu, adieu! Hamlet, remember me. *[Exit.*

HAMLET O all you host of heaven! O earth! What else?
And shall I couple hell? O fie! – Hold, hold, my heart;
And you, my sinews, grow not instant old,
But bear me stiffly up! – Remember thee!
Ay thou poor ghost, while memory holds a seat

In this distracted globe. Remember thee!
Yea, from the table of my memory
I'll wipe away all trivial fond records,
All saws of books, all forms, all pressures past,
That youth and observation copied there;
And thy commandment all alone shall live
Within the book and volume of my brain,
Unmix'd with baser matter: yes, by Heaven!
O most pernicious woman!
O villain, villain, smiling, damned villain!
My tables, – meet it is, I set it down,
That one may smile, and smile, and be a villain;
At least, I am sure, it may be so in Denmark:
[Writing.
So, uncle, there you are. Now to my word;
It is, 'Adieu, adieu! remember me.'
I have sworn't.

HORATIO *[Within.]* My Lord! my lord!

MARCELLUS *[Within.]* Lord Hamlet!

HORATIO *[Within.]* Heaven secure him!

MARCELLUS *[Within.]* So be it!

HORATIO *[Within.]* Illo, ho, ho, my lord!

HAMLET Hillo, ho, ho, boy! come, bird, come.

Enter Horatio and Marcellus.

MARCELLUS How is't, my noble lord?

HORATIO What news, my lord?

HAMLET O, wonderful!

HORATIO Good my lord, tell it.

HAMLET No; you will reveal it.

HORATIO Not I, my lord, by Heaven.

MARCELLUS Nor I, my lord.

HAMLET How say you, then; would heart of man once think it? –
But you'll be secret?

HORATIO, MARCELLUS Ay, by Heaven, my lord.

HAMLET There's ne'er a villain dwelling in all Denmark,
But he's an arrant knave.

HORATIO There needs no ghost, my lord, come from the grave,
To tell us this.

HAMLET Why, right; you are i' the right;
And so, without more circumstance at all,
I hold it fit that we shake hands, and part:
You, as your business and desire shall point you,
For every man hath business and desire,
Such as it is; and, for mine own poor part,
Look you, I'll go pray.

HORATIO These are but wild and whirling words, my lord.

HAMLET I am sorry they offend you, heartily; yes,
'Faith, heartily.

HORATIO There's no offence, my lord.

HAMLET Yes, by Saint Patrick, but there is, Horatio,
And much offence too. Touching this vision here,
It is an honest ghost, that let me tell you:
For your desire to know what is between us,
O'ermaster 't as you may. And now, good friends,
As you are friends, scholars, and soldiers,
Give me one poor request.

HORATIO What is 't, my lord? we will.

HAMLET Never make known what you have seen tonight.

HORATIO, MARCELLUS My lord, we will not.

HAMLET Nay, but swear 't.

HORATIO In faith,
My lord, not I.

MARCELLUS Nor I, my lord, in faith.
HAMLET Upon my sword.
MARCELLUS We have sworn, my lord, already.
HAMLET Indeed, upon my sword, indeed.
GHOST *[Beneath.]* Swear.
HAMLET Ha, ha, boy! say'st thou so? art thou there, true-penny?
Come on, – you hear this fellow in the cellarage, –
Consent to swear.
HORATIO Propose the oath, my lord.
HAMLET Never to speak of this that you have seen,
Swear by my sword.
GHOST *[Beneath.]* Swear.
HAMLET *Hic et ubique?* then, we'll shift our ground. –
Come hither, gentlemen,
And lay your hands again upon my sword:
Never to speak of this that you have heard,
Swear by my sword.
GHOST *[Beneath.]* Swear.
HAMLET Well said, old mole! canst work i' the earth so fast?
A worthy pioner! – Once more remove, good friends.
HORATIO O day and night, but this is wondrous strange!
HAMLET And therefore as a stranger give it welcome.
There are more things in heaven and earth, Horatio,
Than are dreamt of in your philosophy.
But come; –
Here, as before, never, so help you mercy,
How strange or odd soe'er I bear myself, –
As I, perchance, hereafter shall think meet
To put an antick disposition on, –
That you, at such times seeing me, never shall,
With arms encumber'd thus, or this head-shake,

Or by pronouncing of some doubtful phrase,
As, 'Well, well, we know;' – 'We could, an if we would;' –
Or, 'If we list to speak;' – or, 'There be, an if they might;' –
Or such ambiguous giving out, to note
That you know aught of me: – this not to do,
So grace and mercy at your most need help you,
Swear.

GHOST *[Beneath.]* Swear.

HAMLET Rest, rest, perturbed spirit! – So, gentlemen,
With all my love I do commend me to you:
And what so poor a man as Hamlet is
May do, to express his love and friending to you,
God willing, shall not lack. Let us go in together;
And still your fingers on your lips, I pray.
The time is out of joint: – O cursed spite,
That ever I was born to set it right!
Nay, come; let's go together. *[Exeunt.*

ACT TWO

SCÈNE I – A ROOM IN POLONIUS' HOUSE.

Enter Polonius and Reynaldo.

POLONIUS Give him this money, and these notes, Reynaldo.
REYNALDO I will, my lord.
POLONIUS You shall do marvellous wisely, good Reynaldo,
Before you visit him, to make inquiry
Of his behaviour.
REYNALDO My lord, I did intend it.
POLONIUS Marry, well said: very well said. Look you, sir,
Inquire me first what Danskers are in Paris;
And how, and who, what means, and where they keep,
What company, at what expense; and finding,
By this encompassment and drift of question,
That they do know my son, come you more nearer
Than your particular demands will touch it:
Take you, as 't were, some distant knowledge of him;
As thus, – 'I know his father, and his friends,
And, in part, him:' – do you mark this, Reynaldo?
REYNALDO Ay, very well, my lord.
POLONIUS 'And, in part, him; but,' you may say, 'not well:
But if 't be he I mean, he's very wild,
Addicted so and so;' – and there put on him
What forgeries you please; marry, none so rank
As may dishonour him: take heed of that;

But, sir, such wanton, wild, and usual slips,
As are companions noted and most known
To youth and liberty.

REYNALDO As gaming, my lord.

POLONIUS Ay, or drinking, fencing, swearing, quarrelling,
Drabbing: you may go so far.

REYNALDO My lord, that would dishonour him.

POLONIUS 'Faith, no; as you may season it in the charge.
You must not put another scandal on him,
That he is open to incontinency:
That's not my meaning; but breathe his faults so quaintly,
That they may seem the taints of liberty;
The flash and outbreak of a fiery mind;
A savageness in unreclaimed blood,
Of general assault.

REYNALDO But, my good lord, –

POLONIUS Wherefore should you do this?

REYNALDO Ay, my lord,
I would know that.

POLONIUS Marry, sir, here's my drift;
And, I believe, it is a fetch of warrant:
You laying these slight sullies on my son,
As 't were a thing a little soil'd i' the working,
Mark you,
Your party in converse, him you would sound,
Having ever seen in the prenominate crimes
The youth you breathe of guilty, be assur'd,
He closes with you in this consequence:
'Good sir,' or so; or 'friend,' or 'gentleman,' –
According to the phrase, or the addition,
Of man, and country.

REYNALDO Very good, my lord.

POLONIUS And then, sir, does he this, – he does –
What was I about to say? – By the mass, I was
About to say something: – where did I leave?

REYNALDO At 'closes in the consequence,'
At 'friend or so,' and 'gentleman.'

POLONIUS At, closes in the consequence, – ay, marry:
He closes with you thus: – 'I know the gentleman;
I saw him yesterday, or t' other day,
Or then, or then; with such, or such; and, as you say,
There was he gaming; there o'ertook in 's rouse;
There falling out at tennis;' or, perchance,
'I saw him enter such a house of sale,'
Videlicet, a brothel, or so forth. –
See you now;
Your bait of falsehood takes this carp of truth:
And thus do we of wisdom and of reach,
With windlaces, and with assays of bias,
By indirections find directions out:
So, by my former lecture and advice,
Shall you my son. You have me, have you not?

REYNALDO My lord, I have.

POLONIUS God be wi' you; fare you well.

REYNALDO Good my lord!

POLONIUS Observe his inclination in yourself.

REYNALDO I shall, my lord.

POLONIUS And let him ply his music.

REYNALDO Well, my lord.

POLONIUS Farewell! *[Exit Reynaldo.*

Enter Ophelia.

How now, Ophelia? What's the matter?
OPHELIA Alas, my lord, I have been so affrighted!
POLONIUS With what, in the name of God?
OPHELIA My lord, as I was sewing in my chamber,
Lord Hamlet, – with his doublet all unbrac'd;
No hat upon his head; his stockings foul'd,
Ungarter'd, anddown-gyved to his ancle;
Pale as his shirt; his knees knocking each other;
And with a look so piteous in purport,
As if he had been loosed out of hell,
To speak of horrors, – he comes before me.
POLONIUS Mad for thy love?
OPHELIA My lord, I do not know;
But, truly, I do fear it.
POLONIUS What said he?
OPHELIA He took me by the wrist, and held me hard;
Then goes he to the length of all his arm,
And, with his other hand thus o'er his brow,
He falls to such perusal of my face,
As he would draw it. Long stay'd he so:
At last, – a little shaking of mine arm,
And thrice his head thus waving up and down, –
He rais'd a sigh so piteous and profound,
That it did seem to shatter all his bulk,
And end his being. That done, he lets me go,
And, with his head over his shoulder turn'd,
He seem'd to find his way without his eyes;
For out o' doors he went without their help,
And to the last bended their light on me.
POLONIUS Come, go with me: I will go seek the king.

This is the very ecstacy of love,
Whose violent property fordoes itself.
And leads the will to desperate undertakings,
As oft as any passion under heaven,
That does afflict our natures. I am sorry –
What! have you given him any hard words of late?

OPHELIA No, my good lord; but, as you did command,
I did repel his letters, and denied
His access to me.

POLONIUS That hath made him mad.
I am sorry that with better heed and judgment
I had not quoted him: I fear'd he did but trifle,
And meant to wrack thee; but, beshrew my jealousy!
It seems, it is as proper to our age
To cast beyond ourselves in our opinions,
As it is common for the younger sort
To lack discretion. Come, go we to the king:
This must be known; which, being kept close, might move
More grief to hide, than hate to utter love.
Come. *[Exeunt.*

SCENE II – A ROOM IN THE CASTLE.

Enter King, Queen, Rosencrantz, Guildenstern, and Attendants.

KING Welcome, dear Rosencrantz, and Guildenstern!
Moreover that we much did long to see you,
The need we have to use you did provoke
Our hasty sending. Something have you heard

Of Hamlet's transformation; so I call it,
Since not the exterior nor the inward man
Resembles that it was. What it should be,
More than his father's death, that thus hath put him
So much from the understanding of himself,
I cannot dream of: I entreat you both,
That, being of so young days brought up with him,
And since so neighbour'd to his youth and humour,
That you vouchsafe your rest here in our court
Some little time; so by your companies
To draw him on to pleasures, and to gather,
So much as from occasions you may glean,
Whether aught, to us unknown, afflicts him thus,
That, open'd, lies within our remedy.

QUEEN Good gentlemen, he hath much talk'd of you;
And, sure I am, two men there are not living,
To whom he more adheres. If it will please you
To show us so much gentry, and good will,
As to expend your time with us awhile,
For the supply and profit of our hope,
Your visitation shall receive such thanks
As fits a king's remembrance.

ROSENCRANTZ Both your majesties
Might, by the sovereign power you have of us,
Put your dread pleasures more into command
Than to entreaty.

GUILDENSTERN We both obey;
And here give up ourselves, in the full bent,
To lay our services freely at your feet,
To be commanded.

KING Thanks, Rosencrantz, and gentle Guildenstern.

QUEEN Thanks, Guildenstern, and gentle Rosencrantz:
And I beseech you instantly to visit
My too much changed son. – Go, some of you,
And bring these gentlemen where Hamlet is.

GUILDENSTERN Heavens make our presence, and our practices,
Pleasant and helpful to him!

QUEEN Ay, Amen!

[Exeunt Rosencrantz, Guildenstern, and some Attendants.

Enter Polonius.

POLONIUS The ambassadors from Norway, my good lord,
Are joyfully return'd.

KING Thou still hast been the father of good news.

POLONIUS Have I, my lord? Assure you, my good liege,
I hold my duty, as I hold my soul,
Both to my God, and to my gracious king:
And I do think (or else this brain of mine
Hunts not the trail of policy so sure
As it hath us'd to do), that I have found
The very cause of Hamlet's lunacy.

KING O! speak of that; that do I long to hear.

POLONIUS Give first admittance to the ambassadors;
My news shall be the fruit to that great feast.

KING Thyself do grace to them, and bring them in. –

[Exit Polonius.

He tells me, my sweet queen, that he hath found
The head and source of all your son's distemper.

QUEEN I doubt, it is no other but the main;
His father's death, and our o'erhasty marriage.

KING Well, we shall sift him. –

Re-enter Polonius, with Voltimand, and Cornelius.

Welcome, my good friends.
Say, Voltimand, what from our brother Norway?

VOLTIMAND Most fair return of greetings and desires.
Upon our first, he sent out to suppress
His nephew's levies; which to him appear'd
To be a preparation 'gainst the Polack:
But, better look'd into, he truly found
It was against your highness: whereat griev'd, –
That so his sickness, age, and impotence,
Was falsely borne in hand, – sends out arrests
On Fortinbras; which he, in brief, obeys,
Receives rebuke from Norway, and, in fine,
Makes vow before his uncle, never more
To give the assay of arms against your majesty.
Whereon old Norway, overcome with joy,
Gives him three thousand crowns in annual fee,
And his commission to employ those soldiers,
So levied as before, against the Polack;
With an entreaty, herein further shown. *[Giving a paper.*
That it might please you to give quiet pass
Through your dominions for this enterprise;
On such regards of safety, and allowance,
As therein are set down.

KING It likes us well;
And, at our more consider'd time, we'll read,
Answer, and think upon this business:
Meantime, we thank you for your well-took labour.
Go to your rest; at night we'll feast together:
Most welcome home! *[Exeunt Voltimand and Cornelius.*

POLONIUS This business is well ended.

My liege, and madam, to expostulate
What majesty should be, what duty is,
Why day is day, night, night, and time is time,
Were nothing but to waste night, day, and time,
Therefore, since brevity is the soul of wit,
And tediousness the limbs and outward flourishes,
I will be brief. Your noble son is mad:
Mad call I it; for, to define true madness,
What is 't, but to be nothing else but mad?
But let that go.

QUEEN More matter, with less art.

POLONIUS Madam, I swear, I use no art at all.
That he is mad, 't is true: 't is true 't is pity;
And pity 't is 't is true: a foolish figure;
But farewell it, for I will use no art.
Mad let us grant him, then; and now remains,
That we find out the cause of this effect;
Or rather say, the cause of this defect,
For this effect defective comes by cause:
Thus it remains, and the remainder thus.
Perpend.
I have a daughter; have, whilst she is mine;
Who, in her duty and obedience, mark,
Hath given me this. Now gather, and surmise.
– 'To the celestial, and my soul's idol, the most beautified Ophelia,' –
That 's an ill phrase, a vile phrase: 'beautified' is a vile phrase; but you shall hear. – Thus:
'In her excellent-white bosom, these,' &c. –

QUEEN Came this from Hamlet to her?

POLONIUS Good madam, stay awhile; I will be faithful. –

[Reads.] 'Doubt thou, the stars are fire;
Doubt, that the sun doth move;
Doubt truth to be a liar;
But never doubt, I love.

'O dear Ophelia! I am ill at these numbers: I have not art to reckon my groans; but that I love thee best, O most best! believe it. Adieu.

'Thine evermore, most dear lady, whilst this machine is to him, HAMLET.'

This in obedience hath my daughter show'd me;
And more above, hath his solicitings,
As they fell out by time, by means, and place,
All given to mine ear.

KING But how hath she
Receiv'd his love?

POLONIUS What do you think of me?

KING As of a man faithful and honourable.

POLONIUS I would fain prove so. But what might you think.
When I had seen this hot love on the wing,
(As I perceiv'd it, I must tell you that,
Before my daughter told me,) what might you,
Or my dear majesty, your queen here, think,
If I had play'd the desk, or table-book;
Or given my heart a winking, mute and dumb;
Or look'd upon this love with idle sight:
What might you think? No, I went round to work.
And my young mistress thus I did bespeak:
'Lord Hamlet is a prince, out of thy star;
This must not be:' and then I precepts gave her,
That she should lock herself from his resort,
Admit no messengers, receive no tokens.

Which done, she took the fruits of my advice;
And he, repulsed, – a short tale to make, –
Fell into a sadness; then into a fast;
Thence to a watch; thence into a weakness;
Thence to a lightness; and, by this declension,
Into the madness wherein now he raves,
And all we wail for.

KING Do you think 't is this?

QUEEN It may be, very likely.

POLONIUS Hath there been such a time, I'd fain know that,
That I have positively said, ''T is so,'
When it prov'd otherwise?

KING Not that I know.

POLONIUS Take this from this, if this be otherwise.
If circumstances lead me, I will find
Where truth is hid, though it were hid indeed
Within the centre.

KING How may we try it further?

POLONIUS You know, sometimes he walks four hours together.
Here in the lobby.

QUEEN So he does, indeed.

POLONIUS At such a time I'll loose my daughter to him:
Be you and I behind an arras then;
Mark the encounter: if he love her not,
And be not from his reason fall'n thereon,
Let me be no assistant for a state,
But keep a farm, and carters.

KING We will try it.

QUEEN But, look, where sadly the poor wretch comes reading.

POLONIUS Away! I do beseech you, both away.
I'll board him presently: – O! give me leave. –
[Exeunt King, Queen, and Attendants.

Enter Hamlet, reading.

How does my good Lord Hamlet?

HAMLET Well, God-a-mercy.

POLONIUS Do you know me, my lord?

HAMLET Excellent well; you are a fishmonger.

POLONIUS Not I, my lord.

HAMLET Then I would you were so honest a man.

POLONIUS Honest, my lord?

HAMLET Ay, sir: to be honest, as this world goes, is to be one man picked out of ten thousand.

POLONIUS That 's very true, my lord.

HAMLET For if the sun breed maggots in a dead dog, being a god kissing carrion, – Have you a daughter?

POLONIUS I have, my lord.

HAMLET Let her not walk i' the sun: conception is a blessing; but not as your daughter may conceive. – Friend, look to 't.

POLONIUS How say you by that? – *[Aside.]* Still harping on my daughter: – yet he knew me not at first: he said, I was a fishmonger. He is far gone, far gone: and truly in my youth I suffered much extremity for love; very near this. I'll speak to him again. – What do you read, my lord?

HAMLET Words, words, words.

POLONIUS What is the matter, my lord?

HAMLET Between who?

POLONIUS I mean, the matter that you read, my lord.

HAMLET Slanders, sir: for the satirical slave says here, that old men have grey beards; that their faces are wrinkled; their eyes purging thick amber and plum-tree gum; and that they have a plentiful lack of wit, together with most weak hams: all of which, sir, though I most powerfully and potently believe, yet I hold it not honesty to have it thus set down; for you yourself, sir, should be old as I am, if like a crab you could go backward.

POLONIUS *[Aside.]* Though this be madness, yet there is method in 't. – Will you walk out of the air, my lord?

HAMLET Into my grave?

POLONIUS Indeed, that is out o' the air. – *[Aside.]* How pregnant sometimes his replies are! a happiness that often madness hits on, which reason and sanity could not so prosperously be delivered of. I will leave him, and suddenly contrive the means of meeting between him and my daughter. – My honourable lord, I will most humbly take my leave of you.

HAMLET You cannot, sir, take from me anything that I will more willingly part withal; except my life, except my life, except my life.

POLONIUS Fare you well, my lord.

HAMLET These tedious old fools!

Enter Rosencrantz and Guildenstern.

POLONIUS You go to seek the Lord Hamlet; there he is.

ROSENCRANTZ *[To Polonius.]* God save you, sir!

[Exit Polonius.

GUILDENSTERN Mine honour'd lord! –

ROSENCRANTZ My most dear lord!

HAMLET My excellent good friends! How dost thou, Guildenstern? Ah, Rosencrantz! Good lads, how do ye both?

ROSENCRANTZ As the indifferent children of the earth.

GUILDENSTERN Happy, in that we are not overhappy;
On Fortune's cap we are not the very button.

HAMLET Nor the soles of her shoe?

ROSENCRANTZ Neither, my lord.

HAMLET Then you live about her waist, or in the middle of her favours?

GUILDENSTERN 'Faith, her privates we.

HAMLET In the secret parts of Fortune? O! most true; she is a strumpet. What news?

ROSENCRANTZ None, my lord, but that the world's grown honest.

HAMLET Then is doomsday near; but your news is not true. Let me question more in particular: what have you, my good friends, deserved at the hands of Fortune, that she sends you to prison hither?

GUILDENSTERN Prison, my lord?

HAMLET Denmark's a prison.

ROSENCRANTZ Then is the world one.

HAMLET A goodly one; in which there are many confines, wards, and dungeons, Denmark being one of the worst.

ROSENCRANTZ We think not so, my lord.

HAMLET Why, then 't is none to you; for there is nothing either good or bad, but thinking makes it so: to me it is a prison.

ROSENCRANTZ Why, then your ambition makes it one: 't is too narrow for your mind.

HAMLET O God! I could be bounded in a nut-shell, and count myself a king of infinite space, were it not that I have bad dreams.

GUILDENSTERN Which dreams, indeed, are ambition; for the very substance of the ambitious is merely the shadow of a dream.

HAMLET A dream itself is but a shadow.

ROSENCRANTZ Truly, and I hold ambition of so airy and light a quality, that it is but a shadow's shadow.

HAMLET Then are our beggars bodies, and our monarchs, and outstretched heroes, the beggars' shadows. Shall we to the court? for, by my fay, I cannot reason.

ROSENCRANTZ, GUILDENSTERN We'll wait upon you.

HAMLET No such matter: I will not sort you with the rest of my servants; for, to speak to you like an honest man, I am most dreadfully attended. But, in the beaten way of friendship, what make you at Elsinore?

ROSENCRANTZ To visit you, my lord; no other occasion.

HAMLET Beggar that I am, I am even poor in thanks; but I thank you: and sure, dear friends, my thanks are too dear, a halfpenny. Were you not sent for? Is it your own inclining? Is it a free visitation? Come, come; deal justly with me: come, come; nay, speak.

GUILDENSTERN What should we say, my lord?

HAMLET Why, anything, – but to the purpose. You were sent for; and there is a kind of confession in your looks, which your modesties have not craft enough to colour; I know, the good king and queen have sent for you.

ROSENCRANTZ To what end, my lord?

HAMLET That you must teach me. But let me conjure you, by the rights of our fellowship, by the consonancy of our youth, by the obligation of our ever-preserved love, and by what more dear a better proposer could charge you withal, be even and direct with me, whether you were sent for, or no.

ROSENCRANTZ What say you?

HAMLET Nay, then I have an eye of you. – If you love me, hold not off.

GUILDENSTERN My lord, we were sent for.

HAMLET I will tell you why; so shall my anticipation prevent your discovery, and your secrecy to the king and queen moult no feather. I have of late (but wherefore I know not) lost all my mirth, forgone all custom of exercises; and, indeed, it goes so heavily with my disposition, that this goodly frame, the earth, seems to me a steril promontory; this most excellent canopy, the air, look you, this brave o'erhanging firmament, this majestical roof fretted with golden fire, why, it appeareth no other thing to me than a foul and pestilent congregation of vapours. What a piece of work is a man! how noble in reason! how infinite in faculty! in form and moving, how express and admirable! in action, how like an angel! in apprehension, how like a god! the beauty of the world! the paragon of animals! And yet, to me, what is this quintessence of dust? man delights not me; no, nor woman neither, though by your smiling you seem to say so.

ROSENCRANTZ My lord, there was no such stuff in my thoughts.

HAMLET Why did you laugh then, when I said, man delights not me?

ROSENCRANTZ To think, my lord, if you delight not in man, what lenten entertainment the players shall receive from you: we coted them on the way, and hither are they coming to offer you service.

HAMLET He that plays the king shall be welcome; his majesty shall have tribute of me: the adventurous knight shall use his foil and target: the lover shall not sigh gratis: the humorous man shall end his part in peace: the clown shall make those laugh, whose lungs are tickled o' the sere: and the lady shall say her mind freely, or the blank verse shall halt for 't. What players are they?

ROSENCRANTZ Even those you were wont to take such delight in, the tragedians of the city.

HAMLET How chances it they travel? their residence, both in reputation and profit, was better both ways.

ROSENCRANTZ I think, their inhibition comes by the means of the late innovation.

HAMLET Do they hold the same estimation they did when I was in the city? Are they so followed?

ROSENCRANTZ No, indeed, they are not.

HAMLET How comes it? Do they grow rusty?

ROSENCRANTZ Nay, their endeavour keeps in the wonted pace: but there is, sir, an aery of children, little eyases, that cry out on the top of the question, and are most tyrannically clapped for 't: these are now the fashion; and so berattle the common stages (so they call them), that many wearing rapiers are afraid of goose-quills, and dare scarce come thither.

HAMLET What! are they children? who maintains them? how are they escoted? Will they pursue the quality no longer than they can sing? will they not say afterwards, if they should grow themselves to common players, (as it is most like, if their means are not better,) their writers do them wrong, to make them exclaim against their own succession?

ROSENCRANTZ 'Faith, there has been much to do on both sides; and the nation holds it no sin, to tarre them to controversy: there was, for a while, no money bid for argument, unless the poet and the player went to cuffs in the question.

HAMLET Is it possible?

GUILDENSTERN O! there has been much throwing about of brains.

HAMLET Do the boys carry it away?

ROSENCRANTZ Ay, that they do, my lord; Hercules, and his load too.

HAMLET It is not strange; for my uncle is King of Denmark, and those that would make mows at him while my father lived, give twenty, forty, fifty, an hundred ducats a-piece, for his picture in little. 'Sblood, there is something in this more than natural, if philosophy could find it out.

[Flourish of trumpets within.

GUILDENSTERN There are the players.

HAMLET Gentlemen, you are welcome to Elsinore. Your hands. Come, then; the appurtenance of welcome is fashion and ceremony: let me comply with you in this garb, lest my extent to the players (which, I tell you, must show fairly outward) should more appear like entertainment than yours. You are welcome; but my uncle-father, and aunt-mother, are deceived.

GUILDENSTERN In what, my dear lord?

HAMLET I am but mad north-north-west: when the wind is southerly, I know a hawk from a handsaw.

Re-enter Polonius.

POLONIUS Well be with you, gentlemen!

HAMLET Mark you, Guildenstern; – and you too; – at each ear a hearer: that great baby, you see there, is not yet out of his swathing-clouts.

ROSENCRANTZ Happily he's the second time come to them; for, they say, an old man is twice a child.

HAMLET I will prophesy, he comes to tell me of the players; mark it. – You say right, sir: for o' Monday morning: 't was so indeed.

POLONIUS My lord, I have news to tell you.

HAMLET My lord, I have news to tell you. When Roscius was an actor in Rome. –

POLONIUS The actors are come hither, my lord.

HAMLET Buz, buz!

POLONIUS Upon my honour, –

HAMLET Then came each actor on his ass, –

POLONIUS The best actors in the world, either for tragedy, comedy, history, pastoral, pastoral-comical, historical-pastoral, tragical-historical, tragical-comical-historical-pastoral, scene individable, or poem unlimited: Seneca cannot be too heavy, nor Plautus too light. For the law of writ, and the liberty, these are the only men.

HAMLET 'O Jephthah, judge of Israel,' what a treasure hadst thou!

POLONIUS What a treasure had he, my lord?

HAMLET Why,

'One fair daughter, and no more,
The which he loved passing well.'

POLONIUS *[Aside.]* Still on my daughter.

HAMLET Am I not i' the right, old Jephthah?

POLONIUS If you call me Jephthah, my lord, I have a daughter that I love passing well.

HAMLET Nay, that follows not.

POLONIUS What follows then, my lord?

HAMLET Why,

'As by lot, God wot,'

and then, you know,

'It came to pass, as most like it was,' –

the first row of the pious chanson will show you more; for look, where my abridgement comes.

Enter four or five Players.

You are welcome, masters; welcome, all. – I am glad to see thee well: – welcome, good friends. – O, my old friend! why, thy face is valanced since I saw thee last: com'st thou to beard me in Denmark? – What! my young lady and mistress! By 'r lady, your ladyship is nearer to heaven, than when I saw you last, by the altitude of a chopine. Pray God, your voice, like a piece of uncurrent gold, be not cracked within the ring.

Masters, you are all welcome. We 'll e'en to 't like French falconers, fly at anything we see: we'll have a speech straight. Come, give us a taste of your quality; come, a passionate speech.

1 PLAYER What speech, my good lord?

HAMLET I heard thee speak me a speech once, – but it was never acted; or, if it was, not above once; for the play, I remember, pleased not the million; 't was caviare to the general: but it was (as I received it, and others, whose judgments in such matters cried in the top of mine) an excellent play, well digested in the scenes, set down with as much modesty as cunning. I remember, one said, there were no sallets in the lines to make the matter savoury, nor no matter in the phrase that might indite the author of affectation, but called it an honest method, as wholesome as sweet, and by very much more handsome than fine. One speech in it I chiefly loved: 't was Æneas' tale to Dido; and thereabout of it especially, where he speaks of Priam's slaughter. If it live in your memory, begin at this line: – let me see, let me see: –

'The rugged Pyrrhus, like the Hyrcanian beast,'
– 't is not so; it begins with Pyrrhus: –
'The rugged Pyrrhus, – he, whose sable arms,
Black as his purpose, did the night resemble
When he lay couched in the ominous horse,
Hath now this dread and black complexion smear'd
With heraldry more dismal; head to foot
Now is he total gules; horridly trick'd
With blood of fathers, mothers, daughters, sons;
Bak'd and impasted with the parching streets,
That lend a tyrannous and a damned light
To their vile murders: roasted in wrath and fire,

And thus o'er-sized with coagulate gore,
With eyes like carbuncles, the hellish Pyrrhus
Old grandsire Priam seeks.' –
So, proceed you.

POLONIUS 'Fore God, my lord, well spoken; with good accent, and good discretion.

1 PLAYER 'Anon he finds him
Striking too short at Greeks: his antique sword,
Rebellious to his arm, lies where it falls,
Repugnant to command. Unequal match'd,
Pyrrhus at Priam drives; in rage, strikes wide;
But with the whiff and wind of his fell sword
The unnerved father falls. Then senseless Ilium,
Seeming to feel this blow, with flaming top
Stoops to his base; and with a hideous crash
Takes prisoner Pyrrhus' ear: for, lo! his sword,
Which was declining on the milky head
Of reverend Priam, seem'd i' the air to stick:
So, as a painted tyrant, Pyrrhus stood;
And, like a neutral to his will and matter,
Did nothing.
But, as we often see, against some storm,
A silence in the heavens, the rack stand still,
The bold winds speechless, and the orb below
As hush as death, anon the dreadful thunder
Doth rend the region: so, after Pyrrhus' pause,
Aroused vengeance sets him new a-work;
And never did the Cyclops' hammers fall
On Mars his armour, forg'd for proof eterne,
With less remorse than Pyrrhus' bleeding sword
Now falls on Priam. –

Out, out, thou strumpet, Fortune! All you gods,
In general synod, take away her power;
Break all the spokes and fellies from her wheel,
And bowl the round nave down the hill of heaven.
As low as to the fiends!'

POLONIUS This is too long.

HAMLET It shall to the barber's, with your beard. Pr'ythee, say on: – he's for a jig, or a tale of bawdry, or he sleeps. – Say on: come to Hecuba.

1 PLAYER 'But who, O! who had seen the mobled queen' –

HAMLET The mobled queen?

POLONIUS That's good; mobled queen is good.

1 PLAYER 'Run barefoot up and down, threat'ning the flames
With bisson rheum; a clout upon that head,
Where late the diadem stood; and, for a robe,
About her lank and all o'er-teemed loins,
A blanket, in the alarm of fear caught up;
Who this had seen, with tongue in venom steep'd,
'Gainst Fortune's state would treason have pronounc'd:
But if the gods themselves did see her then,
When she saw Pyrrhus make malicious sport
In mincing with his sword her husband's limbs,
The instant burst of clamour that she made,
(Unless things mortal move them not at all,)
Would have made milch the burning eyes of heaven,
And passion in the gods.'

POLONIUS Look, whe'er he has not turned his colour, and has tears in 's eyes! – Pr'ythee, no more.

HAMLET 'T is well; I'll have thee speak out the rest of this soon. – Good my lord, will you see the players well bestowed? Do you hear, let them be well used: for they are the abstracts, and brief chronicles, of the time: after your death you were better have a bad epitaph, than their ill report while you lived.

POLONIUS My lord, I will use them according to their desert.

HAMLET God's bodikin, man, much better: use every man after his desert, and who should 'scape whipping? Use them after your own honour and dignity: the less they deserve, the more merit is in your bounty. Take them in.

POLONIUS Come, sirs.

HAMLET Follow him, friends: we'll hear a play tomorrow. *[Exit Polonius, with all the Players except the First.]* Dost thou hear me, old friend? can you play the Murder of Gonzago?

1 PLAYER Aye, my lord.

HAMLET We'll have it to-morrow night. You could, for a need, study a speech of some dozen or sixteen lines, which I would set down and insert in 't, could you not?

1 PLAYER Ay, my lord.

HAMLET Very well. – Follow that lord: and look you mock him not. *[Exit First Player.]* My good friends *[to Rosencrantz and Guildenstern.]*, I'll leave you till night: you are welcome to Elsinore.

ROSENCRANTZ Good my lord!

HAMLET Ay, so, God be wi' ye. –

[Exeunt Rosencrantz and Guildenstern.

Now I am alone.

O, what a rogue and peasant slave am I!
Is it not monstrous, that this player here,
But in a fiction, in a dream of passion,
Could force his soul so to his whole conceit,
That, from her working, all his visage wann'd;
Tears in his eyes, distraction in 's aspect,
A broken voice, and his whole function suiting

With forms to his conceit? and all for nothing!
For Hecuba!
What's Hecuba to him, or he to Hecuba,
That he should weep for her? What would he do,
Had he the motive and the cue for passion,
That I have? He would drown the stage with tears,
And cleave the general ear with horrid speech;
Make mad the guilty, and appal the free,
Confound the ignorant; and amaze, indeed,
The very faculties of eyes and ears.
Yet I,
A dull and muddy-mettled rascal, peak,
Like John-a-dreams, unpregnant of my cause,
And can say nothing; no, not for a king,
Upon whose property, and most dear life,
A damn'd defeat was made. Am I a coward?
Who calls me villain? breaks my pate across?
Plucks off my beard, and blows it in my face?
Tweaks me by the nose? gives me the lie i' the throat,
As deep as to the lungs? Who does me this?
Ha!
'Swounds! I should take it; for it cannot be,
But I am pigeon-liver'd, and lack gall
To make oppression bitter, or, ere this,
I should have fatted all the region kites
With this slave's offal. Bloody, bawdy villain!
Remorseless, treacherous, lecherous, kindless villain!
O, vengeance!
Why, what an ass am I! Ay, sure, this is most brave;
That I, the son of a dear father murder'd,
Prompted to my revenge by heaven and hell,

Must, like a whore, unpack my heart with words,
And fall a-cursing, like a very drab,
A scullion!
Fie upon 't! foh! About, my brain! – I have heard,
That guilty creatures, sitting at a play,
Have by the very cunning of the scene
Been struck so to the soul, that presently
They have proclaim'd their malefactions;
For murder, though it have no tongue, will speak
With most miraculous organ. I'll have these players
Play something like the murder of my father,
Before mine uncle: I'll observe his looks;
I'll tent him to the quick: if he but blench,
I know my course. The spirit that I have seen
May be the devil: and the devil hath power
To assume a pleasing shape; yea, and, perhaps,
Out of my weakness, and my melancholy,
As he is very potent with such spirits,
Abuses me to damn me. I'll have grounds
More relative than this: – the play's the thing,
Wherein I'll catch the conscience of the king. *[Exit.*

ACT THREE

SCENE I – A ROOM IN THE CASTLE.

Enter King, Queen, Polonius, Ophelia, Rosencrantz, and Guildenstern.

KING And can you, by no drift of circumstance,
Get from him, why he puts on this confusion,
Grating so harshly all his days of quiet
With turbulent and dangerous lunacy?

ROSENCRANTZ He does confess, he feels himself distracted;
But from what cause he will by no means speak.

GUILDENSTERN Nor do we find him foward to be sounded,
But, with a crafty madness, keeps aloof,
When we would bring him on to some confession
Of his true state.

QUEEN Did he receive you well?

ROSENCRANTZ Most like a gentleman.

GUILDENSTERN But with much forcing of his disposition.

ROSENCRANTZ Niggard of question; but, of our demands,
Most free in his reply.

QUEEN Did you assay him
To any pastime?

ROSENCRANTZ Madam, it so fell out, that certain players
We o'er-raught on the way: of these we told him;
And there did seem in him a kind of joy
To hear of it. They are about the court;

And, as I think, they have already order
This night to play before him.

POLONIUS 'T is most true:
And he beseech'd me to entreat your majesties,
To hear and see the matter.

KING With all my heart; and it doth much content me
To hear him so inclin'd.
Good gentlemen, give him a further edge,
And drive his purpose on to these delights.

ROSENCRANTZ We shall, my lord.

[Exeunt Rosencrantz and Guildenstern.

KING Sweet Gertrude, leave us too;
For we have closely sent for Hamlet hither,
That he, as 't were by accident, may here
Affront Ophelia.
Her father, and myself, (lawful espials,)
Will so bestow ourselves, that, seeing, unseen,
We may of their encounter frankly judge;
And gather by him, as he is behav'd,
If't be the affliction of his love, or no,
That thus he suffers for.

QUEEN I shall obey you. –
And, for your part, Ophelia, I do wish,
That your good beauties be the happy cause
Of Hamlet's wildness; so shall I hope, your virtues
Will bring him to his wonted way again,
To both your honours.

OPHELIA Madam, I wish it may. *[Exit Queen.*

POLONIUS Ophelia, walk you here. – Gracious, so please you,
We will bestow ourselves. – *[To Ophelia.]* Read on this book;
That show of such an exercise may colour

Your loneliness. – We are oft to blame in this, –
'T is too much prov'd, that, with devotion's visage,
And pious action, we do sugar o'er
The devil himself.

KING *[Aside.]* O! 't is too true!
How smart a lash that speech doth give my conscience!
The harlot's cheek, beautified with plastering art,
Is not more ugly to the thing that helps it,
Than is my deed to my most painted word.
O heavy burden!

POLONIUS I hear him coming: let's withdraw, my lord.

[Exeunt King and Polonius.

Enter Hamlet.

HAMLET To be, or not to be, that is the question: –
Whether 't is nobler in the mind, to suffer
The slings and arrows of outrageous fortune;
Or to take arms against a sea of troubles,
And by opposing end them? – To die, – to sleep,
No more; – and, by a sleep, to say we end
The heart-ache, and the thousand natural shocks
That flesh is heir to, – 't is a consummation
Devoutly to be wish'd. To die, – to sleep: –
To sleep! perchance to dream: – ay, there's the rub;
For in that sleep of death what dreams may come,
When we have shuffled off this mortal coil,
Must give us pause. There's the respect,
That makes calamity of so long life:
For who would bear the whips and scorns of time,
The oppressor's wrong, the proud man's contumely,
The pangs of despis'd love, the law's delay,

The insolence of office, and the spurns
That patient merit of the unworthy takes,
When he himself might his quietus make
With a bare bodkin? who would these fardels bear,
To grunt and sweat under a weary life,
But that the dread of something after death, –
The undiscover'd country, from whose bourn
No traveller returns, – puzzles the will,
And makes us rather bear those ills we have,
Than fly to others that we know not of?
Thus conscience does make cowards of us all;
And thus the native hue of resolution
Is sicklied o'er with the pale cast of thought;
And enterprises of great pith and moment
With this regard their currents turn awry,
And lose the name of action. – Soft you, now!
The fair Ophelia. – Nymph, in thy orisons
Be all my sins remember'd.

OPHELIA Good my lord,
How does your honour for this many a day?

HAMLET I humbly thank you; well, well, well.

OPHELIA My lord, I have remembrances of yours,
That I have longed long to re-deliver;
I pray you, now receive them.

HAMLET No, not I;
I never gave you aught.

OPHELIA My honour'd lord, you know right well you did;
And, with them, words of so sweet breath compos'd,
As made the things more rich: their perfume lost,
Take these again; for, to the noble mind,
Rich gifts wax poor when givers prove unkind.
There, my lord.

HAMLET Ha, ha! are you honest?

OPHELIA My lord!

HAMLET Are you fair?

OPHELIA What means your lordship?

HAMLET That if you be honest, and fair, your honesty should admit no discourse to your beauty.

OPHELIA Could beauty, my lord, have better commerce than with honesty?

HAMLET Ay, truly; for the power of beauty will sooner transform honesty from what it is to a bawd than the force of honesty can translate beauty into his likeness: this was sometime a paradox, but now the time gives it proof. I did love you once.

OPHELIA Indeed, my lord, you made me believe so.

HAMLET You should not have believed me; for virtue cannot so inoculate our old stock, but we shall relish of it. I loved you not.

OPHELIA I was the more deceived.

HAMLET Get thee to a nunnery: why wouldst thou be a breeder of sinners? I am myself indifferent honest; but yet I could accuse me of such things, that it were better, my mother had not borne me. I am very proud, revengeful, ambitious; with more offences at my beck, than I have thoughts to put them in, imagination to give them shape, or time to act them in. What should such fellows as I do crawling between heaven and earth? We are arrant knaves, all; believe none of us. Go thy ways to a nunnery. Where's your father?

OPHELIA At home, my lord.

HAMLET Let the doors be shut upon him, that he may play the fool nowhere but in 's own house. Farewell.

OPHELIA O! help him, you sweet heavens!

HAMLET If thou dost marry, I'll give thee this plague for thy dowry: be thou as chaste as ice, as pure as snow, thou shalt not escape calumny. Get thee to a nunnery; go, farewell. Or, if thou wilt needs marry, marry a fool; for wise men know well enough what monsters you make of them. To a nunnery, go; and quickly too. Farewell.

OPHELIA O heavenly powers, restore him!

HAMLET I have heard of your paintings too, well enough: God hath given you one face, and you make yourselves another: you jig, you amble, and you lisp, and nickname God's creatures, and make your wantonness your ignorance. Go to; I'll no more on 't: it hath made me mad. I say, we will have no more marriages: those that are married already, all but one, shall live; the rest shall keep as they are. To a nunnery, go. *[Exit.*

OPHELIA O, what a noble mind is here o'erthrown!
The courtier's, soldier's, scholar's, eye, tongue, sword:
The expectancy and rose of the fair state,
The glass of fashion, and the mould of form,
The observ'd of all observers, quite, quite down!
And I, of ladies most deject and wretched,
That suck'd the honey of his music vows,
Now see that noble and most sovereign reason,
Like sweet bells jangled, out of tune and harsh;
That unmatch'd form and feature of blown youth
Blasted with ecstacy. O, woe is me,
To have seen what I have seen, see what I see!

Re-enter King and Polonius.

KING Love! his affections do not that way tend;
Nor what he spake, though it lack'd form a little,

Was not like madness. There's something in his soul,
O'er which his melancholy sits on brood;
And, I do doubt, the hatch, and the disclose,
Will be some danger: which for to prevent,
I have, in quick determination,
Thus set it down. He shall with speed to England,
For the demand of our neglected tribute:
Haply, the seas, and countries different,
With variable objects, shall expel
This something-settled matter in his heart:
Whereon his brains still beating puts him thus
From fashion of himself. What think you on 't?

POLONIUS It shall do well: but yet do I believe,
The origin and commencement of his grief
Sprung from neglected love, – How now, Ophelia!
You need not tell us what Lord Hamlet said;
We heard it all. – My lord, do as you please;
But, if you hold it fit, after the play,
Let his queen mother all alone entreat him
To show his griefs: let her be round with him;
And I'll be plac'd, so please you, in the ear
Of all their conference. If she find him not,
To England send him; or confine him, where
Your wisdom best shall think.

KING It shall be so:
Madness in great ones must not unwatch'd go. *[Exeunt.*

SCENE II – A HALL IN THE SAME.

Enter Hamlet and certain Players.

HAMLET Speak the speech, I pray you, as I pronounced it to you, trippingly on the tongue; but if you mouth it, as many of your players do, I have as lief the town-crier spoke my lines. Nor do not saw the air too much with your hand, thus; but use all gently: for in the very torrent, tempest, and (as I may say) the whirlwind of passion, you must acquire and beget a temperance, that may give it smoothness. O! it offends me to the soul, to hear a robustious periwig-pated fellow tear a passion to tatters, to very rags, to split the ears of the groundlings; who, for the most part, are capable of nothing but inexplicable dumb-shows, and noise: I would have such a fellow whipped for o'erdoing Termagant; it out-herods Herod: pray you, avoid it.

1 PLAYER I warrant your honour.

HAMLET Be not too tame neither, but let your own discretion be your tutor: suit the action to the word, the word to the action, with this special observance, that you o'erstep not the modesty of nature; for anything so overdone is from the purpose of playing, whose end, both at the first, and now, was, and is, to hold, as 't were, the mirror up to nature; to show virtue her own feature, scorn her own image, and the very age and body of the time, his form and pressure. Now, this overdone, or come tardy off, though it make the unskilful laugh, cannot but make the judicious grieve; the censure of the which one must, in your allowance, o'erweigh a whole theatre of others. O! there be players, that I have seen play, – and heard others praise, and that highly, – not to speak it profanely, that, neither having the accent of Christians, nor the gait of Christian, pagan, nor man, have so strutted, and bellowed, that I have thought some of nature's journeymen had made men, and not made them well, they imitated humanity so abominably.

1 PLAYER I hope, we have reformed that indifferently with us.

HAMLET O! reform it altogether. And let those that play your clowns speak no more than is set down for them: for there be of them, that will themselves laugh, to set on some quantity of barren spectators to laugh too; though, in the meantime, some necessary question of the play be then to be considered: that 's villainous, and shows a most pitiful ambition in the fool that uses it. Go, make you ready. – *[Exeunt Players.*

Enter Polonius, Rosencrantz, and Guildenstern.

How now, my lord? will the king hear this piece of work?

POLONIUS And the queen too, and that presently.

HAMLET Bid the players make haste. – *[Exit Polonius.*
Will you two help to hasten them?

ROSENCRANTZ, GUILDENSTERN We will, my lord.
[Exeunt Rosencrantz and Guildenstern.

HAMLET What, ho! Horatio!

Enter Horatio.

HORATIO Here, sweet lord, at your service.

HAMLET Horatio, thou art e'en as just a man
As e'er my conversation cop'd withal.

HORATIO O! my dear lord, –

HAMLET Nay, do not think I flatter;
For what advancement may I hope from thee,
That no revenue hast but thy good spirits,
To feed and clothe thee? Why should the poor be flatter'd?

No; let the candied tongue lick absurd pomp,
And crook the pregnant hinges of the knee,
Where thrift may follow fawning. Dost thou hear?
Since my dear soul was mistress of her choice,
And could of men distinguish, her election
Hath seal'd thee for herself: for thou hast been
As one, in suffering all, that suffers nothing
A man, that Fortune's buffets and rewards
Hast ta'en with equal thanks: and bless'd are those,
Whose blood and judgment are so well co-mingled,
That they are not a pipe for Fortune's finger
To sound what stop she please. Give me that man
That is not passion's slave, and I will wear him
In my heart's core, ay, in my heart of heart,
As I do thee. – Something too much of this. –
There is a play to-night before the king;
One scene of it comes near the circumstance,
Which I have told thee, of my father's death:
I pr'ythee, when thou seest that act afoot,
Even with the very comment of thy soul
Observe mine uncle: if his occulted guilt
Do not itself unkennel in one speech,
It is a damned ghost that we have seen,
And my imaginations are as foul
As Vulcan's stithy. Give him heedful note:
For I mine eyes will rivet to his face;
And, after, we will both our judgments join
In censure of his seeming.

HORATIO Well, my lord:
If he steal aught, the whilst this play is playing,
And 'scape detecting, I will pay the theft.

HAMLET They are coming to the play: I must be idle;
Get you a place.

Danish march. A flourish. Enter King, Queen, Polonius, Ophelia, Rosencrantz, Guildenstern, and others.

KING How fares our cousin Hamlet?

HAMLET Excellent, i' faith; of the chameleon's dish: I eat the air, promise-crammed. You cannot feed capons so.

KING I have nothing with this answer, Hamlet: these words are not mine.

HAMLET No, nor mine now. – *[To Polonius.]* My lord, you played once in the university, you say?

POLONIUS That did I, my lord; and was accounted a good actor.

HAMLET And what did you enact?

POLONIUS I did enact Julius Cæsar: I was killed i' the Capitol; Brutus killed me.

HAMLET It was a brute part of him to kill so capital a calf there. – Be the players ready?

ROSENCRANTZ Ay, my lord; they stay upon your patience.

QUEEN Come hither, my good Hamlet, sit by me.

HAMLET No, good mother, here's metal more attractive.

POLONIUS O ho! do you mark that?

HAMLET Lady, shall I lie in your lap?

[Lying down at Ophelia's feet.

OPHELIA No, my lord.

HAMLET I mean, my head upon your lap?

OPHELIA Ay, my lord.

HAMLET Do you think, I meant country matters?

OPHELIA I think nothing, my lord.

HAMLET That's a fair thought to lie between maids' legs.

OPHELIA What is, my lord?

HAMLET Nothing.

OPHELIA You are merry, my lord.

HAMLET Who, I?

OPHELIA Ay, my lord.

HAMLET O God! your only jig-maker. What should a man do, but be merry? for, look you, how cheerfully my mother looks, and my father died within 's two hours.

OPHELIA Nay, 't is twice two months, my lord.

HAMLET So long? Nay then, let the devil wear black, for I'll have a suit of sables. O heavens! die two months ago, and not forgotten yet? Then there 's hope, a great man's memory may outlive his life half a year; but, by 'r lady, he must build churches then, or else shall he suffer not thinking on, with the hobby-horse; whose epitaph is, 'For, O! for, O! the hobby-horse is forgot.'

Hautboys play. The dumb-show enters.

Enter a King and a Queen, very lovingly; the Queen embracing him, and he her. She kneels, and makes show of protestation unto him. He takes her up, and declines his head upon her neck; lays him down upon a bank of flowers; she, seeing him asleep, leaves him. Anon comes in a fellow, takes off his crown, kisses it, and pours poison in the King's ears, and exit. The Queen returns, finds the King dead, and makes passionate action. The Poisoner, with some two or three Mutes, comes in again, seeming to lament with her. The dead body is carried away. The Poisoner woos the Queen with gifts: she seems loath and unwilling awhile; but in the end accepts his love.

[Exeunt.

OPHELIA What means this, my lord?

HAMLET Marry, this is miching mallecho; it means mischief.

OPHELIA Belike, this show imports the argument of the play.

Enter Prologue.

HAMLET We shall know by this fellow: the players cannot keep counsel; they'll tell all.

OPHELIA Will he tell us what this show meant?

HAMLET Ay, or any show that you will show him: be not you ashamed to show, he'll not shame to tell you what it means.

OPHELIA You are naught, you are naught. I'll mark the play.

PROLOGUE For us, and for our tragedy,
Here stooping to your clemency.
We beg your hearing patiently. *[Exit.*

HAMLET Is this a prologue, or the posy of a ring?

OPHELIA 'T is brief, my lord.

HAMLET As woman's love.

Enter a King and a Queen.

P. KING Full thirty times hath Phœbus' cart gone round
Neptune's salt wash, and Tellus' orbed ground;
And thirty dozen moons, with borrow'd sheen,
About the world have times twelve thirties been;
Since love our hearts, and Hymen did our hands,
United commutual in most sacred bands.

P. QUEEN So many journeys may the sun and moon
Make us again count o'er, ere love be done.
But, woe is me! you are so sick of late,
So far from cheer, and from your former state,
That I distrust you. Yet, though I distrust,
Discomfort you, my lord, it nothing must;
For women's fear and love holds quantity,
In neither aught, or in extremity.
Now, what my love is, proof hath made you know;
And as my love is siz'd, my fear is so.

Where love is great, the littlest doubts are fear;
Where little fears grow great, great love grows there.

P. KING 'Faith, I must leave thee, love, and shortly too;
My operant powers their functions leave to do:
And thou shalt live in this fair world behind,
Honour'd, belov'd; and, haply, one as kind
For husband shalt thou –

P. QUEEN O, confound the rest!
Such love must needs be treason in my breast:
In second husband let me be accurst;
None wed the second, but who kill'd the first.

HAMLET *[Aside.]* Wormwood, wormwood.

P. QUEEN The instances, that second marriage move,
Are base respects of thrift, but none of love:
A second time I kill my husband dead,
When second husband kisses me in bed.

P. KING I do believe you think what now you speak;
But what we do determine oft we break.
Purpose is but the slave of memory,
Of violent birth, but poor validity;
Which now, like fruit unripe, sticks on the tree,
But fall unshaken, when they mellow be.
Most necessary 't is, that we forget
To pay ourselves what to ourselves is debt:
What to ourselves in passion we propose,
The passion ending, doth the purpose lose.
The violence of either grief or joy
Their own enactures with themselves destroy:
Where joy most revels, grief doth most lament;
Grief joys, joy grieves, on slender accident.
This world is not for aye; nor 't is not strange,

That even our love should with our fortunes change:
For 't is a question left us yet to prove,
Whether love lead fortune, or else fortune love.
The great man down, you mark, his favourite flies;
The poor advanc'd makes friends of enemies.
And hitherto doth love on fortune tend:
For who not needs shall never lack a friend;
And who in want a hollow friend doth try,
Directly seasons him his enemy.
But, orderly to end where I begun,
Our wills and fates do so contrary run,
That our devices still are overthrown;
Our thoughts are ours, their ends none of our own:
So think thou wilt no second husband wed;
But die thy thoughts, when thy first lord is dead.

P. QUEEN Nor earth to me give food, nor heaven light!
Sport and repose lock from me, day and night!
To desperation turn my trust and hope!
An anchor's cheer in prison be my scope!
Each opposite, that blanks the face of joy,
Meet what I would have well, and it destroy!
Both here, and hence, pursue me lasting strife,
If, once a widow, ever I be wife!

HAMLET If she should break it now?

P. KING 'T is deeply sworn. Sweet, leave me here awhile:
My spirits grow dull, and fain I would beguile
The tedious day with sleep. *[Sleeps.*

P. QUEEN Sleep rock thy brain;
And never come mischance between us twain! *[Exit.*

HAMLET Madam, how like you this play?

QUEEN The lady protests too much, methinks.

HAMLET O! but she'll keep her word.

KING Have you heard the argument? Is there no offence in 't?

HAMLET No, no; they do but jest, poison in jest: no offence i'the world.

KING What do you call the play?

HAMLET The Mouse-trap. Marry, how? Tropically. This play is the image of a murder done in Vienna: Gonzago is the duke's name; his wife, Baptista. You shall see anon; 't is a knavish piece of work: but what of that? your majesty, and we, that have free souls, it touches us not: let the galled jade wince, our withers are unwrung.

Enter Lucianus.

This is one Lucianus, nephew to the king.

OPHELIA You are a good chorus, my lord.

HAMLET I could interpret between you and your love, if I could see the puppets dallying.

OPHELIA You are keen, my lord, you are keen.

HAMLET It would cost you a groaning to take off my edge.

OPHELIA Still better, and worse.

HAMLET So you must take your husbands. – Begin, murderer: pox, leave thy damnable faces, and begin. Come: – the croaking raven doth bellow for revenge.

LUCIANUS Thoughts black, hands apt, drugs fit, and time agreeing;
Confederate season, else no creature seeing;
Thou mixture rank, of midnight weeds collected,
With Hecate's ban thrice blasted, thrice infected,
Thy natural magic and dire property,
On wholesome life usurp immediately.

[Pours the poison into the Sleeper's ears.

HAMLET He poisons him i' the garden for 's estate. His name 's Gonzago: the story is extant and writ in choice Italian. You shall see anon, how the murderer gets the love of Gonzago's wife.

OPHELIA The king rises.

HAMLET What! frighted with false fire?

QUEEN How fares my lord?

POLONIUS Give o'er the play.

KING Give me some light! – away!

ALL Lights, lights, lights! *[Exeunt all but Hamlet and Horatio.*

HAMLET Why, let the strucken deer go weep,
The hart ungalled play;
For some must watch, while some must sleep:
Thus runs the world away.
Would not this, sir, and a forest of feathers, (if the rest of my fortunes turn Turk with me) with two Provincial roses on my razed shoes, get me a fellowship in a cry of players, sir?

HORATIO Half a share.

HAMLET A whole one, I.
For thou dost know, O Damon dear,
This realm dismantled was
Of Jove himself; and now reigns here
A very, very – pajock.

HORATIO You might have rhymed.

HAMLET O good Horatio! I'll take the ghost's word for a thousand pound. Didst perceive?

HORATIO Very well, my lord.

HAMLET Upon the talk of the poisoning, –

HORATIO I did very well note him.

HAMLET Ah, ha! – Come, some music! come, the recorders!
For if the king like not the comedy.

Why then, belike, – he likes it not, perdy. –
Come, some music!

Enter Rosencrantz and Guildenstern.

GUILDENSTERN Good my lord, vouchsafe me a word with you.

HAMLET Sir, a whole history.

GUILDENSTERN The king, sir, –

HAMLET Ay, sir, what of him?

GUILDENSTERN Is, in his retirement, marvellous distempered.

HAMLET With drink, sir?

GUILDENSTERN No, my lord, rather with choler.

HAMLET Your wisdom should show itself more richer, to signify this to his doctor; for, for me to put him to his purgation, would, perhaps, plunge him into far more choler.

GUILDENSTERN Good my lord, put your discourse into some frame, and start not so wildly from my affair.

HAMLET I am tame, sir; – pronounce.

GUILDENSTERN The queen, your mother, in most great affliction of spirit, hath sent me to you.

HAMLET You are welcome.

GUILDENSTERN Nay, good my lord, this courtesy is not of the right breed. If it shall please you to make me a wholesome answer, I will do your mother's commandment; if not, your pardon and my return shall be the end of my business.

HAMLET Sir, I cannot.

GUILDENSTERN What, my lord?

HAMLET Make you a wholesome answer; my wit's diseased; but, sir, such answer as I can make, you shall command; or, rather, as you say, my mother: therefore no more, but to the matter. My mother, you say, –

ROSENCRANTZ Then, thus she says. Your behaviour hath struck her into amazement and admiration.

HAMLET O wonderful son, that can so astonish a mother! – But is there no sequel at the heels of this mother's admiration? impart.

ROSENCRANTZ She desires to speak with you in her closet, ere you go to bed.

HAMLET We shall obey, were she ten times our mother. Have you any further trade with us?

ROSENCRANTZ My lord, you once did love me.

HAMLET And do still, by these pickers and stealers.

ROSENCRANTZ Good my lord, what is your cause of distemper? you do freely bar the door of your own liberty, if you deny your griefs to your friend.

HAMLET Sir, I lack advancement.

ROSENCRANTZ How can that be, when you have the voice of the king himself for your succession in Denmark?

HAMLET Ay, sir, but 'While the grass grows;' – the proverb is something musty.

Enter Players with recorders.

O! the recorders: let me see one. – To withdraw with you. – Why do you go about to recover the wind of me, as if you would drive me into a toil?

GUILDENSTERN O, my lord, if my duty be too bold, my love is too unmannerly.

HAMLET I do not well understand that. Will you play upon this pipe?

GUILDENSTERN My lord, I cannot.

HAMLET I pray you.

GUILDENSTERN Believe me, I cannot.

HAMLET I do beseech you.

GUILDENSTERN I know no touch of it, my lord.

HAMLET It is as easy as lying: govern these vantages with your finger and thumb, give it breath with your mouth, and it will discourse most eloquent music. Look you, these are the stops.

GUILDENSTERN But these cannot I command to any utterance of harmony: I have not the skill.

HAMLET Why, look you now, how unworthy a thing you make of me. You would play upon me; you would seem to know my stops; you would pluck out the heart of my mystery; you would sound me from my lowest note to the top of my compass; and there is much music, excellent voice, in this little organ, yet cannot you make it speak. 'Sblood! do you think I am easier to be played on than a pipe? Call me what instrument you will, though you can fret me, you cannot play upon me. –

Enter Polonius.

God bless you, sir!

POLONIUS My lord, the queen would speak with you, and presently.

HAMLET Do you see yonder cloud, that's almost in shape of a camel?

POLONIUS By the mass, and 't is like a camel, indeed.

HAMLET Methinks, it is like a weasel.

POLONIUS It is backed like a weasel.

HAMLET Or, like a whale?

POLONIUS Very like a whale.

HAMLET Then will I come to my mother by-and-by. They fool me to the top of my bent. – I will come by-and-by.

POLONIUS I will say so. *[Exit.*

HAMLET By-and-by is easily said. – Leave me, friends.

[Exeunt Rosencrantz, Guildenstern, Horatio, &c.

'T is now the very witching time of night,
When churchyards yawn, and hell itself breathes out
Contagion to this world: now could I drink hot blood,
And do such bitter business as the day
Would quake to look on. Soft! now to my mother.
O heart! lose not thy nature; let not ever
The soul of Nero enter this firm bosom:
Let me be cruel, not unnatural.
I will speak daggers to her, but use none;
My tongue and soul in this be hypocrites:
How in my words soever she be shent,
To give them seals never, my soul, consent!

[Exit.

SCENE III – A ROOM IN THE SAME.

Enter King, Rosencrantz, and Guildenstern.

KING I like him not; nor stands it safe with us,
To let his madness range. Therefore, prepare you:
I your commission will forthwith despatch,
And he to England shall along with you.
The terms of our estate may not endure
Hazard so dangerous, as doth hourly grow
Out of his lunacies.

GUILDENSTERN We will ourselves provide.
Most holy and religious fear it is,
To keep those many many bodies safe,
That live and feed upon your majesty.

ROSENCRANTZ The single and peculiar life is bound,
With all the strength and armour of the mind,
To keep itself from noyance; but much more

That spirit, upon whose weal depends and rests
The lives of many. The cease of majesty
Dies not alone; but, like a gulf, doth draw
What's near it with it: it is a massy wheel,
Fix'd on the summit of the highest mount,
To whose huge spokes ten thousand lesser things
Are mortis'd and adjoin'd; which, when it falls,
Each small annexment, petty consequence,
Attends the boisterous ruin. Never alone
Did the king sigh, but with a general groan.

KING Arm you, I pray you, to this speedy voyage;
For we will fetters put upon this fear,
Which now goest too free-footed.

ROSENCRANTZ, GUILDENSTERN We will haste us.

[Exeunt Rosencrantz and Guildenstern.

Enter Polonius.

POLONIUS My lord, he's going to his mother's closet.
Behind the arras I'll convey myself,
To hear the process: I'll warrant, she'll tax him home;
And, as you said, and wisely was it said,
'T is meet that some more audience, than a mother,
Since nature makes them partial, should o'erhear
The speech, of vantage. Fare you well, my liege:
I'll call upon you ere you go to bed,
And tell you what I know.

KING Thanks, dear my lord.

[Exit Polonius.

O! my offence is rank, it smells to heaven;
It hath the primal eldest curse upon 't,
A brother's murder! – Pray can I not,

Though inclination be as sharp as will:
My stronger guilt defeats my strong intent;
And, like a man a double business bound,
I stand in pause where I shall first begin,
And both neglect. What if this cursed hand
Were thicker than itself with brother's blood,
Is there not rain enough in the sweet heavens,
To wash it white as snow? Whereto serves mercy,
But to confront the visage of offence?
And what's in prayer, but this two-fold force, –
To be forestalled, ere we come to fall,
Or pardon'd, being down? Then, I'll look up:
My fault is past. But, O! what form of prayer
Can serve my turn? Forgive me my foul murder! –
That cannot be; since I am still possess'd
Of those effects for which I did the murder,
My crown, mine own ambition, and my queen.
May one be pardon'd, and retain the offence?
In the corrupted currents of this world,
Offence's gilded hand may shove by justice;
And oft 't is seen, the wicked prize itself
Buys out the law: but 't is not so above;
There is no shuffling, there the action lies
In his true nature; and we ourselves compell'd,
Even to the teeth and forehead of our faults,
To give in evidence. What then? what rests?
Try what repentance can: what can it not?
Yet what can it, when one can not repent?
O wretched state! O bosom, black as death!
O limed soul, that, struggling to be free,
Art more engaged! Help, angels! make assay:

Bow, stubborn knees; and, heart, with strings of steel,
Be soft as sinews of the new-born babe.
All may be well. *[Retires and kneels.*

Enter Hamlet.

HAMLET Now might I do it, pat, now he is praying;
And now I'll do 't: – and so he goes to heaven;
And so am I reveng'd? That would be scann'd:
A villain kills my father; and, for that,
I, his sold son, do this same villain send
To heaven.
Why, this is hire and salary, not revenge.
He took my father grossly, full of bread;
With all his crimes broad blown, as flush as May;
And how his audit stands, who knows, save Heaven?
But in our circumstance and course of thought,
'T is heavy with him. And am I then reveng'd,
To take him in the purging of his soul,
When he is fit and season'd for his passage?
No.
Up, sword; and know thou a more horrid hent:
When he is drunk, asleep, or in his rage;
Or in the incestuous pleasures of his bed;
At gaming, swearing; or about some act,
That has no relish of salvation in 't;
Then trip him, that his heels may kick at heaven,
And that his soul may be as damn'd, and black,
As hell, whereto it goes. My mother stays:
This physic but prolongs thy sickly days. *[Exit.*

The King rises and advances.

KING My words fly up, my thoughts remain below:
Words without thoughts never to heaven go. *[Exit.*

SCENE IV – A ROOM IN THE SAME.

Enter Queen and Polonius.

POLONIUS He will come straight. Look, you lay home to him;
Tell him, his pranks have been too broad to bear with,
And that your grace hath screen'd and stood between
Much heat and him. I'll silence me e'en here.
Pray you, be round with him.
HAMLET *[Within.]* Mother, mother, mother!
QUEEN I'll warrant you; fear me not:
Withdraw, I hear him coming.
[Polonius hides himself behind the arras.

Enter Hamlet.

HAMLET Now, mother, what's the matter?
QUEEN Hamlet, thou hast thy father much offended.
HAMLET Mother, you have my father much offended.
QUEEN Come, come; you answer with an idle tongue.
HAMLET Go, go; you question with a wicked tongue.
QUEEN Why, how now, Hamlet?
HAMLET What's the matter now?
QUEEN Have you forgot me?
HAMLET No, by the rood, not so:
You are the queen, your husband's brother's wife;
But – 'would you were not so! – you are my mother.

QUEEN Nay then, I'll set those to you that can speak.

HAMLET Come, come, and sit you down; you shall not budge:
You go not, till I set you up a glass
Where you may see the inmost part of you.

QUEEN What wilt thou do? thou wilt not murder me?
Help, help, ho!

POLONIUS *[Behind.]* What, ho! help, help, help!

HAMLET How now! a rat? *[Draws.]* Dead! for a ducat, dead!
[Makes a pass through the arras.

POLONIUS *[Behind.]* O! I am slain. *[Falls, and dies.*

QUEEN O me! what hast thou done?

HAMLET Nay, I know not:
Is it the king?

QUEEN O, what a rash and bloody deed is this!

HAMLET A bloody deed; almost as bad, good mother,
As kill a king, and marry with his brother.

QUEEN As kill a king!

HAMLET Ay, lady, 't was my word.
[Lifts up the arras, and draws forth Polonius.
Thou wretched, rash, intruding fool, farewell!
I took thee for thy better; take thy fortune:
Thou find'st, to be too busy is some danger. –
Leave wringing of your hands. Peace! sit you down,
And let me wring your heart: for so I shall,
If it be made of penetrable stuff;
If damned custom have not braz'd it so,
That it is proof and bulwark against sense.

QUEEN What have I done, that thou dar'st wag thy tongue
In noise so rude against me?

HAMLET Such an act.
That blurs the grace and blush of modesty;

Calls virtue, hypocrite; takes off the rose
From the fair forehead of an innocent love,
And sets a blister there; makes marriage vows
As false as dicers' oaths: O! such a deed,
As from the body of contraction plucks
The very soul; and sweet religion makes
A rhapsody of words: heaven's face doth glow;
Yea, this solidity and compound mass,
With tristful visage, as against the doom,
Is thought-sick at the act.

QUEEN Ah me! what act,
That roars so loud, and thunders in the index?

HAMLET Look here, upon this picture, and on this;
The counterfeit presentment of two brothers.
See, what a grace was seated on this brow:
Hyperion's curls; the front of Jove himself;
An eye like Mars, to threaten and command;
A station like the herald Mercury,
New-lighted on a heaven-kissing hill;
A combination, and a form, indeed,
Where every god did seem to set his seal,
To give the world assurance of a man.
This was your husband: look you now, what follows.
Here is your husband; like a mildew'd ear.
Blasting his wholesome brother. Have you eyes?
Could you on this fair mountain leave to feed,
And batten on this moor? Ha! have you eyes?
You cannot call it love; for, at your age,
The hey-day in the blood is tame, it's humble,
And waits upon the judgment; and what judgment
Would step from this to this? Sense, sure, you have,

Else could you not have motion; but, sure, that sense
Is apoplex'd; for madness would not err,
Nor sense to ecstacy was ne'er so thrall'd,
But it reserv'd some quantity of choice,
To serve in such a difference. What devil was 't,
That thus hath cozen'd you at hoodman-blind?
Eyes without feeling, feeling without sight,
Ears without hands or eyes, smelling sans all,
Or but a sickly part of one true sense
Could not so mope.
O shame! where is thy blush? Rebellious hell,
If thou canst mutine in a matron's bones,
To flaming youth let virtue be as wax,
And melt in her own fire: proclaim no shame,
When the compulsive ardour gives the charge;
Since frost itself as actively doth burn,
And reason panders will.

QUEEN O Hamlet! speak no more!
Thou turn'st mine eyes into my very soul;
And there I see such black and grained spots,
As will not leave their tinct.

HAMLET Nay, but to live
In the rank sweat of an enseamed bed;
Stew'd in corruption; honeying, and making love
Over the nasty sty; –

QUEEN O, speak to me no more!
These words like daggers enter in mine ears:
No more, sweet Hamlet!

HAMLET A murderer, and a villain;
A slave, that is not twentieth part the tithe
Of your precedent lord: – a Vice of kings;

A cutpurse of the empire and the rule,
That from a shelf the precious diadem stole,
And put it in his pocket!

QUEEN No more!

HAMLET A king of shreds and patches. –

Enter Ghost.

Save me, and hover o'er me with your wings,
You heavenly guards! – What would your gracious figure?

QUEEN Alas! he's mad.

HAMLET Do you not come your tardy son to chide,
That, laps'd in time and passion, lets go by
The important acting of your dread command?
O, say!

GHOST Do not forget. This visition
Is but to whet thy almost blunted purpose.
But, look! amazement on thy mother sits;
O, step between her and her fighting soul;
Conceit in weakest bodies strongest works:
Speak to her, Hamlet.

HAMLET How is it with you, lady?

QUEEN Alas! how is 't with you,
That you do bend your eye on vacancy,
And with the incorporal air do hold discourse?
Forth at your eyes your spirits wildly peep;
And, as the sleeping soldiers in the alarm,
Your bedded hair, like life in excrements,
Starts up, and stands on end. O gentle son!
Upon the heat and flame of thy distemper
Sprinkle cool patience. Whereon do you look?

HAMLET On him, on him! – Look you, how pale he glares!

His form and cause conjoin'd, preaching to stones,
Would make them capable. – Do not look upon me;
Lest with this piteous action you convert
My stern effects: then, what I have to do
Will want true colour; tears, perchance, for blood.

QUEEN To whom do you speak this?

HAMLET Do you see nothing there?

QUEEN Nothing at all; yet all, that is, I see.

HAMLET Nor did you nothing hear?

QUEEN No, nothing but ourselves.

HAMLET Why, look you there! look, how it steals away!
My father, in his habit as he liv'd!
Look, where he goes, even now, out at the portal!

[Exit Ghost.

QUEEN This is the very coinage of your brain:
This bodiless creation ecstacy
Is very cunning in.

HAMLET Ecstacy!
My pulse, as yours, doth temperately keep time,
And make as healthful music. It is not madness
That I have utter'd: bring me to the test,
And I the matter will re-word; which madness
Would gambol from. Mother, for love of grace,
Lay not that flattering unction to your soul,
That not your trespass, but my madness speaks:
It will but skin and film the ulcerous place;
Whilst rank corruption, mining all within,
Infects unseen. Confess yourself to Heaven;
Repent what's past; avoid what is to come;
And do not spread the compost on the weeds,
To make them ranker. Forgive me this my virtue;

For, in the fatness of these pursy times,
Virtue itself of vice must pardon beg,
Yea, curb and woo, for leave to do him good.

QUEEN O Hamlet! thou hast cleft my heart in twain.

HAMLET O, throw away the worser part of it,
And live the purer with the other half.
Good night; but go not to mine uncle's bed:
Assume a virtue, if you have it not.
That monster, custom, who all sense doth eat,
Oft habits' devil, is angel yet in this,
That to the use of actions fair and good
He likewise gives a frock, or livery,
That aptly is put on. Refrain to-night;
And that shall lend a kind of easiness
To the next abstinence: the next more easy;
For use almost can change the stamp of nature,
And master the devil, or throw him out
With wondrous potency. Once more, good night:
And when you are desirous to be bless'd,
I'll blessing beg of you. – For this same lord.
[Pointing to Polonius.
I do repent: but Heaven hath pleas'd it so, –
To punish me with this, and this with me, –
That I must be their scourge and minister.
I will bestow him, and will answer well
The death I gave him. So, again, good night. –
I must be cruel, only to be kind:
Thus bad begins, and worse remains behind. –
One word more, good lady.

QUEEN What shall I do?

HAMLET Not this, by no means, what I bid you do:

Let the bloat king tempt you again to bed;
Pinch wanton on your cheek; call you his mouse;
And let him, for a pair of reechy kisses,
Or paddling in your neck with his damn'd fingers,
Make you to ravel all this matter out,
That I essentially am not in madness,
But mad in craft. 'T were good, you let him know;
For who, that's but a queen, fair, sober, wise,
Would for a paddock, from a bat, a gib,
Such dear concernings hide? who would do so?
No, in despite of sense, and secrecy,
Unpeg the basket on the house's top,
Let the birds fly, and, like the famous ape,
To try conclusions, in the basket creep,
And break your own neck down.

QUEEN Be thou assur'd, if words be made of breath,
And breath of life, I have no life to breathe
What thou hast said to me.

HAMLET I must to England; you know that.

QUEEN Alack!
I had forgot: 't is so concluded on.

HAMLET There's letters seal'd: and my two school-fellows, –
Whom I will trust, as I will adders fang'd, –
They bear the mandate; they must sweep my way,
And marshal me to knavery. Let it work;
For 't is the sport, to have the engineer
Hoist with his own petar: and 't shall go hard,
But I will delve one yard below their mines,
And blow them at the moon. O! 't is most sweet,
When in one line two crafts directly meet. –
This man shall set me packing:

I'll lug the guts into the neighbour room. –
Mother, good night. – Indeed, this counsellor
Is now most still, most secret, and most grave,
Who was in life a foolish prating knave.
Come, sir, to draw toward an end with you.
Good night, mother.

[Exeunt severally; Hamlet dragging in Polonius.

ACT FOUR

SCENE I – THE SAME.

Enter King, Queen, Rosencrantz, and Guildenstern.

KING There's matter in these signs: these profound heaves
You must translate; 't is fit we understand them.
Where is your son?

QUEEN Bestow this place on us a little while. –
[Exeunt Rosencrantz and Guildenstern.
Ah, my good lord, what have I seen to-night!

KING What, Gertrude? How does Hamlet?

QUEEN Mad as the sea, and wind, when both contend
Which is the mightier. In his lawless fit,
Behind the arras hearing something stir,
He whips his rapier out, and cries, 'A rat! a rat!'
And, in this brainish apprehension, kills
The unseen good old man.

KING O heavy deed!
It had been so with us, had we been there.
His liberty is full of threats to all;
To you yourself, to us, to every one.
Alas! how shall this bloody deed be answer'd
It will be laid to us, whose providence
Should have kept short, restrain'd, and out of haunt,
This mad young man; but so much was our love,
We would not understand what was most fit;

But, like the owner of a foul disease,
To keep it from divulging, let it feed
Even on the pith of life. Where is he gone?

QUEEN To draw apart the body he hath kill'd;
O'er whom his very madness, like some ore
Among a mineral of metals base,
Shows itself pure: he weeps for what is done.

KING O Gertrude! come away.
The sun no sooner shall the mountains touch,
But we will ship him hence; and this vile deed
We must, with all our majesty and skill,
Both countenance and excuse. – Ho! Guildenstern!

Re-enter Rosencrantz and Guildenstern.

Friends both, go join you with some further aid.
Hamlet in madness hath Polonius slain,
And from his mother's closet hath he dragg'd him:
Go, seek him out; speak fair, and bring the body
Into the chapel. I pray you, haste in this.
[Exeunt Rosencrantz and Guildenstern.
Come, Gertrude, we'll call up our wisest friends;
And let them know, both what we mean to do,
And what's untimely done: so, haply, slander –
Whose whisper o'er the world's diameter,
As level as the cannon to his blank,
Transports his poison'd shot – may miss our name,
And hit the woundless air. O, come away!
My soul is full of discord, and dismay. *[Exeunt.*

SCENE II – ANOTHER ROOM IN THE SAME.

Enter Hamlet.

HAMLET Safely stowed.

ROSENCRANTZ, GUILDENSTERN *[Within.]* Hamlet! Lord Hamlet!

HAMLET What noise? who calls on Hamlet? O! here they come.

Enter Rosencrantz and Guildenstern.

ROSENCRANTZ What have you done, my lord, with the dead body?

HAMLET Compounded it with dust, whereto 't is kin.

ROSENCRANTZ Tell us where 't is; that we may take it thence,
And bear it to the chapel.

HAMLET Do not believe it.

ROSENCRANTZ Believe what?

HAMLET That I can keep your counsel, and not mine own. Besides, to be demanded of a sponge, what replication should be made by the son of a king?

ROSENCRANTZ Take you me for a sponge, my lord?

HAMLET Ay, sir; that soaks up the king's countenance, his rewards, his authorities. But such officers do the king best service in the end: he keeps them, like an ape, in the corner of his jaw; first mouthed, to be last swallowed: when he needs what you have gleaned, it is but squeezing you, and, sponge, you shall be dry again.

ROSENCRANTZ I understand you not, my lord.

HAMLET I am glad of it: a knavish speech sleeps in a foolish ear.

ROSENCRANTZ My lord, you must tell us where the body is, and go with us to the king.

HAMLET The body is with the king, but the king is not with the body. The king is a thing –

GUILDENSTERN A thing, my lord!

HAMLET Of nothing: bring me to him. Hide fox, and all after.

[Exeunt.

SCENE III – ANOTHER ROOM IN THE SAME.

Enter King, attended.

KING I have sent to seek him, and to find the body.
How dangerous is it, that this man goes loose!
Yet must not we put the strong law on him:
He's lov'd of the distracted multitude,
Who like not in their judgment, but their eyes;
And where 't is so, the offender's scourge is weigh'd,
But never the offence. To bear all smooth and even,
This sudden sending him away must seem
Deliberate pause: diseases, desperate grown,
By desperate appliance are reliev'd,
Or not at all. –

Enter Rosencrantz.

How now! what hath befallen?

ROSENCRANTZ Where the dead body is bestow'd, my lord,
We cannot get from him.

KING But where is he?

ROSENCRANTZ Without, my lord; guarded, to know your pleasure.

KING Bring him before us.

ROSENCRANTZ Ho, Guildenstern! bring in my lord.

Enter Hamlet and Guildenstern.

KING Now, Hamlet, where's Polonius?

HAMLET At supper.

KING At supper! Where?

HAMLET Not where he eats, but where he is eaten: a certain convocation of politic worms are e'en at him. Your worm is your only emperor for diet: we fat all creatures else, to fat us, and we fat ourselves for maggots: your fat king, and your lean beggar, is but variable service; two dishes, but to one table; that's the end.

KING Alas, alas!

HAMLET A man may fish with the worm that hath eat of a king; and eat of the fish that hath fed of that worm.

KING What dost thou mean by this?

HAMLET Nothing, but to show you how a king may go a progress through the guts of a beggar.

KING Where is Polonius?

HAMLET In heaven: send thither to see; if your messenger find him not there, seek him i' the other place yourself. But, indeed, if you find him not within this month, you shall nose him as you go up the stairs into the lobby.

KING *[To some Attendants.]* Go seek him there.

HAMLET He will stay till you come. *[Exeunt Attendants.*

KING Hamlet, this deed, for thine especial safety,
Which we do tender, as we dearly grieve
For that which thou hast done, – must send thee hence
With fiery quickness; therefore, prepare thyself.
The bark is ready, and the wind at help,
The associates tend, and everything is bent
For England.

HAMLET For England?

KING Ay, Hamlet.

HAMLET Good.

KING So is it, if thou knew'st our purposes.

HAMLET I see a cherub that sees them. – But, come; for England! – Farewell, dear mother.

KING Thy loving father, Hamlet.

HAMLET My mother; father and mother is man and wife, man and wife is one flesh; and so, my mother. Come, for England!

KING Follow him at foot; tempt him with speed aboard:
Delay it not, I'll have him hence to-night.
Away, for everything is seal'd and done,
That else leans on the affair: pray you, make haste.
[Exeunt Rosencrantz and Guildenstern.
And, England, if my love thou hold'st at aught,
(As my great power thereof may give thee sense,
Since yet thy cicatrice looks raw and red
After the Danish sword, and thy free awe
Pays homage to us,) thou may'st not coldly set
Our sovereign process, which imports at full,
By letters conjuring to that effect,
The present death of Hamlet. Do it, England;
For like the hectic in my blood he rages,
And thou must cure me. Till I know 't is done.
Howe'er my haps, my joys were ne'er begun. *[Exit.*

SCENE IV – A PLAIN IN DENMARK.

Enter Fortinbras, a Captain, and Soldiers, marching.

FORTINBRAS Go, captain: from me greet the Danish king:

Tell him, that, by his license, Fortinbras
Claims the conveyance of a promis'd march
Over his kingdom. You know the rendezvous.
If that his majesty would aught with us,
We shall express our duty in his eye,
And let him know so.

CAPTAIN I will do 't, my lord.

FORTINBRAS Go softly on. *[Exeunt Fortinbras and Soldiers.*

Enter Hamlet, Rosencrantz, Guildenstern, &c.

HAMLET Good sir, whose powers are these?

CAPTAIN They are of Norway, sir.

HAMLET How purpos'd, sir, I pray you?

CAPTAIN Against some part of Poland.

HAMLET Who commands them, sir?

CAPTAIN The nephew to old Norway, Fortinbras.

HAMLET Goes it against the main of Poland, sir,
Or for some frontier?

CAPTAIN Truly to speak, sir, and with no addition,
We go to gain a little patch of ground,
That hath in it no profit but the name.
To pay five ducats, five, I would not farm it;
Nor will it yield to Norway, or the Pole,
A ranker rate, should it be sold in fee.

HAMLET Why, then the Polack never will defend it.

CAPTAIN Yes, 't is already garrison'd.

HAMLET Two thousand souls, and twenty thousand ducats,
Will not debate the question of this straw:
This is the imposthume of much wealth and peace,
That inward breaks, and shows no cause without
Why the man dies. – I humbly thank you, sir.

CAPTAIN God be wi' you, sir. *[Exit.*

ROSENCRANTZ Will't please you go, my lord?

HAMLET I'll be with you straight. Go a little before.

[Exeunt Rosencrantz, Guildenstern, &c.

How all occasions do inform against me,
And spur my dull revenge! What is a man,
If his chief good, and market of his time,
Be but to sleep, and feed? a beast, no more.
Sure, He, that made us with such large discourse,
Looking before and after, gave us not
That capability and godlike reason
To fast in us unus'd. Now, whether it be
Bestial oblivion, or some craven scruple
Of thinking too precisely on the event, –
A thought, which, quarter'd, hath but one part wisdom,
And ever three parts coward, – I do not know
Why yet I live to say, 'This thing's to do;'
Sith I have cause, and will, and strength, and means,
To do 't. Examples, gross as earth, exhort me:
Witness this army, of such mass and charge,
Led by a delicate and tender prince,
Whose spirit, with divine ambition puff'd,
Makes mouths at the invisible event;
Exposing what is mortal, and unsure,
To all that fortune, death, and danger, dare,
Even for an egg-shell. Rightly to be great
Is not to stir without great argument,
But greatly to find quarrel in a straw,
When honour 's at the stake. How stand I then,
That have a father kill'd, a mother stain'd,
Excitements of my reason, and my blood,

And let all sleep? while, to my shame, I see
The imminent death of twenty thousand men,
That, for a fantasy and trick of fame,
Go to their graves like beds; fight for a plot
Whereon the numbers cannot try the cause;
Which is not tomb enough, and continent,
To hide the slain? – O! from this time forth,
My thoughts be bloody, or be nothing worth! *[Exit.*

SCENE V – ELSINORE. A ROOM IN THE CASTLE.

Enter Queen and Horatio.

QUEEN I will not speak with her.
HORATIO She is importunate; indeed, distract:
Her mood will needs be pitied.
QUEEN What would she have?
HORATIO She speaks much of her father; says, she hears,
There's tricks i' the world; and hems, and beats her heart;
Spurns enviously at straws; speaks things in doubt,
That carry but half sense: her speech is nothing,
Yet the unshaped use of it doth move
The hearers to collection; they aim at it.
And botch the words up fit to their own thoughts;
Which, as her winks, and nods, and gestures yield them,
Indeed would make one think, there might be thought,
Though nothing sure, yet much unhappily.
'T were good she were spoken with, for she may strew
Dangerous conjectures in ill-breeding minds.
QUEEN Let her come in. *[Exit Horatio.*

To my sick soul, as sin's true nature is,
Each toy seems prologue to some great amiss:
So full of artless jealousy is guilt,
It spills itself in fearing to be spilt.

Re-enter Horatio, with Ophelia.

OPHELIA Where is the beauteous majesty of Denmark?
QUEEN How now, Ophelia?
OPHELIA *[Sings.] How should I your true love know*
From another one?
By his cockle hat and staff,
And his sandal shoon.
QUEEN Alas, sweet lady, what imports this song?
OPHELIA Say you? nay, pray you, mark.
He is dead and gone, lady,
He is dead and gone;
At his head a grass-green turf,
At his heels a stone.
O, ho!
QUEEN Nay, but, Ophelia, –
OPHELIA Pray you, mark.
White his shroud as the mountain snow, –

Enter King.

QUEEN Alas! look here, my lord.
OPHELIA *Larded with sweet flowers;*
Which bewept to the grave did go,
With true-love showers.
KING How do you, pretty lady?
OPHELIA Well, God 'ield you! They say, the owl was a baker's daughter. Lord! we know what we are, but know not what we

may be. God be at your table!

KING Conceit upon her father.

OPHELIA Pray you, let's have no words of this; but when they ask you what it means, say you this:

To-morrow is Saint Valentine's day.
All-in the morning betime,
And I a maid at your window,
To be your Valentine:
Then up he rose, and donn'd his clothes,
And dupp'd the chamber door;
Let in the maid, that out a maid
Never departed more.

KING Pretty Ophelia!

OPHELIA Indeed, la! without an oath, I'll make an end on 't:

By Gis, and by Saint Charity,
Alack, and fie for shame!
Young men will do 't, if they come to 't;
By cock, they are to blame.
Quoth she, before you tumbled me,
You promis'd me to wed:
So would I ha' done, by yonder sun,
An thou hadst not come to my bed.

KING How long hath she been thus?

OPHELIA I hope, all will be well. We must be patient: but I cannot choose but weep, to think, they should lay him i' the cold ground. My brother shall know of it, and so I thank you for your good counsel. Come, my coach! Good night, ladies; good night, sweet ladies; good night, good night. *[Exit.*

KING Follow her close; give her good watch, I pray you.

[Exit Horatio.

O! this is the poison of deep grief; it springs

All from her father's death. And now, behold,
O Gertrude, Gertrude!
When sorrows come, they come not single spies,
But in battalions. First, her father slain:
Next, your son gone; and he most violent author
Of his own just remove: the people muddied,
Thick and unwholesome in their thoughts and whispers.
For good Polonius' death; and we have done but greenly,
In hugger-mugger to inter him: poor Ophelia
Divided from herself, and her fair judgment,
Without the which we are pictures, or mere beasts:
Last, and as much contained as all these,
Her brother is in secret come from France,
Feeds on his wonder, keeps himself in clouds,
And wants not buzzers to infect his ear
With pestilent speeches of his father's death;
Wherein necessity, of matter beggar'd,
Will nothing stick our person to arraign
In ear and ear. O my dear Gertrude! this,
Like to a murdering-piece, in many places
Gives me superfluous death. *[A noise within.*

QUEEN Alack! what noise is this?

Enter a Gentleman.

KING Where are my Switzers? Let them guard the door.
What is the matter?

GENTLEMAN Save yourself, my lord;
The ocean, overpeering of his list,
Eats not the flats with more impetuous haste,
Than young Laertes, in a riotous head,
O'erbears your officers. The rabble call him lord;

And, as the world were now but to begin,
Antiquity forgot, custom not known,
The ratifiers and props of every word.
They cry, 'Choose we; Laertes shall be king!'
Caps, hands, and tongues, applaud it to the clouds,
'Laertes shall be king, Laertes king!'

QUEEN How cheerfully on the false trail they cry!
O! this is counter, you false Danish dogs.

KING The doors are broke. *[Noise within.*

Enter Laertes, armed; Danes following.

LAERTES Where is this king? – Sirs, stand you all without.

DANE No, let's come in.

LAERTES I pray you, give me leave.

DANE We will, we will. *[They retire without the door.*

LAERTES I thank you: keep the door. – O thou vile king.
Give me my father.

QUEEN Calmly, good Laertes.

LAERTES That drop of blood that's calm proclaims me bastard;
Cries, cuckold, to my father; brands the harlot
Even here, between the chaste unsmirched brow
Of my true mother.

KING What is the cause, Laertes,
That thy rebellion looks so giant-like? –
Let him go, Gertrude; do not fear our person
There's such divinity doth hedge a king,
That treason can but peep to what it would,
Acts little of his will. – Tell me, Laertes,
Why thou art thus incens'd. – Let him go, Gertrude. –
Speak, man.

LAERTES Where is my father?

KING Dead.

QUEEN But not by him.

KING Let him demand his fill.

LAERTES How came he dead? I'll not be juggled with.
To hell, allegiance! vows, to the blackest devil!
Conscience, and grace, to the profoundest pit!
I dare damnation. To this point I stand,
That both the worlds I give to negligence;
Let come what comes, only I'll be reveng'd
Most throughly for my father.

KING Who shall stay you?

LAERTES My will, not all the world;
And, for my means, I'll husband them so well,
They shall go far with little.

KING Good Laertes,
If you desire to know the certainty
Of your dear father's death, is 't writ in your revenge,
That, swoopstake, you will draw both friend and foe,
Winner and loser?

LAERTES None but his enemies.

KING Will you know them then?

LAERTES To his good friends thus wide I'll ope my arms;
And, like the kind life-rendering pelican,
Repast them with my blood.

KING Why, now you speak
Like a good child, and a true gentleman.
That I am guiltless of your father's death,
And am most sensibly in grief for it,
It shall be level to your judgment pierce,
As day does to your eye.

DANES *[Within.]* Let her come in.

LAERTES How now! what noise is that?

Re-enter Ophelia.

O heat, dry up my brains! tears seven times salt,
Burn out the sense and virtue of mine eye! –
By heaven, thy madness shall be paid by weight,
Till our scale turn the beam. O rose of May!
Dear maid, kind sister, sweet Ophelia! –
O heavens! is't possible, a young maid's wits
Should be as mortal as an old man's life?
Nature is fine in love; and, where 't is fine,
It sends some precious instance of itself
After the thing it loves.

OPHELIA *They bore him barefac'd on the bier;*
Hey non nonny, nonny, hey nonny:
And in his grave rain'd many a tear; –
Fare you well, my dove!

LAERTES Hadst thou thy wits, and didst persuade revenge,
It could not move thus.

OPHELIA You must sing, *Down a-down, an you call him a-down-a.* O, how the wheel becomes it! It is the false steward, that stole his master's daughter.

LAERTES This nothing's more than matter.

OPHELIA There's rosemary, that's for remembrance; pray you, love, remember: and there is pansies, that's for thoughts.

LAERTES A document in madness; thoughts and remembrance fitted.

OPHELIA There's fennel for you, and columbines; there's rue for you; and here's some for me: we may call it herb-grace o' Sundays: – O, you must wear your rue with a difference. – There's a daisy: I would give you some violets; but they

withered all when my father died. – They say, he made a good end, –
For bonny sweet Robin is all my joy, –

LAERTES Thought and affliction, passion, hell itself,
She turns to favour, and to prettiness.

OPHELIA *And will he not come again?*
And will he not come again?
No, no, he is dead:
Go to thy death-bed:
He never will come again.

His beard as white as snow,
All flaxen was his poll;
He is gone, he is gone,
And we cast away moan;
God ha' mercy on his soul!
And of all Christian souls, I pray God. God be wi' you!
[*Exit.*

LAERTES Do you see this? O God!

KING Laertes, I must commune with your grief,
Or you deny me right. Go but apart,
Make choice of whom your wisest friends you will,
And they shall hear and judge 'twixt you and me.
If you direct, or by collateral hand
They find us touch'd, we will our kingdom give,
Our crown, our life, and all that we call ours,
To you in satisfaction; but if not,
Be you content to lend your patience to us,
And we shall jointly labour with your soul
To give it due content.

LAERTES Let this be so:

His means of death, his obscure burial, –
No trophy, sword, nor hatchment, o'er his bones,
No noble rite, nor formal ostentation, –
Cry to be heard, as 't were from heaven to earth,
That I must call't in question.

KING So you shall;
And, where the offence is, let the great axe fall.
I pray you, go with me. *[Exeunt.*

SCENE VI – ANOTHER ROOM IN THE SAME.

Enter Horatio and a Servant.

HORATIO What are they, that would speak with me?

SERVANT Sailors, sir: they say, they have letters for you.

HORATIO Le them come in. – *[Exit Servant.*
I do not know from what part of the world
I should be greeted, if not from Lord Hamlet.

Enter Sailors.

1 SAILOR God bless you, sir.

HORATIO Let him bless thee too.

1 SAILOR He shall, sir, an't please him. There's a letter for you, sir: it comes from the ambassador that was bound for England, if your name be Horatio, as I am let to know it is.

HORATIO *[Reads.]* 'Horatio, when thou shalt have overlooked this, give these fellows some means to the king: they have letters for him. Ere we were two days old at sea, a pirate of very warlike appointment gave us chase. Finding ourselves too slow of sail, we put on a compelled valour; in the grapple I boarded them: on the instant they got clear of our ship, so I alone became their prisoner. They have dealt with me like thieves of mercy; but they knew what they did; I am to do a good turn for them. Let the king have the letters I have sent; and repair thou to me with as much haste as thou wouldst fly death. I have words to speak in thine ear, will make thee dumb; yet are they much too light for the bore of the matter. These good fellows will bring thee where I am. Rosencrantz and Guildenstern hold their course for England: of them I have much to tell thee. Farewell.

He that thou knowest thine, HAMLET.'

Come, I will give you way for these your letters;
And do 't the speedier, that you may direct me
To him from whom you brought them. *[Exeunt.*

SCENE VII – ANOTHER ROOM IN THE SAME.

Enter King and Laertes.

KING Now must your conscience my acquittance seal,
And you must put me in your heart for friend,
Sith you have heard, and with a knowing ear,
That he, which hath your noble father slain,
Pursu'd my life.

LAERTES It well appears: but tell me
Why you proceeded not against these feats,
So crimeful and so capital in nature,
As by your safety, wisdom, all things else,
You mainly were stirr'd up.

KING O! for two special reasons;
Which may to you, perhaps, seem much unsinew'd,

And yet to me they are strong. The queen, his mother,
Lives almost by his looks; and for myself,
(My virtue, or my plague, be it either which,)
She 's so conjunctive to my life and soul,
That, as the star moves not but in his sphere,
I could not but by her. The other motive,
Why to a public count I might not go,
Is the great love the general gender bear him;
Who, dipping all his faults in their affection,
Would, like the spring that turneth wood to stone,
Convert his gyves to graces; so that my arrows,
Too slightly timber'd for so loud a wind,
Would have reverted to my bow again,
And not where I had aim'd them.

LAERTES And so have I a noble father lost;
A sister driven into desperate terms;
Whose worth, if praises may go back again,
Stood challenger on mount of all the age
For her perfections. But my revenge will come.

KING Break not your sleeps for that; you must not think,
That we are made of stuff so flat and dull,
That we can let our beard be shook with danger,
And think it pastime. You shortly shall hear more:
I lov'd your father, and we love ourself;
And that, I hope, will teach you to imagine, –

Enter a Messenger.

How now! what news?

MESSENGER Letters; my lord, from Hamlet.
This to your majesty: this to the queen.

KING From Hamlet! who brought them?

MESSENGER Sailors, my lord, they say; I saw them not:
They were given me by Claudio, he receiv'd them
Of him that brought them.
KING Laertes, you shall hear them. –
Leave us. *[Exit Messenger.*
[Reads.] 'High and mighty, you shall know, I am set naked on your kingdom. To-morrow shall I beg leave to see your kingly eyes; when I shall, first asking your pardon thereunto, recount the occasions of my sudden and more strange return. HAMLET.'
What should this mean? Are all the rest come back?
Or is it some abuse, and no such thing?
LAERTES Know you the hand?
KING 'T is Hamlet's character. 'Naked,' –
And, in a postscript here, he says, 'alone.'
Can you advise me?
LAERTES I'm lost in it, my lord. But let him come:
It warms the very sickness in my heart.
That I shall live and tell him to his teeth,
'Thus diddest thou.'
KING If it be so, Laertes,
(As how should it be so? how otherwise?)
Will you be ruled by me?
LAERTES Ay, my lord;
So you will not o'er-rule me to a peace.
KING To thine own peace. If he be now return'd, –
As checking at his voyage, and that he means
No more to undertake it, – I will work him
To an exploit, now ripe in my device,
Under the which he shall not choose but fall;
And for his death no wind of blame shall breathe,

But even his mother shall uncharge the practice,
And call it accident.

LAERTES My lord, I will be rul'd;
The rather, if you could devise it so,
That I might be the organ.

KING It falls right.
You have been talk'd of since your travel much,
And that in Hamlet's hearing, for a quality
Wherein, they say, you shine: your sum of parts
Did not together pluck such envy from him,
As did that one; and that, in my regard,
Of the unworthiest siege.

LAERTES What part is that, my lord.

KING A very riband in the cap of youth,
Yet needful too; for youth no less becomes
The light and careless livery that it wears,
Than settled age his sables, and his weeds,
Importing health and graveness. – Two months since,
Here was a gentleman of Normandy: –
I have seen myself, and serv'd against, the French,
And they can well on horseback; but this gallant
Had witchcraft in 't; he grew unto his seat;
And to such wondrous doing brought his horse,
As he had been incorps'd and demi-natur'd
With the brave beast; so far he topp'd my thought,
That I, in forgery of shapes and tricks,
Come short of what he did.

LAERTES A Norman, was 't?

KING A Norman.

LAERTES Upon my life, Lamord.

KING The very same.

LAERTES I know him well: he is the brooch, indeed,
And gem of all the nation.
KING He made confession of you;
And gave you such a masterly report,
For art and exercise in your defence,
And for your rapier most especially,
That he cried out, 't would be a sight indeed,
If one could match you: the scrimers of their nation,
He swore, had neither motion, guard, nor eye,
If you oppos'd them. Sir, this report of his
Did Hamlet so envenom with his envy,
That he could nothing do, but wish and beg
Your sudden coming o'er, to play with him.
Now, out of this, –
LAERTES What out of this, my lord?
KING Laertes, was your father dear to you?
Or are you like the painting of a sorrow,
A face without a heart?
LAERTES Why ask you this?
KING Not that I think you did not love your father;
But that I know love is begun by time;
And that I see, in passages of proof,
Time qualifies the spark and fire of it.
There lives within the very flame of love
A kind of wick, or snuff, that will abate it;
And nothing is at a like goodness still;
For goodness, growing to a plurisy,
Dies in his own too-much. That we would do,
We should do when we would; for this 'would' changes,
And hath abatements and delays as many,
As there are tongues, are hands, are accidents,

And then this 'should' is like a spendthrift sigh,
That hurts by easing. But, to the quick o' the ulcer:
Hamlet comes back: what would you undertake,
To show yourself your father's son in deed,
More than in words?

LAERTES To cut his throat i' the church.

KING No place, indeed, should murder sanctuarise:
Revenge should have no bounds. But, good Laertes,
Will you do this, keep close within your chamber.
Hamlet, return'd, shall know you are come home:
We'll put on those shall praise your excellence,
And set a double varnish on the fame
The Frenchman gave you; bring you, in fine, together,
And wager on your heads: he, being remiss,
Most generous, and free from all contriving,
Will not peruse the foils; so that with ease,
Or with a little shuffling, you may choose
A sword unbated, and, in a pass of practice,
Requite him for your father.

LAERTES I will do 't;
And, for that purpose, I 'll anoint my sword.
I bought an unction of a mountebank,
So mortal, that but dip a knife in it,
Where it draws blood, no cataplasm so rare,
Collected from all simples that have virtue
Under the moon, can save the thing from death,
That is but scratch'd withal: I'll touch my point
With this contagion, that, if I gall him slightly,
It may be death.

KING Let's further think of this;
Weigh, what convenience, both of time and means,

May fit us to our shape. If this should fail,
And that our drift look through our bad performance,
'T were better not assay'd: therefore, this project
Should have a back, or second, that might hold,
If this should blast in proof. Soft! – let me see: –
We'll make a solemn wager on your cunnings, –
I ha 't:
When in your motion you are hot and dry,
(As make your bouts more violent to that end.)
And that he calls for drink, I'll have prepar'd him
A chalice for the nonce; whereon but sipping,
If he by chance escape your venom'd stuck,
Our purpose may hold there. But stay! what noise?

Enter Queen.

How now, sweet queen?
QUEEN One woe doth tread upon another's heel,
So fast they follow. – Your sister's drown'd, Laertes.
LAERTES Drown'd! – O, where?
QUEEN There is a willow grows aslant a brook,
That shows his hoar leaves in the glassy stream;
There with fantastic garlands did she come,
Of crow-flowers, nettles, daisies, and long purples,
That liberal shepherds give a grosser name,
But our cold maids do dead men's fingers call them:
There, on the pendant boughs her coronet weeds
Clambering to hang, an envious sliver broke,
When down her weedy trophies, and herself,
Fell in the weeping brook. Her clothes spread wide,
And, mermaid-like, awhile they bore her up:
Which time, she chanted snatches of old tunes,

As one incapable of her own distress,
Or like a creature native and indu'd
Unto that element: but long it could not be,
Till that her garments, heavy with their drink,
Pull'd the poor wretch from her melodious lay
To muddy death.

LAERTES Alas! then, is she drown'd?

QUEEN Drown'd, drown'd.

LAERTES Too much of water hast thou, poor Ophelia,
And therefore I forbid my tears: but yet
It is our trick; nature her custom holds.
Let shame say what it will: when these are gone,
The woman will be out. – Adieu, my lord!
I have a speech of fire, that fain would blaze,
But that this folly douts it. *[Exit.*

KING Let's follow, Gertrude.
How much I had to do to calm his rage!
Now fear I, this will give it start again;
Therefore, let's follow. *Exeunt.*

ACT FIVE

SCENE I – A CHURCHYARD.

Enter two Clowns, with spades and mattocks.

1 CLOWN Is she to be buried in Christian burial, that wilfully seeks her own salvation?

2 CLOWN I tell thee, she is; and therefore make her grave straight: the crowner hath sat on her, and finds it Christian burial.

1 CLOWN How can that be, unless she drowned herself in her own defence?

2 CLOWN Why, 't is found so.

1 CLOWN It must be *se offendendo*; it cannot be else. For here lies the point: if I drown myself wittingly, it argues an act, and an act hath three branches; it is, to act, to do, and to perform: argal, she drowned herself wittingly.

2 CLOWN Nay, but hear you, goodman delver. –

1 CLOWN Give me leave. Here lies the water; good: here stands the man; good: if the man go to this water, and drown himself, it is will he, nill he, he goes; mark you that: but if the water come to him, and drowns him, he drowns not himself: argal, he that is not guilty of his own death shortens not his own life.

2 CLOWN But is this law?

1 CLOWN Ay, marry, is't, crowner's quest-law.

2 CLOWN Will you ha' the truth on 't? If this had not been a gentlewoman, she should have been buried out of Christian burial.

1 CLOWN Why, there thou say'st; and the more pity, that great folk shall have countenance in this world to drown or hang themselves, more than their even-Christian. Come, my spade. There is no ancient gentlemen but gardeners, ditchers, and grave-makers; they hold up Adam's profession.

2 CLOWN Was he a gentleman?

1 CLOWN He was the first that ever bore arms.

2 CLOWN Why, he had none.

1 CLOWN What, art a heathen? How dost thou understand the Scripture? The Scripture says, Adam digged: could he dig without arms? I'll put another question to thee: if thou answerest me not to the purpose, confess thyself –

2 CLOWN Go to.

1 CLOWN What is he, that builds stronger than either the mason, the shipwright, or the carpenter?

2 CLOWN The gallows-maker; for that frame outlives a thousand tenants.

1 CLOWN I like thy wit well, in good faith: the gallows does well; but how does it well? it does well to those that do ill: now, thou dost ill to say the gallows is built stronger than the church; argal, the gallows may do well to thee. To 't again; come.

2 CLOWN Who builds stronger than a mason, a shipwright, or a carpenter?

1 CLOWN Ay, tell me that, and unyoke.

2 CLOWN Marry, now I can tell.

1 CLOWN To 't.

2 CLOWN Mass, I cannot tell.

Enter Hamlet and Horatio, at a distance.

1 CLOWN Cudgel thy brains no more about it, for your dull ass will not mend his pace with beating; and, when you are asked this question next, say, a grave-maker: the houses that he makes last till doomsday. Go, get thee to Yaughan; fetch me a stoop of liquor. *[Exit 2 Clown*

1 Clown digs, and sings.

In youth, when I dìd love, did love,
Methought it was very sweet,
To contract, O! the time, for-a! my behove,
O, methought, there was nothing-a meet.

HAMLET Hath this fellow no feeling of his business, that he sings at grave-making?

HORATIO Custom hath made it in him a property of easiness.

HAMLET 'T is e'en so: the hand of little employment hath the daintier sense.

1 CLOWN *But age, with his stealing steps,*
Hath claw'd me in his clutch,
And hath shipped me intil the land.
As if I had never been such. *[Throws up a skull.*

HAMLET That skull had a tongue in it, and could sing once: how the knave jowls it to the ground, as if it were Cain's jaw-bone, that did the first murder! This might be the pate of a politician, which this ass now o'er-offices, one that would circumvent God, might it not?

HORATIO It might, my lord.

HAMLET Or of a courtier, which could say, 'Good morrow, sweet lord! How dost thou, good lord?' This might be my Lord Such-a-one, that praised my Lord Such-a-one's horse, when he meant to beg it, might it not?

HORATIO Ay, my lord.

HAMLET Why, e'en so, and now my Lady Worm's; chapless, and knocked about the mazzard with a sexton's spade. Here's fine revolution, an we had the trick to see't. Did these bones cost no more the breeding, but to play at loggats with 'em? mine ache to think on 't.

1 CLOWN *A pick-axe, and a spade, a spade,*
For and a shrouding sheet:
O! a pit of clay for to be made
For such a guest is meet. *[Throws up another skull.*

HAMLET There's another: why may not that be the skull of a lawyer? Where be his quiddits now, his quillets, his cases, his tenures, and his tricks? why does he suffer this rude knave now to knock him about the sconce with a dirty shovel, and will not tell him of his action of battery? Humph! This fellow might be in 's time a great buyer of land, with his statutes, his recognisances, his fines, his double vouchers, his recoveries: is this the fine of his fines, and the recovery of his recoveries, to have his fine pate full of fine dirt? will his vouchers vouch him no more of his purchases, and double ones too, than the length and breadth of a pair of indentures? The very conveyances of his lands will hardly lie in this box, and must the inheritor himself have no more? ha?

HORATIO Not a jot more, my lord.

HAMLET Is not parchment made of sheep-skins?

HORATIO Ay, my lord, and of calf-skins too.

HAMLET They are sheep, and calves, which seek out assurance in that. I will speak to this fellow. – Whose grave's this, sir?

1 CLOWN Mine, sir. –
O! a pit of clay for to be made
For such a guest is meet.

HAMLET I think it be thine, indeed; for thou liest in 't.

1 CLOWN You lie out on 't, sir, and therefore it is not yours; for my part, I do not lie in 't, and yet it is mine.

HAMLET Thou dost lie in 't, to be in 't, and say it is thine: 't is for the dead, not for the quick; therefore, thou liest.

1 CLOWN 'T is a quick lie, sir; 't will away again, from me to you.

HAMLET What man dost thou dig it for?

1 CLOWN For no man, sir.

HAMLET What woman, then?

1 CLOWN For none, neither.

HAMLET Who is to be buried in 't?

1 CLOWN One, that was a woman, sir; but, rest her soul, she's dead.

HAMLET How absolute the knave is! we must speak by the card, or equivocation will undo us. By the Lord, Horatio, this three years I have taken note of it; the age is grown so picked, that the toe of the peasant comes so near the heel of the courtier, he galls his kibe. – How long hast thou been a grave-maker?

1 CLOWN Of all the days i' the year, I came to 't that day that our last King Hamlet o'ercame Fortinbras.

HAMLET How long is that since?

1 CLOWN Cannot you tell that? every fool can tell that. It was the very day that young Hamlet was born; he that is mad, and sent into England.

HAMLET Ay, marry; why was he sent into England?

1 CLOWN Why, because he was mad: he shall recover his wits there; or, if he do not, 't is no great matter there.

HAMLET Why?

1 CLOWN 'T will not be seen in him there; there the men are as mad as he.

HAMLET How came he mad?

1 CLOWN Very strangely, they say.

HAMLET How strangely?

1 CLOWN 'Faith, e'en with losing his wits.

HAMLET Upon what ground?

1 CLOWN Why, here in Denmark: I have been sexton here, man, and boy, thirty years.

HAMLET How long will a man lie i' the earth ere he rot?

1 CLOWN 'Faith, if he be not rotten before he die, (as we have many pocky corses now-a-day, that will scarce hold the laying in,) he will last you some eight year, or nine year: a tanner will last you nine year.

HAMLET Why he more than another?

1 CLOWN Why, sir, his hide is so tanned with his trade, that he will keep out water a great while; and your water is a sore decayer of your whoreson dead body. Here's a skull now; this skull hath lain i' the earth three-and-twenty years.

HAMLET Whose was it?

1 CLOWN A whoreson mad fellow's it was: whose do you think it was?

HAMLET Nay, I know not.

1 CLOWN A pestilence on him for a mad rogue! 'a poured a flagon of Rhenish on my head once. This same skull, sir, this same skull, sir, was Yorick's skull, the king's jester.

HAMLET This?

1 CLOWN E'en that.

HAMLET Let me see. *[Takes the skull.]* Alas, poor Yorick! – I knew him, Horatio: a fellow of infinite jest, of most excellent fancy: he hath borne me on his back a thousand times; and now, how abhorred my imagination is! my gorge rises at it. Here hung those lips, that I have kissed I know not how oft. Where be your gibes now? your gambols? your songs? your flashes of merriment, that were wont to set the table on a roar? Not one now, to mock your own grinning? quite chap-fallen? Now, get you to my lady's chamber, and tell her, let her paint an inch thick, to this favour she must come; make her laugh at that, – Pr'ythee, Horatio, tell me one thing.

HORATIO What's that, my lord?

HAMLET Dost thou think, Alexander looked o' this fashion i' the earth?

HORATIO E'en so.

HAMLET And smelt so? pah! *[Puts down the skull.*

HORATIO E'en so, my lord.

HAMLET To what base uses we may return, Horatio! Why may not imagination trace the noble dust of Alexander, till he find it stopping a bung-hole?

HORATIO 'T were to consider too curiously, to consider so.

HAMLET No, faith, not a jot; but to follow him thither with modesty enough, and likelihood to lead it: as thus: Alexander died, Alexander was buried, Alexander returneth into dust; the dust is earth; of earth we make loam; and why of that loam, whereto he was converted, might they not stop a beer-barrel?

Imperious Cæsar, dead, and turn'd to clay,
Might stop a hole to keep the wind away:
O! that that earth, which kept the world in awe,
Should patch a wall to expel the winter's flaw!

But soft! but soft! aside: – here comes the king,

Enter Priests, &c., in procession; the Corse of Ophelia, Laertes and Mourners following; King, Queen, their Trains, &c.

The queen, the courtiers. Who is that they follow,
And with such maimed rites? This doth betoken,
The corse they follow did with desperate hand

Fordo its own life; 't was of some estate.
Couch we awhile, and mark. *[Retiring with Horatio.*

LAERTES What ceremony else?

HAMLET That is Laertes,
A very noble youth: mark.

LAERTES What ceremony else?

PRIEST Her obsequies have been as far enlarg'd
As we have warrantise: her death was doubtful;
And, but that great command o'ersways the order,
She should in ground unsanctified have lodg'd,
Till the last trumpet; for charitable prayers,
Shards, flints, and pebbles, should be thrown on her;
Yet here she is allow'd her virgin erants,
Her maiden strewments, and the bringing home
Of bell and burial.

LAERTES Must there no more be done?

PRIEST No more be done:
We should profane the service of the dead,
To sing a requiem, and such rest to her,
As to peace-parted souls.

LAERTES Lay her i' the earth;
And from her fair and unpolluted flesh
May violets spring! – I tell thee, churlish priest,
A ministering angel shall my sister be,
When thou liest howling.

HAMLET What! the fair Ophelia?

QUEEN Sweets to the sweet: farewell. *[Scattering flowers.*
I hop'd thou shouldst have been my Hamlet's wife:
I thought thy bride-bed to have deck'd, sweet maid,
And not have strew'd thy grave.

LAERTES O! treble woe

Fall ten times treble on that cursed head,
Whose wicked deed thy most ingenious sense
Depriv'd thee of! – Hold off the earth awhile,
Till I have caught her once more in mine arms.
[Leaping into the grave.
Now pile your dust upon the quick and dead,
Till of this flat a mountain you have made,
To o'er-top old Pelion, or the skyish head
Of blue Olympus.

HAMLET *[Advancing.]* What is he, whose grief
Bears such an emphasis? whose phrase of sorrow
Conjures the wandering stars, and makes them stand,
Like wonder-wounded hearers? This is I,
Hamlet the Dane. *[Leaping into the grave.*

LAERTES The devil take thy soul!
[Grappling with him.

HAMLET Thou pray'st not well.
I pr'ythee, take thy fingers from my throat;
For though I am not splenitive and rash,
Yet have I something in me dangerous,
Which let thy wiseness fear. Away thy hand!

KING Pluck them asunder.

QUEEN Hamlet! Hamlet!

ALL Gentlemen, –

HORATIO Good my lord, be quiet.
[The Attendants part them, and they come out of the grave.

HAMLET Why, I will fight with him upon this theme,
Until my eyelids will no longer wag.

QUEEN O my son! what theme?

HAMLET I lov'd Ophelia: forty thousand brothers
Could not, with all their quantity of love,

Make up my sum. – What wilt thou do for her?

KING O! he is mad, Laertes.

QUEEN For love of God, forbear him.

HAMLET 'Swounds! show me what thou'lt do:
Woo't weep? woo't fight? woo't fast? woo't tear thyself?
Woo't drink up Esill? eat a crocodile?
I'll do 't. – Dost thou come here to whine?
To outface me with leaping in her grave?
Be buried quick with her, and so will I:
And, if thou prate of mountains, let them throw
Millions of acres on us, till our ground,
Singeing his pate against the burning zone,
Make Ossa like a wart! Nay, an thou'lt mouth,
I'll rant as well as thou.

QUEEN This is mere madness:
And thus awhile the fit will work on him;
Anon, as patient as the female dove,
When that her golden couplet are disclos'd,
His silence will sit drooping.

HAMLET Hear you, sir:
What is the reason that you use me thus?
I lov'd you ever: but it is no matter;
Let Hercules himself do what he may,
The cat will mew, and dog will have his day. *[Exit.*

KING I pray you, good Horatio, wait upon him. *[Exit Horatio.*
[To Laertes.] Strengthen your patience in our last night's speech;
We'll put the matter to the present push. –
Good Gertrude, set some watch over your son.
This grave shall have a living monument:
An hour of quiet shortly shall we see;
Till then, in patience our proceeding be. *[Exeunt.*

SCENE II – A HALL IN THE CASTLE.

Enter Hamlet and Horatio.

HAMLET So much for this, sir: now let me see the other; –
You do remember all the circumstance?
HORATIO Remember it, my lord!
HAMLET Sir, in my heart there was a kind of fighting,
That would not let me sleep: methought, I lay
Worse than the mutines in the bilboes. Rashly, –
And prais'd be rashness for it, – let us know,
Our indiscretion sometimes serves us well,
When our dear plots do pall; and that should teach us,
There's a divinity that shapes our ends,
Rough-hew them how we will, –
HORATIO That is most certain.
HAMLET Up from my cabin,
My sea-glown scarf'd about me, in the dark
Grop'd I to find out them; had my desire;
Finger'd their packet; and, in fine, withdrew
To mine own room again: making so bold,
My fears forgetting manners, to unseal
Their grand commission; where I found, Horatio,
O royal knavery! an exact command, –
Larded with many several sorts of reason,
Importing Denmark's health, and England's too,
With, ho! such bugs and goblins in my life, –
That, on the supervise, no leisure bated,
No, not to stay the grinding of the axe,
My head should be struck off.
HORATIO Is't possible?

HAMLET Here's the commission: read it at more leisure.
But wilt thou hear me how I did proceed?

HORATIO Ay, 'beseech you.

HAMLET Being thus benetted round with villainies, –
Ere I could make a prologue to my brains,
They had begun the play, – I sat me down,
Devis'd a new commission; wrote it fair:
I once did hold it, as our statists do,
A baseness to write fair, and labour'd much
How to forget that learning; but, sir, now
It did me yeoman's service. Wilt thou know
The effect of what I wrote?

HORATIO Ay, good my lord.

HAMLET An earnest conjuration from the king, –
As England was his faithful tributary,
As love between them as the palm should flourish,
As peace should still her wheaten garland wear,
And stand a comma 'tween their amities,
and many such-like as's of great charge, –
That, on the view and know of these contents,
Without debatement further, more or less,
He should the bearers put to sudden death,
Not shriving-time allow'd.

HORATIO How was this seal'd?

HAMLET Why, even in that was Heaven ordinant.
I had my father's signet in my purse,
Which was the model of that Danish seal;
Folded the writ up in form of the other;
Subscrib'd it; gave 't the impression; plac'd it safely,
The changeling never known. Now, the next day
Was our sea-fight; and what to this was sequent
Thou know'st already.

HORATIO So Guildenstern and Rosencrantz go to 't.

HAMLET Why, man, they did make love to this employment:
They are not near my conscience: their defeat
Does by their own insinuation grow.
'T is dangerous, when the baser nature comes
Between the pass and fell-incensed points
Of mighty opposites.

HORATIO Why, what a king is this!

HAMLET Does it not, thinks 't thee, stand me now upon –
He that hath kill'd my king, and whor'd my mother;
Popp'd in between the election and my hopes;
Thrown out his angle for my proper life,
And with such cozenage – is 't not perfect conscience,
To quit him with this arm? and is 't not to be damn'd.
To let this canker of our nature come
In further evil?

HORATIO It must be shortly known to him from England.
What is the issue of the business there.

HAMLET It will be short: the interim is mine;
And a man's life no more than to say, one.
But I am very sorry, good Horatio,
That to Laertes I forgot myself;
For, by the image of my cause, I see
The portraiture of his: I'll court his favours:
But, sure, the bravery of his grief did put me
Into a towering passion.

HORATIO Peace! who comes here?

Enter Osrick.

OSRICK Your lordship is right welcome back to Denmark.

HAMLET I humbly thank you, sir. – Dost know this water-fly?

HORATIO No, my good lord.

HAMLET Thy state is the more gracious; for 't is a vice to know him. He hath much land, and fertile: let a beast be lord of beasts, and his crib shall stand at the king's mess: 't is a chough; but, as I say, spacious in the possession of dirt.

OSRICK Sweet lord, if your lordship were at leisure, I should impart a thing to you from his majesty.

HAMLET I will receive it, sir, with all diligence of spirit. Your bonnet to his right use; 't is for the head.

OSRICK I thank your lordship, 't is very hot.

HAMLET No, believe me, 't is very cold; the wind is northerly.

OSRICK It is indifferent cold, my lord, indeed.

HAMLET But yet, methinks, it is very sultry and hot, for my complexion.

OSRICK Exceedingly, my lord; it is very sultry, – as 't were, – I cannot tell how. – But, my lord, his majesty bade me signify to you, that he has laid a great wager on your head. Sir, this is the matter, –

HAMLET I beseech you, remember –

[Hamlet moves him to put on his hat.

OSRICK Nay, in good faith; for mine ease, in good faith. Sir, here is newly come to court, Laertes; believe me, an absolute gentleman, full of most excellent differences, of very soft society, and great showing: indeed, to speak feelingly of him, he is the card or calendar of gentry, for you shall find in him the continent of what part a gentleman would see.

HAMLET Sir, his definement suffers no perdition in you; though, I know, to divide him inventorially, would dizzy the arithmetic of memory, and it but yaw neither, in respect of his quick sale. But, in the verity of extolment, I take him to be a soul of great article; and his infusion of such dearth and rareness, as, to make true diction of him, his semblable is his mirror; and who else would trace him, his umbrage, nothing more.

OSRICK Your lordship speaks most infallibly of him.

HAMLET The concernancy, sir? why do we wrap the gentleman in our more rawer breath?

OSRICK Sir?

HORATIO Is't not possible to understand in another tongue? You will do 't, sir, really.

HAMLET What imports the nomination of this gentleman?

OSRICK Of Laertes?

HORATIO His purse if empty already; all's golden words are spent.

HAMLET Of him, sir.

OSRICK I know, you are not ignorant –

HAMLET I would, you did, sir; yet, in faith, if you did, it would not much approve me. – Well, sir.

OSRICK You are not ignorant of what excellence Laertes is –

HAMLET I dare not confess that, lest I should compare with him in excellence; but, to know a man well, were to know himself.

OSRICK I mean, sir, for his weapon; but in the imputation laid on him by them, in his meed he's unfellowed.

HAMLET What 's his weapon?

OSRICK Rapier and dagger.

HAMLET That's two of his weapons: but, well.

OSRICK The king, sir, hath wagered with him six Barbary horses: against the which he has imponed, as I take it, six French rapiers and poniards, with their assigns, as girdle, hangers, and so. Three of the carriages, in faith, are very dear to fancy, very responsive to the hilts, most delicate carriages, and of very liberal conceit.

HAMLET What call you the carriages?

HORATIO I knew, you must be edified by the margent ere you had done.

OSRICK The carriages, sir, are the hangers.

HAMLET The phrase would be more german to the matter, if we could carry cannon by our sides: I would it might be hangers till then. But, on: six Barbary horses against six French swords, their assigns, and three liberal-conceited carriages; that's the French bet against the Danish. Why is this imponed, as you call it?

OSRICK The king, sir, hath laid, sir, that in a dozen passes between yourself and him, he shall not exceed you three hits: he hath laid on twelve for nine; and that would come to immediate trial, if your lordship would vouchsafe the answer.

HAMLET How, if I answer no?

OSRICK I mean, my lord, the opposition of your person in trial.

HAMLET Sir, I will walk here in the hall: if it please his majesty, it is the breathing time of day with me; let the foils be brought, the gentleman willing, and the king hold his purpose, I will win for him, if I can; if not, I will gain nothing but my shame, and the odd hits.

OSRICK Shall I re-deliver you e'en so?

HAMLET To this effect, sir; after what flourish your nature will.

OSRICK I commend my duty to your lordship.

HAMLET Yours, yours. *[Exit Osrick.]* – He does well to commend it himself; there are no tongues else for 's turn.

HORATIO This lapwing runs away with the shell on his head.

HAMLET He did comply with his dug before he sucked it. Thus has he (and many more of the same bevy, that, I know, the drossy age dotes on) only got the tune of the time, and outward habit of encounter, a kind of yesty collection, which carries them through and through the most fond and winnowed opinions; and do but blow them to their trial, the bubbles are out.

Enter a Lord.

LORD My lord, his majesty commended him to you by young Osrick, who brings back to him, that you attend him in the hall: he sends to know, if your pleasure hold to play with Laertes, or that you will take longer time.

HAMLET I am constant to my purposes; they follow the king's pleasure: if his fitness speaks, mine is ready; now, or whensoever, provided I be so able as now.

LORD The king, and queen, and all are coming down.

HAMLET In happy time.

LORD The queen desires you to use some gentle entertainment to Laertes, before you fall to play.

HAMLET She well instructs me. *[Exit Lord.*

HORATIO You will lose this wager, my lord.

HAMLET I do not think so: since he went into France, I have been in continual practice; I shall win at the odds. Thou wouldst not think, how ill all 's here about my heart; but it is no matter.

HORATIO Nay, good my lord, –

HAMLET It is but foolery; but it is such a kind of gain-giving, as would, perhaps, trouble a woman.

HORATIO If your mind dislike anything, obey it: I will forestall their repair hither, and say, you are not fit.

HAMLET Not a whit, we defy augury: there is a special providence in the fall of a sparrow. If it be now, 't is not to come; if it be not to come, it will be now; if it be not now, yet it will come: the readiness is all. Since no man has aught of what he leaves, what is 't to leave betimes? Let be.

Enter King, Queen, Laertes, Lords, Osrick, and Attendants with foils, &c.

KING Come, Hamlet, come, and take this hand from me.

[The King puts the hand of Laertes into that of Hamlet.

HAMLET Give me your pardon, sir: I've done you wrong;
But pardon 't, as you are a gentleman.
This presence knows,
And you must needs have heard, how I am punish'd
With sore distraction. What I have done,
That might your nature, honour, and exception,
Roughly awake, I here proclaim was madness.
Was 't Hamlet wrong'd Laertes? Never Hamlet:
If Hamlet from himself be ta'en away,
And, when he's not himself, does wrong Laertes,
Then Hamlet does it not; Hamlet denies it.
Who does it then? His madness. If 't be so,
Hamlet is of the faction that is wrong'd;
His madness is poor Hamlet's enemy.
Sir, in this audience,
Let my disclaiming from a purpos'd evil
Free me so far in your most generous thoughts,
That I have shot mine arrow o'er the house,
And hurt my brother.

LAERTES I am satisfied in nature,
Whose motive, in this case, should stir me most
To my revenge: but in my terms of honour,
I stand aloof, and will no reconcilement,
Till by some elder masters, of known honour,

I have a voice and precedent of peace,
To keep my name ungor'd. But till that time,
I do receive your offer'd love like love,
And will not wrong it.

HAMLET I embrace it freely;
And will this brother's wager frankly play. –
Give us the foils. – Come on.

LAERTES Come, one for me.

HAMLET I'll be your foil, Laertes: in mine ignorance,
Your skill shall, like a star i' the darkest night,
Stick fiery off indeed.

LAERTES You mock me, sir.

HAMLET No, by this hand.

KING Give them the foils, young Osrick. – Cousin Hamlet,
You know the wager?

HAMLET Very well, my lord;
Your grace hath laid the odds o' the weaker side.

KING I do not fear it: I have seen you both;
But since he's better'd, we have therefore odds.

LAERTES This is too heavy; let me see another.

HAMLET This likes me well. these foils have all a length?

[They prepare to play.

OSRICK Ay, my good lord.

KING Set me the stoops of wine upon that table. –
If Hamlet give the first or second hit,
Or quit in answer of the third exchange,
Let all the battlements their ordnance fire;
The king shall drink to Hamlet's better breath:
And in the cup an union shall he throw,
Richer than that which four successive kings
In Denmark's crown have worn. Give me the cups:

And let the kettle to the trumpet speak,
The trumpet to the cannoneer without,
The cannons to the heavens, the heavens to earth,
'Now the king drinks to Hamlet!' – Come, begin; –
And you, the judges, bear a wary eye.

HAMLET Come on, sir.

LAERTES Come, my lord. *[They play.*

HAMLET One.

LAERTES No.

HAMLET Judgment.

OSRICK A hit, a very palpable hit.

LAERTES Well: – again.

KING Stay; give me drink. Hamlet, this pearl is thine;
Here's to thy health. – Give him the cup,
[Trumpets sound; and cannon shot off within.

HAMLET I'll play this bout first: set it by awhile.
Come. – *[They play.]* Another hit: what say you?

LAERTES A touch, a touch, I do confess.

KING Our son shall win.

QUEEN He's fat, and scant of breath. –
Here, Hamlet, take my napkin, rub thy brows:
The queen carouses to thy fortune, Hamlet.

HAMLET Good madam!

KING Gertrude, do not drink.

QUEEN I will, my lord: I pray you, pardon me.

KING *[Aside.]* It is the poison'd cup! it is too late.

HAMLET I dare not drink yet, madam; by-and-by.

QUEEN Come, let me wipe thy face.

LAERTES My lord, I'll hit him now.

KING I do not think it.

LAERTES *[Aside.]* And yet it is almost against my conscience.

HAMLET Come, for the third, Laertes. You but dally:
I pray you, pass with your best violence.
I am afeard, you make a wanton of me.
LAERTES Say you so? come on. *[They play.*
OSRICK Nothing, neither way.
LAERTES Have at you now.
[Laertes wounds Hamlet: then, in scuffling, they change rapiers, and Hamlet wounds Laertes.
KING Part them! they are incens'd.
HAMLET Nay, come again *[The Queen falls.*
OSRICK Look to the queen there. – Ho!
HORATIO They bleed on both sides. – How is it, my lord?
OSRICK How is 't, Laertes?
LAERTES Why, as a woodcock to mine own springe, Osrick;
I am justly kill'd with mine own treachery.
HAMLET How does the queen?
KING She swoonds to see them bleed.
QUEEN No, no, the drink, the drink, – O my dear Hamlet!
The drink, the drink: I am poison'd. *[Dies.*
HAMLET O villainy! – Ho! let the door be lock'd:
Treachery! seek it out. *[Laertes falls.*
LAERTES It is here, Hamlet. Hamlet, thou art slain:
No medicine in the world can do thee good;
In thee there is not half an hour of life;
The treacherous instrument is in thy hand,
Unbated and envenom'd. The foul practice
Hath turn'd itself on me: lo! here I lie,
Never to rise again. Thy mother's poison'd.
I can no more. The king, the king 's to blame.
HAMLET The point – envenom'd too!
Then, venom, to thy work. *[Stabs the King.*

ALL Treason! treason!

KING O! yet defend me, friends, I am but hurt.

HAMLET Here, thou incestuous, murderous, damned Dane,
Drink off this potion: – is thy union here?
Follow my mother. *[King dies.*

LAERTES He is justly serv'd;
It is a poison temper'd by himself. –
Exchange forgiveness with me, noble Hamlet;
Mine and my father's death come not upon thee,
Nor thine on me! *[Dies.*

HAMLET Heaven make thee free of it! I follow thee.
I am dead, Horatio. – Wretched queen, adieu! –
You that look pale and tremble at this chance,
That are but mutes or audience to this act,
Had I but time, (as this fell sergeant, death,
Is strict in his arrest,) O! I could tell you, –
But let it be. – Horatio, I am dead;
Thou liv'st: report me and my cause aright
To the unsatisfied.

HORATIO Never believe it:
I am more an antique Roman than a Dane:
Here's yet some liquor left.

HAMLET As thou 'rt a man,
Give me the cup: let go; by Heaven, I'll have it. –
O good Horatio, what a wounded name,
Things standing thus unknown, shall live behind me!
If thou didst ever hold me in thy heart,
Absent thee from felicity awhile,
And in this harsh world draw thy breath in pain,
To tell my story. *[March afar off, and shot within.*
What warlike noise is this?

OSRICK Young Fortinbras, with conquest come from Poland,
To the ambassadors of England gives
This warlike volley.

HAMLET O! I die, Horatio;
The potent poison quite o'er-crows my spirit:
I cannot live to hear the news from England;
But I do prophesy the election lights
On Fortinbras: he has my dying voice;
So tell him, with the occurrents, more and less,
Which have solicited. – The rest is silence. *[Dies.*

HORATIO Now cracks a noble heart. – Good night, sweet prince;
And flights of angels sing thee to thy rest! –
Why does the drum come hither? *[March within.*

Enter Fortinbras, the English Ambassadors, and others.

FORTINBRAS Where is this sight?

HORATIO What is it ye would see?
If aught of woe, or wonder, cease your search.

FORTINBRAS This quarry cries on havock. – O proud death!
What feast is toward in thine eternal cell,
That thou so many princes at a shot
So bloodily hast struck?

1 AMBASSADOR The sight is dismal,
And our affairs from England come too late:
The ears are senseless that should give us hearing,
To tell him his commandment is fulfill'd,
That Rosencrantz and Guildenstern are dead.
Where should we have our thanks?

HORATIO Not from his mouth.
Had it the ability of life to thank you:
He never gave commandment for their death.

But since, so jump upon this bloody question,
You from the Polack wars, and you from England,
Are here arriv'd, give order that these bodies
High on a stage be placed to the view;
And let me speak to the yet unknowing world,
How these things came about: so shall you hear
Of carnal, bloody, and unnatural acts.
Of accidental judgments, casual slaughters,
Of deaths put on by cunning, and forc'd cause,
And, in this upshot, purposes mistook
Fall'n on the inventors' heads: all this can I
Truly deliver.

FORTINBRAS Let us haste to hear it,
And call the noblest to the audience.
For me, with sorrow I embrace my fortune:
I have some rights of memory in this kingdom,
Which now to claim my vantage doth invite me.

HORATIO Of that I shall have also cause to speak,
And from his mouth whose voice will draw on more:
But let this same be presently perform'd.
Even while men's minds are wild, lest more mischance,
On plots and errors, happen.

FORTINBRAS Let four captains
Bear Hamlet, like a soldier, to the stage;
For he was likely, had he been put on,
To have prov'd most royally: and for his passage,
The soldiers' music, and the rites of war,
Speak loudly for him.
Take up the bodies: – such a sight as this
Becomes the field, but here shows much amiss.
Go, bid the soldiers shoot.

[Exeunt, bearing off the bodies; after which, a peal of ordnance is shot off.

MACBETH

DRAMATIS PERSONAE

Duncan – *King of Scotland*
Malcolm, Donalbain – *His Sons*
Macbeth, Banquo – *Generals of the King's Army*
Macduff, Lenox, Rosse, Menteth, Angus, Cathness – *Noblemen of Scotland*
Fleance – *Son to Banquo*
Siward – *Earl of Northumberland, General of the English Forces*
Young Siward – *his Son*
Seyton – *an Officer attending on Macbeth*
Boy – *Son to Macduff*
An English Doctor
A Scotch Doctor
A Soldier
A Porter
An Old Man
Lady Macbeth
Lady Macduff
Gentlewoman attending on Lady Macbeth
Hecate, and Three Witches
Lords, Gentlemen, Officers, Soldiers, Murderers, Attendants, and Messengers
The Ghost of Banquo, and other Apparitions

SCENE

IN THE END OF THE FOURTH ACT, IN ENGLAND; THROUGH THE REST OF THE PLAY, IN SCOTLAND.

ACT ONE

SCENE I – AN OPEN PLACE.

Thunder and lightning. Enter three Witches.

1 WITCH When shall we three meet again,
In thunder, lightning, or in rain?
2 WITCH When the hurlyburly's done,
When the battle's lost and won.
3 WITCH That will be ere the set of sun.
1 WITCH Where the place?
2 WITCH Upon the heath.
3 WITCH There to meet with Macbeth.
1 WITCH I come, Graymalkin!
ALL Paddock calls. – Anon! –
Fair is foul, and foul is fair:
Hover through the fog and filthy air. *[Exeunt.*

SCENE II – A CAMP NEAR FORES.

Alarum within. Enter King Duncan, Malcolm, Donalbain, Lenox, with Attendants, meeting a bleeding Captain.

DUNCAN What bloody man is that? He can report,
As seemeth by his plight, of the revolt
The newest state.

MALCOLM This is the sergeant,
Who, like a good and hardy soldier, fought
'Gainst my captivity. – Hail, brave friend!
Say to the king the knowledge of the broil,
As thou didst leave it.
CAPTAIN Doubtful it stood;
As two spent swimmers, that do cling together
And choke their art. The merciless Macdonwald
(Worthy to be a rebel, for to that
The multiplying villainies of nature
Do swarm upon him) from the western isles
Of Kernes and Gallowglasses is supplied;
And fortune, on his damned quarrel smiling,
Show'd like a rebel's whore: but all's too weak:
For brave Macbeth (well he deserves that name),
Disdaining fortune, with his brandish'd steel,
Which smok'd with bloody execution,
Like valour's minion, carv'd out his passage,
Till he fac'd the slave;
Which ne'er shook hands, nor bade farewell to him.
Till he unseam'd him from the nave to the chaps,
And fix'd his head upon our battlements.
DUNCAN O valiant cousin! worthy gentleman!
CAPTAIN As whence the sun 'gins his reflection
Shipwracking storms and direful thunders break,
So from that spring, whence comfort seem'd to come,
Discomfort swells. Mark, King of Scotland, mark;
No sooner justice had, with valour arm'd,
Compell'd these skipping Kernes to trust their heels,
But the Norweyan lord, surveying vantage,
With furbish'd arms, and new supplies of men,
Began a fresh assault.

DUNCAN Dismay'd not this
Our captains, Macbeth and Banquo?
CAPTAIN Yes;
As sparrows eagles, or the hare the lion.
If I say sooth, I must report they were
As cannons overcharg'd with double cracks;
So they
Doubly redoubled strokes upon the foe:
Except they meant to bathe in reeking wounds,
Or memorise another Golgatha,
I cannot tell –
But I am faint, my gashes cry for help.
DUNCAN So well thy words become thee, as thy wounds:
They smack of honour both. – Go, get him surgeons.
[Exit Captain, attended.

Enter Rosse.

Who comes here?
MALCOLM The worthy thane of Rosse.
LENOX What a haste looks through his eyes!
So should he look that seems to speak things strange.
ROSSE God save the king!
DUNCAN Whence cam'st thou, worthy thane?
ROSSE From Fife, great king,
Where the Norweyan banners flout the sky
And fan our people cold.
Norway himself, with terrible numbers,
Assisted by that most disloyal traitor,
The thane of Cawdor, began a dismal conflict;
Till that Bellona's bridgroom, lapp'd in proof,
Confronted him with self-comparisons,

Point against point, rebellious arm 'gainst arm,
Curbing his lavish spirit: and, to conclude,
The victory fell on us; –

DUNCAN Great happiness!

ROSSE That now
Sweno, the Norways' king, craves composition;
Nor would we deign him burial of his men
Till he disbursed at Saint Colme's Inch
Ten thousand dollars to our general use.

DUNCAN No more that thane of Cawdor shall deceive
Our bosom interest. – Go, pronounce his present death,
And with his former title greet Macbeth.

ROSSE I'll see it done.

DUNCAN What he hath lost, noble Macbeth hath won.

[Exeunt.

SCENE III – A HEATH.

Thunder. Enter the three Witches.

1 WITCH Where hast thou been, sister?

2 WITCH Killing swine.

3 WITCH Sister, where thou?

1 WITCH A sailor's wife had chestnuts in her lap.
And mounch'd, and mounch'd, and mounch'd: 'Give me,' quoth I: –
'Aroint thee, witch!' the rump-fed ronyon cries.
Her husband's to Aleppo gone, master o' the Tiger:
But in a sieve I 'll thither sail,
And like a rat without a tail;
I 'll do, I 'll do, and I 'll do.

2 WITCH I 'll give thee a wind.
1 WITCH Th' art kind.
3 WITCH And I another.
1 WITCH I myself have all the other;
And the very ports they blow,
All the quarters that they know
I' the shipman's card.
I 'll drain him dry as hay:
Sleep shall neither night nor day
Hang upon his penthouse lid;
He shall live a man forbid.
Weary sev'n-nights, nine times nine,
Shall he dwindle, peak, and pine:
Though his bark cannot be lost,
Yet it shall be tempest-tost.
Look what I have.
2 WITCH Show me, show me.
1 WITCH Here I have a pilot's thumb.
Wrack'd, as homeward he did come. *[Drum within.*
3 WITCH A drum! a drum!
Macbeth doth come.
ALL The weird sisters, hand in hand,
Posters of the sea and land,
Thus do go about, about:
Thrice to thine, and thrice to mine,
And thrice again, to make up nine.
Peace! – the charm's wound up.

Enter Macbeth and Banquo.

MACBETH So foul and fair a day I have not seen.
BANQUO How far is 't call'd to Fores? – What are these,

So wither'd and so wild in their attire,
That look not like th' inhabitants o' the earth,
And yet are on 't? Live you? or are you aught
That man may question? You seem to understand me,
By each at once her choppy finger laying
Upon her skinny lips: – you should be women,
And yet your beards forbid me to interpret
That you are so.

MACBETH Speak, if you can: – what are you?

1 WITCH All hail, Macbeth! hail to thee, thane of Glamis!

2 WITCH All hail, Macbeth! hail to thee, thane of Cawdor!

3 WITCH All hail, Macbeth! that shalt be king hereafter.

BANQUO Good sir, why do you start, and seem to fear
Things that do sound so fair? – I' the name of truth,
Are ye fantastical, or that indeed
Which outwardly ye show? My noble partner
You greet with present grace, and great prediction
Of noble having, and of royal hope,
That he seems rapt withal: to me you speak not.
If you can look into the seeds of time,
And say which grain will grow, and which will not,
Speak then to me, who neither beg, nor fear,
Your favours nor your hate.

1 WITCH Hail!

2 WITCH Hail!

3 WITCH Hail!

1 WITCH Lesser than Macbeth, and greater.

2 WITCH Not so happy, yet much happier.

3 WITCH Thou shalt get kings, though thou be none:
So, all hail, Macbeth and Banquo!

1 WITCH Banquo and Macbeth, all hail!

MACBETH Stay, you imperfect speakers, tell me more.
By Sinel's death, I know, I am thane of Glamis;
But how of Cawdor? the thane of Cawdor lives,
A prosperous gentleman; and to be king
Stands not within the prospect of belief,
No more than to be Cawdor. Say, from whence
You owe this strange intelligence? or why
Upon this blasted heath you stop our way
With such prophetic greeting? – Speak, I charge you.
[Witches vanish.

BANQUO The earth hath bubbles, as the water has.
And these are of them. – Wither are they vanish'd?

MACBETH Into the air; and what seem'd corporal, melted
As breath into the wind. – 'Would they had stay'd!

BANQUO Were such things here, as we do speak about,
Or have we eaten on the insane root,
That takes the reason prisoner?

MACBETH Your children shall be kings.

BANQUO You shall be king.

MACBETH And than of Cawdor too; went it not so?

BANQUO To the selfsame tune, and words. Who's here?

Enter Rosse and Angus.

ROSSE The king hath happily receiv'd, Macbeth,
The news of thy success; and when he reads
Thy personal venture in the rebel's fight,
His wonders and his praises do contend,
Which should be thine, or his. Silenc'd with that,
In viewing o'er the rest o' the selfsame day,
He finds thee in the stout Norweyan ranks,
Nothing afeard of what thyself didst make,

Strange images of death. As thick as hail,
Came post with post; and every one did bear
Thy praises in his kingdom's great defence,
And pour'd them down before him.

ANGUS We are sent,
To give thee from our royal master thanks;
Only to herald thee into his sight,
Not pay thee.

ROSSE And, for an earnest of a greater honour,
He bade me, from him, call thee thane of Cawdor:
In which addition, hail, most worthy thane,
For it is thine.

BANQUO What! can the devil speak true?

MACBETH The thane of Cawdor lives: why do you dress me
In borrow'd robes?

ANGUS Who was the thane, lives yet:
But under heavy judgment bears that life
Which he deserves to lose. Whether he was combin'd
With those of Norway, or did line the rebel
With hidden help and vantage, or that with both
He labour'd in his country's wrack, I know not;
But treasons capital, confess'd and prov'd,
Have overthrown him.

MACBETH Glamis, and thane of Cawdor:
The greatest is behind. – Thanks for your pains. –
Do you not hope your children shall be kings,
When those that gave the thane of Cawdor to me
Promis'd no less to them?

BANQUO That, trusted home,
Might yet enkindle you unto the crown,
Besides the thane of Cawdor. But 't is strange:

And oftentimes, to win us to our harm,
The instruments of darkness tell us truths;
Win us with honest trifles, to betray 's
In deepest consequence. –
Cousins, a word, I pray you.

MACBETH *[Aside.]* Two truths are told,
As happy prologues to the swelling act
Of the imperial theme. – I thank you, gentlemen. –
[Aside.] This supernatural soliciting
Cannot be ill; cannot be good: – if ill,
Why hath it given me earnest of success,
Commencing in a truth? I am thane of Cawdor:
If good, why do I yield to that suggestion
Whose horrid image doth unfix my hair,
And make my seated heart knock at my ribs,
Against the use of nature? Present fears
Are less than horrible imaginings.
My thought, whose murder yet is but fantastical,
Shakes so my single state of man, that function
Is smother'd in surmise, and nothing is,
But what is not.

BANQUO Look, how our partner's rapt.

MACBETH *[Aside.]* If chance will have me king, why, chance may crown me,
Without my stir.

BANQUO New honours come upon him,
Like our strange garments, cleave not to their mould,
But with the aid of use.

MACBETH *[Aside.]* Come what come may,
Time and the hour runs through the roughest day.

BANQUO Worthy Macbeth, we stay upon your leisure.

MACBETH Give me your favour: my dull brain was wrought
With things forgotten. Kind gentlemen, your pains
Are register'd where every day I turn
The leaf to read them. – Let us toward the king. –
Think upon what hath chanc'd; and at more time,
The interim having weigh'd it, let us speak
Our free hearts each to other.
BANQUO Very gladly.
MACBETH Till then, enough. – Come, friends. *[Exeunt.*

SCENE IV – FORES. A ROOM IN THE PALACE

Flourish. Enter Duncan, Malcolm, Donalbain, Lenox, and Attendants.

DUNCAN Is execution done on Cawdor? Are not
Those in commission yet return'd?
MALCOLM My liege,
They are not yet come back; but I have spoke
With one that saw him die: who did report,
That very frankly he confess'd his treasons,
Implor'd your highness' pardon, and set forth
A deep repentance. Nothing in his life
Became him like the leaving it: he died
As one that had been studied in his death,
To throw away the dearest thing he ow'd,
As 't were a careless trifle.
DUNCAN There's no art
To find the mind's construction in the face:
He was a gentleman on whom I built
An absolute trust –

Enter Macbeth, Banquo, Rosse, and Angus.

O worthiest cousin!
The sin of my ingratitude even now
Was heavy on me. Thou art so far before,
That swiftest wing of recompense is slow
To overtake thee: 'would thou hadst less deserv'd,
That the proportion both of thanks and payment
Might have been mine! only I have left to say,
More is thy due than more than all can pay.

MACBETH The service and the loyalty I owe,
In doing it, pays itself. Your highness' part
Is to receive our duties: and our duties
Are to your throne and state, children and servants;
Which do but what they should, by doing everything
Safe toward your love and honour.

DUNCAN Welcome hither:
I have begun to plant thee, and will labour
To make thee full of growing. – Noble Banquo,
That hast no less deserv'd, nor must be known
No less to have done so, let me infold thee,
And hold thee to my heart.

BANQUO There if I grow,
The harvest is your own.

DUNCAN My plenteous joys,
Wanton in fulness, seek to hide themselves
In drops of sorrow. – Sons, kinsmen, thanes,
And you whose places are the nearest, know,
We will establish our estate upon
Our eldest, Malcolm; whom we name hereafter
The Prince of Cumberland: which honour must
Not, unaccompanied, invest him only,

But signs of nobleness, like stars, shall shine
On all deservers. – From hence to Inverness,
And bind us further to you.

MACBETH The rest is labour, which is not us'd for you:
I'll be myself the harbinger, and make joyful
The hearing of my wife with your approach;
So, humbly take my leave.

DUNCAN My worthy Cawdor!

MACBETH *[Aside.]* The Prince of Cumberland! – That is a step,
On which I must fall down, or else o'erleap,
For in my way it lies. Stars, hide your fires!
Let not light see my black and deep desires;
The eye wink at the hand; yet let that be,
Which the eye fears, when it is done, to see. *[Exit.*

DUNCAN True, worthy Banquo: he is full so valiant
And in his commendations I am fed;
It is a banquet to me. Let us after him,
Whose care is gone before to bid us welcome:
It is a peerless kinsman. *[Flourish. Exeunt.*

SCENE V – INVERNESS. A ROOM IN MACBETH'S CASTLE.

Enter Lady Macbeth, reading a letter.

LADY MACBETH 'They met me in the day of success; and I have learned by the perfectest report, they have more in them than mortal knowledge. When I burned in desire to question them further, they made themselves air, into which they vanished. Whiles I stood rapt in the wonder of it, came missives from the king, who all-hailed me, "Thane of Cawdor;" by which title, before, these weird sisters saluted me, and referred me to the coming on of time, with "Hail, king that shalt be!" This have I thought good to deliver thee, my dearest partner of greatness, that thou mightest not lose the dues of rejoicing, by being ignorant of what greatness is promised thee. Lay it to thy heart, and farewell.'

Glamis thou art, and Cawdor; and shalt be
What thou art promis'd. – Yet do I fear thy nature:
It is too full o' the milk of human kindness,
To catch the nearest way. Thou wouldst be great;
Art not without ambition, but without
The illness should attend it: what thou wouldst highly,
That wouldst thou holily; wouldst not play false,
And yet wouldst wrongly win; thou'dst have, great Glamis,
That which cries, 'Thus thou must do, if thou have it;'
And that which rather thou dost fear to do,
Than wishest should be undone. Hie thee hither,
That I may pour my spirits in thine ear,
And chastise with the valour of my tongue
All that impedes thee from the golden round,
Which fate and metaphysical aid doth seem
To have three crown'd withal. –

Enter a Messenger.

What is your tidings?

MESSENGER The king comes here to-night.

LADY MACBETH Thou'rt mad to say it.
Is not thy master with him? who, were't so,
Would have inform'd for preparation.

MESSENGER So please you, it is true: our thane is coming;
One of my fellows had the speed of him,
Who, almost dead for breath, had scarcely more
Than would make up his message.

LADY MACBETH Give him tending:
He brings great news. *[Exit Messenger.]* The raven himself is hoarse,
That croaks the fatal entrance of Duncan
Under my battlements. Come, you spirits
That tend on mortal thoughts, unsex me here.
And fill me, from the crown to the toe, top-full
Of direst cruelty! make thick my blood,
Stop up th' access and passage to remorse;
That no compunctious visitings of nature
Shake my fell purpose, nor keep peace between
Th' effect and it! Come to my woman's breasts,
And take my milk for gall, you murdering ministers,
Wherever in your sightless substances
You wait on nature's mischief! Come, thick night,
And pall thee in the dunnest smoke of hell,
That my keen knife see not the wound it makes.
Nor heaven peep through the blanket of the dark,
To cry, 'Hold, hold!' –

Enter Macbeth.

Great Glamis! worthy Cawdor;
Greater than both, by the all-hail hereafter!
Thy letters have transported me beyond
This ignorant present, and I feel now
The future in the instant.

MACBETH My dearest love,
Duncan comes here to-night.

LADY MACBETH And when goes he hence?

MACBETH To-morrow, as he proposes.

LADY MACBETH O! never

Shall sun that morrow see!
Your face, my thane, is as a book, where men
May read strange matters. To beguile the time,
Look like the time; bear welcome in your eye,
Your hand, your tongue: look like the innocent flower,
But be the serpent under't. He that's coming
Must be provided for; and you shall put
This night's great business into my despatch;
Which shall to all our nights and days to come
Give solely sovereign sway and masterdom.

MACBETH We will speak further.

LADY MACBETH Only look up clear;
To alter favour ever is to fear.
Leave all the rest to me. *[Exeunt.*

SCENE VI – THE SAME. BEFORE THE CASTLE.

Hautboys and torches. Enter Duncan, Malcolm, Donalbain, Banquo, Lenox, Macduff, Rosse, Angus, and Attendants.

DUNCAN This castle hath a pleasant seat; the air
Nimbly and sweetly recommends itself
Unto our gentle senses.

BANQUO This guest of summer,
The temple-haunting martlet, does approve,
By his lov'd mansionry, that the heaven's breath
Smells wooingly here: no jutty, frieze,
Buttress, nor coign of vantage, but this bird
Hath made his pendent bed, and procreant cradle:
Where they most breed and haunt, I have observ'd,
The air is delicate.

Enter Lady Macbeth.

DUNCAN See, see! our honour'd hostess. –
The love that follows us sometime is our trouble,
Which still we thank as love. Herein I teach you,
How you shall bid God yield us for your pains,
And thank us for your trouble.

LADY MACBETH All our service,
In every point twice done, and then done double,
Were poor and single business, to contend
Against those honours deep and broad, wherewith
Your majesty loads our house: for those of old,
And the late dignities heap'd up to them,
We rest your hermits.

DUNCAN Where's the thane of Cawdor
We cours'd him at the heels, and had a purpose
To be his purveyor: but he rides well;
And his great love, sharp as his spur, hath holp him
To his home before us. Fair and noble hostess,
We are your guest to-night.

LADY MACBETH Your servants ever
Have theirs, themselves, and what is theirs, in compt,
To make their audit at your highness' pleasure,
Still to return your own.

DUNCAN Give me your hand;
Conduct me to mine host: we love him highly,
And shall continue our graces towards him.
By your leave, hostess. *[Exeunt.*

SCENE VII – THE SAME. A ROOM IN THE CASTLE.

Hautboys and torches. Enter, and pass over the stage, a Sewer, and divers Servants with dishes and service. Then enter Macbeth.

MACBETH If it were done, when 't is done, then 't were well
It were done quickly: if the assassination
Could trammel up the consequence, and catch
With his surcease success; that but this blow
Might be the be-all and the end-all here,
But here, upon this bank and shoal of time,
We'd jump the life to come. – But in these cases,
We still have judgment here; that we but teach
Bloody instructions, which, being taught, return
To plague th' inventor: this even-handed justice
Commends th' ingredients of our poison'd chalice
To our own lips. He's here in double trust:
First, as I am his kinsman and his subject,
Strong both against the deed; then, as his host,
Who should against his murderer shut the door,
Not bear the knife myself. Besides, this Duncan
Hath borne his faculties so meek, hath been
So clear in his great office, that his virtues
Will plead like angels, trumpet-tongued, against
The deep damnation of his taking off;
And pity, like a naked new-born babe,
Striding the blast, or heaven's cherubin, hors'd
Upon the sightless couriers of the air,
Shall blow the horrid deed in every eye,
That tears shall drown the wind. – I have no spur

To prick the sides of my intent, but only
Vaulting ambition, which o'erleaps itself,
And falls on the other –

Enter Lady Macbeth.

How now! what news?

LADY MACBETH He has almost supp'd. Why have you left the chamber?

MACBETH Hath he ask'd for me?

LADY MACBETH Know you not, he has?

MACBETH We will proceed no further in this business:
He hath honour'd me of late; and I have bought
Golden opinions from all sorts of people,
Which would be worn now in their newest gloss,
Not cast aside so soon.

LADY MACBETH Was the hope drunk,
Wherein you dress'd yourself? hath it slept since,
And wakes it now, to look so green and pale
At what it did so freely? From this time,
Such I account thy love. Art thou afeard
To be the same in thine own act and valour,
As thou art in desire? Wouldst thou have that
Which thou esteem'st the ornament of life,
And live a coward in thine own esteem,
Letting 'I dare not' wait upon 'I would,'
Like the poor cat i' the adage?

MACBETH Pr'ythee, peace.
I dare do all that may become a man;
Who dares do more, is none.

LADY MACBETH What beast was't then,
That made you break this enterprise to me?

When you durst do it, then you were a man;
And, to be more than what you were, you would
Be so much more the man. Nor time, nor place,
Did then adhere, and yet you would make both:
They have made themselves, and that their fitness now
Does unmake you. I have given suck, and know
How tender 't is to love the babe that milks me:
I would, while it was smiling in my face,
Have pluck'd my nipple from his boneless gums,
And dash'd the brains out, had I so sworn as you
Have done to this.

MACBETH If we should fail, –

LADY MACBETH We fail!
But screw your courage to the sticking-place,
And we'll not fail. When Duncan is asleep
(Whereto the rather shall his day's hard journey
Soundly invite him), his two chamberlains
Will I with wine and wassail so convince,
That memory, the warder of the brain,
Shall be a fume, and the receipt of reason
A limbeck only: when in swinish sleep
Their drenched natures lie, as in a death,
What cannot you and I perform upon
Th' unguarded Duncan? what not put upon
His spongy officers, who shall bear the guilt
Of our great quell?

MACBETH Bring forth men-children only!
For thy undaunted mettle should compose
Nothing but males. Will it not be receiv'd,
When we have mark'd with blood those sleepy two
Of his own chamber, and us'd their very daggers,
That they have done 't?

LADY MACBETH Who dares receive it other,
As we shall make our griefs and clamour roar
Upon his death?

MACBETH I am settled, and bend up
Each corporal agent to this terrible feat.
Away, and mock the time with fairest show:
False face must hide what the false heart doth know.

[Exeunt.

ACT TWO

SCENE I – THE SAME. COURT WITHIN THE CASTLE.

Enter Banquo, and Fleance, with a torch before him.

BANQUO How goes the night, boy?
FLLEANCE The moon is down; I have not heard the clock.
BANQUO And she goes down at twelve.
FLLEANCE I take 't, 't is later, sir.
BANQUO Hold, take my sword. – There's husbandry in heaven;
Their candles are all out. – Take thee that too.
A heavy summons lies like lead upon me,
And yet I would not sleep: merciful powers!
Restrain in me the cursed thoughts that nature
Gives way to in repose! – Give me my sword.

Enter Macbeth, and a Servant with a torch.

Who's there?
MACBETH A friend.
BANQUO What, sir! not yet at rest? The king's a-bed:
He hath been in unusual pleasure, and
Sent forth great largess to your offices.
This diamond he greets your wife withal,
By the name of most kind hostess, and shut up
In measureless content.
MACBETH Being unprepar'd,
Our will became the servant to defect,

Which else should free have wrought.

BANQUO All's well.

I dreamt last night of the three weird sisters:

To you they have show'd some truth.

MACBETH I think not of them:

Yet, when we can entreat an hour to serve,

We would spend it in some words upon that business,

If you would grant the time.

BANQUO At your kind'st leisure.

MACBETH If you shall cleave to my consent, when 't is,

It shall make honour for you.

BANQUO So I lose none

In seeking to augment it, but still keep

My bosom franchis'd, and allegiance clear,

I shall be counsell'd.

MACBETH Good repose, the while!

BANQUO Thanks, sir: the like to you.

[Exeunt Banquo and Fleance.

MACBETH Go, bid thy mistress, when my drink is ready,

She strike upon the bell. Get thee to bed. – *[Exit Servant.*

Is this a dagger, which I see before me,

The handle toward my hand? Come, let me clutch thee: –

I have thee not, and yet I see thee still.

Art thou not, fatal vision, sensible

To feeling, as to sight? or art thou but

A dagger of the mind, a false creation,

Proceeding from the heat-oppressed brain?

I see thee yet, in form as palpable

As this which now I draw.

Thou marshall'st me the way that I was going;

And such an instrument I was to use. –

Mine eyes are made the fools o' the other senses,
Or else worth all the rest: I see thee still;
And on thy blade, and dudgeon, gouts of blood,
Which was not so before. – There's no such thing.
It is the bloody business which informs
Thus to mine eyes. – Now o'er the one half-world
Nature seems dead, and wicked dreams abuse
The curtain'd sleep: witchcraft celebrates
Pale Hecate's offerings; and wither'd murder,
Alarum'd by his sentinel, the wolf,
Whose howl's his watch, thus with his stealthy pace,
With Tarquin's ravishing strides, towards his design
Moves like a ghost, – Thou sure and firm-set earth,
Hear not my steps, which way they walk, for fear
Thy very stones prate of my where-about,
And take the present horror from the time,
Which now suits with it. – Whiles I threat, he lives:
Words to the heat of deeds too cold breath gives.

[A bell rings.

I go, and it is done: the bell invites me.
Hear it not, Duncan; for it is a knell
That summons thee to heaven, or to hell. *[Exit.*

SCENE II – THE SAME.

Enter Lady Macbeth.

LADY MACBETH That which hath made them drunk hath made me bold:
What hath quench'd them hath given me fire. – Hark! – Peace!
It was the owl that shriek'd, the fatal bellman,

Which gives the stern'st good-night. He is about it.
The doors are open; and the surfeited grooms
Do mock their charge with snores: I have drugg'd their possets,
That death and nature do contend about them,
Whether they live, or die.

MACBETH *[Within.]* Who's there? – what, ho!

LADY MACBETH Alack! I am afraid they have awak'd,
And 't is not done: – the attempt and not the deed
Confounds us. – Hark! – I laid their daggers ready;
He could not miss them. – had he not resembled
My father as he slept, I had done 't. – My husband!

Enter Macbeth.

MACBETH I have done the deed. – Didst thou not hear a noise?

LADY MACBETH I heard the owl scream, and the crickets cry.
Did not you speak?

MACBETH When?

LADY MACBETH Now.

MACBETH As I descended?

LADY MACBETH Ay.

MACBETH Hark!
Who lies i' the second chamber?

LADY MACBETH Donalbain.

MACBETH This is a sorry sight.

LADY MACBETH A foolish thought to say a sorry sight.

MACBETH There's one did laugh in 's sleep, and one cried, 'Murder!'
That they did wake each other: I stood and heard them;
But they did say their prayers, and address'd them
Again to sleep.

LADY MACBETH There are two lodg'd togther.

MACBETH One cried, 'God bless us!' and, 'Amen,' the other,
As they had seen me with these hangman's hands,
Listening their fear, I could not say, 'Amen,'
When they did say, 'God bless us.'

LADY MACBETH Consider it not so deeply.

MACBETH But wherefore could not I pronounce 'Amen?'
I had most need of blessing, and 'Amen'
Stuck in my throat.

LADY MACBETH These deeds must not be thought
After these ways: so, it will make us mad.

MACBETH Methought, I heard a voice cry, 'Sleep no more!
Macbeth does murder sleep,' – the innocent sleep:
Sleep, that knits up the ravell'd sleave of care,
The death of each day's life, sore labour's bath,
Balm of hurt minds, great nature's second course,
Chief nourisher in life's feast; –

LADY MACBETH What do you mean?

MACBETH Still it cried, 'Sleep no more!' to all the house:
Glamis hath murder'd sleep, and therefore Cawdor
Shall sleep no more, Macbeth shall sleep no more!

LADY MACBETH Who was it that thus cried? Why, worthy thane,
You do unbend your noble strength, to think
So brainsickly of things. Go, get some water,
And wash this filthy witness from your hand.
Why did you bring these daggers from the place?
They must lie there: go, carry them, and smear
The sleepy grooms with blood.

MACBETH I'll go no more:
I am afraid to think what I have done;
Look on 't again I dare not.

LADY MACBETH Infirm of purpose!
Give me the daggers. The sleeping, and the dead,
Are but as pictures; 't is the eye of childhood
That fears a painted devil. If he do bleed,
I'll gild the faces of the grooms withal,
For it must seem their guilt.
[Exit – Knocking within.

MACBETH Whence is that knocking?
How is 't with me, when every noise appals me?
What hands are here? Ha! they pluck out mine eyes.
Will all great Neptune's ocean wash this blood
Clean from my hand! No, this my hand will rather
The multitudinous seas incarnardine,
Making the green one red.

Re-enter Lady Macbeth.

LADY MACBETH My hands are of your colour; but I shame
To wear a heart so white. *[Knock.]* I hear a knocking
At the south entry: – retire we to our chamber.
A little water clears us of this deed:
How easy is it then! Your constancy
Hath left you unattended. – *[Knock.]* Hark! more knocking.
Get on your night-gown, lest occasion call us,
And show us to be watchers. – Be not lost
So poorly in your thoughts.
MACBETH To know my deed, 't were best not know myself.
[Knock.
Wake Duncan with thy knocking: I would thou couldst!
[Exeunt.

SCENE III – THE SAME.

Enter a Porter.

[Knocking within.

PORTER Here's a knocking, indeed! If a man were porter of hell-gate, he should have old turning the key. *[Knocking.]* Knock, knock, knock. Who's there, i' the name of Belzebub? – Here's a farmer, that hanged himself on the expectation of plenty: come in time; have napkins enough about you; here you'll sweat for 't. *[Knocking.]* Knock, knock. Who's there, i' the other devil's name? – 'Faith, here's an equivocator, that could swear in both the scales against either scale; who committed treason enough for God's sake, yet could not equivocate to heaven: O! come in, equivocator. *[Knocking.]* Knock, knock, knock. Who's there? – 'Faith, here's an English tailor come hither for stealing out of a French hose: come in, tailor; here you may roast your goose. *[Knocking.]* Knock, knock. Never at quiet! What are you? – But this place is too cold for hell. I'll devil-porter it no further: I had thought to have let in some of all professions, that go the primrose way to the everlasting bonfire. *[Knocking.]* Anon, anon: I pray you, remember the porter.

[Opens the gate.

Enter Macduff and Lenox.

MACDUFF Was it so late, friend, ere you went to bed,
That you do lie so late?

PORTER 'Faith, sir, we were carousing till the second cock;
And drink, sir, is a great provoker of three things.

MACDUFF What three things does drink especially provoke?

PORTER Marry, sir, nose-painting, sleep, and urine. Lechery, sir, it provokes, and unprovokes: it provokes the desire, but it takes away the performance. Therefore, much drink may be said to be an equivocator with lechery: it makes him, and it mars him; it sets him on, and it takes him off; it persuades him, and disheartens him; makes him stand to, and not stand to: in conclusion, equivocates him in a sleep, and, giving him the lie, leaves him.

MACDUFF I believe, drink gave thee the lie last night.

PORTER That it did, sir, i' the very throat o' me: but I requited him for his lie; and, I think, being too strong for him, though he took up my legs sometime, yet I made a shift to cast him.

MACDUFF Is thy master stirring?

Enter Macbeth.

Our knocking has awak'd him; here he comes.

LENOX Good morrow, noble sir!

MACBETH Good morrow, both!

MACDUFF Is the king stirring, worthy thane?

MACBETH Not yet.

MACDUFF Hs did command me to call timely on him:
I have almost slipp'd the hour.

MACBETH I'll bring you to him.

MACDUFF I know, this is a joyful trouble to you;
But yet 't is one.

MACBETH The labour we delight on physics pain.
This is the door.

MACDUFF I'll make so bold to call,
For 't is my limited service. *[Exit.*

LENOX Goes the king hence to-day?

MACBETH He does: – he did appoint so.

LENOX The night has been unruly: where we lay,

Our chimneys were blown down; and, as they say,
Lamentings heard i' the air; strange screams of death,
And prophesying with accents terrible
Of dire combustion, and confus'd events,
New hatch'd to the woful time.
The obscure bird clamour'd the livelong night:
Some say, the earth was feverous, and did shake.

MACBETH 'T was a rough night.

LENOX My young remembrance cannot parallel
A fellow to it.

Re-enter Macduff.

MACDUFF O horror! horror! horror! Tongue, nor heart,
Cannot conceive, nor name thee!

MACBETH, LENOX What's the matter?

MACDUFF Confusion now hath made his master-piece!
Most sacrilegious murder hath broke ope
The Lord's anointed temple, and stole thence
The life o' the building.

MACBETH What is 't you say? the life?

LENOX Mean you his majesty?

MACDUFF Approach the chamber, and destroy your sight
With a new Gorgon. – Do not bid me speak:
See, and then speak yourselves. –

[Exeunt Macbeth and Lenox.

Awake! awake! –
Ring the alarum-bell. – Murder, and treason!
Banquo, and Donalbain! Malcolm! awake!
Shake off this downy sleep, death's counterfeit,
And look on death itself! – up, up, and see
The great doom's image! – Malcolm! Banquo!

As from your graves rise up, and walk like sprites,
To countenance this horror! Ring the bell. *[Bell rings.*

Enter Lady Macbeth.

LADY MACBETH What's the business,
That such a hideous trumpet calls to parley
The sleepers of the house? speak, speak!

MACDUFF O gentle lady,
'T is not for you to hear what I can speak:
The repetition, in a woman's ear,
Would murder as it fell.

Enter Banquo.

O Banquo! Banquo!
Our royal master's murder'd!

LADY MACBETH Woe, alas!
What! in our house?

BANQUO Too cruel, anywhere.
Dear Duff, I pr'ythee, contradict thyself,
And say, it is not so.

Re-enter Macbeth and Lenox.

MACBETH Had I but died an hour before this chance,
I have liv'd a blessed time; for, from this instant,
There's nothing serious in mortality;
All is but toys: renown, and grace, is dead;
The wine of life is drawn, and the mere lees
Is left this vault to brag of.

Enter Malcolm and Donalbain.

DONALBAIN What is amiss?

MACBETH You are, and do not know 't:
The spring, the head, the fountain of your blood
Is stopp'd; the very source of it is stopp'd.
MACDUFF Your royal father's murder'd.
MALCOLM O! by whom?
LENOX Those of his chamber, as it seem'd, had done 't:
Their hands and faces were all badg'd with blood;
So were their daggers, which, unwip'd, we found
Upon their pillows:
They star'd, and were distracted; no man's life
Was to be trusted with them.
MACBETH O! yet I do repent me of my fury,
That I did kill them.
MACDUFF Wherefore did you so?
MACBETH Who can be wise, amaz'd, temperate and furious,
Loyal and neutral, in a moment? No man:
The expedition of my violent love
Outrun the pauser reason. – Here lay Duncan,
His silver skin lac'd with his golden blood;
And his gash'd stabs look'd like a breach in nature
For ruin's wasteful entrance: there, the murderers,
Steep'd in the colours of their trade, their daggers
Unmannerly breech'd with gore. Who could refrain,
That had a heart to love, and in that heart
Courage, to make 's love known?
LADY MACBETH Help me hence, ho!
MACDUFF Look to the lady.
MALCOLM Why do we hold our tongues,
That most may claim this argument for ours?
DONALBAIN What should be spoken
Here, where our fate, hid in an auger-hole,

May rush, and seize us? Let's away: our tears
Are not yet brew'd.

MALCOLM Nor our strong sorrow
Upon the foot of motion.

BANQUO Look to the lady: –

[Lady Macbeth is carried out.

And when we have our naked frailties hid,
That suffer in exposure, let us meet,
And question this most bloody piece of work,
To know it further. Fears and scruples shake us:
In the great hand of God I stand; and, thence,
Against the undivulg'd pretence I fight
Of treasonous malice.

MACDUFF And so do I.

ALL So all.

MACDUFF Let's briefly put on manly readiness,
And meet i' the hall together.

ALL Well contented.

[Exeunt all but Malcolm and Donalbain.

MALCOLM What will you do? Let's not consort with them:
To show an unfelt sorrow in an office
Which the false man does easy. I'll to England.

DONALBAIN To Ireland, I: our separated fortune
Shall keep us both the safer; where we are,
There's daggers in men's smiles: the near' in blood,
The nearer bloody.

MALCOLM The murderous shaft that's shot
Hath not yet lighted, and our safest way
Is to avoid the aim: therefore, to horse;
And let us not be dainty of leave-taking,
But shift away. There's warrant in that theft
Which steals itself, when there's no mercy left. *[Exeunt.*

SCENE IV – WITHOUT THE CASTLE.

Enter Rosse and an Old Man.

OLD MAN Threescore and ten I can remember well;
Within the volume of which time I have seen
Hours dreadful, and things strange, but this sore night
Hath trifled former knowings.

ROSSE Ah! good father,
Thou seest, the heavens, as troubled with man's act,
Threaten his bloody stage: by the clock 't is day,
And yet dark night strangles the travelling lamp.
Is 't night's predominance, or the day's shame,
That darkness does the face of earth entomb,
When living light should kiss it?

OLD MAN 'T is unnatural,
Even like the deed that's done. On Tuesday last,
A falcon, towering in her pride of place,
Was by a mousing owl hawk'd at, and kill'd.

ROSSE And Duncan's horses (a thing most strange and certain),
Beauteous and swift, the minions of their race,
Turn'd wild in nature, broke their stalls, flung out,
Contending 'gainst obedience, as they would make
War with mankind.

OLD MAN 'T is said, they eat each other.

ROSSE They did so; to th'amazement of mine eyes,
That look'd upon't. Here comes the good Macduff. –

Enter Macduff.

How goes the world, sir, now?

MACDUFF Why, see you not?

ROSSE Is't known, who did this more than bloody deed?
MACDUFF Those that Macbeth hath slain.
ROSSE Alas, the day!
What good could they pretend?
MACDUFF They were suborn'd.
Malcolm, and Donalbain, the king's two sons,
Are stol'n away and fled; which puts upon them
Suspicion of the deed.
ROSSE 'Gainst nature still:
Thriftless ambition, that wilt ravin up
Thine own life's means! – Then 't is most like
The sovereignty will fall upon Macbeth.
MACDUFF He is already nam'd, and gone to Scone
To be invested.
ROSSE Where is Duncan's body?
MACDUFF Carried to Colme-kill,
The sacred storehouse of his predecessors,
And guardian of their bones.
ROSSE Will you to Scone?
MACDUFF No, cousin: I 'll to Fife.
ROSSE Well, I will thither.
MACDUFF Well, may you see things well done there: – adieu! –
Lest our old robes sit easier than our new!
ROSSE Farewell, father.
OLD MAN God's benison go with you; and with those
That would make good of bad, and friends of foes! *[Exeunt.*

ACT THREE

SCENE I – FORES. A ROOM IN THE PALACE.

Enter Banquo.

BANQUO Thou hast it now, king, Cawdor, Glamis, all,
As the weird woman promis'd; and, I fear,
Thou play'dst most foully for 't; yet it was said,
It should not stand in thy posterity;
But that myself should be the root and father
Of many kings. If there come truth from them,
(As upon thee, Macbeth, their speeches shine,)
Why, by the verities on thee made good,
May they not be my oracles as well,
And set me up in hope? But, hush; no more.

Sennet sounded. Enter Macbeth, as King; Lady Macbeth, as Queen; Lenox, Rosse, Lords and Attendants.

MACBETH Here's our chief guest.
LADY MACBETH If he had been forgotten,
It had been as a gap in our great feast,
And all-thing unbecoming.
MACBETH To-night we hold a solemn supper, sir,
And I'll request your presence.
BANQUO Let your highness
Command upon me, to the which my duties
Are with a most indissoluble tie
For ever knit.

MACBETH Ride you this afternoon?
BANQUO Ay, my good lord.
MACBETH We should have else desir'd your good advice
(Which still hath been both grave and prosperous)
In this day's council; but we'll take to-morrow.
Is't far you ride?
BANQUO As far, my lord, as will fill up the time
'Twixt this and supper: go not my horse the better,
I must become a borrower of the night,
For a dark hour, or twain.
MACBETH Fail not our feast.
BANQUO My lord, I will not.
MACBETH We hear, our bloody cousins are bestow'd
In England, and in Ireland; not confessing
Their cruel parricide, filling their hearers
With strange invention. But of that to-morrow,
When, therewithal, we shall have cause of state,
Craving us jointly. Hie you to horse: adieu,
Till you return at night. Goes Fleance with you?
BANQUO Ay, my good lord: our time does call upon 's.
MACBETH I wish your horses swift, and sure of foot;
And so I do commend you to their backs.
Farewell. – *[Exit Banquo.*
Let every man be master of his time
Till seven at night, to make society
The sweeter welcome: we will keep ourself
Till supper-time alone: while then, God be with you.
[Exeunt Lady Macbeth, Lords, &c.
Sirrah, a word with you. Attend those men
Our pleasure?
ATTENDANT They are, my lord, without the palace gate.

MACBETH Bring them before us. *[Exit Attendant.]* – To be thus is nothing,
But to be safely thus. – Our fears in Banquo
Stick deep, and in his royalty of nature
Reigns that which would be fear'd: 't is much he dares;
And, to that dauntless temper of his mind,
He hath a wisdom that doth guide his valour
To act in safety. There is none but he
Whose being I do fear: and under him
My genius is rebuk'd; as, it is said,
Mark Antony's was by Caesar. He chid the sisters,
When first they put the name of king upon me,
And bade them speak to him; then, prophet-like,
They hail'd him father to a line of kings.
Upon my head they plac'd a fruitless crown,
And put a barren sceptre in my gripe,
Thence to be wrench'd with an unlineal hand,
No son of mine succeeding. If 't be so,
For Banquo's issue have I fil'd my mind;
For them the gracious Duncan have I murder'd;
Put rancours in the vessel of my peace,
Only for them; and mine eternal jewel
Given to the common enemy of man,
To make them kings, the seed of Banquo kings!
Rather than so, come, fate, into the list,
And champion me to the utterance! – Who's there? –

Re-enter Attendant, with two Murderers.

Now, go to the door, and stay there till we call.
[Exit Attendant.
Was it not yesterday we spoke together?

1 MURDERER It was, so please your highness.
MACBETH Well then, now
Have you consider'd of my speeches? Know,
That it was he, in the times past, which held you
So under fortune, which, you thought, had been
Our innocent self. This I made good to you
In our last conference; pass'd in probation with you,
How you were borne in hand; how cross'd; the instruments;
Who wrought with them; and all things else, that might,
To half a soul, and to a notion craz'd,
Say, 'Thus did Banquo.'
1 MURDERER You made it known to us.
MACBETH I did so; and went further, which is now
Our point of second meeting. Do you find
Your patience so predominant in your nature,
That you can let this go? Are you so gospell'd,
To pray for this good man, and for his issue,
Whose heavy hand hath bow'd you to the grave,
And beggar'd yours for ever?
1 MURDERER We are men, my liege.
MACBETH Ay, in the catalogue ye go for men;
As hounds, and greyhounds, mongrels, spaniels, curs,
Shoughs, water-rugs, and demi-wolves, are clept
All by the name of dogs: the valu'd file
Distinguishes the swift, the slow, the subtle,
The housekeeper, the hunter, every one
According to the gift which bounteous nature
Hath in him clos'd; whereby he does receive
Particular addition, from the bill
That writes them all alike; and so of men.
Now, if you have a station in the file,

Not i' the worst rank of manhood, say it;
And I will put that business in your bosoms,
Whose execution takes your enemy off,
Grapples you to the heart and love of us,
Who wear our health but sickly in his life,
Which in his death were perfect.

2 MURDERER I am one, my liege,
Whom the vile blows and buffets of the world
Have so incens'd, that I am reckless what
I do, to spite the world.

1 MURDERER And I another,
So weary with disasters, tugg'd with fortune,
That I would set my life on any chance,
To mend it, or be rid on 't.

MACBETH Both of you
Know, Banquo was your enemy.

2 MURDERER True, my lord.

MACBETH So is he mine; and in such bloody distance,
That every minute of his being thrusts
Against my near'st of life: and though I could
With bare-fac'd power sweep him from my sight,
And bid my will avouch it, yet I must not,
For certain friends that are both his and mine,
Whose loves I may not drop, but wail his fall
Who I myself struck down: and thence it is
That I to your assistance do make love,
Masking the business from the common eye,
For sundry weighty reasons.

2 MURDERER We shall, my lord,
Perform what you command us.

1 MURDERER Though our lives –

MACBETH Your spirits shine through you. Within this hour, at most,
I will advise you where to plant yourselves,
Acquaint you with the perfect spy o' the time,
The moment on 't; for 't must be done to-night,
And something from the palace; always thought,
That I require a clearness: and with him,
(To leave no rubs, nor botches, in the work,)
Fleance his son, that keeps him company,
Whose absence is no less material to me
Than is his father's, must embrace the fate
Of that dark hour. Resolve yourselves apart;
I'll come to you anon.

2 MURDERER We are resolv'd, my lord.

MACBETH I'll call upon you straight: abide within. –
[Exeunt Murderers.
It is concluded: Banquo, thy soul's flight,
If it find heaven, must find it out to-night. *[Exit.*

SCENE II – THE SAME. ANOTHER ROOM.

Enter Lady Macbeth and a Servant.

LADY MACBETH Is Banquo gone from court?

SERVANT Ay, madam, but returns again to-night.

LADY MACBETH Say to the king, I would attend his leisure
For a few words.

SERVANT Madam, I will. *[Exit.*

LADY MACBETH Nought's had, all's spent,
Where our desire is got without content:

'T is safer to be that which we destroy,
Than by destruction dwell in doubtful joy.

Enter Macbeth.

How now, my lord? why do you keep alone,
Of sorriest fancies your companions making,
Using those thoughts, which should indeed have died
With them they think on? Things without all remedy
Should be without regard: what's done is done.

MACBETH We have scotch'd the snake, not kill'd it:
She'll close, and be herself; whilst our poor malice
Remains in danger of her former tooth.
But let the frame of things disjoint, both the worlds suffer,
Ere we will eat our meal in fear, and sleep
In the affliction of these terrible dreams,
That shake us nightly. Better be with the dead,
Whom we, to gain our peace, have sent to peace,
Than on the torture of the mind to lie
In restless ecstacy. Duncan is in his grave;
After life's fitful fever he sleeps well;
Treason has done his worst: nor steel, nor poison,
Malice domestic, foreign levy, nothing
Can touch him further!

LADY MACBETH Come on:
Gentle my lord, sleek o'er your rugged looks;
Be bright and jovial among your guests to-night.

MACBETH So shall I, love; and so, I pray, be you.
Let your remembrance apply to Banquo:
Present him eminence, both with eye and tongue:
Unsafe the while, that we
Must lave our honours in these flattering streams,

And make our faces visards to our hearts,
Disguising what they are.

LADY MACBETH You must leave this.

MACBETH O! full of scorpions is my mind, dear wife!
Thou know'st that Banquo, and his Fleance, lives.

LADY MACBETH But in them nature's copy's not eterne.

MACBETH There's comfort yet; they are assailable:
Then be thou jocund. Ere the bat hath flown
His cloister'd flight; ere to black Hecate's summons
The shard-borne beetle, with his drowsy hums,
Hath rung night's yawning peal,
There shall be done a deed of dreadful note.

LADY MACBETH What's to be done?

MACBETH Be innocent of the knowledge, dearest chuck,
Till thou applaud the deed. Come, seeling night,
Scarf up the tender eye of pitiful day,
And, with thy bloody and invisible hand,
Cancel, and tear to pieces, that great bond
Which keeps me pale! – Light thickens; and the crow
Makes wing to the rooky wood;
Good things of day begin to droop and drowse,
Whiles night's black agents to their preys do rouse.
Thou marvell'st at my words: but hold thee still;
Things bad begun make strong themselves by ill.
So, pr'ythee, go with me. *[Exeunt.*

SCENE III – THE SAME. A PARK, WITH A ROAD LEADING TO THE PALACE.

Enter three Murderers.

1 MURDERER But who did bid thee join with us?
3 MURDERER Macbeth.
2 MURDERER He needs not our mistrust; since he delivers
Our offices, and what we have to do,
To the direction just.
1 MURDERER Then stand with us.
The west yet glimmers with some streaks of day:
Now spurs the lated traveller apace,
To gain the timely inn; and near approaches
The subject of our watch.
3 MURDERER Hark! I hear horses.
BANQUO *[Within.]* Give us a light there, ho!
2 MURDERER Then it is he: the rest
That are within the note of expectation,
Already are i' the court.
1 MURDERER His horses go about.
3 MURDERER Almost a mile; but he does usually,
So all men do, from hence to the palace gate
Make it their walk.

Enter Banquo, and Fleance, with a torch.

2 MURDERER A light, a light!
3 MURDERER 'T is he.
1 MURDERER Stand to 't.
BANQUO It will be rain to-night.
1 MURDERER Let it come down.
[Assaults Banquo.

BANQUO O, treachery! Fly, good Fleance, fly, fly, fly!
Thou may'st revenge – O slave!
[Dies. Fleance escapes.
3 MURDERER Who did strike out the light?
1 MURDERER Was't not the way?
3 MURDERER There's but one down: the son is fled.
2 MURDERER We have lost
Best half of our affair.
1 MURDERER Well, let's away, and say how much is done.
[Exeunt.

SCENE IV – A ROOM OF STATE IN THE PALACE.

A Banquet prepared. Enter Macbeth, Lady Macbeth, Rosse, Lenox, Lords and Attendants.

MACBETH You know your own degrees, sit down: at first and last,
The hearty welcome.
LORDS Thanks to your majesty.
MACBETH Ourself will mingle with society,
And play the humble host.
Our hostess keeps her state; but, in best time,
We will require her welcome.
LADY MACBETH Pronounce it for me, sir, to all our friends;
For my heart speaks, they are welcome.

Enter first Murderer, to the door.

MACBETH See, they encounter thee with their hearts' thanks.
Both sides are even: here I'll sit i' the midst.
Be large in mirth; anon, we'll drink a measure

The table round. – There's blood upon thy face.
MURDERER 'T is Banquo's then.
MACBETH 'T is better thee without, than he within.
Is he despatch'd?
MURDERER My lord, his throat is cut; that I did for him.
MACBETH Thou art the best o' the cut-throats; yet he's good.
That did the like for Fleance: if thou didst it,
Thou art the nonpareil.
MURDERER Most royal sir,
Fleance is 'scap'd.
MACBETH Then comes my fit again: I had else been perfect;
Whole as the marble, founded as the rock,
As broad and general as the casing air:
But now, I am cabin'd, cribb'd, confin'd, bound in
To saucy doubts and fears. – But Banquo's safe?
MURDERER Ay, my good lord, safe in a ditch he bides,
With twenty trenched gashes on his head;
The least a death to nature.
MACBETH Thanks for that. –
There the grown serpent lies: the worm, that's fled,
Hath nature that in time will venom breed,
No teeth for the present. – Get thee gone; to-morrow
We'll hear ourselves again. *[Exit Murderer.*
LADY MACBETH My royal lord,
You do not give the cheer: the feast is sold,
That is not often vouch'd, while 't is a-making,
'T is given with welcome. To feed were best at home;
From thence, the sauce to meat is ceremony;
Meeting were bare without it.
MACBETH Sweet remembrancer! –
Now, good digestion wait on appetite,
And health on both!

LENOX May it please your highness sit?

The Ghost of Banquo enters, and sits in Macbeth's place.

MACBETH Here had we now our country's honour roof'd,
Were the grac'd person of our Banquo present;
Who may I rather challenge for unkindness,
Than pity for mischance!

ROSSE His absence, sir.
Lays blame upon his promise. Please it your highness
To grace us with your royal company?

MACBETH The table's full.

LENOX Here is a place reserv'd, sir.

MACBETH Where?

LENOX Here, my good lord. What is't that moves your highness?

MACBETH Which of you have done this?

LORDS What, my good lord?

MACBETH Thou canst not say, I did it: never shake
Thy gory locks at me.

ROSSE Gentlemen, rise; his highness is not well.

LADY MACBETH Sit, worthy friends. My lord is often thus.
And hath been from his youth: pray you, keep seat;
The fit is momentary; upon a thought
He will again be well. If much you note him,
You shall offend him, and extend his passion;
Feed, and regard him not, – Are you a man?

MACBETH Ay, and a bold one, that dare look on that
Which might appal the devil.

LADY MACBETH O proper stuff!
This is the very painting of your fear:
This is the air-drawn dagger, which, you said,
Led you to Duncan. O! these flaws, and starts,

(Impostors to true fear,) would well become
A woman's story at a winter's fire,
Authoris'd by her grandam. Shame itself!
Why do you make such faces? When all's done,
You look but on a stool.

MACBETH Pr'ythee, see there! behold! look! lo! how say you? –
Why, what care I? If thou canst nod, speak too. –
If charnel-houses, and our graves, must send
Those that we bury, back, our monuments
Shall be the maws of kites. *[Ghost disappears.*

LADY MACBETH What! quite unmann'd in folly?

MACBETH If I stand here, I saw him.

LADY MACBETH Fie! for shame!

MACBETH Blood hath been shed ere now, i' th' olden time,
Ere human statute purg'd the gentle weal;
Ay, and since too, murders have been perform'd
Too terrible for the ear: the time has been,
That, when the brains were out, the man would die,
And there an end; but now, they rise again,
With twenty mortal murders on their crowns,
And push us from our stools. This is more strange
Than such a murder is.

LADY MACBETH My worthy lord,
Your noble friends do lack you.

MACBETH I do forget. –
Do not muse at me, my most worthy friends;
I have a strange infirmity, which is nothing
To those that know me. Come, love and health to all;
Then, I'll sit down. – Give me some wine: fill full: –
I drink to the general joy of the whole table,
And to our dear friend Banquo, whom we miss;

Would he were here! to all, and him, we thirst,
And all to all.

LORDS Our duties, and the pledge.

Re-enter Ghost.

MACBETH Avaunt! and quit my sight! Let the earth hide thee!
Thy bones are marrowless, thy blood is cold;
Thou hast no speculation in those eyes,
Which thou dost glare with.

LADY MACBETH Think of this, good peers,
But as a thing of custom: 't is no other;
Only it spoils the pleasure of the time.

MACBETH What man dare, I dare:
Approach thou like the rugged Russian bear,
The arm'd rhinoceros, or the Hyrcan tiger;
Take any shape but that, and my firm nerves
Shall never tremble: or, be alive again,
And dare me to the desert with thy sword;
If trembling I inhabit then, protest me
The baby of a girl. Hence, horrible shadow!
Unreal mockery, hence! *[Ghost disappears.]* – Why, so; – being gone,
I am a man again. – Pray you, sit still.

LADY MACBETH You have displaced the mirth, broke the good meeting,
With most admir'd disorder.

MACBETH Can such things be,
And overcome us like a summer's cloud,
Without our special wonder? You make me strange
Even to the disposition that I owe,
When now I think you can behold such sights,

And keep the natural ruby of your cheeks,
When mine is blanch'd with fear.

ROSSE What sights, my lord?

LADY MACBETH I pray you, speak not: he grows worse and worse;
Question enrages him. At once, good night: –
Stand not upon the order of your going,
But go at once.

LENOX Good night, and better health
Attend his majesty!

LADY MACBETH A kind good night to all!

[Exeunt Lords and Attendants.

MACBETH It will have blood, they say; blood will have blood:
Stones have been known to move, and trees to speak;
Augurs, and understood relations, have
By magot-pies, and choughs, and rooks, brought forth
The secret'st man of blood. – What is the night?

LADY MACBETH Almost at odds with morning, which is which.

MACBETH How say'st thou, that Macduff denies his person,
At our great bidding?

LADY MACBETH Did you send to him, sir?

MACBETH I hear it by the way; but I will send.
There's not a one of them, but in his house
I keep a servant fee'd. I will to-morrow
(And betimes I will) to the weird sisters:
More shall they speak; for now I am bent to know,
By the worst means, the worst. For mine own good,
All causes shall give way: I am in blood
Stepp'd in so far, that, should I wade no more,
Returning were as tedious as go o'er.
Strange things I have in head, that will to hand,

Which must be acted, ere they may be scann'd.

LADY MACBETH You lack the season of all natures, sleep.

MACBETH Come, we'll to sleep. My strange and self-abuse
Is the initiate fear, that wants hard use:
We are yet but young in deed. *[Exeunt.*

SCENE V – THE HEATH.

Thunder. Enter the three Witches, meeting Hecate.

1 WITCH Why, how now, Hecate? you look angerly.

HECATE Have I not reason, beldams as you are,
Saucy, and overbold? How did you dare
To trade and traffic with Macbeth,
In riddles, and affairs of death;
And I, the mistress of your charms,
The close contriver of all harms,
Was never call'd to bear my part,
Or show the glory of our art?
And, which is worse, all you have done
Hath been but for a wayward son,
Spiteful, and wrathful; who, as others do,
Loves for his own ends, not for you.
But make amends now: get you gone,
And at the pit of Acheron
Meet me i' the morning: thither he
Will come to know his destiny.
Your vessels, and your spells, provide,
Your charms, and everything beside.
I am for the air; this night I'll spend
Unto a dismal and a fatal end:

Great business must be wrought ere noon.
Upon the corner of the moon
There hangs a vaporous drop profound;
I'll catch it ere it come to ground:
And that, distill'd by magic sleights,
Shall raise such artificial sprites,
As, by the strength of their illusion,
Shall draw him on to his confusion.
He shall spurn fate, scorn death, and bear
His hopes 'bove wisdom, grace, and fear;
And you all know, security
Is mortals' chiefest enemy.
[Song, within: 'Come away, come away,' &c.
Hark! I am call'd: my little spirit, see,
Sits in a foggy cloud, and stays for me. *[Exit.*

1 WITCH Come, let's make haste: she'll soon be back again.
[Exeunt.

SCENE VI – FORES. A ROOM IN THE PALACE.

Enter Lenox and another Lord.

LENOX My former speeches have but hit your thoughts,
Which can interpret further: only, I say,
Things have been strangely borne. The gracious Duncan
Was pitied of Macbeth: – marry, he was dead: –
And the right-valiant Banquo walk'd too late;
Whom, you may say, if't please you, Fleance kill'd,
For Fleance fled. Men must not walk too late,
Who cannot want the thought, how monstrous
It was for Malcolm, and for Donalbain.

To kill their gracious father? damned fact!
How it did grieve Macbeth! did he not straight,
In pious rage, the two delinquents tear,
That were the slaves of drink, and thralls of sleep?
Was not that nobly done? Ay, and wisely too:
For 't would have anger'd any heart alive
To hear the men deny it. So that, I say,
He has borne all things well: and I do think,
That, had he Duncan's sons under his key,
(As, an 't please Heaven, he shall not,) they should find
What 't were to kill a father; so should Fleance.
But, peace! – for from broad words, and 'cause he fail'd
His presence at the tyrant's feast, I hear,
Macduff lives in disgrace. Sir, can you tell
Where he bestows himself?

LORD The son of Duncan,
From whom this tyrant holds the due of birth,
Lives in the English court; and is receiv'd
Of the most pious Edward with such grace,
That the malevolence of fortune nothing
Takes from his high respect. Thither Macduff
Is gone to pray the holy king, upon his aid
To wake Northumberland, and warlike Siward;
That, by the help of these, (with Him above
To ratify the work,) we may again
Give to our tables meat, sleep to our nights,
Free from our feasts and banquets bloody knives,
Do faithful homage, and receive free honours,
All which we pine for now. And this report
Hath so exasperate the king, that he
Prepares for some attempt of war.

LENOX Sent he to Macduff?

LORD He did: and with an absolute 'Sir, not I,'
The cloudy messenger turns me his back,
And hums, as who should say, 'You'll rue the time
That clogs me with this answer.'

LENOX And that well might
Advise him to a caution, to hold what distance
His wisdom can provide. Some holy angel
Fly to the court of England, and unfold
His message ere he come, that a swift blessing
May soon return to this our suffering country
Under a hand accurs'd!

LORD I'll send my prayers with him.

[Exeunt.

ACT FOUR

SCENE I – A DARK CAVE. IN THE MIDDLE, A BOILING CAULDRON.

Thunder. Enter the three Witches.

1 WITCH Thrice the brinded cat hath mew'd.
2 WITCH Thrice and once the hedge-pig whin'd.
3 WITCH Harpier cries: – 'T is time, 't is time.
1 WITCH Round about the cauldron go;
In the poison'd entrails throw. –
Toad, that under cold stone
Days and nights has thirty-one
Swelter'd venom, sleeping got,
Boil thou first i' the charmed pot.
ALL Double, double toil and trouble:
Fire, burn; and, cauldron, bubble.
2 WITCH Fillet of a fenny snake,
In the cauldron boil and bake;
Eye of newt, and toe of frog,
Wool of bat, and tongue of dog,
Adder's fork, and blind-worm's sting,
Lizard's leg, and howlet's wing,
For a charm of powerful trouble,
Like a hell-broth boil and bubble.
ALL Double, double toil and trouble:
Fire, burn; and, cauldron, bubble.

3 WITCH Scale of dragon, tooth of wolf;
Witches' mummy; maw, and gulf,
Of the ravin'd salt-sea shark;
Root of hemlock, digg'd i' the dark;
Liver of blaspheming Jew;
Gall of goat, and slips of yew,
Sliver'd in the moon's eclipse;
Nose of Turk, and Tartar's lips;
Finger of birth-strangled babe,
Ditch-deliver'd by a drab,
Make the gruel thick and slab:
Add thereto a tiger's chaudron.
For the ingredients of our cauldron.
ALL Double, double toil and trouble:
Fire, burn; and, cauldron, bubble.
2 WITCH Cool it with a baboon's blood;
Then the charm is firm and good.

Enter Hecate.

HECATE O, well done! I commend your pains,
And every one shall share i' the gains.
And now about the cauldron sing,
Like elves and fairies in a ring,
Enchanting all that you put in.
[Music and a Song, 'Black spirits,' &c.
2 WITCH By the pricking of my thumbs,
Something wicked this way comes. – *[Knocking.*
Open, locks.
Whoever knocks.

Enter Macbeth.

MACBETH How now, you secret, black, and midnight hags!
What is't you do?
ALL A deed without a name.
MACBETH I conjure you, by that which you profess,
Howe'er you come to know it, answer me:
Though you untie the winds, and let them fight
Against the churches; though the yesty waves
Confound and swallow navigation up;
Though bladed corn be lodg'd, and trees blown down;
Though castles topple on their warders' heads;
Though palaces, and pyramids, do slope
Their heads to their foundations; though the treasure
Of nature's germen tumble all together,
Even till destruction sicken, answer me
To what I ask you.
1 WITCH Speak.
2 WITCH Demand.
3 WITCH We'll answer.
1 WITCH Say, if thou'dst rather hear it from our mouths.
Or from our masters?
MACBETH Call 'em; let me see 'em.
1 WITCH Pour in sow's blood, that hath eaten
Her nine farrow; grease, that's sweaten
From the murderer's gibbet, throw
Into the flame.
ALL Come, high, or low;
Thyself, and office, deftly show.

Thunder. First Apparition, an armed Head.

MACBETH Tell me, thou unknown power, –

1 WITCH He knows thy thought:
Hear his speech, but say thou nought.
1 APPARITION Macbeth! Macbeth! Macbeth! beware Macduff;
Beware the thane of Fife. – Dismiss me. – Enough. *[Descends.*
MACBETH Whate'er thou art, for thy good caution, thanks:
Thou hast harp'd my fear aright. – But one word more: –
1 WITCH He will not be commanded. Here's another,
More potent than the first.

Thunder. Second Apparition, a bloody Child.

2 APPARITION Macbeth! Macbeth! Macbeth! –
MACBETH Had I three ears, I'd hear thee.
2 APPARITION Be bloody, bold, and resolute: laugh to scorn
The power of man, for none of woman born
Shall harm Macbeth. *[Descends.*
MACBETH Then live, Macduff: what need I fear of thee?
But yet I'll make assurance double sure,
And take a bond of fate: thou shalt not live;
That I may tell pale-hearted fear it lies,
And sleep in spite of thunder. –

Thunder. Third Apparition, a Child crowned, with a tree in his hand.

What is this,
That rises like the issue of a king;
And wears upon his baby brow the round
And top of sovereignty?
ALL Listen, but speak not to 't.
3 APPARITION Be lion-mettled, proud, and take no care
Who chafes, who frets, or where conspirers are:
Macbeth shall never vanquish'd be, until

Great Birnam wood to high Dunsinane hill
Shall come against him. *[Descends.*

MACBETH That will never be:
Who can impress the forest; bid the tree
Unfix his earth-bound root? Sweet bodements! good!
Rebellious head, rise never, till the wood
Of Birnam rise; and our high-plac'd Macbeth
Shall live the lease of nature, pay his breath
To time, and mortal custom. – Yet my heart
Throbs to know one thing: tell me (if your art
Can tell so much), shall Banquo's issue ever
Reign in this kingdom?

ALL Seek to know no more.

MACBETH I will be satisfied: deny me this,
And an eternal curse fall on you! Let me know. –
Why sinks that cauldron? and what noise is this?
[Hautboys.

1 WITCH Show!

2 WITCH Show!

3 WITCH Show!

ALL Show his eyes, and grieve his heart;
Come like shadows, so depart.

A show of eight Kings, the last with a glass in his hand; Banquo following.

MACBETH Thou art too like the spirit of Banquo: down!
Thy crown does sear mine eye-balls: – and thy hair,
Thou other gold-bound brow, is like the first: –
A third is like the former: – filthy hags!
Why do you show me this? – A fourth? – Start, eyes,
What! will the line stretch out to the crack of doom.

Another yet? – A seventh? – I'll see no more: –
And yet the eighth appears, who bears a glass,
Which shows me many more; and some I see,
That two-fold balls and treble scepters carry.
Horrible sight! – Now, I see, 't is true;
For the blood-bolter'd Banquo smiles upon me,
And points at them for his. – What! is this so?

1 WITCH Ay, sir, all this is so: – but why
Stands Macbeth thus amazedly? –
Come, sisters, cheer we up his sprites,
And show the best of our delights.
I'll charm the air to give a sound,
While you perform your antick round;
That this great king may kindly say,
Our duties did his welcome pay.

[Music. The Witches dance, and vanish.

MACBETH Where are they? Gone? – Let this pernicious hour
Stand aye accursed in the calendar! –
Come in, without there!

Enter Lenox.

LENOX What's your grace's will?

MACBETH Saw you the weird sisters?

LENOX No, my lord.

MACBETH Came they not by you?

LENOX No, indeed, my lord.

MACBETH Infected be the air whereon they ride,
And damn'd all those that trust them! – I did hear
The galloping of horse: who was 't came by?

LENOX 'T is two or three, my lord, that bring you word,
Macduff is fled to England.

MACBETH Fled to England?

LENOX Ay, my good lord.

MACBETH Time, thou anticipat'st my dread exploits:
The flighty purpose never is o'ertook,
Unless the deed go with it. From this moment,
The very firstlings of my heart shall be
The firstlings of my hand. And even now,
To crown my thoughts with acts, be it thought and done:
The castle of Macduff I will surprise;
Seize upon Fife; give to the edge o' the sword
His wife, his babes, and all unfortunate souls
That trace him in his line. No boasting like a fool;
This deed I'll do, before this purpose cool:
But no more sights! – Where are these gentlemen?
Come, bring me where they are. *[Exeunt.*

SCENE II – FIFE. A ROOM IN MACDUFF'S CASTLE.

Enter Lady Macduff, her Son, and Rosse.

LADY MACDUFF What had he done, to make him fly the land?

ROSSE You must have patience, madam.

LADY MACDUFF He had none:
His flight was madness: when our actions do not,
Our fears do make us traitors.

ROSSE You know not,
Whether it was his wisdom, or his fear.

LADY MACDUFF Wisdom! to leave his wife, to leave his babes,
His mansion, and his titles, in a place
From whence himself does fly? He loves us not:
He wants the natural touch; for the poor wren,

The most diminutive of birds, will fight,
Her young ones in her nest, against the owl.
All is the fear, and nothing is the love;
As little is the wisdom, where the flight
So runs against all reason.

ROSSE My dearest coz,
I pray you, school yourself: but, for your husband,
He is noble, wise, judicious, and best knows
The fits o' the season. I dare not speak much further:
But cruel are the times, when we are traitors,
And do not know ourselves; when we hold rumour
From what we fear, yet know not what we fear,
But float upon a wild and violent sea.
Each way, and move. – I take my leave of you:
Shall not be long but I'll be here again.
Things at the worst will cease, or else climb upward
To what they were before. – My pretty cousin,
Blessing upon you!

LADY MACDUFF Father'd he is, and yet he's fatherless.

ROSSE I am so much a fool, should I stay longer,
It would be my disgrace, and your discomfort:
I take my leave at once. *[Exit.*

LADY MACDUFF Sirrah, your father's dead:
And what will you do now? How will you live?

SON As birds do, mother.

LADY MACDUFF What, with worms and flies?

SON With what I get, I mean; and so do they.

LADY MACDUFF Poor bird! thou'dst never fear the net, nor lime,
The pit-fall, nor the gin.

SON Why should I, mother? Poor birds they are not set for.
My father is not dead, for all your saying.

LADY MACDUFF Yes, he is dead: how wilt thou do for a father?

SON Nay, how will you do for a husband?

LADY MACDUFF Why, I can buy me twenty at any market.

SON Then you'll buy 'em to sell again.

LADY MACDUFF Thou speak'st with all thy wit;
And yet, i' faith, with wit enough for thee.

SON Was my father a traitor, mother?

LADY MACDUFF Ay, that he was.

SON What is a traitor?

LADY MACDUFF Why, one that swears and lies.

SON And be all traitors that do so?

LADY MACDUFF Every one that does so is a traitor, and must be hanged.

SON And must they all be hanged that swear and lie?

LADY MACDUFF Every one.

SON Who must hang them?

LADY MACDUFF Why, the honest men.

SON Then the liars and swearers are fools; for there are liars and swearers enough to beat the honest men, and hang up them.

LADY MACDUFF Now God help thee, poor monkey! But how wilt thou do for a father?

SON If he were dead, you'd weep for him: if you would not, it were a good sign that I should quickly have a new father.

LADY MACDUFF Poor prattler, how thou talk'st!

Enter a Messenger.

MESSENGER Bless you, fair dame! I am not to you known,
Though in your state of honour I am perfect.
I doubt, some danger does approach you nearly:
If you will take a homely man's advice,
Be not found here; hence, with your little ones.

To fright you thus, methinks, I am too savage;
To do worse to you were fell cruelty,
Which is too nigh your person. Heaven preserve you!
I dare abide no longer. [Exit.

LADY MACDUFF Whither should I fly?
I have done no harm. But I remember now
I am in this earthly world, where, to do harm,
Is often laudable; to do good, sometime,
Accounted dangerous folly: why then, alas!
Do I put up that womanly defence,
To say, I have done no harm? What are these faces?

Enter Murderers.

MURDERER Where is your husband?

LADY MACDUFF I hope, in no place so unsanctified,
Where such as thou may'st find him.

MURDERER He's a traitor.

SON Thou liest, thou shag-hair'd villain!

MURDERER What, you egg! *[Stabbing him.*
Young fry of treachery!

SON He has kill'd me, mother; run away, I pray you. *[Dies.*

[Exit Lady Macduff, crying 'Murder!' and pursued by the Murderers.

SCENE III – ENGLAND. A ROOM IN THE KING'S PALACE.

Enter Malcolm and Macduff.

MALCOLM Let us seek out some desolate shade, and there
Weep our sad bosoms empty.

MACDUFF Let us rather
Hold fast the mortal sword, and like good men

Bestride our down-fall'n birthdom. Each new morn,
New widows howl, new orphans cry; new sorrows
Strike heaven on the face, that it resounds
As if it felt with Scotland, and yell'd out
Like syllable of dolour.

MALCOLM What I believe, I'll wail;
What know, believe; and what I can redress,
As I shall find the time to friend, I will.
What you have spoke, it may be so, perchance.
This tyrant, whose sole name blisters our tongues,
Was once thought honest: you have lov'd him well;
He hath not touch'd you yet. I am young; but something
You may deserve of him through me, and wisdom
To offer up a weak, poor, innocent lamb,
To appease an angry God.

MACDUFF I am not treacherous.

MALCOLM But Macbeth is.
A good and virtuous nature may recoil,
In an imperial charge. But I shall crave your pardon:
That which you are my thoughts cannot transpose;
Angels are bright still, though the brightest fell:
Though all things foul would wear the brows of grace,
Yet grace must still look so.

MACDUFF I have lost my hopes.

MALCOLM Perchance even there where I did find my doubts.
Why in that rawness left you wife and child,
(Those precious motives, those strong knots of love,)
Without leave-taking? – I pray you,
Let not my jealousies be your dishonours,
But mine own safeties: you may be rightly just,
Whatever I shall think.

MACDUFF Bleed, bleed, poor country!
Great tyranny, lay thou thy basis sure,
For goodness dare not check thee! wear thou thy wrongs;
The title is affeer'd! – Fare thee well, lord:
I would not be the villain that thou think'st
For the whole space that's in the tyrant's grasp,
And the rich East to boot.

MALCOLM Be not offended:
I speak not as in absolute fear of you.
I think our country sinks beneath the yoke;
It weeps, it bleeds; and each new day a gash
Is added to her wounds: I think, withal,
There would be hands uplifted in my right;
And here, from gracious England, have I offer
Of goodly thousands: but, for all this,
When I shall tread upon the tyrant's head,
Or wear it on my sword, yet my poor country
Shall have more vices than it had before,
More suffer, and more sundry ways than ever,
By him that shall succeed.

MACDUFF What should he be?

MALCOLM It is myself I mean; in whom I know
All the particulars of vice so grafted,
That, when they shall be open'd, black Macbeth
Will seem as pure as snow; and the poor state
Esteem him as a lamb, being compar'd
With my confineless harms.

MACDUFF Not in the legions
Of horrid hell can come a devil more damn'd
In evils, to top Macbeth.

MALCOLM I grant him bloody,

Luxurious, avaricious, false, deceitful,
Sudden, malicious, smacking of every sin
That has a name; but there's no bottom, none,
In my voluptuousness: your wives, your daughters,
Your matrons, and your maids, could not fill up
The cistern of my lust; and my desire
All continent impediments would o'erbear,
That did oppose my will: better Macbeth,
Than such a one to reign.

MACDUFF Boundless intemperance
In nature is a tyranny; it hath been
The untimely emptying of the happy throne,
And fall of many kings. But fear not yet
To take upon you what is yours: you may
Convey your pleasures in a spacious plenty,
And yet seem cold, the time you may so hoodwink.
We have willing dames enough; there cannot be
That vulture in you, to devour so many
As will to greatness dedicate themselves,
Finding it so inclin'd.

MALCOLM With this, there grows
In my most ill-compos'd affection such
A staunchless avarice, that, were I king,
I should cut off the nobles for their lands;
Desire his jewels, and this other's house:
And my more-having would be as a sauce
To make me hunger more; that I should forge
Quarrels unjust against the good and loyal,
Destroying them for wealth.

MACDUFF This avarice
Sticks deeper, grows with more pernicious root

Than summer-seeming lust; and it hath been
The sword of our slain kings: yet do not fear;
Scotland hath foisons to fill up your will,
Of your mere own. All these are portable,
With other graces weigh'd.

MALCOLM But I have none: the king-becoming graces,
As justice, verity, temperance, stableness,
Bounty, perseverance, mercy, lowliness,
Devotion, patience, courage, fortitude,
I have no relish of them; but abound
In the division of each several crime,
Acting it many ways. Nay, had I power, I should
Pour the sweet milk of concord into hell,
Uproar the universal peace, confound
All unity on earth.

MACDUFF O Scotland, Scotland!

MALCOLM If such a one be fit to govern, speak:
I am as I have spoken.

MACDUFF Fit to govern!
No, not to live. – O nation miserable,
With an untitled tyrant bloody-scepter'd,
When shalt thou see thy wholesome days again,
Since that the truest issue of thy throne
By his own interdiction stands accurs'd,
And does blaspheme his breed? Thy royal father
Was a most sainted king: the queen, that bore thee,
Oft'ner upon her knees than on her feet,
Died every day she liv'd. Fare thee well!
These evils thou repeat'st upon thyself
Have banish'd me from Scotland. – O my breast,
Thy hope ends here!

MALCOLM Macduff, this noble passion,
Child of integrity, hath from my soul
Wip'd the black scruples, reconcil'd my thoughts
To thy good truth and honour. Devilish Macbeth
By many of these trains hath sought to win me
Into his power, and modest wisdom plucks me
From over-credulous haste: but God above
Deal between thee and me! for even now
I put myself to thy direction, and
Unspeak mine own detraction; here abjure
The taints and blames I laid upon myself,
For strangers to my nature. I am yet
Unknown to woman; never was forsworn;
Scarcely have coveted what was mine own;
At no time broke my faith: would not betray
The devil to his fellow; and delight
No less in truth, than life; my first false speaking
Was this upon myself. What I am truly,
Is thine, and my poor country's, to command:
Whither, indeed, before thy here-approach,
Old Siward, with ten thousand warlike men,
Already at a point, was setting forth.
Now, we'll together, and the chance of goodness
Be like our warranted quarrel. Why are you silent?

MACDUFF Such welcome and unwelcome things at once,
'T is hard to reconcile.

Enter a Doctor.

MALCOLM Well; more anon. – Comes the king forth, I pray you?

DOCTOR Ay, sir; there are a crew of wretched souls,
That stay his cure: their malady convinces

The great assay of art; but at his touch,
Such sanctity hath Heaven given his hand,
They presently amend.

MALCOLM I thank you, doctor. *[Exit Doctor.*

MACDUFF What's the disease he means?

MALCOLM 'T is call'd the evil;
A most miraculous work in this good king,
Which often, since my here-remain in England,
I have seen him do. How he solicits Heaven,
Himself best knows; but strangely-visited people,
All swoln and ulcerous, pitiful to the eye,
The mere despair of surgery, he cures;
Hanging a golden stamp about their necks,
Put on with holy prayers: and 't is spoken,
To the succeeding royalty he leaves
The healing benediction. With this strange virtue,
He hath a heavenly gift of prophecy;
And sundry blessings hang about his throne,
That speak him full of grace.

Enter Rosse.

MACDUFF See, who comes here?

MALCOLM My countryman; but yet I know him not.

MACDUFF My ever-gentle cousin, welcome hither.

MALCOLM I know him now. Good God, betimes remove
The means that makes us strangers!

ROSSE Sir, Amen.

MACDUFF Stands Scotland where it did?

ROSSE Alas, poor country!
Almost afraid to know itself. It cannot
Be call'd our mother, but our grave; where nothing,

But who knows nothing, is once seen to smile;
Where sighs, and groans, and shrieks that rent the air,
Are made, not mark'd; where violent sorrow seems
A modern ecstacy: the dead man's knell
Is there scarce ask'd for who; and good men's lives
Expire before the flowers in their caps,
Dying or ere they sicken.

MACDUFF O relation,
Too nice, and yet too true!

MALCOLM What is the newest grief?

ROSSE That of an hour's age doth hiss the speaker;
Each minute seems a new one.

MACDUFF How does my wife?

ROSSE Why, well.

MACDUFF And all my children?

ROSSE Well too.

MACDUFF The tyrant has not batter'd at their peace?

ROSSE No; they were well at peace, when I did leave them.

MACDUFF Be not a niggard of your speech: how goes it?

ROSSE When I came hither to transport the tidings,
Which I have heavily borne, there ran a rumour
Of many worthy fellows that were out;
Which was to my belief witness'd the rather,
For that I saw the tyrant's power afoot.
Now is the time of help. Your eye in Scotland
Would create soldiers, make our women fight,
To doff their dire distresses.

MALCOLM Be 't their comfort,
We are coming thither. Gracious England hath
Lent us good Siward, and ten thousand men;
An older, and a better soldier, none
That Christendom gives out.

ROSSE 'Would I could answer
This comfort with the like! But I have words,
That would be howl'd out in the desert air,
Where hearing should not latch them.

MACDUFF What concern they?
The general cause? or is it a fee-grief,
Due to some single breast?

ROSSE No mind that's honest
But in it shares some woe, though the main part
Pertains to you alone.

MACDUFF If it be mine,
Keep it not from me; quickly let me have it.

ROSSE Let not your ears despise my tongue for ever,
Which shall possess them with the heaviest sound,
That ever yet they heard.

MACDUFF Humph! I guess at it.

ROSSE Your castle is surpris'd; your wife, and babes,
Savagely slaughtered: to relate the manner,
Were, on the quarry of these murder'd deer,
To add the death of you.

MALCOLM Merciful Heaven! –
What, man! ne'er pull your hat upon your brows:
Give sorrow words; the grief, that does not speak,
Whispers the o'er-fraught heart, and bids it break.

MACDUFF My children too?

ROSSE Wife, children, servants, all
That could be found.

MACDUFF And I must be from thence!
My wife kill'd too?

ROSSE I have said.

MALCOLM Be comforted:

Let's make us medicines of our great revenge,
To cure this deadly grief.

MACDUFF He has no children. – All my pretty ones?
Did you say, all? – O hell-kite! – All?
What, all my pretty chickens, and their dam,
At one fell swoop?

MALCOLM Dispute it like a man.

MACDUFF I shall do so;
But I must also feel it as a man:
I cannot but remember such things were,
That were most precious to me. – Did Heaven look on,
And would not take their part? Sinful Macduff!
They were all struck for thee. Naught that I am,
Not for their own demerits, but for mine,
Fell slaughter on their souls. Heaven rest them now!

MALCOLM Be this the whetstone of your sword: let grief
Convert to anger; blunt not the heart, enrage it.

MACDUFF O! I could play the woman with mine eyes,
And braggart with my tongue. – But, gentle heavens,
Cut short all intermission; front to front,
Bring thou this fiend of Scotland, and myself;
Within my sword's length set him; if he 'scape,
Heaven forgive him too!

MALCOLM This tune goes manly.
Come, go we to the king: our power is ready;
Our lack is nothing but our leave. Macbeth
Is ripe for shaking, and the powers above
Put on their instruments. Receive what cheer you may;
The night is long that never finds the day. *[Exeunt.*

ACT FIVE

SCENE I – DUNSINANE. A ROOM IN THE CASTLE.

Enter a Doctor of Physic and a waiting Gentlewoman.

DOCTOR I have two nights watched with you, but can perceive no truth in your report. When was it she last walked?

GENTLEWOMAN Since his majesty went into the field, I have seen her rise from her bed, throw her night-gown upon her, unlock her closet, take forth paper, fold it, write upon it, read it, afterwards seal it, and again return to bed; yet all this while in a most fast sleep.

DOCTOR A great perturbation in nature, to receive at once the benefit of sleep, and do the effects of watching. In this slumbery agitation, besides her walking and other actual performances, what, at any time, have you heard her say?

GENTLEWOMAN That, sir, which I will not report after her.

DOCTOR You may, to me; and 't is most meet you should.

GENTLEWOMAN Neither to you, nor any one; having no witness to confirm my speech.

Enter Lady Macbeth, with a taper.

Lo you! here she comes. This is her very guise; and, upon my life, fast asleep. Observe her: stand close.

DOCTOR How came she by that light?

GENTLEWOMAN Why, it stood by her: she has light by her continually; 't is her command.

DOCTOR You see, her eyes are open.

GENTLEWOMAN Ay, but their sense' are shut.

DOCTOR What is it she does now? Look, how she rubs her hands.

GENTLEWOMAN It is an accustomed action with her, to seem thus washing her hands. I have known her continue in this a quarter of an hour.

LADY MACBETH Yet here's a spot.

DOCTOR Hark! she speaks. I will set down what comes from her, to satisfy my remembrance the more strongly.

LADY MACBETH Out, damned spot! out, I say! – One; two, why, then 't is time to do 't. – Hell is murky! – Fie, my lord, fie! a soldier, and afeard? – What need we fear who knows it, when none can call our power to account? – Yet who would have thought the old man to have had so much blood in him?

DOCTOR Do you mark that?

LADY MACBETH The thane of Fife had a wife: where is she now? – What, will these hands ne'er be clean? – No more o' that, my lord, no more o' that: you mar all with this starting.

DOCTOR Go to, go to: you have known what you should not.

GENTLEWOMAN She has spoke what she should not, I am sure of that: Heaven knows what she has known.

LADY MACBETH Here's the smell of the blood still: all the perfumes of Arabia will not sweeten this little hand. Oh! oh! oh!

DOCTOR What a sigh is there! The heart is sorely charged.

GENTLEWOMAN I would not have such a heart in my bosom, for the dignity of the whole body.

DOCTOR Well, well, well.

GENTLEWOMAN 'Pray God, it be sir.

DOCTOR This disease is beyond my practice: yet I have known those which have walked in their sleep, who have died holily in their beds.

LADY MACBETH Wash your hands, put on your night-gown; look not so pale. – I tell you yet again, Banquo's buried: he cannot come out on 's grave.

DOCTOR Even so?

LADY MACBETH To bed, to bed: there's knocking at the gate. Come, come, come, come, give me your hand. What's done cannot be undone. To bed, to bed, to bed. *[Exit.*

DOCTOR Will she go now to bed?

GENTLEWOMAN Directly.

DOCTOR Foul whisperings are abroad. Unnatural deeds
Do breed unnatural troubles: infected minds
To their deaf pillows will discharge their secrets.
More needs she the divine than the physician. –
God, God, forgive us all! Look after her;
Remove from her the means of all annoyance,
And still keep eyes upon her. – So, good night:
My mind she has mated, and amaz'd my sight.
I think, but dare not speak.

GENTLEWOMAN Good night, good doctor. *[Exeunt.*

SCENE II – THE COUNTRY NEAR DUNSINANE.

Enter, with drum and colours, Menteth, Cathness, Angus, Lenox, and Soldiers.

MENTETH The English power is near, led on by Malcolm,
His uncle Siward, and the good Macduff.
Revenges burn in them; for their dear causes
Would, to the bleeding and the grim alarm,
Excite the mortified man.

ANGUS Near Birnam wood

Shall we well meet them: that way are they coming.
CATHNESS Who knows if Donalbain be with his brother?
LENOX For certain, sir, he is not. I have a file
Of all the gentry: there is Siward's son,
And many unrough youths, that even now
Protest their first of manhood.
MENTETH What does the tyrant?
CATHNESS Great Dunsinane he strongly fortifies.
Some say he's mad; others, that lesser hate him,
Do call it valiant fury: but, for certain,
He cannot buckle his distemper'd cause
Within the belt of rule.
ANGUS Now does he feel
His secret murders sticking on his hands;
Now minutely revolts upbraid his faith-breach:
Those he commands move only in command,
Nothing in love: now does he feel his title
Hang loose about him, like a giant's robe
Upon a dwarfish thief.
MENTETH Who then shall blame
His pester'd senses to recoil and start,
When all that is within him does condemn
Itself, for being there?
CATHNESS Well; march we on,
To give obedience where 't is truly ow'd:
Meet we the medicine of the sickly weal;
And with him pour we, in our country's purge,
Each drop of us.
LENOX Or so much as it needs
To dew and sovereign flower, and drown the weeds.
Make we our march towards Birnam. *[Exeunt, marching.*

SCENE III – DUNSINANE. A ROOM IN THE CASTLE.

Enter Macbeth, Doctor, and Attendants.

MACBETH Bring me no more reports; let them fly all
Till Birnam wood remove to Dunsinane,
I cannot taint with fear. What's the boy Malcolm?
Was he not born of woman? The spirits that know
All mortal consequences have pronounc'd me thus:
'Fear not, Macbeth; no man that's born of woman
Shall e'er have power upon thee.' – Then fly, false thanes,
And mingle with the English epicures:
The mind I sway by, and the heart I bear,
Shall never sag with doubt, nor shake with fear.

Enter a Servant.

The devil damn thee black, thou cream-fac'd loon!
Where gott'st thou that goose look?
SERVANT There is ten thousand –
MACBETH Geese, villain?
SERVANT Soldiers, sir.
MACBETH Go, prick thy face, and over-red thy fear,
Thou lily-liver'd boy. What soldiers, patch?
Death of thy soul! those linen cheeks of thine
Are counsellors to fear. What soldiers, whey-face?
SERVANT The English force, so please you.
MACBETH Take thy face hence. *[Exit Servant.]* – Seyton! – I am sick at heart.
When I behold – Seyton, I say! – This push
Will cheer me ever, or disseat me now.
I have liv'd long enough: my way of life

Is fall'n into the sere, the yellow leaf;
And that which should accompany old age,
As honour, love, obedience, troops of friends,
I must not look to have; but, in their stead,
Curses, not loud, but deep, mouth-honour, breath,
Which the poor heart would fain deny, and dare not.
Seyton! –

Enter Seyton.

SEYTON What is your gracious pleasure?
MACBETH What news more?
SEYTON All is confirm'd, my lord, which was reported.
MACBETH I'll fight, till from my bones my flesh be hack'd.
Give me my armour.
SEYTON 'T is not needed yet.
MACBETH I'll put it on.
Send out moe horses, skir the country round;
Hang those that talk of fear. Give me mine armour.
How does your patient, doctor?
DOCTOR Not so sick, my lord.
As she is troubled with thick-coming fancies,
That keep her from her rest.
MACBETH Cure her of that:
Canst thou not minister to a mind diseas'd,
Pluck from the memory a rooted sorrow,
Raze out the written troubles of the brain,
And with some sweet oblivious antidote
Cleanse the stuff'd bosom of that perilous stuff,
Which weighs upon the heart?
DOCTOR Therein the patient
Must minister to himself.

MACBETH Throw physic to the dogs; I'll none of it. –
Come, put mine armour on; give me my staff. –
Seyton, send out – Doctor, the thanes fly from me. –
Come, sir, despatch. – If thou couldst, doctor, cast
The water of my mind, find her disease,
And purge it to a sound and pristine health,
I would applaud thee to the very echo,
That should applaud again. – Pull 't off, I say. –
What rhubarb, senna, or what purgative drug,
Would scour these English hence? – Hear'st thou of them?
DOCTOR Ay, my good lord: your royal preparation
Makes us hear something.
MACBETH Bring it after me. –
I will not be afraid of death and bane,
Till Birnam forest come to Dunsinane. *[Exit.*
DOCTOR *[Aside.]* Were I from Dunsinane away and clear.
Profit again should hardly draw me here. *[Exeunt.*

SCENE IV – COUNTRY NEAR DUNSINANE. A WOOD IN VIEW.

Enter, with drum and colours, Malcolm, Old Siward and his Son, Macduff, Menteth, Cathness, Angus, Lenox, Rosse, and Soldiers, marching.

MALCOLM Cousins, I hope the days are near at hand,
That chambers will be safe.
MENTETH We doubt it nothing.
SIWARD What wood is this before us?
MENTETH The wood of Birnam.
MALCOLM Let every soldier hew him down a bough,
And bear't before him: thereby shall we shadow

The numbers of our host, and make discovery
Err in report of us.

SOLDIER It shall be done.

SIWARD We learn no other, but the confident tyrant
Keeps still in Dunsinane, and will endure
Our setting down before 't.

MALCOLM 'T is his main hope;
For where there is advantage to be given,
Both more and less have given him the revolt,
And none serve with him but constrained things,
Whose hearts are absent too.

MACDUFF Let our just censures
Attend the true event, and put we on
Industrious soldiership.

SIWARD The time approaches,
That will with due decision make us know
What we shall say we have, and what we owe.
Thoughts speculative their unsure hopes relate,
But certain issue strokes must arbitrate;
Towards which advance the war. *[Exeunt, marching.*

SCENE V – DUNSINANE. WITHIN THE CASTLE.

Enter, with drum and colours, Macbeth, Seyton, and Soldiers.

MACBETH Hang out our banners on the outward walls;
The cry is still, 'They come!' Our castle's strength
Will laugh a siege to scorn: here let them lie,
Till famine and the ague eat them up.
Were they not forc'd with those that should be ours,
We might have met them dareful, beard to beard, *[Exit.*

And beat them backward home. What is that noise?
[A cry within, of Women.

SEYTON It is the cry of women, my good lord. *[Exit.*

MACBETH I have almost forgot the taste of fears.
The time has been, my senses would have cool'd
To hear a night-shriek; and my fell of hair
Would at a dismal treatise rouse and stir,
As life were in 't. I have supp'd full with horrors:
Direness, familiar to my slaughterous thoughts,
Cannot once start me.

Re-enter Seyton.

Wherefore was that cry?

SEYTON The queen, my lord, is dead.

MACBETH She should have died hereafter:
There would have been a time for such a word. –
To-morrow, and to-morrow, and to-morrow,
Creeps in this pretty pace from day to day,
To the last syllable of recorded time;
And all our yesterdays have lighted fools
The way to dusty death. Out, out, brief candle!
Life's but a walking shadow; a poor player,
That struts and frets his hour upon the stage,
And then is heard no more: it is a tale
Told by an idiot, full of sound and fury,
Signifying nothing.

Enter a Messenger.

Thou com'st to use thy tongue; thy story quickly.

MESSENGER Gracious my lord,
I should report that which I say I saw,
But know not how to do it.

MACBETH Well, say, sir.

MESSENGER As I did stand my watch upon the hill,
I look'd toward Birnham, and anon, methought,
The wood began to move.

MACBETH Liar, and slave!

MESSENGER Let me endure your wrath, if 't be not so.
Within this three mile may you see it coming;
I say, a moving grove.

MACBETH If thou speak'st false,
Upon the next tree shalt thou hang alive,
Till famine cling thee: if thy speech be sooth,
I care not if thou dost for me as much. –
I pull in resolution; and begin
To doubt the equivocation of the fiend,
That lies like truth: 'Fear not, till Birnam wood
Do come to Dunsinane;' – and now a wood
Comes toward Dunsinane. – Arm, arm, and out! –
If this which he avouches does appear,
There is nor flying hence, nor tarrying here.
I 'gin to be aweary of the sun,
And wish the estate o' the world were now undone. –
Ring the alarum-bell! – Blow, wind! come, wrack!
At least we'll die with harness on our back. *[Exeunt.*

SCENE VI – THE SAME. A PLAIN BEFORE THE CASTLE.

Enter, with drum and colours, Malcolm, Old Siward, Macduff, &c., and their Army, with boughs.

MALCOLM Now, near enough: your leavy screens throw down.
And show like those you are. – You, worthy uncle,

Shall, with my cousin, your right-noble son,
Lead our first battle: worthy Macduff, and we,
Shall take upon 's what else remains to do,
According to our order.

SIWARD Fare you well. –
Do we but find the tyrant's power to-night,
Let us be beaten, if we cannot fight.

MACDUFF Make all our trumpets speak; give them all breath,
Those clamorous harbingers of blood and death.

[Exeunt. Alarums continued.

SCENE VII – THE SAME. ANOTHER PART OF THE PLAIN.

Enter Macbeth.

MACBETH They have tied me to a stake: I cannot fly,
But, bear-like, I must fight the course, – What's he,
That was not born of woman? Such a one
Am I to fear, or none.

Enter Young Siward.

YOUNG SIWARD What is thy name?

MACBETH Thou'lt be afraid to hear it.

YOUNG SIWARD No; though thou call'st thyself a hotter name
Than any is in hell.

MACBETH My name's Macbeth.

YOUNG SIWARD The devil himself could not pronounce a title
More hateful to mine ear.

MACBETH No, nor more fearful.

YOUNG SIWARD Thou liest, abhorred tyrant: with my sword
I'll prove the lie thou speak'st.

[They fight, and Young Siward is slain.

MACBETH Thou wast born of woman: –
But swords I smile at, weapons laugh to scorn,
Brandish'd by man that's of a woman born. *[Exit.*

Alarums. Enter Macduff.

MACDUFF That way the noise is. – Tyrant, show thy face:
If thou be'st slain, and with no stroke of mine,
My wife and children's ghosts will haunt me still.
I cannot strike at wretched Kernes, whose arms
Are hir'd to bear their staves: either thou, Macbeth,
Or else my sword, with an unbatter'd edge,
I sheathe again undeeded. There thou shouldst be;
By this great clatter, one of greatest note
Seems bruited. Let me find him, fortune!
And more I beg not. *[Exit. Alarum.*

Enter Malcolm and Old Siward.

SIWARD This way, my lord; – the castle's gently render'd:
The tyrant's people on both sides do fight;
The noble thanes do bravely in the war.
The day almost itself professes yours,
And little is to do.

MALCOLM We have met with foes
That strike beside us.

SIWARD Enter, sir, the castle.
[Exeunt. Alarum.

Re-enter Macbeth.

MACBETH Why should I play the Roman fool, and die
On mine own sword? whiles I see lives, the gashes
Do better upon them.

Re-enter Macduff.

MACDUFF Turn, hell-hound, turn!
MACBETH Of all men else I have avoided thee:
But get thee back, my soul is too much charg'd
With blood of thine already.
MACDUFF I have no words;
My voice is in my sword: thou bloodier villain
Than terms can give thee out! *[They fight.*
MACBETH Thou losest labour:
As easy may'st thou the intrenchant air
With thy keen sword impress, as make me bleed:
Let fall thy blade on vulnerable crests;
I bear a charmed life; which must not yield
To one of woman born.
MACDUFF Despair thy charm;
And let the angel, whom thou still hast serv'd,
Tell thee, Macduff was from his mother's womb
Untimely ripp'd.
MACBETH Accursed be that tongue that tells me so,
For it hath cow'd my better part of man:
And be these juggling fiends no more believ'd,
That palter with us in a double sense;
That keep the word of promise to our ear,
And break it to our hope. – I'll not fight with thee.
MACDUFF Then yield thee, coward,
And live to be the show and gaze o' the time:
We'll have thee, as our rarer monsters are,
Painted upon a pole, and underwrit,
'Here may you see the tyrant.'
MACBETH I will not yield,
To kiss the ground before young Malcolm's feet,

And to be baited with the rabble's curse.
Though Birnam wood be come to Dunsinane,
And thou oppos'd, being of no woman born,
Yet I will try the last: before my body
I throw my warlike shield: lay on, Macduff;
And damn'd be him that first cries, 'Hold, enough!'
[Exeunt, fighting.

Retreat. Flourish. Re-enter, with drum and colours, Malcolm, Old Siward, Rosse, Thanes, and Soldiers.

MALCOLM I would the friends we miss were safe arriv'd.
SIWARD Some must go off: and yet, by these I see,
So great a day as this is cheaply bought.
MALCOLM Macduff is missing, and your noble son.
ROSSE Your son, my lord, has paid a soldier's debt:
He only liv'd but till he was a man;
The which no sooner had his prowess confirm'd,
In the unshrinking station where he fought,
But like a man he died.
SIWARD Then he is dead?
ROSSE Ay, and brought off the field. Your cause of sorrow
Must not be measur'd by his worth, for then
It hath no end.
SIWARD Had he his hurts before?
ROSSE Ay, on the front.
SIWARD Why then, God's soldier be he!
Had I as many sons as I have hairs,
I would not wish them to a fairer death:
And so, his knell is knoll'd.
MALCOLM He's worth more sorrow,
And that I'll spend for him.

SIWARD He's worth no more;
They say, he parted well, and paid his score:
And so, God be with him! – Here comes newer comfort.

Re-enter Macduff, with Macbeth's head.

MACDUFF Hail, king! for so thou art. Behold, where stands
The usurper's cursed head: the time is free.
I see thee compass'd with thy kingdom's pearl,
That speak my salutation in their minds;
Whose voices I desire aloud with mine, –
Hail, King of Scotland!

ALL Hail, King of Scotland! *[Flourish.*

MALCOLM We shall not spend a large expense of time,
Before we reckon with your several loves,
And make us even with you. My thanes and kinsmen,
Henceforth be earls; the first that ever Scotland
In such an honour nam'd. What's more to do,
Which would be planted newly with the time, –
As calling home our exil'd friends abroad,
That fled the snares of watchful tyranny;
Producing forth the cruel ministers
Of this dead butcher, and this fiend-like queen,
Who, as 't is thought, by self and violent hands
Took off her life; – this, and what needful else
That calls upon us, by the grace of Grace
We will perform in measure, time, and place.
So thanks to all at once, and to each one,
Whom we invite to see us crown'd at Scone.

[Flourish. Exeunt.

KING LEAR

DRAMATIS PERSONAE

Lear – *King of Britain*
King of France
Duke of Burgundy
Duke of Cornwall
Duke of Albany
Earl of Kent
Earl of Gloster
Edgar – *Son to Gloster*
Edmund – *Bastard Son to Gloster*
Curan – *a Courtier*
Oswald – *Steward to Goneril*
Old Man – *Tenant to Gloster*
Physician
Fool
An Officer – *employed by Edmund*
Gentleman – *Attendant on Cordelia*
A Herald
Servants to Cornwall
Goneril – *Daughters*
Regan – *to*
Cordelia – *Lear*

Knights of Lear's Train, Officers, Messengers, Soldiers and Attendants

SCENE

BRITAIN

ACT ONE

SCENE I – A ROOM OF STATE IN KING LEAR'S PALACE.

Enter Kent, Gloster, and Edmund.

KENT I thought, the king had more affected the Duke of Albany, than Cornwall.

GLOSTER It did always seem so to us: but now, in the division of the kingdom, it appears not which of the dukes he values most; for equalities are so weighed, that curiosity in neither can make choice of either's moiety.

KENT Is not this your son, my lord?

GLOSTER His breeding, sir, hath been at my charge: I have so often blushed to acknowledge him, that now I am brazed to it.

KENT I cannot conceive you.

GLOSTER Sir, this young fellow's mother could; whereupon she grew round-wombed, and had indeed, sir, a son for her cradle, ere she had a husband for her bed. Do you smell a fault?

KENT I cannot wish the fault undone, the issue of it being so proper.

GLOSTER But I have a son, sir, by order of law, some year elder than this, who yet is no dearer in my account: though this knave came somewhat saucily into the world, before he was sent for, yet was his mother fair; there was good sport at his making, and the whoreson must be acknowledged. – Do you know this noble gentleman, Edmund?

EDMUND No, my lord.

GLOSTER My Lord of Kent: remember him hereafter as my honourable friend.

EDMUND My services to your lordship.

KENT I must love you, and sue to know you better.

EDMUND Sir, I shall study deserving.

GLOSTER He hath been out nine years, and away he shall again. – The king is coming. *[Sennet within.*

Enter Lear, Cornwall, Albany, Goneril, Regan, Cordelia, and Attendants.

LEAR Attend the Lords of France and Burgundy, Gloster.

GLOSTER I shall, my liege. *[Exeunt Gloster and Edmund.*

LEAR Meantime we shall express our darker purpose.
Give me the map there. – Know, that we have divided,
In three, our kingdom; and 'tis our fast intent
To shake all cares and business from our age,
Conferring them on younger strengths, while we
Unburden'd crawl toward death. – Our son of Cornwall,
And you, our no less loving son of Albany,
We have this hour a constant will to publish
Our daughters' several dowers, that future strife
May be prevented now. The princes, France and Burgundy,
Great rivals in our youngest daughter's love,
Long in our court have made their amorous sojourn,
And here are to be answer'd. – Tell me, my daughters,
(Since now we will divest us, both of rule,
Interest of territory, cares of state,)
Which of you, shall we say, doth love us most?
That we our largest bounty may extend
Where nature doth with merit challenge. – Goneril,

Our eldest-born, speak first.
GONERIL Sir, I love you more than words can wield the matter;
Dearer than eye-sight, space, and liberty;
Beyond what can be valued, rich or rare;
No less than life, with grace, health, beauty, honour;
As much as child e'er lov'd, or father found;
A love that makes breath poor, and speech unable;
Beyond all manner of so much I love you.
CORDELIA *[Aside]* What shall Cordelia do? Love, and be silent.
LEAR Of all these bounds, even from this line to this,
With shadowy forests and with champains rich'd,
With plenteous rivers and wide-skirted meads,
We make thee lady: to thine and Albany's issue
Be this perpetual. – What says our second daughter,
Our dearest Regan, wife to Cornwall? Speak.
REGAN I am made of that self metal as my sister,
And prize me at her worth. In my true heart
I find, she names my very deed of love;
Only she comes too short, – that I profess
Myself an enemy to all other joys,
Which the most precious square of sense possesses,
And find, I am alone felicitate
In your dear highness' love.
CORDELIA *[Aside]* Then, poor Cordelia!
And yet not so; since, I am sure, my love's
More ponderous than my tongue.
LEAR To thee, and thine, hereditary ever,
Remain this ample third of our fair kingdom;
No less in space, validity, and pleasure,
Than that conferr'd on Goneril. – Now, our joy,
Although our last, not least; to whose young love

The vines of France, and milk of Burgundy,
Strive to be interess'd; what can you say, to draw
A third more opulent than your sisters? Speak.

CORDELIA Nothing, my lord.

LEAR Nothing?

CORDELIA Nothing.

LEAR Nothing will come of nothing: speak again.

CORDELIA Unhappy that I am, I cannot heave
My heart into my mouth: I love your majesty
According to my bond; nor more, nor less.

LEAR How, how, Cordelia! mend your speech a little,
Lest you may mar your fortunes.

CORDELIA Good my lord,
You have begot me, bred me, lov'd me: I
Return those duties back as are right fit,
Obey you, love you, and most honour you.
Why have my sisters husbands, if they say,
They love you all? Haply, when I shall wed,
That lord, whose hand must take my plight, shall carry
Half my love with him, half my care, and duty:
Sure, I shall never marry like my sisters,
To love my father all.

LEAR But goes thy heart with this?

CORDELIA Ay, my good lord.

LEAR So young, and so untender?

CORDELIA So young, my lord, and true.

LEAR Let it be so: thy truth then be thy dower;
For, by the sacred radiance of the sun,
The mysteries of Hecate, and the night,
By all the operation of the orbs,
From whom we do exist, and cease to be,

Here I disclaim all my paternal care,
Propinquity and property of blood,
And as a stranger to my heart and me
Hold thee, from this, for ever. The barbarous Scythian,
Or he that makes his generation messes
To gorge his appetite, shall to my bosom
Be as well neighbour'd, pitied, and reliev'd,
As thou my sometime daughter.

KENT Good my liege, –

LEAR Peace, Kent!
Come not between the dragon and his wrath.
I lov'd her most, and thought to set my rest
On her kind nursery. – Hence, and avoid my sight! –
So be my grave my peace, as here I give
Her father's heart from her! – Call France. – Who stirs? –
Call Burgundy. – Cornwall, and Albany.
With my two daughters' dowers digest the third:
Let pride, which she calls plainness, marry her.
I do invest you jointly with my power,
Pre-eminence, and all the large effects
That troop with majesty. – Ourself, by monthly course,
With reservation of an hundred knights,
By you to be sustain'd, shall our abode
Make with you by due turn. Only, we shall retain
The name, and all the additions to a king;
The sway, revenue, execution of the rest,
Beloved sons, be yours: which to confirm,
This coronet part between you.

KENT Royal Lear,
Whom I have ever honour'd as my king,
Lov'd as my father, as my master follow'd,

As my great patron thought on in my prayers, –
LEAR The bow is bent and drawn; make from the shaft.
KENT Let it fall rather, though the fork invade
The region of my heart: be Kent unmannerly,
When Lear is mad. – What wouldst thou do, old man?
Think'st thou, that duty shall have dread to speak,
When power to flattery bows? To plainness honour's bound,
When majesty falls to folly. Reserve thy state;
And, in thy best consideration, check
This hideous rashness: answer my life my judgment,
Thy youngest daughter does not love thee least;
Nor are those empty-hearted, whose low sound
Reverbs no hollowness.
LEAR Kent, on thy life, no more.
KENT My life I never held but as a pawn
To wage against thine enemies; ne'er fear to lose it,
Thy safety being the motive.
LEAR Out of my sight!
KENT See better, Lear; and let me still remain
The true blank of thine eye.
LEAR Now, by Apollo, –
KENT Now, by Apollo, king,
Thou swear'st thy gods in vain.
LEAR O, vassal! miscreant!
[Laying his hand upon his sword.
ALBANY, CORNWALL Dear, sir, forbear.
KENT Do;
Kill thy physician, and the fee bestow
Upon the foul disease. Revoke thy gift;
Or, whilst I can vent clamour from my throat,
I'll tell thee, thou dost evil.

LEAR Hear me, recreant!
On thine allegiance, hear me!
Since thou hast sought to make us break our vow
(Which we durst never yet), and, with strain'd pride,
To come betwixt our sentence and our power
(Which nor our nature nor our place can bear),
Our potency made good, take thy reward.
Five days we do allot thee for provision
To shield thee from disasters of the world;
And on the sixth to turn thy hated back
Upon our kingdom: if, on the tenth day following,
Thy banish'd trunk be found in our dominions,
The moment is thy death. Away! By Jupiter,
This shall not be revok'd.

KENT Fare thee well, king: since thus thou wilt appear,
Freedom lives hence, and banishment is here. –
[To Cordelia.] The gods to their dear shelter take thee, maid,
That justly think'st, and hast most rightly said! –
[To Regan and Goneril.] And your large speeches may your deeds approve,
That good effects may spring from words of love. –
Thus Kent, O princes! bids you all adieu;
He'll shape his old course in a country new. *[Exit.*

Flourish. Re-enter Gloster; with France, Burgundy, and Attendants.

GLOSTER Here's France and Burgundy, my noble lord.

LEAR My Lord of Burgundy,
We first address toward you, who with this king
Hath rivall'd for our daughter. What, in the least,
Will you require in present dower with her,

Or cease your quest of love?

BURGUNDY Most royal majesty,
I crave no more than hath your highness offer'd,
Nor will you tender less.

LEAR Right noble Burgundy,
When she was dear to us, we did hold her so;
But now her price is fall'n. Sir, there she stands:
If aught within that little seeming substance,
Or all of it, with our displeasure piec'd,
And nothing more, may fitly like your grace,
She's there, and she is yours.

BURGUNDY I know no answer.

LEAR Will you, with those infirmities she owes,
Unfriended, new-adopted to our hate,
Dower'd with our curse, and stranger'd with our oath,
Take her, or leave her?

BURGUNDY Pardon me, royal sir;
Election makes not up on such conditions.

LEAR Then leave her, sir; for, by the power that made me,
I tell you all her wealth. – *[To France.]* For you, great king,
I would not from your love make such a stray,
To match you where I hate: therefore, beseech you
To avert your liking a more worthier way,
Than on a wretch whom Nature is asham'd
Almost to acknowledge hers.

FRANCE This is most strange,
That she, who even but now was your best object,
The argument of your praise, balm of your age,
Most best, most dearest, should in this trice of time
Commit a thing so monstrous, to dismantle
So many folds of favour. Sure, her offence

Must be of such unnatural degree,
That monsters it, or your fore-vouch'd affection
Fall into taint: which to believe of her,
Must be a faith that reason without miracle
Could never plant in me.

CORDELIA* I yet beseech your majesty
(If for I want that glib and oily art,
To speak and purpose not; since what I well intend,
I'll do't before I speak) that you make known
It is no vicious blot, murder, or foulness,
No unchaste action, or dishonour'd step,
That hath depriv'd me of your grace and favour;
But even for want of that for which I am richer,
A still-soliciting eye, and such a tongue
That I am glad I have not, though not to have it
Hath lost me in your liking.

LEAR Better thou
Hadst not been born, than not to have pleas'd me better.

FRANCE Is it but this? A tardiness in nature,
Which often leaves the history unspoke,
That it intends to do? – My Lord of Burgundy,
What say you to the lady? Love's not love,
When it is mingled with regards, that stand
Aloof from the entire point. Will you have her?
She is herself a dowry.

BURGUNDY Royal king,
Give but that portion which yourself propos'd,
And here I take Cordelia by the hand,
Duchess of Burgundy.

LEAR Nothing: I have sworn; I am firm.

BURGUNDY I am sorry, then, you have so lost a father,

That you must lose a husband.

CORDELIA Peace be with Burgundy!
Since that respects of fortune are his love,
I shall not be his wife.

FRANCE Fairest Cordelia, that art most rich, being poor:
Most choice, forsaken; and most lov'd, despised;
Thee and thy virtues here I seize upon:
Be it lawful, I take up what 's cast away.
Gods, gods! 'tis strange, that from their cold'st neglect
My love should kindle to inflam'd respect. –
Thy dowerless daughter, king, thrown to my chance,
Is queen of us, of ours, and our fair France:
Not all the dukes of waterish Burgundy
Shall buy this unpriz'd precious maid of me. –
Bid them farewell, Cordelia, though unkind:
Thou losest here, a better where to find.

LEAR Thou hast her, France: let her be thine; for we
Have no such daughter, nor shall ever see
That face of hers again: – therefore, be gone
Without our grace, our love, our benison. –
Come, noble Burgundy.

[Flourish. Exeunt Lear, Burgundy, Cornwall, Albany, Gloster, and Attendants.

FRANCE Bid farewell to your sisters.

CORDELIA The jewels of our father, with wash'd eyes
Cordelia leaves you: I know you what you are;
And, like a sister, am most loath to call
Your faults as they are nam'd. Love well our father:
To your professed bosoms I commit him;
But yet, alas! stood I within his grace,
I would prefer him to a better place.
So farewell to you both.

REGAN Prescribe not us our duty.

GONERIL Let your study
Be, to content your lord, who hath receiv'd you
At fortune's alms: you have obedience scanted,
And well are worth the want that you have wanted.

CORDELIA Time shall unfold what plighted cunning hides;
Who cover faults, at last shame them derides.
Well may you prosper!

FRANCE Come, my fair Cordelia.

[Exeunt France and Cordelia.

GONERIL Sister, it is not little I have to say of what most nearly appertains to us both. I think, our father will hence to-night.

REGAN That's most certain, and with you; next month with us.

GONERIL You see how full of changes his age is; the observation we have made of it hath not been little: he always loved our sister most; and with what poor judgment he hath now cast her off, appears too grossly.

REGAN 'Tis the infirmity of his age; yet he hath ever but slenderly known himself.

GONERIL The best and soundest of his time hath been but rash; then must we look to receive from his age, not alone the imperfections of long-engraffed condition, but, therewithal, the unruly waywardness that infirm and choleric years bring with them.

REGAN Such unconstant starts are we like to have from him, as this of Kent's banishment.

GONERIL There is further compliment of leave-taking between France and him. Pray you, let us hit together: if our father carry authority with such disposition as he bears, this last surrender of his will but offend us.

REGAN We shall further think of it.

GONERIL We must do something, and i' the heat. *[Exeunt.*

SCENE II – A HALL IN THE EARL OF GLOSTER'S CASTLE.

Enter Edmund, with a letter.

EDMUND Thou, Nature, art my goddess; to thy law
My services are bound. Wherefore should I
Stand in the plague of custom, and permit
The curiosity of nations to deprive me,
For that I am some twelve or fourteen moonshines
Lag of a brother? Why bastard? wherefore base?
When my dimensions are as well compact,
My mind as generous, and my shape as true,
As honest madam's issue? Why brand they us
With base? with baseness? bastardy? base, base?
Who in the lusty stealth of nature take
More composition and fierce quality,
Than doth, within a dull, stale, tired bed,
Go to the creating a whole tribe of fops,
Got 'tween asleep and wake? – Well then,
Legitimate Edgar, I must have your land:
Our father's love is to the bastard Edmund,
As to the legitimate. Fine word, – legitimate!
Well, my legitimate, if this letter speed,
And my invention thrive, Edmund the base
Shall to the legitimate: – I grow, I prosper; –
Now, gods, stand up for bastards!

Enter Gloster.

GLOSTER Kent banish'd thus! And France in choler parted!
And the king gone to-night! subscrib'd his power!
Confin'd to exhibition! All this done

Upon the gad! – Edmund! How now! what news?

EDMUND So please your lordship, none. *[Putting up the letter.*

GLOSTER Why so earnestly seek you to put up that letter?

EDMUND I know no news, my lord.

GLOSTER What paper were you reading?

EDMUND Nothing, my lord.

GLOSTER No? What needed then that terrible despatch of it into your pocket? the quality of nothing hath not such need to hide itself. Let's see; come; if it be nothing, I shall not need spectacles.

EDMUND I beseech you, sir, pardon me; it is a letter from my brother, that I have not all o'er-read: and for so much as I have perused, I find it not fit for your o'erlooking.

GLOSTER Give me the letter, sir.

EDMUND I shall offend, either to detain or give it. The contents, as in part I understand them, are to blame.

GLOSTER Let's see, let's see.

EDMUND I hope, for my brother's justification, he wrote this but as an essay or taste of my virtue.

GLOSTER *[Reads.]* 'This policy, and reverence of age, makes the world bitter to the best of our times; keeps our fortunes from us, till our oldness cannot relish them. I begin to find an idle and fond bondage in the oppression of aged tyranny, who sways, not as it hath power, but as it is suffered. Come to me, that of this I may speak more. If our father would sleep till I waked him, you should enjoy half his revenue for ever, and live the beloved of your brother, EDGAR.' – Humph! – Conspiracy! – 'Sleep till I waked him, – you should enjoy half his revenue.' – My son Edgar! Had he a hand to write this? a heart and brain to breed it in? – When came this to you? Who brought it?

EDMUND It was not brought me, my lord; there's the cunning of it: I found it thrown in at the casement of my closet.

GLOSTER You know the character to be your brother's?

EDMUND If the matter were good, my lord, I durst swear it were his; but, in respect of that, I would fain think it were not.

GLOSTER It is his.

EDMUND It is his hand, my lord; but, I hope, his heart is not in the contents.

GLOSTER Has he never before sounded you in this business?

EDMUND Never, my lord: but I have often heard him maintain it to be fit, that, sons at perfect age, and fathers declined, the father should be as ward to the son, and the son manage his revenue.

GLOSTER O villain, villain! – His very opinion in the letter! – Abhorred villain! Unnatural, detested, brutish villain! worse than brutish! – Go, sirrah, seek him; I'll apprehend him. – Abominable villain! – Where is he?

EDMUND I do not well know, my lord. If it shall please you to suspend your indignation against my brother, till you can derive from him better testimony of his intent, you shall run a certain course; where, if you violently proceed against him, mistaking his purpose, it would make a great gap in your own honour, and shake in pieces the heart of his obedience. I dare pawn down my life for him, that he hath writ this to feel my affection to your honour, and to no other pretence of danger.

GLOSTER Think you so?

EDMUND If your honour judge it meet, I will place you where you shall hear us confer of this, and by an auricular assurance have your satisfaction; and that without any further delay than this very evening.

GLOSTER He cannot be such a monster –

EDMUND Nor is not, sure.

GLOSTER To his father, that so tenderly and entirely loves him. – Heaven and earth! – Edmund, seek him out; wind me into him, I pray you: frame the business after your own wisdom. I would unstate myself to be in a due resolution.

EDMUND I will seek him, sir, presently; convey the business as I shall find means, and acquaint you withal.

GLOSTER These late eclipses in the sun and moon portend no good to us: though the wisdom of nature can reason it thus and thus, yet nature finds itself scourged by the sequent effects. Love cools, friendship falls off, brothers divide: in cities, mutinies; in countries, discord; in palaces, treason; and the bond cracked between son and father. This villain of mine comes under the prediction; there's son against father: the king falls from bias of nature; there's father against child. We have seen the best of our time: machinations, hollowness, treachery, and all ruinous disorders, follow us disquietly to our graves. – Find out this villain, Edmund; it shall lose thee nothing: do it carefully. – And the noble and true-hearted Kent banished! his offence, honesty! – 'Tis strange. *[Exit.*

EDMUND This is the excellent foppery of the world, that, when we are sick in fortune (often the surfeit of our own behaviour), we make guilty of our disasters the sun, the moon, and the stars: as if we were villains by necessity; fools by heavenly compulsion: knaves, thieves, and treachers, by spherical predominance; drunkards, liars, and adulterers, by an enforced obedience of planetary influence; and all that we are evil in, by a divine thrusting on. An admirable evasion of whoremaster man, to lay his goatish disposition on the charge of a star! My father compounded with my mother under the dragon's tail: and my nativity was under *ursa major*: so that it follows, I am rough and lecherous. – Tut! I should have been that I am, had the maidenliest star in the firmament twinkled on my bastardising.

Enter Edgar.

Pat: he comes, like the catastrophe of the old comedy: my cue is villainous melancholy, with a sigh like Tom o' Bedlam. – O! these eclipses do portend these divisions. Fa, sol, la, mi.

EDGAR How now, brother Edmund! What serious contemplation are you in?

EDMUND I am thinking, brother, of a prediction I read this other day, what should follow these eclipses.

EDGAR Do you busy yourself with that?

EDMUND I promise you, the effects he writes of succeed unhappily: as of unnaturalness between the child and the parent; death, dearth, dissolutions of ancient amities; divisions in state; menaces and maledictions against king and nobles; needless diffidences, banishment of friends, dissipation of cohorts, nuptial breaches, and I know not what.

EDGAR How long have you been a sectary astronomical?

EDMUND Come, come; when saw you my father last?

EDGAR The night gone by.

EDMUND Spake you with him?

EDGAR Ay, two hours together.

EDMUND Parted you in good terms? Found you no displeasure in him, by word, or countenance?

EDGAR None at all.

EDMUND Bethink yourself, wherein you may have offended him: and at my entreaty forbear his presence, till some little time hath qualified the heat of his displeasure, which at this instant so rageth in him, that with the mischief of your person it would scarcely allay.

EDGAR Some villain hath done me wrong.

EDMUND That's my fear. I pray you, have a continent forbearance, till the speed of his rage goes slower; and, as I say, retire with me to my lodging, from whence I will fitly bring you to hear my lord speak. Pray you, go: there's my key. – If you do stir abroad, go armed.

EDGAR Armed, brother?

EDMUND Brother, I advise you to the best; I am no honest man, if there be any good meaning towards you: I have told you what I have seen and heard, but faintly; nothing like the image and horror of it. Pray you, away.

EDGAR Shall I hear from you anon?

EDMUND I do serve you in this business. – *[Exit Edgar.*
A credulous father, and a brother noble,
Whose nature is so far from doing harms,
That he suspects none; on whose foolish honesty
My practices ride easy! – I see the business. –
Let me, if not by birth, have lands by wit:
All with me's meet, that I can fashion fit. *[Exit.*

SCENE III – A ROOM IN THE DUKE OF ALBANY'S PALACE.

Enter Goneril, and Oswald, her Steward.

GONERIL Did my father strike my gentleman for chiding of his fool?

OSWALD Ay, madam.

GONERIL By day and night he wrongs me: every hour
He flashes into one gross crime or other,
That sets us all at odds: I'll not endure it.
His knights grow riotous, and himself upbraids us

On every trifle. – When he returns from hunting,
I will not speak with him; say, I am sick:
If you come slack of former services,
You shall do well; the fault of it I'll answer.

OSWALD He's coming, madam; I hear him. *[Horns within.*

GONERIL Put on what weary negligence you please.
You and your fellows; I'd have it come to question:
If he distaste it, let him to my sister,
Whose mind and mine, I know, in that are one,
Not to be over-rul'd. Idle old man,
That still would manage those authorities
That he hath given away! – Now, by my life,
Old fools are babes again; and must be us'd
With checks, as flatteries, when they are seen abus'd.
Remember what I have said.

OSWALD Well, madam.

GONERIL And let his knights have colder looks among you;
What grows of it, no matter; advise your fellows so:
I would breed from hence occasions, and I shall,
That I may speak: – I'll write straight to my sister,
To hold my course. – Prepare for dinner. *[Exeunt.*

SCENE IV – A HALL IN THE SAME.

Enter Kent, disguised.

KENT If but as well I other accents borrow,
That can my speech diffuse, my good intent
May carry through itself to that full issue
For which I raz'd my likeness. – Now, banish'd Kent,
If thou canst serve where thou dost stand condemn'd,

(So may it come!) thy master, whom thou lov'st,
Shall find thee full of labours.

Horns within. Enter Lear, Knights, and Attendants.

LEAR Let me not stay a jot for dinner: go, get it ready. *[Exit an Attendant.]* How now! what art thou?

KENT A man, sir.

LEAR What dost thou profess? What wouldst thou with us?

KENT I do profess to be no less than I seem; to serve him truly that will put me in trust; to love him that is honest; to converse with him that is wise, and says little; to fear judgment; to fight when I cannot choose; and to eat no fish.

LEAR What art thou?

KENT A very honest-hearted fellow, and as poor as the king.

LEAR If thou be as poor for a subject, as he is for a king, thou art poor enough. What wouldst thou?

KENT Service.

LEAR Whom wouldst thou serve?

KENT You.

LEAR Dost thou know me, fellow?

KENT No, sir; but you have that in your countenance, which I would fain call master.

LEAR What's that?

KENT Authority.

LEAR What services canst thou do?

KENT I can keep honest counsel, ride, run, mar a curious tale in telling it, and deliver a plain message bluntly: that which ordinary men are fit for, I am qualified in; and the best of me is diligence.

LEAR How old art thou?

KENT Not so young, sir, to love a woman for singing; nor so old, to dote on her for anything: I have years on my back forty-eight.

LEAR Follow me; thou shalt serve me: if I like thee no worse after dinner, I will not part from thee yet. – Dinner, ho! dinner! – Where's my knave? my fool? Go you, and call my fool hither. *[Exit an Attendant.*

Enter Oswald.

You, you, sirrah, where's my daughter?

OSWALD So please you, – *[Exit.*

LEAR What says the fellow there? Call the clotpoll back. *[Exit a Knight.]* – Where's my fool, ho? – I think the world's asleep.

Re-enter Knight.

How now! where's that mongrel?

KNIGHT He says, my lord, your daughter is not well.

LEAR Why came not the slave back to me, when I called him?

KNIGHT Sir, he answered me in the roundest manner, he would not.

LEAR He would not!

KNIGHT My lord, I know not what the matter is; but, to my judgment, your highness is not entertained with that ceremonious affection as you were wont: there's a great abatement of kindness appears, as well in the general dependants, as in the duke himself also, and your daughter.

LEAR Ha! sayest thou so?

KNIGHT I beseech you, pardon me, my lord, if I be mistaken; for my duty cannot be silent, when I think your highness wronged.

LEAR Thou but rememberest me of mine own conception. I have perceived a most faint neglect of late; which I have rather blamed as mine own jealous curiosity, than as a very pretence and purpose of unkindness: I will look further into 't. – But where's my fool? I have not seen him this two days.

KNIGHT Since my young lady's going into France, sir, the fool hath much pined away.

LEAR No more of that; I have noted it well. – Go you, and tell my daughter I would speak with her. *[Exit an Attendant]* – Go you, call hither my fool. *[Exit an Attendant.*

Re-enter Oswald.

O! you sir, you, come you hither, sir. Who am I, sir?

OSWALD My lady's father.

LEAR My lady's father! my lord's knave: you whoreson dog! you slave! you cur!

OSWALD I am none of these, my lord; I beseech your pardon.

LEAR Do you bandy looks with me, you rascal? *[Striking him.*

OSWALD I'll not be struck, my lord.

KENT Nor tripped neither, you base foot-ball player. *[Tripping up his heels.*

LEAR I thank thee, fellow; thou servest me, and I'll love thee.

KENT Come, sir, arise, away! I'll teach you differences: away, away! If you will measure your lubber's length again, tarry; but away! Go to: have your wisdom? so. *[Pushes Oswald out.*

LEAR Now, my friendly knave, I thank thee: there's earnest of thy service. *[Giving Kent money.*

Enter Fool.

FOOL Let me hire him too: – here's my coxcomb. *[Giving Kent his cap.*

LEAR How now, my pretty knave! how dost thou?

FOOL Sirrah, you were best take my coxcomb.

KENT Why, fool?

FOOL Why, for taking one's part that's out of favour. – Nay, an thou canst not smile as the wind sits, thou'lt catch cold shortly:

there, take my coxcomb. Why, this fellow has banished two on 's daughters, and did the third a blessing against his will: if thou follow him, thou must needs wear my coxcomb. – How now, nuncle? 'Would I had two coxcombs, and two daughters!

LEAR Why, my boy?

FOOL If I gave them all my living, I'd keep my coxcombs myself. There's mine; beg another of thy daughters.

LEAR Take heed, sirrah, – the whip.

FOOL Truth's a dog must to kennel; he must be whipped out, when the lady brach may stand by the fire and stink.

LEAR A pestilent gall to me!

FOOL Sirrah, I'll teach thee a speech.

LEAR Do.

FOOL Mark it, nuncle: –

Have more than thou showest,
Speak less than thou knowest,
Lend less than thou owest,
Ride more than thou goest,
Learn more than thou trowest,
Set less than thou throwest;
Leave thy drink and thy whore,
And keep in-a-door,
And thou shalt have more
Than two tens to a score.

KENT This is nothing, fool.

FOOL Then 'tis like the breath of an unfee'd lawyer; you gave me nothing for 't. – Can you make no use of nothing, nuncle?

LEAR Why, no, boy; nothing can be made out of nothing.

FOOL *[To Kent.]* Pr'ythee, tell him, so much the rent of his land comes to: he will not believe a fool.

LEAR A bitter fool!

FOOL Dost thou know the difference, my boy, between a bitter fool and a sweet one?

LEAR No, lad; teach me.

FOOL That lord, that counsell'd thee
To give away thy land,
Come place him here by me;
Do thou for him stand:
The sweet and bitter fool
Will presently appear;
The one in motley here.
The other found out there.

LEAR Dost thou call me fool, boy?

FOOL All thy other titles thou hast given away; that thou wast born with.

KENT This is not altogether fool, my lord.

FOOL No, 'faith; lords and great men will not let me: if I had a monopoly out, they would have part on 't; and ladies too: they will not let me have all fool to myself; they'll be snatching. – Nuncle, give me an egg, and I'll give thee two crowns.

LEAR What two crowns shall they be?

FOOL Why, after I have cut the egg i' the middle, and eat up the meat, the two crowns of the egg. When thou clovest thy crown i' the middle, and gavest away both parts, thou borest thine ass on thy back o'er the dirt: thou hadst little wit in thy bald crown, when thou gavest thy golden one away. If I speak like myself in this, let him be whipped that first finds it so.

[Singing.

Fools had ne'er less grace in a year;
For wise men are grown foppish,
And know not how their wits to wear,
Their manners are so apish.

LEAR When were you wont to be so full of songs, sirrah?

FOOL I have used it, nuncle, ever since thou madest thy daughters thy mothers: for when thou gavest them the rod and putt'st down thine own breeches, *[Singing.*

Then they for sudden joy did weep,
And I for sorrow sung,
That such a king should play bo-peep,
And go the fools among.

Pr'ythee, nuncle, keep a schoolmaster that can teach thy fool a lie: I would fain learn to lie.

LEAR An you lie, sirrah, we'll have you whipped.

FOOL I marvel, what kin thou and thy daughters are: they'll have me whipped for speaking true, thou'lt have me whipped for lying; and sometimes I am whipped for holding my peace. I had rather be any kind o' thing than a fool; and yet I would not be thee, nuncle: thou hast pared thy wit o' both sides, and left nothing i' the middle. Here comes one o' the parings.

Enter Goneril.

LEAR How now, daughter? what makes that frontlet on? Methinks, you are too much of late i' the frown.

FOOL Thou wast a pretty fellow, when thou hadst no need to care for her frowning; now thou art an O without a figure. I am better than thou art now: I am a fool, thou art nothing. – Yes, forsooth, I will hold my tongue; so your face *[to Goneril]* bids me, though you say nothing.

Mum, mum:
He that keeps nor crust nor crum,
Weary of all, shall want some.

That's a sheal'd peascod.

GONERIL Not only, sir, this your all-licens'd fool,
But other of your insolent retinue
Do hourly carp and quarrel; breaking forth
In rank and not-to-be-endured riots. Sir,
I had thought, by making this well known unto you,
To have found a safe redress; but now grow fearful,
By what yourself too late have spoke and done,
That you protect this course, and put it on
By your allowance; which if you should, the fault
Would not 'scape censure, nor the redresses sleep,
Which, in the tender of a wholesome weal,
Might in their working do you that offence,
Which else were shame, that then necessity
Will call discreet proceeding.
FOOL For you know, nuncle,
The hedge-sparrow fed the cuckoo so long,
That it had it head bit off by it young.
So, out went the candle, and we were left darkling.
LEAR Are you our daughter?
GONERIL I would you would make use of your good wisdom,
Whereof I know you are fraught, and put away
These dispositions, which of late transport you
From what you rightly are.
FOOL May not an ass know when the cart draws the horse? –
Whoop, Jug! I love thee.
LEAR Does any here know me? This is not Lear:
Does Lear walk thus? speak thus? Where are his eyes?
Either his notion weakens, his discernings
Are lethargied. – Ha! waking? 'tis not so. –
Who is it that can tell me who I am? –
FOOL Lear's shadow.

LEAR I would learn that; for by the marks of sovereignty, knowledge, and reason, I should be false persuaded I had daughters.

FOOL Which they will make an obedient father.

LEAR Your name, fair gentlewoman?

GONERIL This admiration, sir, is much o' the savour
Of other your new pranks. I do beseech you
To understand my purposes aright:
As you are old and reverend, should be wise.
Here do you keep a hundred knights and squires;
Men so disorder'd, so debosh'd, and bold,
That this our court, infected with their manners,
Shows like a riotous inn: epicurism and lust
Make it more like a tavern, or a brothel,
Then a grac'd palace. The shame itself doth speak
For instant remedy: be then desir'd
By her, that else will take the thing she begs,
A little to disquantity your train;
And the remainder, that shall still depend,
To be such men as may besort your age,
Which know themselves and you.

LEAR Darkness and devils! –
Saddle my horses; call my train together. –
Degenerate bastard! I'll not trouble thee:
Yet have I left a daughter.

GONERIL You strike my people; and your disorder'd rabble
Make servants of their betters.

Enter Albany.

LEAR Woe, that too late repents, – *[To Albany.]* O, sir, are you come?

Is it your will? Speak, sir. – Prepare my horses.
Ingratitude, thou marble-hearted fiend,
More hideous, when thou show'st thee in a child,
Than the sea-monster!

ALBANY Pray, sir, be patient.

LEAR *[To Goneril.]* Detested kite! thou liest:
My train are men of choice and rarest parts,
That all particulars of duty know,
And in the most exact regard support
The worships of their name. – O most small fault,
How ugly didst thou in Cordelia show!
Which, like an engine, wrench'd my frame of nature
From the fix'd place, drew from my heart all love,
And added to the gall. O Lear, Lear, Lear!
Beat at this gate, that let thy folly in. *[Striking his head.*
And thy dear judgment out! – Go, go, my people.

ALBANY My lord, I am guiltless, as I am ignorant
Of what hath mov'd you.

LEAR It may be so, my lord. –
Hear, Nature, hear! dear goddess, hear!
Suspend thy purpose, if thou didst intend
To make this creature fruitful!
Into her womb convey sterility!
Dry up in her the organs of increase,
And from her derogate body never spring
A babe to honour her! If she must teem,
Create her child of spleen; that it may live,
And be a thwart disnatur'd torment to her!
Let it stamp wrinkles in her brow of youth;
With cadent tears fret channels in her cheeks;
Turn all her mother's pains, and benefits,

To laughter and contempt; that she may feel
How sharper than a serpent's tooth it is
To have a thankless child! – Away, away! *[Exit.*

ALBANY Now, gods, that we adore, whereof comes this?

GONERIL Never afflict yourself to know more of it;
But let his disposition have that scope
As dotage gives it.

Re-enter Lear.

LEAR What, fifty of my followers at a clap!
Within a fortnight?

ALBANY What's the matter, sir?

LEAR I'll tell thee: – Life and death! *[To Goneril.]* I am ashamed,
That thou hast power to shake my manhood thus;
That these hot tears, which break from me perforce,
Should make thee worth them. Blasts and fogs upon thee!
The untented woundings of a father's curse
Pierce every sense about thee! – Old fond eyes,
Beweep this cause again, I'll pluck ye out,
And cast you, with the waters that you lose,
To temper clay. – Yea, is it come to this?
Let it be so: – yet have I left a daughter.
Who, I am sure, is kind and comfortable:
When she shall hear this of thee, with her nails
She'll flay thy wolfish visage. Thou shalt find,
That I'll resume the shape which thou dost think
I have cast off for ever. *[Exeunt Lear, Kent, and Attendants.*

GONERIL Do you mark that?

ALBANY I cannot be so partial, Goneril,
To the great love I bear you. –

GONERIL Pray you, content. – What, Oswald, ho! –

[To the Fool.] You, sir, more knave than fool, after your master.

FOOL Nuncle Lear, nuncle Lear! tarry, and take the fool with thee.

A fox, when one has caught her,
And such a daughter,
Should sure to the slaughter,
If my cap would buy a halter;
So the fool follows after. *[Exit.*

GONERIL This man hath had good counsel. – A hundred knights!
'Tis politic, and safe, to let him keep
At point a hundred knights: yes, that on every dream,
Each buz, each fancy, each complaint, dislike,
He may enguard his dotage with their powers,
And hold our lives in mercy. – Oswald, I say! –

ALBANY Well, you may fear too far.

GONERIL Safer than trust too far.
Let me still take away the harms I fear,
Not fear still to be taken: I know his heart.
What he hath utter'd, I have writ my sister:
If she sustain him and his hundred knights,
When I have show'd the unfitness, –

Re-enter Oswald.

How now, Oswald!
What, have you writ that letter to my sister?

OSWALD Ay, madam.

GONERIL Take you some company, and away to horse:
Inform her full of my particular fear;
And thereto add such reasons of your own,
As may compact it more. Get you gone,

And hasten your return. *[Exit Oswald]* No, no, my lord,
This milky gentleness and course of yours
Though I condemn not, yet, under pardon,
You are much more attask'd for want of wisdom,
Than prais'd for harmful mildness.

ALBANY How far your eyes may pierce, I cannot tell:
Striving to better, oft we mar what's well.

GONERIL Nay, then –

ALBANY Well, well; the event. *[Exeunt.*

SCENE V – COURT BEFORE THE SAME.

Enter Lear, Kent, and Fool.

LEAR Go you before to Gloster with these letters. Acquaint my daughter no further with anything you know, than comes from her demand out of the letter. If your diligence be not speedy, I shall be there before you.

KENT I will not sleep, my lord, till I have delivered your letter. *[Exit.*

FOOL If a man's brains were in his heels, were 't not in danger of kibes?

LEAR Ay, boy.

FOOL Then, I pr'ythee, be merry; thy wit shall not go slip-shod.

LEAR Ha, ha, ha!

FOOL Shalt see, thy other daughter will use thee kindly; for though she's as like this as a crab is like an apple, yet I can tell what I can tell.

LEAR What canst tell, boy?

FOOL She will taste as like this as a crab does to a crab. Thou canst tell why one's nose stands i' the middle on 's face?

LEAR No.

FOOL Why, to keep one's eyes of either side 's nose; that what a man cannot smell out, he may spy into.

LEAR I did her wrong: –

FOOL Canst tell how an oyster makes his shell?

LEAR No.

FOOL Nor I neither; but I can tell you why a snail has a house.

LEAR Why?

FOOL Why, to put his head in; not to give it away to his daughters, and leave his horns without a case.

LEAR I will forget my nature. – So kind a father! – Be my horses ready?

FOOL Thy asses are gone about 'em. The reason why the seven stars are no more than seven is a pretty reason.

LEAR Because they are not eight?

FOOL Yes, indeed. Thou wouldst make a good fool.

LEAR To take it again perforce! – Monster ingratitude!

FOOL If thou wert my fool, nuncle, I'd have thee beaten for being old before thy time.

LEAR How's that?

FOOL Thou shouldst not have been old till thou hadst been wise.

LEAR O, let me not be mad, not mad, sweet heaven!
Keep me in temper: I would not be mad! –

Enter Gentleman.

How now! Are the horses ready?

GENTLEMAN Ready, my lord.

LEAR Come, boy.

FOOL She that's a maid now, laughs at my departure,
Shall not be a maid long, unless things be cut shorter.

[Exeunt.

ACT TWO

SCENE 1 – A COURT WITHIN THE CASTLE OF THE EARL OF GLOSTER.

Enter Edmund and Curan, meeting.

EDMUND Save thee, Curan.

CURAN And you, sir. I have been with your father, and given him notice, that the Duke of Cornwall, and Regan his duchess, will be here with him to-night.

EDMUND How comes that?

CURAN Nay, I know not. You have heard of the news abroad? I mean, the whispered ones, for they are yet but ear-kissing arguments.

EDMUND Not I: pray you, what are they?

CURAN Have you heard of no likely wars toward, 'twixt the Dukes of Cornwall and Albany?

EDMUND Not a word.

CURAN You may do then, in time. Fare you well, sir. *[Exit.*

EDMUND The duke be here to-night? The better! best!
This weaves itself perforce into my business.
My father hath set guard to take my brother;
And I have one thing, of a queasy question,
Which I must act. – Briefness, and fortune, work! –
Brother, a word; – descend: – brother, I say!

Enter Edgar

My father watches. – O sir! fly this place;
Intelligence is given where you are hid:
You have now the good advantage of the night. –
Have you not spoken 'gainst the Duke of Cornwall?
He's coming hither; now, i' the night, i' the haste,
And Regan with him: have you nothing said
Upon his party 'gainst the Duke of Albany?
Advise yourself.

EDGAR I am sure on 't, not a word.

EDMUND I hear my father coming. – Pardon me.
In cunning, I must draw my sword upon you:
Draw: seem to defend yourself. Now quit you well.
Yield: – come before my father. – Light, ho! here! –
Fly, brother. – Torches! torches! – So, farewell. –
[Exit Edgar.
Some blood drawn on me would beget opinion
[Wounds his arm.
Of my more fierce endeavour: I have seen drunkards
Do more than this in sport. – Father! father!
Stop, stop! No help?

Enter Gloster, and Servants with torches.

GLOSTER Now, Edmund, where's the villain?

EDMUND Here stood he in the dark, his sharp sword out,
Mumbling of wicked charms, conjuring the moon
To stand auspicious mistress, –

GLOSTER But where is he?

EDMUND Look, sir, I bleed.

GLOSTER Where is the villain, Edmund?

EDMUND Fled this way, sir. When by no means he could –

GLOSTER Pursue him, ho! – Go after. *[Exit Servant.]*
By no means, – what?
EDMUND Persuade me to the murder of your lordship;
But that I told him, the revenging gods
'Gainst parricides did all their thunders bend;
Spoke, with how manifold and strong a bond
The child was bound to the father; – sir, in fine,
Seeing how loathly opposite I stood
To his unnatural purpose, in fell motion,
With his prepared sword he charges home
My unprovided body, lanc'd mine arm:
But when he saw my best alarum'd spirits,
Bold in the quarrel's right, rous'd to the encounter,
Or whether ghasted by the noise I made,
Full suddenly he fled.
GLOSTER Let him fly far:
Not in this land shall he remain uncaught;
And found – despatch. – The noble duke my master,
My worthy arch and patron, comes to-night:
By his authority I will proclaim it,
That he which finds him shall deserve our thanks,
Bringing the murderous coward to the stake;
He that conceals him, death.
EDMUND When I dissuaded him from his intent,
And found him pight to do it, with curst speech
I threaten'd to discover him: he replied,
'Thou unpossessing bastard! dost thou think,
If I would stand against thee, would the reposal
Of any trust, virtue, or worth, in thee
Make thy words faith'd? No: what I should deny,
(As this I would; ay, though thou didst produce

My very character,) I'd turn it all
To thy suggestion, plot, and damned practice:
And thou must make a dullard of the world,
If they not thought the profits of my death
Were very pregnant and potential spurs
To make thee seek it.'

GLOSTER Strong and fasten'd villain!
Would he deny his letter? – I never got him. *[Tucket within.*
Hark! the duke's trumpets. I know not why he comes.
All ports I'll bar; the villain shall not 'scape;
The duke must grant me that: besides, his picture
I will send far and near, that all the kingdom
May have due note of him; and of my land,
Loyal and natural boy, I'll work the means
To make thee capable.

Enter Cornwall, Regan, and Attendants.

CORNWALL How now, my noble friend! since I came hither
(Which I can call but now), I have heard strange news.
REGAN If it be true, all vengeance comes too short,
Which can pursue the offender. How dost, my lord?
GLOSTER O, madam, my old heart is crack'd, it's crack'd!
REGAN What! did my father's godson seek your life?
He whom my father nam'd? your Edgar?
GLOSTER O, lady, lady! shame would have it hid.
REGAN Was he not companion with the riotous knights
That tend upon my father?
GLOSTER I know not, madam, 'tis too bad, too bad.
EDMUND Yes, madam, he was of that consort.
REGAN No marvel then, though he were ill affected:
'Tis they have put him on the old man's death,

To have the expense and waste of his revenues.
I have this present evening from my sister
Been well inform'd of them; and with such cautions,
That if they come to sojourn at my house,
I'll not be there.

CORNWALL Nor I, assure thee, Regan. –
Edmund, I hear that you have shown your father
A child-like office.

EDMUND 'Twas my duty, sir.

GLOSTER He did bewray his practice; and receiv'd
This hurt you see, striving to apprehend him.

CORNWALL Is he pursued?

GLOSTER Ay, my good lord.

CORNWALL If he be taken, he shall never more
Be fear'd of doing harm: make your own purpose,
How in my strength you please. – For you, Edmund,
Whose virtue and obedience doth this instant
So much commend itself, you shall be ours:
Natures of such deep trust we shall much need;
You we first seize on.

EDMUND I shall serve you, sir,
Truly, however else.

GLOSTER For him I thank your grace.

CORNWALL You know not why we came to visit you, –

REGAN Thus out of season, threading dark-ey'd night.
Occasions, noble Gloster, of some poise,
Wherein we must have use of your advice.
Our father he hath writ, so hath our sister,
Of differences, which I best thought it fit
To answer from our home: the several messengers
From hence attend despatch. Our good old friend,

Lay comforts to your bosom, and bestow
Your needful counsel to our businesses,
Which crave the instant use.

GLOSTER I serve you, madam.
Your graces are right welcome. *[Exeunt.*

SCENE II – BEFORE GLOSTER'S CASTLE.

Enter Kent and Oswald, severally.

OSWALD Good dawning to thee, friend: art of this house?

KENT Ay.

OSWALD Where may we set our horses?

KENT I' the mire.

OSWALD Pr'ythee, if thou lov'st me, tell me.

KENT I love thee not.

OSWALD Why, then I care not for thee.

KENT If I had thee in Lipsbury pinfold, I would make thee care for me.

OSWALD Why dost thou use me thus? I know thee not.

KENT Fellow, I know thee.

OSWALD What dost thou know me for?

KENT A knave, a rascal, an eater of broken meats; a base, proud, shallow, beggarly, three-suited, hundred-pound, filthy, worsted-stocking knave; a lily-liver'd, action-taking knave; a whoreson, glass-gazing, super-serviceable, finical rogue; one-trunk-inheriting slave; one that wouldst be a bawd, in way of good service, and art nothing but the composition of a knave, beggar, coward, pander, and the son and heir of a mongrel bitch: one whom I will beat into clamorous whining, if thou deniest the least syllable of thy addition.

OSWALD Why, what a monstrous fellow art thou, thus to rail on one, that is neither known of thee, nor knows thee!

KENT What a brazen-faced varlet art thou, to deny thou knowest me! Is it two days since I tripped up thy heels, and beat thee, before the king? Draw, you rogue; for though it be night, yet the moon shines: I'll make a sop o' the moonshine of you. *[Drawing his sword.]* Draw, you whoreson cullionly barber-monger, draw.

OSWALD Away! I have nothing to do with thee.

KENT Draw, you rascal: you come with letters against the king, and take Vanity the puppet's part, against the royalty of her father. Draw, you rogue, or I'll so carbonado your shanks: – draw, you rascal; come your ways.

OSWALD Help, ho! murder! help!

KENT Strike, you slave: stand, rogue, stand; you neat slave, strike. *[Beating him.*

OSWALD Help, ho! murder! murder!

Enter Edmund.

EDMUND How now! What's the matter?

KENT With you, goodman boy, if you please: come, I'll flesh you, come on, young master.

Enter Cornwall, Regan, Gloster, and Servants.

GLOSTER Weapons! arms! What's the matter here?

CORNWALL Keep peace, upon your lives:
He dies that strikes again. What is the matter?

REGAN The messengers from our sister and the king.

CORNWALL What is your difference? speak.

OSWALD I am scarce in breath, my lord.

KENT No marvel, you have so bestirred your valour. You

cowardly rascal, nature disclaims in thee: a tailor made thee.

CORNWALL Thou art a strange fellow: a tailor make a man?

KENT Ay, a tailor, sir: a stone-cutter, or a painter, could not have made him so ill, though they had been but two hours o' the trade.

CORNWALL Speak yet, how grew your quarrel?

OSWALD This ancient ruffian, sir, whose life I have spar'd,
At suit of his grey beard, –

KENT Thou whoreson zed! thou unnecessary letter! – My lord, if you will give me leave, I will tread this unbolted villain into mortar, and daub the wall of a jakes with him. – Spare my grey beard, you wag-tail?

CORNWALL Peace, sirrah!
You beastly knave, know you no reverence?

KENT Yes, sir; but anger hath a privilege.

CORNWALL Why art thou angry?

KENT That such a slave as this should wear a sword,
Who wears no honesty. Such smiling rogues as these,
Like rats, oft bite the holy cords a-twain
Which are too intrinse t' unloose; smooth every passion
That in the natures of their lords rebel;
Bring oil to fire, snow to their colder moods;
Renege, affirm, and turn their halcyon beaks
With every gale and vary of their masters,
Knowing nought, like dogs, but following. –
A plague upon your epileptic visage!
Smile you my speeches, as I were a fool?
Goose, if I had you upon Sarum plain,
I'd drive ye cackling home to Camelot.

CORNWALL What! art thou mad, old fellow?

GLOSTER How fell you out? say that.

KENT No contraries hold more antipathy,
Than I and such a knave.
CORNWALL Why dost thou call him knave? What is his fault?
KENT His countenance likes me not.
CORNWALL No more, perchance, does mine, nor his, nor hers.
KENT Sir, 'tis my occupation to be plain:
I have seen better faces in my time,
Than stands on any shoulder that I see
Before me at this instant.
CORNWALL This is some fellow,
Who, having been prais'd for bluntness, doth affect
A saucy roughness, and constrains the garb,
Quite from his nature: he cannot flatter, he;
An honest mind and plain, – he must speak truth:
An they will take it, so; if not, he's plain.
These kind of knaves I know, which in this plainness
Harbour more craft, and more corrupter ends,
Than twenty silly ducking observants,
That stretch their duties nicely.
KENT Sir, in good sooth, in sincere verity,
Under the allowance of your great aspect,
Whose influence, like the wreath of radiant fire
On flicking Phœbus' front, –
CORNWALL What mean'st by this?
KENT To go out of my dialect, which you discommend so much.
I know, sir, I am no flatterer: he that beguiled you in a plain accent, was a plain knave; which, for my part, I will not be, though I should win your displeasure to entreat me to 't.
CORNWALL What was the offence you gave him?
OSWALD I never gave him any:
It pleas'd the king, his master, very late,

To strike at me, upon his misconstruction;
When he, compact, and flattering his displeasure,
Tripp'd me behind; being down, insulted, rail'd,
And put upon him such a deal of man,
That worthied him, got praises of the king
For him attempting who was self-subdu'd;
And, in the fleshment of this dread exploit,
Drew on me here again.

KENT None of these rogues, and cowards,
But Ajax is their fool.

CORNWALL Fetch forth the stocks!
You stubborn ancient knave, you reverend braggart,
We'll teach you.

KENT Sir, I am too old to learn.
Call not your stocks for me; I serve the king,
On whose employment I was sent to you:
You shall do small respect, show too bold malice
Against the grace and person of my master,
Stocking his messenger.

CORNWALL Fetch forth the stocks!
As I have life and honour, there shall he sit till noon.

REGAN Till noon! till night, my lord; and all night too.

KENT Why, madam, if I were your father's dog,
You should not use me so.

REGAN Sir, being his knave, I will.

CORNWALL This is a fellow of the selfsame colour
Our sister speaks of. – Come, bring away the stocks.
[Stocks brought out.

GLOSTER Let me beseech your grace not to do so.
His fault is much, and the good king his master
Will check him for't: your purpos'd low correction

Is such as basest and contemned'st wretches,
For pilferings and most common trespasses,
Are punish'd with. The king must take it ill,
That he, so slightly valued in his messenger,
Should have him thus restrain'd.

CORNWALL I'll answer that.

REGAN My sister may receive it much more worse,
To have her gentleman abus'd, assaulted,
For following her affairs. – Put in his legs. –
[Kent is put in the stocks.
Come, my lord, away. *[Exeunt all but Gloster and Kent.*

GLOSTER I am sorry for thee, friend; 'tis the duke's pleasure,
Whose disposition, all the world well knows,
Will not be rubb'd, nor stopp'd: I'll entreat for thee.

KENT Pray, do not, sir. I have watch'd, and travell'd hard;
Some time I shall sleep out, the rest I'll whistle.
A good man's fortune may grow out at heels:
Give you good morrow!

GLOSTER The duke's to blame in this: 't will be ill taken *[Exit.*

KENT Good king, that must approve the common saw:
Thou out of heaven's benediction com'st
To the warm sun.
Approach, thou beacon to this under globe,
That by thy comfortable beams I may
Peruse this letter. – Nothing almost sees miracles,
But misery: – I know, 'tis from Cordelia;
Who hath most fortunately been inform'd
Of my obscured course; and shall find time
From this enormous state, – seeking to give
Losses their remedies. – All weary and o'er-watch'd,
Take vantage, heavy eyes, not to behold

This shameful lodging.
Fortune, good night; smile once more; turn thy wheel!
[He sleeps.

SCENE III – A PART OF THE HEATH.

Enter Edgar.

EDGAR I heard myself proclaim'd;
And, by the happy hollow of a tree,
Escap'd the hunt. No port is free; no place,
That guard, and most unusual vigilance,
Does not attend my taking. While I may 'scape,
I will preserve myself; and am bethought
To take the basest and most poorest shape,
That ever penury, in contempt of man,
Brought near to beast; my face I'll grime with filth,
Blanket my loins, elf all my hair in knots,
And with presented nakedness outface
The winds and persecutions of the sky.
The country gives me proof and precedent
Of Bedlam beggars, who, with roaring voices,
Strike with their numb'd and mortified bare arms
Pins, wooden pricks, nails, sprigs of rosemary;
And with this horrible object, from low farms,
Poor pelting villages, sheep-cotes, and mills,
Sometime with lunatic bans, sometime with prayers,
Enforce their charity. – Poor Turlygood! poor Tom!
That's something yet: – Edgar I nothing am. *[Exit.*

SCENE IV – BEFORE GLOSTER'S CASTLE. KENT IN THE STOCKS.

Enter Lear, Fool, and Gentleman.

LEAR 'Tis strange that they should so depart from home,
And not send back my messenger.

GENTLEMAN As I learn'd,
The night before there was no purpose in them
Of this remove.

KENT Hail to thee, noble master!

LEAR Ha!
Mak'st thou this shame thy pastime?

KENT No, my lord.

FOOL Ha, ha! look; he wears cruel garters. Horses are tied by the head, dogs and bears by the neck, monkeys by the loins, and men by the legs: when a man's over-lusty at legs, then he wears wooden nether-stocks.

LEAR What's he that hath so much thy place mistook,
To set thee here?

KENT It is both he and she,
Your son and daughter.

LEAR No.

KENT Yes.

LEAR No, I say.

KENT I say, yea.

LEAR No, no; they would not.

KENT Yes, they have.

LEAR By Jupiter, I swear, no.

KENT By Juno, I swear, ay.

LEAR They durst not do't;

They could not, would not do't: 'tis worse than murder,
To do upon respect such violent outrage.
Resolve me, with all modest haste, which way
Thou mightst deserve, or they impose, this usage,
Coming from us.

KENT My lord, when at their home
I did commend your highness' letters to them,
Ere I was risen from the place that show'd
My duty kneeling, came there a reeking post,
Stew'd in his haste, half breathless, panting forth
From Goneril, his mistress, salutations;
Deliver'd letters, spite of intermission,
Which presently they read: on whose contents
They summon'd up their meiny, straight took horse;
Commanded me to follow, and attend
The leisure of their answer; gave me cold looks:
And meeting here the other messenger,
Whose welcome, I perceiv'd, had poison'd mine,
(Being the very fellow which of late
Display'd so saucily against your highness,)
Having more man than wit about me, drew:
He rais'd the house with loud and coward cries.
Your son and daughter found this trespass worth
The shame which here it suffers.

FOOL Winter's not gone yet, if the wild-geese fly that way.
Fathers, that wear rags,
Do make their children blind;
But fathers, that bear bags,
Shall see their children kind.
Fortune, that arrant whore,
Ne'er turns the key to the poor. –

But, for all this, thou shalt have as many dolours for thy daughters, as thou canst tell in a year.

LEAR O, how this mother swells up toward my heart!
Hysterica passio! down, thou climbing sorrow!
Thy element's below. – Where is this daughter?

KENT With the earl, sir; here, within.

LEAR Follow me not; stay here.

[Exit.

GENTLEMAN Made you no more offence than what you speak of?

KENT None.
How chance the king comes with so small a number?

FOOL An thou hadst been set i' the stocks for that question, thou hadst well deserved it.

KENT Why, fool?

FOOL We'll set thee to school to an ant, to teach thee there's no labouring i' the winter. All that follow their noses are led by their eyes, but blind men; and there's not a nose among twenty but can smell him that's stinking. Let go thy hold, when a great wheel runs down a hill, lest it break thy neck with following it; but the great one that goes up the hill, let him draw thee after. When a wise man gives thee better counsel, give me mine again: I would have none but knaves follow it, since a fool gives it.

That sir, which serves and seeks for gain,
And follows for form,
Will pack when it begins to rain,
And leave thee in the storm.
But I will tarry; the fool will stay,
And let the wise man fly:
The knave turns fool that runs away;
The fool no knave, perdy.

KENT Where learn'd you this, fool?

FOOL Not i' the stocks, fool.

Re-enter Lear, with Gloster.

LEAR Deny to speak with me? They are sick? they are weary?
They have travell'd all the night? Mere fetches,
The images of revolt and flying off!
Fetch me a better answer.

GLOSTER My dear lord,
You know the fiery quality of the duke;
How unremovable and fix'd he is
In his own course.

LEAR Vengeance! plague! death! confusion!
Fiery? what quality? Why, Gloster, Gloster,
I'd speak with the Duke of Cornwall and his wife.

GLOSTER Well, my good lord, I have inform'd them so.

LEAR Inform'd them! Dost thou understand me, man?

GLOSTER Ay, my good lord.

LEAR The king would speak with Cornwall; the dear father
Would with his daughter speak, commands her service:
Are they inform'd of this? My breath and blood! –
Fiery? the fiery duke? – Tell the hot duke, that –
No, but not yet: – may be, he is not well:
Infirmity doth still neglect all office,
Whereto our health is bound; we are not ourselves,
When nature, being oppress'd, commands the mind
To suffer with the body. I'll forbear;
And am fall'n out with my more headier will,
To take the indispos'd and sickly fit
For the sound man. – Death on my state! wherefore
[Looking on Kent.

Should he sit here? This act persuades me,
That this remotion of the duke and her
Is practice only. Give me my servant forth.
Go, tell the duke and 's wife, I 'd speak with them,
Now, presently: bid them come forth and hear me,
Or at their chamber-door I 'll beat the drum,
Till it cry – 'Sleep to death.'

GLOSTER I would have all well betwixt you. *[Exit.*

LEAR O me! my heart, my rising heart! – but, down.

FOOL Cry to it, nuncle, as the cockney did to the eels, when she put them i' the paste alive; she knapp'd 'em o' the coxcombs with a stick, and cried, 'Down wantons, down!' 'Twas her brother that, in pure kindness to his horse, buttered his hay.

Enter Cornwall, Regan, Gloster, and Servants.

LEAR Good morrow to you both.

CORNWALL Hail to your grace!

[Kent is set at liberty.

REGAN I am glad to see your highness.

LEAR Regan, I think you are; I know what reason
I have to think so: if thou shouldst not be glad,
I would divorce me from thy mother's tomb,
Sepulchring an adult'ress. – *[To Kent.]* O! are you free?
Some other time for that. – Beloved Regan,
Thy sister's naught: O Regan! she hath tied
Sharp-tooth'd unkindness, like a vulture, here. –

[Points to his heart.

I can scarce speak to thee: thou'lt not believe,
With how deprav'd a quality – O Regan!

REGAN I pray you, sir, take patience. I have hope,
You less know how to value her desert,
Than she to scant her duty.

LEAR Say, how is that?
REGAN I cannot think my sister in the least
Would fail her obligation: if, sir, perchance,
She have restrain'd the riots of your followers,
'Tis on such ground, and to such wholesome end,
As clears her from all blame.
LEAR My curses on her!
REGAN O, sir! you are old;
Nature in you stands on the very verge
Of her confine: you should be rul'd and led
By some discretion, that discerns your state
Better than you yourself. Therefore, I pray you,
That to our sister you do make return:
Say, you have wrong'd her, sir.
LEAR Ask her forgiveness?
Do you but mark how this becomes the house:
'Dear daughter, I confess that I am old;
Age is unnecessary: on my knees I beg, *[Kneeling.*
That you'll vouchsafe me raiment, bed, and food.'
REGAN Good sir, no more: these are unsightly tricks.
Return you to my sister.
LEAR *[Rising.]* Never, Regan.
She hath abated me of half my train;
Look'd black upon me; struck me with her tongue,
Most serpent-like, upon the very heart. –
All the stor'd vengeances of heaven fall
On her ungrateful top! Strike her young bones,
You taking airs, with lameness!
CORNWALL Fie, sir, fie!
LEAR You nimble lightnings, dart your blinding flames
Into her scornful eyes! Infect her beauty,

You fen-suck'd fogs, drawn by the powerful sun,
To fall and blast her pride!

REGAN O the blest gods! so will you wish on me,
When the rash mood is on.

LEAR No, Regan; thou shalt never have my curse:
Thy tender-hefted nature shall not give
Thee o'er to harshness: her eyes are fierce; but thine
Do comfort, and not burn. 'Tis not in thee
To grudge my pleasures, to cut off my train,
To bandy hasty words, to scant my sizes,
And, in conclusion, to oppose the bolt
Against my coming in: thou better know'st
The offices of nature, bond of childhood,
Effects of courtesy, dues of gratitude;
Thy half o' the kingdom hast thou not forgot,
Wherein I thee endow'd.

REGAN Good sir, to the purpose.

LEAR Who put my man i' the stocks? *[Tucket within.*

CORNWALL What trumpet's that?

REGAN I know't, my sister's: this approves her letter,
That she would soon be here. –

Enter Oswald.

Is your lady come?

LEAR This is a slave, whose easy-borrow'd pride
Dwells in the fickle grace of her he follows. –
Out, varlet, from my sight!

CORNWALL What means your grace?

LEAR Who stock'd my servant? Regan, I have good hope
Thou didst not know on't. – Who comes here? O heavens,

Enter Goneril.

If you do love old men, if your sweet sway
Allow obedience, if yourselves are old,
Make it your cause; send down, and take my part! –
[To Goneril.] Art not asham'd to look up this beard? –
O Regan! wilt thou take her by the hand?

GONERIL Why not by the hand, sir? How have I offended?
All's not offence that indiscretion finds,
And dotage terms so.

LEAR O sides! you are too tough:
Will you yet hold? – How came my man i' the stocks?

CORNWALL I set him there, sir; but his own disorders
Deserv'd much less advancement.

LEAR You! did you?

REGAN I pray you, father, being weak, seem so.
If, till the expiration of your month,
You will return and sojourn with my sister,
Dismissing half your train, come then to me:
I am now from home, and out of that provision
Which shall be needful for your entertainment.

LEAR Return to her? and fifty men dismiss'd?
No, rather I abjure all roofs, and choose
To wage against the enmity o' the air;
To be a comrade with the wolf and owl, –
Necessity's sharp pinch! – Return with her?
Why, the hot-blooded France, that dowerless took
Our youngest-born, I could as well be brought
To knee his throne, and, squire-like, pension beg
To keep base life afoot. – Return with her?
Persuade me rather to be slave and sumpter
To this detested groom. *[Pointing at Oswald.*

GONERIL At your choice, sir.

LEAR I pr'ythee, daughter, do not make me mad:
I will not trouble thee, my child; farewell.
We'll no more meet, no more see one another;
But yet thou art my flesh, my blood, my daughter;
Or, rather, a disease that's in my flesh,
Which I must needs call mine: thou art a bile,
A plague-sore, an embossed carbuncle,
In my corrupted blood. But I'll not chide thee;
Let shame come when it will, I do not call it;
I do not bid the thunder-bearer shoot,
Nor tell tales of thee to high-judging Jove.
Mend, when thou canst; be better, at thy leisure:
I can be patient; I can stay with Regan,
I, and my hundred knights.

REGAN Not altogether so:
I look'd not for you yet, nor am provided
For your fit welcome. Give ear, sir, to my sister;
For those that mingle reason with your passion,
Must be content to think you old, and so –
But she knows what she does.

LEAR Is this well spoken?

REGAN I dare avouch it, sir. What! fifty followers?
Is it not well? What should you need of more?
Yea, or so many, sith that both charge and danger
Speak 'gainst so great a number? How, in one house,
Should many people, under two commands,
Hold amity? 'T is hard; almost impossible.

GONERIL Why might not you, my lord, receive attendance
From those that she calls servants, or from mine?

REGAN Why not, my lord? If then they chanc'd to slack you,

We could control them. If you will come to me
(For now I spy a danger), I entreat you
To bring but five-and-twenty: to no more
Will I give place, or notice.

LEAR I gave you all –

REGAN And in good time you gave it.

LEAR Made you my guardians, my depositaries;
But kept a reservation to be follow'd
With such a number. What! must I come to you
With five-and-twenty? Regan, said you so?

REGAN And speak't again, my lord; no more with me.

LEAR Those wicked creatures yet do look well-favour'd!
When others are more wicked, not being the worst
Stands in some rank of praise. – *[To Goneril.]* I'll go with thee:
Thy fifty yet doth double five-and-twenty,
And thou art twice her love.

GONERIL Hear me, my lord.
What need you five-and-twenty, ten, or five,
To follow in a house, where twice so many
Have a command to tend you?

REGAN What need one?

LEAR O! reason not the need; our basest beggars
Are in the poorest thing superfluous:
Allow not nature more than nature needs,
Man's life is cheap as beast's. Thou art a lady;
If only to go warm were gorgeous,
Why, nature needs not what thou gorgeous wear'st,
Which scarcely keeps thee warm. But, for true need –
You heavens, give me that patience, patience I need!
You see me here, you gods, a poor old man,
As full of grief as age; wretched in both:

If it be you that stir these daughters' hearts
Against their father, fool me not so much
To bear it tamely; touch me with noble anger.
O! let not women's weapons, water-drops,
Stain my man's cheeks. – No, you unnatural hags,
I will have such revenges on you both,
That all the world shall – I will do such things, –
What they are, yet I know not; but they shall be
The terrors of the earth. You think, I'll weep;
No, I'll not weep: –
I have full cause of weeping; but this heart
Shall break into a hundred thousand flaws,
Or ere I'll weep. – O fool, I shall go mad!

[Exeunt Lear, Gloster, Kent, and Fool.

CORNWALL Let us withdraw, 'twill be a storm.

[Storm heard at a distance.

REGAN This house is little: the old man and his people
Cannot be well bestow'd.

GONERIL 'Tis his own blame; hath put himself from rest,
And must needs taste his folly.

REGAN For his particular, I'll receive him gladly,
But not one follower.

GONERIL So am I purpos'd.
Where is my Lord of Gloster?

Re-enter Gloster.

CORNWALL Follow'd the old man forth. – He is return'd.

GLOSTER The king is in high rage.

CORNWALL Whither is he going?

GLOSTER He calls to horse; but will I know not whither.

CORNWALL 'Tis best to give him way; he leads himself.

GONERIL My lord, entreat him by no means to stay.

GLOSTER Alack! the night comes on, and the high winds
Do sorely ruffle; for many miles about
There's scarce a bush.

REGAN O, sir, to wilful men,
The injuries that they themselves procure
Must be their schoolmasters. Shut up your doors:
He is attended with a desperate train;
And what they may incense him to, being apt
To have his ear abus'd, wisdom bids fear.

CORNWALL Shut up your doors, my lord; 'tis a wild night:
My Regan counsels well. Come out o' the storm. *[Exeunt.*

ACT THREE

SCENE I – A HEATH

A storm, with thunder and lightning. Enter Kent and a Gentleman, meeting.

KENT Who's there, beside foul weather?

GENTLEMAN One minded like the weather, most unquietly.

KENT I know you. Where's the king?

GENTLEMAN Contending with the fretful elements;
Bids the wind blow the earth into the sea,
Or swell the curled waters 'bove the main,
That things might change or cease; tears his white hair,
Which the impetuous blasts, with eyeless rage,
Catch in their fury, and make nothing of:
Strives in his little world of man to out-scorn
The to-and-fro conflicting wind and rain.
This night, wherein the cub-drawn bear would couch,
The lion and the belly-pinched wolf
Keep their fur dry, unbonneted he runs,
And bids what will take all.

KENT But who is with him?

GENTLEMAN None but the fool, who labours to out-jest
His heart-struck injuries.

KENT Sir, I do know you;
And dare, upon the warrant of my note,
Commend a dear thing to you. There is division,

Although as yet the face of it be cover'd
With mutual cunning, 'twixt Albany and Cornwall;
Who have (as who have not, that their great stars
Thron'd and set high?) servants; who seem no less,
Which are to France the spies and speculations
Intelligent of our state; what hath been seen,
Either in snuffs and packings of the dukes,
Or the hard rein which both of them have borne
Against the old kind king; or something deeper,
Whereof, perchance, these are but furnishings;
(But, true it is, from France there comes a power
Into this scatter'd kingdom; who already,
Wise in our negligence, have secret feet
In some of our best ports, and are at point
To show their open banner. – Now to you:
If on my credit you dare build so far
To make your speed to Dover, you shall find
Some that will thank you, making just report
Of how unnatural and bemadding sorrow
The king hath cause to plain.
I am a gentleman of blood and breeding,
And from some knowledge and assurance offer
This office to you.)

GENTLEMAN I will talk further with you.

KENT No, do not.
For confirmation that I am much more
Than my out-wall, open this purse, and take
What it contains. If you shall see Cordelia
(As fear not but you shall), show her this ring,
And she will tell you who your fellow is
That yet you do not know. Fie on this storm!
I will go seek the king.

GENTLEMAN Give me your hand. Have you no more to say?

KENT Few words, but, to effect, more than all yet:
That, when we have found the king, (in which your pain
That way, I'll this,) he that first lights on him.
Holla the other. *[Exeunt severally.*

SCENE II – ANOTHER PART OF THE HEATH. STORM CONTINUES.

Enter Lear and Fool.

LEAR Blow, winds, and crack your cheeks! rage! blow!
You cataracts and hurricanoes, spout
Till you have drench'd our steeples, drown'd the cocks!
You sulphurous and thought-executing fires,
Vaunt-couriers of oak-cleaving thunderbolts,
Singe my white head! And thou, all-shaking thunder,
Strike flat the thick rotundity o' the world!
Crack nature's moulds, all germens spill at once,
That make ingrateful man!

FOOL O nuncle, court holy-water in a dry house is better than this rain-water out o' door. Good nuncle, in; ask thy daughters' blessing: here's a night pities neither wise men nor fools.

LEAR Rumble thy bellyful! spit, fire! spout, rain!
Nor rain, wind, thunder, fire, are my daughters:
I tax not you, you elements, with unkindness;
I never gave you kingdom, call'd you children,
You owe me no subscription: then, let fall
Your horrible pleasure; here I stand, your slave,
A poor, infirm, weak, and despis'd old man.
But yet I call you servile ministers,

That will with two pernicious daughters join
Your high-engender'd battles 'gainst a head
So old and white as this. O! O! 'tis foul!

FOOL He that has a house to put 's head in, has a good head-piece.

The cod-piece that will house,
Before the head has any,
The head and he shall louse:–
So beggars marry many.
The man that makes his toe
What he his heart should make,
Shall of a corn cry woe,
And turn his sleep to wake.

For there was never yet fair woman but she made mouths in a glass.

LEAR No, I will be the pattern of all patience;
I will say nothing.

Enter Kent.

KENT Who's there?

FOOL Marry, here's grace, and a cod-piece; that's a wise man, and a fool.

KENT Alas, sir! are you here? things that love night,
Love not such nights as these: the wrathful skies
Gallow the very wanderers of the dark,
And make them keep their caves. Since I was man,
Such sheets of fire, such bursts of horrid thunder,
Such groans of roaring wind and rain, I never
Remember to have heard: man's nature cannot carry
The affliction, nor the fear.

LEAR Let the great gods,

That keep this dreadful pother o'er our heads,
Find out their enemies now. Tremble, thou wretch,
That hast within the undivulged crimes,
Unwhipp'd of justice: hide thee, thou bloody hand;
Thou perjur'd, and thou similar of virtue
That art incestuous: caitiff, to pieces shake,
That under covert and convenient seeming
Hast practis'd on man's life: close pent-up guilts,
Rive your concealing continents, and cry
These dreadful summoners grace. I am a man
More sinn'd against than sinning.

KENT Alack, bare-headed!
Gracious my lord, hard by here is a hovel;
Some friendship will it lend you 'gainst the tempest:
Repose you there, while I to this hard house
(More harder than the stones whereof 'tis rais'd,
Which even but now, demanding after you,
Denied me to come in) return, and force
Their scanted courtesy.

LEAR My wits begin to turn.–
Come on, my boy. How dost, my boy? Art cold?
I am cold myself. – Where is this straw, my fellow?
The art of our necessities is strange,
That can make vile things precious. Come, your hovel.
Poor fool and knave, I have one part in my heart
That's sorry yet for thee.

FOOL *Sings] He that has a little tiny wit,–*
With heigh, ho, the wind and the rain,
Must make content with his fortunes fit,
Though the rain it raineth every day.

LEAR True, my good boy. – Come, bring us to this hovel.
[Exeunt Lear and Kent.

FOOL This is a brave night to cool a courtesan.–
I'll speak a prophecy ere I go:
When priests are more in word than matter;
When brewers mar their malt with water;
When nobles are their tailor's tutors;
No heretics burn'd, but wenches' suitors;
When every case in law is right;
No squire in debt, nor no poor knight;
When slanders do not live in tongues;
Nor cutpurses come not to throngs;
When usurers tell their gold i' the field;
And bawds and whores do churches build;
Then shall the realm of Albion
Come to great confusion:
Then comes the time, who lives to see 't,
That going shall be us'd with feet.
This prophecy Merlin shall make; for I live before his time.
[Exit.

SCENE III – A ROOM IN GLOSTER'S CASTLE.

Enter Gloster and Edmund.

GLOSTER Alack, alack! Edmund, I like not this unnatural dealing. When I desired their leave that I might pity him, they took from me the use of mine own house, charged me, on pain of perpetual displeasure, neither to speak of him, entreat for him, nor any way sustain him.

EDMUND Most savage and unnatural!

GLOSTER Go to: say you nothing. There is division between the dukes, and a worse matter than that. I have received a letter this night; – 'tis dangerous to be spoken; – I have locked the letter in my closet. These injuries the king now bears will be revenged home; there is part of a power already footed; we must incline to the king. I will look him, and privily relieve him: go you, and maintain talk with the duke, that my charity be not of him perceived. If he ask for me, I am ill, and gone to bed. If I die for it, as no less is threatened me, the king, my old master, must be relieved. There is some strange thing toward, Edmund; pray you, be careful. *[Exit.*

EDMUND This courtesy, forbid thee, shall the duke
Instantly know; and of that letter too.
This seems a fair deserving, and must draw me
That which my father loses: no less than all:
The younger rises, when the old doth fall. *[Exit.*

SCENE IV – A PART OF THE HEATH, WITH A HOVEL.

Enter Lear, Kent and Fool.

KENT Here is the place, my lord; good my lord, enter:
The tyranny of the open night's too rough
For nature to endure. *[Storm still.*

LEAR Let me alone.

KENT Good my lord, enter here.

LEAR Wilt break my heart?

KENT I'd rather break mine own. Good my lord, enter.

LEAR Thou think'st 'tis much, that this contentious storm
Invades us to the skin: so 'tis to thee;
But where the greater malady is fix'd,
The lesser is scarce felt. Thou'dst shun a bear;
But if thy flight lay toward the roaring sea,

Thou'dst meet the bear i' the mouth. When the mind's free,
The body's delicate: the tempest in my mind
Doth from my senses take all feeling else,
Save what beats there: filial ingratitude.
Is it not as this mouth should tear this hand,
For lifting food to 't? – But I will punish home:–
No, I will weep no more. – In such a night
To shut me out! – Pour on; I will endure.–
In such a night as this! O Regan, Goneril!–
Your old kind father, whose frank heart gave all,–
O! that way madness lies; let me shun that;
No more of that.

KENT Good my lord, enter here.

LEAR Pr'ythee, go in thyself; seek thine own ease:
This tempest will not give me leave to ponder
On things would hurt me more. – But I'll go in.
[To the Fool] In, boy; go first. You houseless poverty,–
Nay, get thee in. I'll pray, and then I'll sleep.– *[Fool goes in.*
Poor naked wretches, wheresoe'er you are,
That bide the pelting of this pitiless storm,
How shall your houseless heads, and unfed sides,
Your loop'd and window'd raggedness, defend you
From seasons such as these? O! I have ta'en
Too little care of this. Take physic, pomp;
Expose thyself to feel what wretches feel,
That thou may'st shake the superflux to them,
And show the heavens more just.

EDGAR *[Within.]* Fathom and half, fathom and half!
Poor Tom! *[The Fool runs out from the hovel.*

FOOL Come not in here, nuncle; here's a spirit. Help me! help me!

KENT Give me thy hand. – Who's there?

FOOL A spirit, a spirit: he says his name's poor Tom.

KENT What art thou that dost grumble there i' the straw?
Come forth.

Enter Edgar, disguised as a madman.

EDGAR Away! the foul fiend follows me! –
Through the sharp hawthorn blow the winds. –
Humph! go to thy bed, and warm thee.

LEAR Didst thou give all to thy daughters?
And art thou come to this?

EDGAR Who gives anything to poor Tom? whom the foul fiend hath led through fire and through flame, through ford and whirlpool, over bog and quagmire; that hath laid knives under his pillow, and halters in his pew; set ratsbane by his porridge; made him proud of heart, to ride on a bay trotting-horse over four-inched bridges, to course his own shadow for a traitor. – Bless thy five wits! Tom's a-cold. – O! do de, do de, do de. – Bless thee from whirlwinds, star-blasting, and taking! Do poor Tom some charity, whom the foul fiend vexes. – There could I have him now, – and there, – and there, – and there again, and there. *[Storm continues.*

LEAR What! have his daughters brought him to this pass? –
Couldst thou save nothing? Didst thou give them all?

FOOL Nay, he reserved a blanket, else we had been all shamed.

LEAR Now, all the plagues that in the pendulous air
Hang fated o'er men's faults, light on thy daughters!

KENT He hath no daughters, sir.

LEAR Death, traitor! nothing could have subdued nature
To such a lowness, but his unkind daughters.–
Is it the fashion, that discarded fathers

Should have thus little mercy on their flesh?
Judicious punishment! 'twas this flesh begot
Those pelican daughters.

EDGAR Pillicock sat on Pillicock hill:–
Halloo, halloo, loo, loo!

FOOL This cold night will turn us all to fools and madmen.

EDGAR Take heed o' the foul fiend. Obey thy parents; keep thy word justly; swear not; commit not with man's sworn spouse; set not thy sweet heart on proud array. Tom's a-cold.

LEAR What hast thou been?

EDGAR A serving-man, proud in heart and mind; that curled my hair, wore gloves in my cap, served the lust of my mistress's heart, and did the act of darkness with her; swore as many oaths as I spake words, and broke them in the sweet face of heaven: one, that slept in the contriving of lust, and waked to do it. Wine loved I deeply; dice dearly; and in woman, out-paramoured the Turk: false of heart, light of ear, bloody of hand; hog in sloth, fox in stealth, wolf in greediness, dog in madness, lion in prey. Let not the creaking of shoes, nor the rustling of silks, betray thy poor heart to woman: keep thy foot out of brothels, thy hand out of plackets, thy pen from lenders' books, and defy the foul fiend. – Still through the hawthorn blows the cold wind, says suum, mun, ha no nonny. Dolphin my boy, my boy; sessa! let him trot by. *[Storm still continues.*

LEAR Why, thou wert better in thy grave, than to answer with thy uncovered body this extremity of the skies. – Is man no more than this? Consider him well. Thou owest the worm no silk, the beast no hide, the sheep no wool, the cat no perfume. – Ha! here's three on 's are sophisticated: thou art the thing itself: unaccommodated man is no more but such a poor, bare, forked animal as thou art. – Off, off, you lendings. – Come; unbutton here. – *[Tearing off his clothes.*

FOOL Pry'thee, nuncle, be contented; 'tis a naughty night to swim in. – Now, a little fire in a wild field were like an old lecher's heart; a small spark, all the rest on 's body cold. – Look! here comes a walking fire.

EDGAR This is the foul fiend Flibbertigibbet: he begins at curfew, and walks till the first cock; he gives the web and the pin, squints the eye, and makes the hare-lip; mildews the white wheat, and hurts the poor creature of earth.

Swithold footed thrice the wold;
He met the night-mare, and her nine-fold
Bid her alight,
And her troth plight,
And, aroint thee, witch, aroint thee!

KENT How fares your grace?

Enter Gloster, with a torch.

LEAR What's he?

KENT Who's there? What is't you seek?

GLOSTER What are you there? Your names?

EDGAR Poor Tom; that eats the swimming frog, the toad, the tadpole, the wall-newt, and the water; that in the fury of his heart, when the foul fiend rages, eats cow-dung for sallets; swallows the old rat, and the ditch-dog; drinks the green mantle of the standing pool; who is whipped from tithing to tithing, and stocked, punished, and imprisoned; who hath had three suits to his back, six shirts to his body, horse to ride, and weapon to wear,–

But mice, and rats, and such small deer,
Have been Tom's food for seven long year.

Beware my follower. – Peace, Smulkin! peace, thou fiend!

GLOSTER What! hath your grace no better company?

EDGAR The prince of darkness is a gentleman;
Modo he's call'd, and Mahu.
GLOSTER Our flesh and blood, my lord, is grown so vile,
That it doth hate what gets it.
EDGAR Poor Tom's a-cold.
GLOSTER Go in with me. My duty cannot suffer
To obey in all your daughters' hard commands:
Though their injunction be to bar my doors,
And let this tyrannous night take hold upon you,
Yet have I ventur'd to come seek you out,
And bring you where both fire and food is ready.
LEAR First let me talk with this philosopher. –
What is the cause of thunder?
KENT Good my lord, take his offer: go into the house.
LEAR I'll talk a word with this same learned Theban.
What is your study?
EDGAR How to prevent the fiend, and to kill vermin.
LEAR Let me ask you one word in private.
KENT Importune him once more to go, my lord;
His wits begin to unsettle.
GLOSTER Canst thou blame him?
His daughters seek his death. – Ah, that good Kent! –
He said it would be thus, poor banish'd man! –
Thou say'st, the king grows mad: I'll tell thee, friend,
I am almost mad myself. I had a son,
Now outlaw'd from my blood; he sought my life,
But lately, very late: I lov'd him, friend. –
No father his son dearer: true to tell thee,
The grief hath craz'd my wits. What a night's this!
[Storm continues.
I do beseech your grace, –

LEAR O! cry you mercy, sir. –
Noble philosopher, your company.

EDGAR Tom's a-cold.

GLOSTER In, fellow, there, into the hovel: keep thee warm.

LEAR Come, let's in all.

KENT This way, my lord.

LEAR With him:
I will keep still with my philosopher.

KENT Good my lord, soothe him; let him take the fellow.

GLOSTER Take him you on.

KENT Sirrah, come on; go along with us.

LEAR Come, good Athenian.

GLOSTER No words, no words: hush.

EDGAR *Child Rowland to the dark tower came,*
His word was still, – Fie, foh, and fum,
I smell the blood of a British man. [*Exeunt.*

SCENE V – A ROOM IN GLOSTER'S CASTLE.

Enter Cornwall and Edmund.

CORNWALL I will have my revenge, ere I depart his house.

EDMUND How, my lord, I may be censured, that nature thus gives way to loyalty, something fears me to think of.

CORNWALL I now perceive, it was not altogether your brother's evil disposition made him seek his death; but a provoking merit, set a-work by a reprovable badness in himself.

EDMUND How malicious is my fortune, that I must repent to be just! This is the letter which he spoke of, which approves him an intelligent part to the advantages of France. O heavens! that this treason were not, or not I the detector!

CORNWALL Go with me to the duchess.

EDMUND If the matter of this paper be certain, you have mighty business in hand.

CORNWALL True, or false, it hath made thee Earl of Gloster. Seek out where thy father is, that he may be ready for our apprehension.

EDMUND *[Aside.]* If I find him comforting the king, it will stuff his suspicion more fully. – I will persever in my course of loyalty, though the conflict be sore between that and my blood.

CORNWALL I will lay trust upon thee, and thou shalt find a dearer father in my love. *[Exeunt.*

SCENE VI – A CHAMBER IN A FARM-HOUSE, ADJOINING THE CASTLE.

Enter Gloster, Lear, Kent, Fool, and Edgar.

GLOSTER Here is better than the open air; take it thankfully. I will piece out the comfort with what addition I can: I will not be long from you.

KENT All the power of his wits have given way to his impatience. – The gods reward your kindness! *[Exit Gloster*

EDGAR Frateretto calls me, and tells me Nero is an angler in the lake of darkness. Pray, innocent, and beware the foul fiend.

FOOL Pr'ythee, nuncle, tell me whether a madman be a gentleman, or a yeoman?

LEAR A king, a king!

FOOL No: he's a yeoman, that has a gentleman to his son; for he's a mad yeoman, that sees his on a gentleman before him.

LEAR To have a thousand with red-burning spits
Come hissing in upon them:–

EDGAR The foul fiend bites my back.

FOOL He's mad, that trusts in the tameness of a wolf, a horse's health, a boy's love, or a whore's oath.

LEAR It shall be done; I will arraign them straight. –
[To Edgar.] Come, sit thou here, most learned justicer: –
[To the Fool.] Thou, sapient sir, sit here. – Now, you she-foxes! –

EDGAR Look, where he stands and glares! –
Wantest thou eyes at trial, madam?
Come o'er the bourn, Bessy, to me: –

FOOL *Her boat hath a leak,*
And she must not speak
Why she dares not come over to thee.

EDGAR The foul fiend haunts poor Tom in the voice of a nightingale. Hopdance cries in Tom's belly for two white herring. Croak not, black angel; I have no food for thee.

KENT How do you, sir? Stand you not so amaz'd:
Will you lie down and rest upon the cushions?

LEAR I'll see their trial first. – Bring in the evidence. –
[To Edgar.] Thou robed man of justice, take thy place; –
[To the Fool.] And thou, his yoke-fellow of equity,
Bench by his side: –
[To Kent.] You are of the commission, sit you too.

EDGAR Let us deal justly.
Sleepest, or wakest thou, jolly shepherd?
Thy sheep be in the corn;
And for one blast of thy minikin mouth,
Thy sheep shall take no harm.
Pur! the cat is grey.

LEAR Arraign her first; 'tis Goneril. I here take my oath before this honourable assembly, she kicked the poor king her father.

FOOL Come hither, mistress. Is your name Goneril?

LEAR She cannot deny it.

FOOL Cry you mercy, I took you for a joint-stool.

LEAR And here's another, whose warp'd looks proclaim
What store her heart is made of. – Stop her there!
Arms, arms, sword, fire! – corruption in the place!
False justicer, why hast thou let her 'scape?

EDGAR Bless thy five wits!

KENT O pity! – Sir, where is the patience now,
That you so oft have boasted to retain?

EDGAR *[Aside.]* My tears begin to take his part so much,
They'll mar my counterfeiting.

LEAR The little dogs and all,
Tray, Blanch, and Sweet-heart, see, they bark at me.

EDGAR Tom will throw his head at them. – Avaunt, you curs!

Be thy mouth or black or white,
Tooth that poisons if it bite;
Mastiff, greyhound, mongrel, grim,
Hound or spaniel, brach or lym;
Or bobtail tike, or trundle-tail:
Tom will make them weep and wail;
For, with throwing thus my head,
Dogs leap the hatch, and all are fled.

Do, de, de, de. Sessa! Come, march to wakes and fairs, and market-towns. – Poor Tom, thy horn is dry.

LEAR Then let them anatomise Regan, see what breeds about her heart. Is there any cause in nature, that makes these hard hearts? – *[To Edgar.]* You, sir, I entertain you for one of my hundred; only, I do not like the fashion of your garments: you will say, they are Persian; but let them be changed.

KENT Now, good my lord, lie here, and rest awhile.

LEAR Make no noise, make no noise; draw the curtains: so, so, so. We'll go to supper i' the morning: so, so, so.

FOOL And I'll go to bed at noon.

Re-enter Gloster.

GLOSTER Come hither, friend: where is the king my master?

KENT Here, sir; but trouble him not, his wits are gone.

GLOSTER Good friend, I pr'ythee, take him in thy arms;
I have o'erheard a plot of death upon him.
There is a litter ready; lay him in 't,
And drive toward Dover, friend, where thou shalt meet
Both welcome and protection. Take up thy master:
If thou shouldst dally half an hour, his life,
With thine, and all that offer to defend him,
Stand in assured loss. Take up, take up;
And follow me, that will to some provision
Give thee quick conduct.

KENT Oppressed nature sleeps: –
This rest might yet have balm'd thy broken sinews,
Which, if convenience will not allow,
Stand in hard cure. – *[To the Fool.]* Come, help to bear thy master;
Thou must not stay behind.

GLOSTER Come, come away.

[Exeunt Kent, Gloster, and the Fool, bearing off the King.

EDGAR When we our betters see bearing our woes,
We scarcely think our miseries our foes.
Who alone suffers, suffers most i' the mind,
Leaving free things, and happy shows, behind;
But then the mind much sufferance doth o'erskip,
When grief hath mates, and bearing-fellowship.

How light and portable my pain seems now,
When that which makes me bend, makes the king bow:
He childed, as I father'd! – Tom, away!
Mark the high noises, and thyself bewray,
When false opinion, whose wrong thought defiles thee,
In thy just proof, repeals and reconciles thee.
What will hap more to-night, safe 'scape the king!
Lurk, lurk. *[Exit.*

SCENE VII – A ROOM IN GLOSTER'S CASTLE.

Enter Cornwall, Regan, Goneril, Edmund, and Servants.

CORNWALL Post speedily to my lord your husband; show him this letter: – the army of France is landed. – Seek out the traitor Gloster. *[Exeunt some of the Servants.*

REGAN Hang him instantly.

GONERIL Pluck out his eyes.

CORNWALL Leave him to my displeasure. – Edmund, keep you our sister company: the revenges we are bound to take upon your traitorous father are not fit for your beholding. Advise the duke, where you are going, to a most festinate preparation: we are bound to the like. Our posts shall be swift and intelligent betwixt us. Farewell, dear sister: – farewell, my Lord of Gloster.

Enter Oswald.

How now! Where's the king?

OSWALD My Lord of Gloster hath convey'd him hence:
Some five or six and thirty of his knights,
Hot questrists after him, met him at gate;

Who, with some other of the lord's dependants,
Are gone with him towards Dover, where they boast
To have well-armed friends.

CORNWALL Get horses for your mistress.

GONERIL Farewell, sweet lord, and sister.

[Exeunt Goneril, Edmund, and Oswald.

CORNWALL Edmund, farewell. – Go, seek the traitor Gloster,
Pinion him like a thief, bring him before us.

[Exeunt other Servants.

Though well we may not pass upon his life
Without the form of justice, yet our power
Shall do a courtesy to our wrath, which men
May blame, but not control. Who's there? The traitor?

Re-enter Servants, with Gloster.

REGAN Ingrateful fox! 'tis he.

CORNWALL Bind fast his corky arms.

GLOSTER What mean your graces? – Good my friends, consider
You are my guests: do me no foul play, friends.

CORNWALL Bind him, I say. *[Servants bind him.*

REGAN Hard, hard. – O filthy traitor!

GLOSTER Unmerciful lady as you are, I'm none.

CORNWALL To this chair bind him. – Villain, thou shalt find –

[Regan plucks his beard.

GLOSTER By the kind gods, 'tis most ignobly done
To pluck me by the beard.

REGAN So white, and such a traitor!

GLOSTER Naughty lady,
These hairs, which thou dost ravish from my chin,
Will quicken, and accuse thee. I am your host:
With robbers' hands my hospitable favours
You should not ruffle thus. What will you do?

CORNWALL Come, sir, what letters had you late from France?
REGAN Be simple-answer'd, for we know the truth.
CORNWALL And what confederacy have you with the traitors
Late footed in the kingdom?
REGAN To whose hands have you sent the lunatic king? Speak.
GLOSTER I have a letter guessingly set down,
Which came from one that's of a neutral heart,
And not from one oppos'd.
CORNWALL Cunning.
REGAN And false.
CORNWALL Where hast thou sent the king?
GLOSTER To Dover.
REGAN Wherefore to Dover? Wast thou not charg'd at peril –
CORNWALL Wherefore to Dover? Let him answer that.
GLOSTER I am tied to the stake, and I must stand the course.
REGAN Wherefore to Dover?
GLOSTER Because I would not see thy cruel nails
Pluck out his poor old eyes; nor thy fierce sister
In his anointed flesh stick boarish fangs.
The sea, with such a storm as his bare head
In hell-black night endur'd, would have buoy'd up,
And quench'd the stelled fires;
Yet, poor old heart, he holp the heavens to rain.
If wolves had at thy gate howl'd that stern time,
Thou shouldst have said, 'Good porter, turn the key,'
All cruels else subscrib'd: – but I shall see
The winged vengeance overtake such children.
CORNWALL See 't shalt thou never. – Fellows, hold the chair. –
Upon these eyes of thine I'll set my foot.
GLOSTER He, that will think to live till he be old,
Give me some help! – O cruel! – O ye gods!

REGAN One side will mock another; the other too.
CORNWALL If you see vengeance, –
1 SERVANT Hold your hand, my lord.
I have serv'd you ever since I was a child;
But better service have I never done you,
Than now to bid you hold.
REGAN How now, you dog!
1 SERVANT If you did wear a beard upon your chin,
I'd shake it on this quarrel. What do you mean?
CORNWALL My villain! *[Draws and runs at him.*
1 SERVANT Nay then, come on, and take the chance of anger.
[Draws. Cornwall is wounded.
REGAN Give me thy sword. A peasant stand up thus!
1 SERVANT O, I am slain! – My lord, you have one eye left
To see some mischief on him. – O! *[Dies.*
CORNWALL Lest it see more, prevent it. – Out, vile jelly!
Where is thy lustre now?
GLOSTER All dark and comfortless. – Where's my son Edmund?
Edmund, enkindle all the sparks of nature,
To quit this horrid act.
REGAN Out, treacherous villain!
Thou call'st on him that hates thee: it was he
That made the overture of thy treasons to us,
Who is too good to pity thee.
GLOSTER O my follies!
Then Edgar was abus'd. –
Kind gods, forgive me that, and prosper him!
REGAN Go, thrust him out at gates, and let him smell
His way to Dover. – How is 't, my lord? How look you?
CORNWALL I have receiv'd a hurt. – Follow me, lady.
Turn out that eyeless villain; – throw this slave

Upon the dunghill. – Regan, I bleed apace:
Untimely comes this hurt. Give me your arm.

[Exit Cornwall, led by Regan; – Servants unbind Gloster, and lead him out.

2 SERVANT I'll never care what wickedness I do,
If this man come to good.

3 SERVANT If she live long,
And in the end meet the old course of death,
Women will all turn monsters.

2 SERVANT Let's follow the old earl, and get the Bedlam
To lead him where he would: his roguish madness
Allows itself to anything.

3 SERVANT Go thou; I'll fetch some flax, and whites of eggs,
To apply to his bleeding face. Now, heaven help him!

[Exeunt severally.

ACT FOUR

SCENE I – THE HEATH.

Enter Edgar.

EDGAR Yet better thus, and known to be contemn'd,
Than still contemn'd and flatter'd. To be worst,
The lowest and most dejected thing of fortune,
Stands still in esperance, lives not in fear:
The lamentable change is from the best;
The worst returns to laughter. Welcome, then,
Thou unsubstantial air, that I embrace:
The wretch, that thou hast blown unto the worst,
Owes nothing to thy blasts. – But who comes here? –

Enter Gloster, led by an Old Man.

My father, poorly led? – World, world, O world!
But that thy strange mutations make us hate thee,
Life would not yield to age.

OLD MAN O my good lord! I have been your tenant, and your father's tenant, these fourscore years.

GLOSTER Away, get thee away; good friend, be gone:
Thy comforts can do me no good at all;
Thee they may hurt.

OLD MAN You cannot see your way.

GLOSTER I have no way, and therefore want no eyes:
I stumbled when I saw. Full oft 'tis seen,

Our means secure us, and our mere defects
Prove our commodities. – Ah! dear son Edgar,
The food of thy abused father's wrath!
Might I but live to see thee in my touch,
I'd say I had eyes again!

OLD MAN How now! Who's there?

EDGAR *[Aside]* O gods! Who is 't can say 'I am at the worst?'
I am worse than e'er I was.

OLD MAN 'Tis poor mad Tom.

EDGAR *[Aside]* And worse I may be yet: the worst is not
So long as we can say, 'This is the worst.'

OLD MAN Fellow, where goest?

GLOSTER Is it a beggar-man?

OLD MAN Madman and beggar too.

GLOSTER He has some reason, else he could not beg.
I' the last night's storm I such a fellow saw,
Which made me think a man a worm: my son
Came then into my mind; and yet my mind
Was then scarce friends with him: I have heard more since.
As flies to wanton boys, are we to the gods;
They kill us for their sport.

EDGAR *[Aside]* How should this be? –
Bad is the trade that must play fool to sorrow,
Angering itself and others. – Bless thee, master!

GLOSTER Is that the naked fellow?

OLD MAN Ay, my lord.

GLOSTER Get thee away. If, for my sake,
Thou wilt o'ertake us, hence a mile or twain,
I' the way toward Dover, do it for ancient love;
And bring some covering for this naked soul,
Which I'll entreat to lead me.

OLD MAN Alack, sir! he is mad.

GLOSTER 'Tis the times' plague, when madmen lead the blind.
Do as I bid thee, or rather do thy pleasure;
Above the rest, be gone.

OLD MAN I'll bring him the best 'parel that I have,
Come on 't what will. *[Exit.*

GLOSTER Sirrah, naked fellow,

EDGAR Poor Tom's a-cold. – *[Aside]* I cannot daub it further.

GLOSTER Come hither, fellow.

EDGAR *[Aside]* And yet I must. – Bless thy sweet eyes, they bleed.

GLOSTER Know'st thou the way to Dover?

EDGAR Both stile and gate, horse-way and foot-path. Poor Tom hath been scared out of his good wits: bless thee, good man's son, from the foul fiend! Five fiends have been in poor Tom at once; of lust, as Obidicut; Hobbididance, prince of dumbness; Mahu, of stealing; Modo, of murder; Flibbertigibbet, of mopping and mowing; who since possesses chambermaids and waiting-women. So, bless thee, master!

GLOSTER Here, take this purse, thou whom the heaven's plagues
Have humbled to all strokes: that I am wretched,
Makes thee the happier: – heavens, deal so still!
Let the superfluous and lust-dieted man,
That slaves your ordinance, that will not see
Because he doth not feel, feel your power quickly;
So distribution should undo excess,
And each man have enough. – Dost thou know Dover?

EDGAR Ay, master.

GLOSTER There is a cliff, whose high and bending head
Looks fearfully in the confined deep:
Bring me but to the very brim of it,

And I'll repair the misery thou dost bear
With something rich about me: from that place
I shall no leading need.

EDGAR Give me thy arm:
Poor Tom shall lead thee. *[Exeunt.*

SCENE II – BEFORE THE DUKE OF ALBANY'S PALACE.

Enter Goneril and Edmund; Oswald meeting them.

GONERIL Welcome, my lord: I marvel, our mild husband
Not met us on the way. – Now, where's your master?

OSWALD Madam, within; but never man so chang'd.
I told him of the army that was landed;
He smil'd at it: I told him, you were coming;
His answer was, 'The worse:' of Gloster's treachery,
And of the loyal service of his son,
When I inform'd him, then he call'd me sot,
And told me, I had turn'd the wrong side out.
What most he should dislike, seems pleasant to him;
What like, offensive.

GONERIL *[To Edmund]* Then shall you go no further.
It is the cowish terror of his spirit,
That dares not undertake: he'll not feel wrongs
Which tie him to an answer. Our wishes on the way
May prove effects. Back, Edmund, to my brother;
Hasten his musters, and conduct his powers:
I must change arms at home, and give the distaff
Into my husband's hands. This trusty servant
Shall pass between us: ere long you are like to hear,

If you dare venture in your own behalf,
A mistress's command. Wear this; spare speech;
[Giving a favour.
Decline your head: this kiss, if it durst speak,
Would stretch thy spirits up into the air. –
Conceive, and fare thee well.

EDMUND Yours in the ranks of death.

GONERIL My most dear Gloster!
[Exit Edmund.
O, the difference of man and man!
To thee a woman's services are due:
My fool usurps my body.

OSWALD Madam, here comes my lord.
[Exit.

Enter Albany.

GONERIL I have been worth the whistle.

ALBANY O Goneril!
You are not worth the dust which the rude wind
Blows in your face. – I fear your disposition:
That nature, which contemns its origin,
Cannot be border'd certain in itself;
She that herself will sliver and disbranch
From her material sap, perforce must wither,
And come to deadly use.

GONERIL No more: the text is foolish.

ALBANY Wisdom and goodness to the vile seem vile:
Filths savour but themselves. What have you done?
Tigers, not daughters, what have you perform'd?
A father, and a gracious aged man,
Whose reverence the head-lugg'd bear would lick,

Most barbarous, most degenerate! have you madded.
Could my good brother suffer you to do it?
A man, a prince, by him so benefited!
If that the heavens do not their visible spirits
Send quickly down to tame these vile offences,
It will come,
Humanity must perforce prey on itself,
Like monsters of the deep.

GONERIL Milk-liver'd man!
That bear'st a cheek for blows, a head for wrongs:
Who hast not in thy brows an eye discerning
Thine honour from thy suffering; that not know'st,
Fools do those villains pity, who are punish'd
Ere they have done their mischief. Where's thy drum?
France spreads his banners in our noiseless land;
With plumed helm thy slayer begins threats:
Whilst thou, a moral fool, sitt'st still, and criest,
'Alack! why does he so?'

ALBANY See thyself, devil!
Proper deformity seems not in the fiend,
So horrid, as in woman.

GONERIL O vain fool!

ALBANY Thou changed and self-cover'd thing, for shame.
Be-monster not thy feature. Were it my fitness
To let these hands obey my blood,
They are apt enough to dislocate and tear
Thy flesh and bones: – howe'er thou art a fiend,
A woman's shape doth shield thee.

GONERIL Marry, your manhood now! –

Enter a Messenger

ALBANY What news?

MESSENGER O, my good lord, the Duke of Cornwall's dead;
Slain by his servant, going to put out
The other eye of Gloster.

ALBANY Gloster's eyes!

MESSENGER A servant that he bred, thrill'd with remorse,
Oppos'd against the act, bending his sword
To this great master; who, thereat enrag'd,
Flew on him, and amongst them fell'd him dead;
But not without that harmful stroke, which since
Hath pluck'd him after.

ALBANY This shows you are above,
You justicers, that these our nether crimes
So speedily can venge! – But, O poor Gloster!
Lost he his other eye?

MESSENGER Both, both, my lord. –
This letter, madam, craves a speedy answer;
'Tis from your sister.

GONERIL *[Aside]* One way I like this well;
But being widow, and my Gloster with her,
May all the building in my fancy pluck
Upon my hateful life. Another way,
The news is not so tart. – I'll read, and answer. *[Exit.*

ALBANY Where was his son, when they did take his eyes?

MESSENGER Come with my lady hither.

ALBANY He is not here.

MESSENGER No, my good lord; I met him back again.

ALBANY Knows he the wickedness?

MESSENGER Ay, my good lord; 'twas he inform'd against him,
And quit the house on purpose, that their punishment

Might have the freer course.

ALBANY Gloster, I live
To thank thee for the love thou show'dst the king,
And to revenge thine eyes. – Come hither, friend:
Tell me what more thou knowest. *[Exeunt.*

SCENE III – THE FRENCH CAMP NEAR DOVER.

Enter Kent and a Gentleman.

KENT Why the King of France is so suddenly gone back, know you the reason?

GENTLEMAN Something he left imperfect in the state, which since his coming forth is thought of; which imports to the kingdom so much fear and danger, that his personal return was most required, and necessary.

KENT Who hath he left behind him general?

GENTLEMAN The Marshal of France, Monsieur La Far.

KENT Did your letters pierce the queen to any demonstration of grief?

GENTLEMAN Ay, sir; she took them, read them in my presence;
And now and then an ample tear trill'd down
Her delicate cheek: it seem'd, she was a queen
Over her passion, who, most rebel-like,
Sought to be king o'er her.

KENT O! then it mov'd her.

GENTLEMAN Not to a rage: patience and sorrow strove
Who should express her goodliest. You have seen
Sunshine and rain at once; her smiles and tears
Were like a better way: those happy smilets,
That play'd on her ripe lip, seem'd not to know

What guest were in her eyes; which parted thence,
As pearls from diamonds dropp'd. – In brief,
Sorrow would be a rarity most belov'd,
If all could so become it.

KENT Made she no verbal question?

GENTLEMAN 'Faith, once, or twice, she heav'd the name of 'father'
Pantingly forth, as if it press'd her heart;
Cried, 'Sisters! sisters! Shame of ladies! sisters!
Kent! father! sisters! What? i' the storm? i' the night?
Let pity not be believed!' – There she shook
The holy water from her heavenly eyes,
And clamour moisten'd: then away she started
To deal with grief alone.

KENT It is the stars,
The stars above us, govern our conditions;
Else one self mate and mate could not beget
Such different issues. You spoke not with her since?

GENTLEMAN No.

KENT Was this before the king return'd?

GENTLEMAN No, since.

KENT Well, sir; the poor distress'd Lear's i' the town;
Who sometime, in his better tune, remembers
What we are come about, and by no means
Will yield to see his daughter.

GENTLEMAN Why, good sir?

KENT A sovereign shame so elbows him: his own unkindness,
That stripp'd her from his benediction, turn'd her
To foreign casualties; gave her dear rights
To his dog-hearted daughters: these things sting
His mind so venomously, that burning shame
Detains him from Cordelia.

GENTLEMAN Alack, poor gentleman!
KENT Of Albany's and Cornwall's powers you heard not?
GENTLEMAN 'Tis so, they are afoot.
KENT Well, sir, I'll bring you to our master Lear,
And leave you to attend him. Some dear cause
Will in concealment wrap me up awhile:
When I am known aright, you shall not grieve
Lending me this acquaintance.
I pray you, go along with me. *[Exeunt.*

SCENE IV – THE SAME. A CAMP.

Enter Cordelia, Physician, and Soldiers.

CORDELIA Alack! 'tis he: why, he was met even now
As mad as the vex'd sea: singing aloud;
Crown'd with rank fumiter, and furrow-weeds,
With hoar-docks, hemlock, nettles, cuckoo-flowers,
Darnel, and all the idle weeds that grow
In our sustaining corn. – A century send forth;
Search every acre in the high-grown field,
And bring him to our eye. *[Exit an Officer.]* – What can man's wisdom
In the restoring his bereaved sense?
He that helps him, take all my outward worth.
PHYSICIAN There is means, madam;
Our foster-nurse of nature is repose,
The which he lacks; that to provoke in him,
Are many simples operative, whose power
Will close the eye of anguish.
CORDELIA All bless'd secrets,
All you unpublish'd virtues of the earth,

Spring with my tears! be aidant, and remediate,
In the good man's distress! – Seek, seek for him;
Lest his ungovern'd rage dissolve the life
That wants the means to lead it.

Enter a Messenger.

MESSENGER News, madam:
The British powers are marching hitherward.

CORDELIA 'Tis known before; our preparation stands
In expectation of them. – O dear father,
It is thy business that I go about;
Therefore great France
My mourning, and important tears, hath pitied.
No blown ambition doth our arms incite,
But love, dear love, and our ag'd father's right.
Soon may I hear and see him! *[Exeunt.*

SCENE V – A ROOM IN GLOSTER'S CASTLE.

Enter Regan and Oswald.

REGAN But are my brother's powers set forth?

OSWALD Ay, madam.

REGAN Himself in person there?

OSWALD Madam, with much ado:
Your sister is the better soldier.

REGAN Lord Edmund spake not with your lord at home?

OSWALD No, madam.

REGAN What might import my sister's letter to him?

OSWALD I know not, lady.

REGAN 'Faith, he is posted hence on serious matter.

It was great ignorance, Gloster's eyes being out,
To let him live: where he arrives, he moves
All hearts against us. Edmund, I think, is gone,
In pity on his misery, to despatch
His nighted life; moreover, to descry
The strength o' the enemy.

OSWALD I must needs after him, madam, with my letter.

REGAN Our troops set forth to-morrow: stay with us;
The ways are dangerous.

OSWALD I may not, madam;
My lady charg'd my duty in this business.

REGAN Why should she write to Edmund? Might not you
Transport her purposes by word? Belike,
Something – I know not what. – I'll love thee much,
Let me unseal the letter.

OSWALD Madam, I had rather –

REGAN I know your lady does not love her husband;
I am sure of that: and, at her late being here,
She gave strange eyliads, and most speaking looks
To noble Edmund. I know, you are of her bosom.

OSWALD I, madam?

REGAN I speak in understanding; you are, I know't:
Therefore, I do advise you, take this note:
My lord is dead; Edmund and I have talk'd;
And more convenient is he for my hand,
Than for your lady's. – You may gather more.
If you do find him, pray you, give him this;
And when your mistress hears thus much from you,
I pray, desire her call her wisdom to her:
So, fare you well.
If you do chance to hear of that blind traitor,
Preferment falls on him that cuts him off.

OSWALD 'Would I could meet him, madam: I would show
What party I do follow.
REGAN Fare thee well. *[Exeunt.*

SCENE VI – THE COUNTRY NEAR DOVER.

Enter Gloster, and Edgar dressed like a peasant.

GLOSTER When shall I come to the top of that same hill?
EDGAR You do climb up it now: look, how we labour.
GLOSTER Methinks, the ground is even.
EDGAR Horrible steep:
Hark! do you hear the sea?
GLOSTER No, truly.
EDGAR Why, then your other senses grow imperfect
By your eyes' anguish.
GLOSTER So may it be, indeed.
Methinks, thy voice is alter'd; and thou speak'st
In better phrase, and matter, than thou didst.
EDGAR You're much deceiv'd: in nothing am I chang'd,
But in my garments.
GLOSTER Methinks, you're better spoken.
EDGAR Come on, sir; here's the place: stand still. – How fearful
And dizzy 'tis, to cast one's eyes so low!
The crows, and choughs, that wing the midway air,
Show scarce so gross as beetles: half way down
Hangs one that gathers samphire; dreadful trade!
Methinks, he seems no bigger than his head.
The fishermen, that walk upon the beach,
Appear like mice; and yond tall anchoring bark,
Diminish'd to her cock; her cock, a buoy

Almost too small for sight. The murmuring surge,
That on the unnumber'd idle pebbles chafes,
Cannot be heard so high. – I'll look no more;
Lest my brain turn, and the deficient sight
Topple down headlong.

GLOSTER Set me where you stand.

EDGAR Give me your hand; you are now within a foot
Of the extreme verge: for all beneath the moon
Would I not leap upright.

GLOSTER Let go my hand.
Here, friend, 's another purse; in it, a jewel
Well worth a poor man's taking: fairies, and gods,
Prosper it with thee! Go thou further off;
Bid me farewell, and let me hear thee going.

EDGAR Now fare you well, good sir.

GLOSTER With all my heart.

EDGAR Why I do trifle thus with his despair,
Is done to cure it.

GLOSTER O you mighty gods!
This world I do renounce, and in your sights
Shake patiently my great affliction off;
If I could bear it longer, and not fall
To quarrel with your great opposeless wills,
My snuff, and loathed part of nature, should
Burn itself out. If Edgar live, O bless him! –
Now, fellow, fare thee well.

EDGAR Gone, sir: farewell. –
And yet I know not how conceit may rob
The treasury of life, when life itself
Yields to the theft: had he been where he thought,
By this had thought been past. – Alive, or dead?

Ho, you sir! friend! Hear you, sir? – speak! –
Thus might he pass indeed, – yet he revives. –
What are you, sir?

GLOSTER Away, and let me die.

EDGAR Hadst thou been aught but gossamer, feather, air,
So many fathom down precipitating,
Thou'dst shiver'd like an egg: but thou dost breathe:
Hast heavy substance; bleed'st not; speak'st; art sound.
Ten masts at each make not the altitude
Which thou hast perpendicularly fell:
Thy life's a miracle. Speak yet again.

GLOSTER But have I fallen, or no?

EDGAR From the dread summit of this chalky bourn.
Look up a-height; the shrill-gorg'd lark so far
Cannot be seen or heard: do but look up.

GLOSTER Alack! I have no eyes. –
Is wretchedness depriv'd that benefit,
To end itself by death? 'Twas yet some comfort,
When misery could beguile the tyrant's rage,
And frustrate his proud will.

EDGAR Give me your arm;
Up: – so; – how is't? Feel you your legs? You stand.

GLOSTER Too well, too well.

EDGAR This is above all strangeness.
Upon the crown o' the cliff, what thing was that
Which parted from you?

GLOSTER A poor unfortunate beggar.

EDGAR As I stood here below, methought, his eyes
Were two full moons; he had a thousand noses,
Horns whelk'd and wav'd like the enridged sea:
It was some fiend; therefore, thou happy father,

Think that the clearest gods, who make them honours
Of men's impossibilities, have preserv'd thee.

GLOSTER I do remember now: henceforth I'll bear
Affliction, till it do cry out itself
'Enough, enough,' and 'die.' That thing you speak of,
I took it for a man; often 'twould say,
'The fiend, the fiend:' he led me to that place.

EDGAR Bear free and patient thoughts. – But who comes here?

Enter Lear, fantastically dressed with wild flowers.

The safer sense will ne'er acommodate
His master thus.

LEAR No, they cannot touch me for coining; I am the king himself.

EDGAR O thou side-piercing sight!

LEAR Nature's above art in that respect. – There's your press-money. That fellow handles his bow like a crow-keeper: draw me a clothier's yard. – Look, look! a mouse. Peace, peace! – this piece of toasted cheese will do't. – There's my gauntlet, I'll prove it on a giant. – Bring up the brown-bills. – O, well flown, bird! – i' the clout, i' the clout: hewgh! – Give the word.

EDGAR Sweet marjoram.

LEAR Pass.

GLOSTER I know that voice.

LEAR Ha! Goneril! – with a white beard! – They flatter'd me like a dog; and told me I had white hairs in my beard, ere the black ones were there. To say 'ay' and 'no' to everything I said! – 'Ay' and 'no' too was no good divinity. When the rain came to wet me once, and the wind to make me chatter; when the thunder would not peace at my bidding: there I found 'em, there I smelt 'em out. Go to, they are not men o' their words: they told me I was everything; 'tis a lie, I am not ague-proof.

GLOSTER The trick of that voice I do well remember:
Is't not the king?
LEAR Ay, every inch a king:
When I do stare, see, how the subject quakes.
I pardon that man's life. What was thy cause? –
Adultery? –
Thou shalt not die: die for adultery! No:
The wren goes to 't, and the small gilded fly
Does lecher in my sight.
Let copulation thrive: for Gloster's bastard son
Was kinder to his father, than my daughters
Got 'tween the lawful sheets.
To 't, luxury, pell-mell! for I lack soldiers. –
Behold yond simpering dame,
Whose face between her forks presageth snow;
That minces virtue, and does shake the head
To hear of pleasure's name;
The fitchew, nor the soiled horse, goes to 't
With a more riotous appetite.
Down from the waist they are centaurs,
Though women all above:
But to the girdle do the gods inherit,
Beneath is all the fiend's: there's hell, there's darkness, there is the sulphurous pit, burning, scalding, stench, consumption; – fie, fie, fie! pah pah! Give me an ounce of civet, good apothecary, to sweeten my imagination: there's money for thee.
GLOSTER O, let me kiss that hand!
LEAR Let me wipe it first; it smells of mortality.
GLOSTER O ruin'd piece of nature! This great world
Shall so wear out to nought. – Dost thou know me?

LEAR I remember thine eyes well enough. Dost thou squiny at me? No, do thy worst, blind Cupid; I'll not love. – Read thou this challenge: mark but the penning of it.

GLOSTER Were all thy letters suns, I could not see.

EDGAR I would not take this from report; it is,
And my heart breaks at it.

LEAR Read.

GLOSTER What! with the case of eyes?

LEAR O, ho! are you there with me? No eyes in your head, nor no money in your purse? Your eyes are in a heavy case, your purse in a light: yet you see how this world goes.

GLOSTER I see it feelingly.

LEAR What, art mad? A man may see how this world goes, with no eyes. Look with thine ears: see how yond justice rails upon yond simple thief. Hark, in thine ear: change places; and, handy-dandy, which is the justice, which is the thief? – Thou hast seen a farmer's dog bark at a beggar?

GLOSTER Ay, sir.

LEAR And the creature run from the cur? There thou mightst behold the great image of authority: a dog's obey'd in office. –
Thou rascal beadle, hold thy bloody hand!
Why dost thou lash that whore? Strip thine own back;
Thou hotly lust'st to use her in that kind
For which thou whipp'st her. The usurer hangs the cozener.
Through tatter'd clothes small vices do appear:
Robes and furr'd gowns hide all. Plate sin with gold,
And the strong lance of justice hurtless breaks;
Arm it in rags, a pigmy's straw does pierce it,
None does offend, none, I say, none; I'll able 'em:
Take that of me, my friend, who have the power
To seal the accuser's lips. Get thee glass eyes;

And, like a scurvy politician, seem
To see the things thou dost not. – Now, now, now, now,
Pull off my boots: – harder, harder; – so.

EDGAR O, matter and impertinency mix'd!
Reason in madness!

LEAR If thou wilt weep my fortunes, take my eyes.
I know thee well enough: thy name is Gloster:
Thou must be patient. We came crying hither:
Thou know'st, the first time that we smell the air,
We wawl, and cry. I will preach to thee: mark me.

GLOSTER Alack, alack the day!

LEAR When we are born, we cry that we are come
To this great stage of fools. – This a good block! –
It were a delicate stratagem, to shoe
A troop of horse with felt: I'll put 't in proof;
And when I have stol'n upon these sons-in-law,
Then, kill, kill, kill, kill, kill, kill!

Enter a Gentleman, with Attendants.

GENTLEMAN O! here he is: lay hand upon him. – Sir,
Your most dear daughter –

LEAR No rescue? What! a prisoner? I am even
The natural fool of fortune. – Use me well;
You shall have ransom. Let me have surgeons;
I am cut to the brains.

GENTLEMAN You shall have anything.

LEAR No seconds? All myself?
Why, this would make a man a man of salt,
To use his eyes for garden water-pots,
Ay, and laying autumn's dust.

GENTLEMAN Good sir, –

LEAR I will die bravely, like a smug bridegroom. What!
I will be jovial; come, come; I am a king,
My masters, know you that?

GENTLEMAN You are a royal one, and we obey you.

LEAR Then there's life in it. Nay, an you get it, you shall get it by running. Sa, sa, sa, sa. *[Exit; Attendants follow.*

GENTLEMAN A sight most pitiful in the meanest wretch,
Past speaking of in a king! – Thou hast one daughter,
Who redeems nature from the general curse
Which twain have brought her to.

EDGAR Hail, gentle sir!

GENTLEMAN Sir, speed you: what's your will?

EDGAR Do you hear aught, sir, of a battle toward?

GENTLEMAN Most sure, and vulgar: every one hears that,
Which can distinguish sound.

EDGAR But, by your favour,
How near's the other army?

GENTLEMAN Near, and on speedy foot; the main descry
Stands on the hourly thought.

EDGAR I thank you, sir: that's all.

GENTLEMAN Though that the queen on special cause is here;
Her army is mov'd on.

EDGAR I thank you, sir. *[Exit Gentleman.*

GLOSTER You ever-gentle gods, take my breath from me:
Let not my worser spirit tempt me again
To die before you please!

EDGAR Well pray you, father.

GLOSTER Now, good sir, what are you?

EDGAR A most poor man, made tame to fortune's blows;
Who by the art of known and feeling sorrows,
Am pregnant to good pity. Give me your hand,
I'll lead you to some biding.

GLOSTER Hearty thanks:
The bounty and the benison of heaven
To boot, and boot!

Enter Oswald.

OSWALD A proclaim'd prize! Most happy!
That eyeless head of thine was first fram'd flesh
To raise my fortunes. – Thou old unhappy traitor,
Briefly thyself remember: – the sword is out
That must destroy thee.

GLOSTER Now let thy friendly hand
Put strength enough to it. *[Edgar interposes.*

OSWALD Wherefore, bold peasant,
Dar'st thou support a publish'd traitor? Hence;
Lest that the infection of his fortune take
Like hold on thee. Let go his arm.

EDGAR Ch'ill not let go, zir, without vurther 'casion.

OSWALD Let go, slave, or thou diest.

EDGAR Good gentleman, go your gait, and let poor volk pass. An ch'ud ha' been zwagger'd out of my life, 'twould not ha' been zo long as 'tis by a vortnight. Nay, come not near the old man: keep out, che vor'ye, or ise try whether your costard or my ballow be the harder. Ch'ill be plain with you.

OSWALD Out, dunghill!

EDGAR Ch'ill pick your teeth, zir. Come; no matter vor your foins.

[They fight, and Edgar knocks him down.

OSWALD Slave, thou hast slain me. – Villain, take my purse.
If ever thou wilt thrive, bury my body;
And give the letters, which thou find'st about me,
To Edmund Earl of Gloster: seek him out

Upon the English party; – O, untimely death! *[Dies.*

EDGAR I know thee well: a serviceable villain;
As duteous to the vices of thy mistress,
As badness would desire.

GLOSTER What! is he dead?

EDGAR Sit you down, father; rest you. –
Let's see these pockets: the letters, that he speaks of,
May be my friends. – He's dead: I am only sorry
He had no other death's-man. – Let us see: –
Leave, gentle wax; and, manners, blame us not:
To know our enemies' minds, we rip their hearts;
Their papers is more lawful.

[Reads] 'Let our reciprocal vows be remembered. You have many opportunities to cut him off; if your will want not, time and place will be fruitfully offered. There is nothing done, if he return the conqueror; then am I the prisoner, and his bed my gaol; from the loathed warmth whereof deliver me, and supply the place for your labour.

Your (wife, so I would say)
affectionate servant,
GONERIL.'

O, undistinguish'd space of woman's will!
A plot upon her virtuous husband's life;
And the exchange, my brother! – Here, in the sands,
Thee I'll rake up, the post unsanctified
Of murderous lechers; and, in the mature time,
With this ungracious paper strike the sight
Of the death-practis'd duke. For him 't is well,
That of thy death and business I can tell.

GLOSTER The king is mad: how stiff is my vile sense,
That I stand up, and have ingenious feeling

Of my huge sorrows! Better I were distract:
So should my thoughts be sever'd from my griefs;
And woes, by wrong imaginations, lose
The knowledge of themselves. *[Drum afar off.*

EDGAR Give me your hand.
Far off, methinks, I hear the beaten drum.
Come, father; I'll bestow you with a friend. *[Exeunt.*

SCENE VII – A TENT IN THE FRENCH CAMP.

Enter Cordelia, Kent, Doctor, and Gentleman.

CORDELIA O thou good Kent! how shall I live and work,
To match thy goodness? My life will be too short,
And every measure fail me.

KENT To be acknowledg'd, madam, is o'er-paid.
All my reports go with the modest truth;
Nor more, nor clipp'd, but so.

CORDELIA Be better suited:
These weeds are memories of those worser hours:
I pr'ythee, put them off.

KENT Pardon me, dear madam:
Yet to be known shortens my made intent:
My boon I make it, that you know me not,
Till time and I think meet.

CORDELIA Then be 't so, my good lord. – *[To the Doctor.*
How does the king?

DOCTOR Madam, sleeps still.

CORDELIA O you kind gods,
Cure this great breach in his abused nature!
The untun'd and jarring senses, O, wind up
Of this child-changed father!

DOCTOR So please your majesty,
That we may wake the king? he hath slept long.
CORDELIA Be govern'd by your knowledge, and proceed
I' the sway of your own will. Is he array'd?

Enter Lear in a chair carried by Servants.

DOCTOR Ay, madam; in the heaviness of sleep,
We put fresh garments on him.
KENT Be by, good madam, when we do awake him;
I doubt not of his temperance.
CORDELIA Very well. *[Music.*
DOCTOR Please you, draw near. – Louder the music there!
CORDELIA O my dear father! Restoration hang
Thy medicine on my lips, and let this kiss
Repair those violent harms, that my two sisters
Have in thy reverence made!
KENT Kind and dear princess!
CORDELIA Had you not been their father, these white flakes
Had challeng'd pity of them. Was this a face
To be oppos'd against the warring winds?
To stand against the deep dread-bolted thunder?
In the most terrible and nimble stroke
Of quick cross lightning? to watch (poor perdu!)
With this thin helm? Mine enemy's dog,
Though he had bit me, should have stood that night
Against my fire. And wast thou fain, poor father,
To hovel thee with swine, and rogues forlorn,
In short and musty straw? Alack, alack!
'Tis wonder, that thy life and wits at once
Had not concluded all. – He wakes; speak to him.
DOCTOR Madam, do you; 'tis fittest.

CORDELIA How does my royal lord? How fares your majesty?
LEAR You do me wrong, to take me out o' the grave. –
Thou art a soul in bliss; but I am bound
Upon a wheel of fire, that mine own tears
Do scald like molten lead.
CORDELIA Sir, do you know me?
LEAR You are a spirit, I know. When did you die?
CORDELIA Still, still, far wide.
DOCTOR He's scarce awake: let him alone awhile.
LEAR Where have I been? Where am I? – Fair daylight? –
I am mightily abus'd. – I should even die with pity,
To see another thus. – I know not what to say. –
I will not swear, these are my hands: – let's see;
I feel this pin prick. 'Would I were assur'd
Of my condition!
CORDELIA O! look upon me, sir,
And hold your hands in benediction o'er me. –
No, sir, you must not kneel.
LEAR Pray, do not mock me:
I am a very foolish fond old man,
Fourscore and upward, not an hour more, nor less;
And, to deal plainly,
I fear, I am not in my perfect mind.
Methinks, I should know you, and know this man;
Yet I am doubtful, for I am mainly ignorant
What place is this; and all the skill I have
Remembers not these garments; nor I know not
Where I did lodge last night. Do not laugh at me;
For, as I am a man, I think this lady
To be my child Cordelia.
CORDELIA And so I am, I am.

LEAR Be your tears wet? Yes, 'faith. I pray, weep not:
If you have poison for me, I will drink it.
I know, you do not love me; for your sisters
Have, as I do remember, done me wrong:
You have some cause, they have not.

CORDELIA No cause, no cause.

LEAR Am I in France?

KENT In your own kindom, sir.

LEAR Do not abuse me.

DOCTOR Be comforted, good madam: the great rage,
You see, is kill'd in him; and yet it is danger
To make him even o'er the time he has lost.
Desire him to go in; trouble him no more,
Till further settling.

CORDELIA Will 't please your highness walk?

LEAR You must bear with me.
Pray you now, forget and forgive: I am old and foolish.

[Exeunt Lear, Cordelia, Doctor, and Attendants.

GENTLEMAN Holds it true, sir, that the Duke of Cornwall was so slain?

KENT Most certain, sir.

GENTLEMAN Who is conductor of his people?

KENT As 'tis said, the bastard son of Gloster.

GENTLEMAN They say, Edgar, his banished son, is with the Earl of Kent in Germany.

KENT Report is changeable. 'Tis time to look about; the powers of the kingdom approach apace.

GENTLEMAN The arbitrement is like to be bloody. Fare you well, sir. *[Exit.*

KENT My point and period will be thoroughly wrought,
Or well, or ill, as this day's battle's fought. *[Exit.*

ACT FIVE

SCENE I – THE CAMP OF THE BRITISH FORCES, NEAR DOVER.

Enter with drums and colours, Edmund, Regan, Officers, Soldiers, and others.

EDMUND Now of the duke, if his last purpose hold;
Or whether, since, he is advis'd by aught
To change the course. He's full of alteration,
And self-reproving: – bring his constant pleasure.
[To an Officer, who goes out.

REGAN Our sister's man is certainly miscarried.

EDMUND 'Tis to be doubted, madam.

REGAN Now, sweet lord.
You know the goodness I intend upon you:
Tell me, – but truly, – but then speak the truth,
Do you not love my sister?

EDMUND In honour'd love.

REGAN But have you never found my brother's way
To the forfended place?

EDMUND That thought abuses you.

REGAN I am doubtful that you have been conjunct
And bosom'd with her, as far as we call hers.

EDMUND No, by mine honour, madam.

REGAN I never shall endure her. Dear my lord,
Be not familiar with her.

EDMUND Fear me not. –

She, and the duke her husband!

Enter Albany, Goneril, and Soldiers.

GONERIL *[Aside]* I had rather lose the battle, than that sister
Should loosen him and me.

ALBANY Our very loving sister, well be-met. –
Sir, this I heard, – the king is come to his daughter,
With others, whom the rigour of our state
Forc'd to cry out. Where I could not be honest,
I never yet was valiant: for this business,
It toucheth us, as France invades our land,
Not bolds the king, with others, whom, I fear,
Most just and heavy causes make oppose.

EDMUND Sir, you speak nobly.

REGAN Why is this reason'd?

GONERIL Combine together 'gainst the enemy;
For these domestic and particular broils
Are not the question here.

ALBANY Let us then determine
With the ancient of war on our proceeding.

EDMUND I shall attend you presently at your tent.

REGAN Sister, you'll go with us?

GONERIL No.

REGAN 'Tis most convenient; pray you, go with us.

GONERIL *[Aside]* Oh, ho! I know the riddle. – I will go.

Enter Edgar, disguised

EDGAR If e'er your grace had speech with man so poor,
Hear me one word.

ALBANY I'll overtake you. – Speak.
[Exeunt Edmund, Regan, Goneril, Officers.

EDGAR Before you fight the battle, ope this letter.

If you have victory, let the trumpet sound
For him that brought it: wretched though I seem,
I can produce a champion, that will prove
What is avouched there. If you miscarry,
Your business of the world hath so an end,
And machination ceases. Fortune love you!

ALBANY Stay till I have read the letter.

EDGAR I was forbid it.
When time shall serve, let but the herald cry,
And I'll appear again.

ALBANY Why, fare thee well: I will o'erlook thy paper.
[Exit Edgar.

Re-enter Edmund.

EDMUND The enemy's in view; draw up your powers.
Here is the guess of their true strength and forces
By diligent discovery; but your haste
Is now urg'd on you.

ALBANY We will greet the time. *[Exit.*

EDMUND To both these sisters have I sworn my love;
Each jealous of the other, as the stung
Are of the adder. Which of them shall I take?
Both? one? or neither? Neither can be enjoy'd,
If both remain alive: to take the widow,
Exasperates, makes mad, her sister Goneril;
And hardly shall I carry out my side,
Her husband being alive. Now then, we'll use
His countenance for the battle; which being done,
Let her who would be rid of him devise
His speedy taking-off. As for the mercy
Which he intends to Lear and to Cordelia, –

The battle done, and they within our power,
Shall never see his pardon; for my state
Stands on me to defend, not to debate *[Exit.*

SCENE II – A FIELD BETWEEN THE TWO CAMPS.

Alarum within. Enter, with drum and colours, Lear, Cordelia, and their Forces; and exeunt.

Enter Edgar and Gloster.

EDGAR Here, father, take the shadow of this tree
For your good host; pray that the right may thrive.
If ever I return to you again,
I'll bring you comfort.
GLOSTER Grace go with you, sir! *[Exit Edgar.*

Alarum; afterwards a Retreat. Re-enter Edgar.

EDGAR Away, old man! give me thy hand: away!
King Lear hath lost, he and his daughter ta'en.
Give me thy hand; come on.
GLOSTER No further, sir; a man may rot even here.
EDGAR What! in ill thoughts again? Men must endure
Their going hence, even as their coming hither:
Ripeness is all. Come on.
GLOSTER And that's true too. *[Exeunt.*

SCENE III – THE BRITISH CAMP NEAR DOVER

Enter, in conquest, with drum and colours, Edmund: Lear, and Cordelia, as prisoners; Captain, Officers, Soldiers &c.

EDMUND Some officers take them away: good guard,
Until their greater pleasures first be known,
That are to censure them.
CORDELIA We are not the first,
Who, with best meaning, have incurr'd the worst.
For thee, oppressed king, am I cast down;
Myself could else out-frown false fortune's frown.
Shall we not see these daughters, and these sisters?
LEAR No, no, no, no! Come, let's away to prison;
We two alone will sing like birds i' the cage:
When thou dost ask me blessing, I'll kneel down,
And ask of thee forgiveness. So we'll live,
And pray, and sing, and tell old tales, and laugh
At gilded butterflies, and hear poor rogues
Talk of court news; and we'll talk with them too,
Who loses, and who wins; who's in, who's out,
And take upon's the mystery of things,
As if we were God's spies: and we'll wear out,
In a wall'd prison, packs and sects of great ones,
That ebb and flow by the moon.
EDMUND Take them away.
LEAR Upon such sacrifices, my Cordelia,
The gods themselves throw incense. Have I caught thee?
He that parts us shall bring a brand from heaven,
And fire us hence like foxes. Wipe thine eyes;
The goujeers shall devour them, flesh and fell,

Ere they shall make us weep: we'll see 'em starve first.
Come. *[Exeunt Lear and Cordelia, guarded.*

EDMUND Come hither, captain; hark.
Take thou this note *[giving a paper]*; go, follow them to prison.
One step I have advanc'd thee; if thou dost
As this instructs thee, thou dost make thy way
To noble fortunes. Know thou this, that men
Are as the time is: to be tender-minded
Does not become a sword. Thy great employment
Will not bear question; either say, thou'lt do't,
Or thrive by other means.

CAPTAIN I'll do 't, my lord.

EDMUND About it; and write happy, when thou hast done.
Mark, – I say, instantly; and carry it so,
As I have set it down.

CAPTAIN I cannot draw a cart, nor eat dried oats;
If it be a man's work, I will do it. *[Exit.*

Flourish. Enter Albany, Goneril, Regan, Officers, and Attendants.

ALBANY Sir, you have show'd to-day your valiant strain,
And fortune led you well. You have the captives
Who were the opposites of this day's strife:
We do require them of you, so to use them,
As we shall find their merits and our safety
May equally determine.

EDMUND Sir, I thought it fit
To send the old and miserable king
To some retention, and appointed guard;
Whose age has charms in it, whose title more,
To pluck the common bosom on his side,

And turn our impress'd lances in our eyes,
Which do command them. With him I sent the queen;
My reason all the same; and they are ready
To-morrow, or at further space, to appear
Where you shall hold your session. At this time
We sweat and bleed: the friend hath lost his friend;
And the best quarrels, in the heat, are curs'd
By those that feel their sharpness. –
The question of Cordelia and her father
Requires a fitter place.

ALBANY Sir, by your patience,
I hold you but a subject of this war,
Not as a brother.

REGAN That's as we list to grace him:
Methinks, our pleasure might have been demanded,
Ere you had spoke so far. He led our powers,
Bore the commission of my place and person;
The which immediacy may well stand up,
And call itself your brother.

GONERIL Not so hot:
In his own grace he doth exalt himself,
More than in your addition.

REGAN In my rights,
By me invested, he compeers the best.

ALBANY That were the most, if he should husband you.

REGAN Jesters do oft prove prophets.

GONERIL Holla, holla!
That eye that told you so look'd but a-squint.

REGAN Lady, I am not well; else I should answer
From a full-flowing stomach. – General,
Take thou my soldiers, prisoners, patrimony:

Dispose of them, of me; the walls are thine.
Witness the world, that I create thee here
My lord and master.

GONERIL Mean you to enjoy him?

ALBANY The let-alone lies not in your good will.

EDMUND Nor in thine, lord.

ALBANY Half-blooded fellow, yes.

REGAN *[To Edmund]* Let the drum strike, and prove my title thine.

ALBANY Stay yet; hear reason. – Edmund, I arrest thee
On capital treason; and, in thy arrest,
This gilded serpent *[pointing to Goneril]* – For your claim, fair sister,
I bar it in the interest of my wife;
'Tis she is sub-contracted to this lord,
And I, her husband, contradict your bans.
If you will marry, make your loves to me,
My lady is bespoke.

GONERIL An interlude!

ALBANY Thou art arm'd, Gloster: – let the trumpet sound:
If none appear to prove upon thy person
Thy heinous, manifest, and many treasons,
There is my pledge *[throwing down a glove]*; I'll make it on thy heart,
Ere I taste bread, thou art in nothing less
Than I have here proclaim'd thee.

REGAN Sick! O, sick!

GONERIL *[Aside]* If not, I'll ne'er trust medicine.

EDMUND There's my exchange *[throwing down a glove]*: what in the world he is
That names me traitor, villain-like he lies.

Call by thy trumpet: he that dares approach,
On him, on you, – who not? – I will maintain
My truth and honour firmly.

ALBANY A herald, ho!

EDMUND A herald, ho! a herald!

ALBANY Trust to thy single virtue; for thy soldiers,
All levied in my name, have in my name
Took their discharge.

REGAN My sickness grows upon me.

ALBANY She is not well; convey her to my tent.

[Exit Regan, led.

Enter a Herald.

Come hither, herald. – Let the trumpet sound,
And read out this.

CAPTAIN Sound, trumpet! *[A trumpet sounds.*

Herald reads.

'If any man of quality, or degree, within the lists of the army, will maintain upon Edmund, supposed Earl of Gloster, that he is a manifold traitor, let him appear by the third sound of the trumpet. He is bold in his defence.'

EDMUND Sound! *[1 trumpet.*

HERALD Again! *[2 trumpet.*

HERALD Again! *[3 trumpet.*

[Trumpet answers within.

Enter Edgar, armed, preceded by a trumpet.

ALBANY Ask him his purposes, why he appears
Upon this call o' the trumpet.

HERALD What are you?

Your name? your quality? and why you answer
This present summons?

EDGAR Know, my name is lost;
By treasons tooth bare-gnawn, and canker-bit:
Yet am I noble, as the adversary
I come to cope.

ALBANY Which is that adversary?

EDGAR What's he, that speaks for Edmund Earl of Gloster?

EDMUND Himself: what say'st thou to him?

EDGAR Draw thy sword,
That, if my speech offend a noble heart,
Thy arm may do thee justice; here is mine:
Behold, it is the privilege of mine honours,
My oath, and my profession: I protest,
Maugre thy strength, youth, place, and eminence,
Despite thy victor sword, and fire-new fortune,
Thy valour, and thy heart, thou art a traitor:
False to thy gods, thy brother, and thy father;
Conspirant 'gainst this high illustrious prince;
And, from the extremest upward of thy head,
To the descent and dust below thy foot,
A most toad-spotted traitor. Say thou, 'No,'
This sword, this arm, and my best spirits, are bent
To prove upon thy heart, whereto I speak,
Thou liest.

EDMUND In wisdom, I should ask thy name;
But, since thy outside looks so fair and warlike,
And that thy tongue some say of breeding breathes,
What safe and nicely I might well delay
By rule of knighthood, I disdain and spurn.
Back do I toss these treasons to thy head;

With the hell-hated lie o'erwhelm thy heart;
Which, for they yet glance by, and scarcely bruise,
This sword of mine shall give them instant way,
Where they shall rest for ever. – Trumpets, speak.

[Alarums. They fight. Edmund falls.

ALBANY Save him! save him!

GONERIL This is practice, Gloster:
By the law of arms, thou wast not bound to answer:
An unknown opposite; thou art not vanquish'd,
But cozen'd and beguil'd.

ALBANY Shut your mouth, dame;
Or with this paper shall I stop it? – Hold, sir;
Thou worse than any name, read thine own evil: –
No tearing, lady; I perceive, you know it.

[Gives the letter to Edmund.

GONERIL Say, if I do, the laws are mine, not thine:
Who can arraign me for 't?

ALBANY Most monstrous! know'st thou this paper?

GONERIL Ask me not what I know. *[Exit.*

ALBANY Go after her: she's desperate; govern her.

[Exit an Officer.

EDMUND What you have charg'd me with, that have I done,
And more, much more; the time will bring it out:
'Tis past, and so am I. But what art thou,
That hast this fortune on me? If thou art noble,
I do forgive thee.

EDGAR Let's exchange charity.
I am no less in blood than thou art, Edmund;
If more, the more thou hast wrong'd me.
My name is Edgar, and thy father's son.
The gods are just, and of our pleasant vices

Make instruments to plague us:
The dark and vicious place where thee he got,
Cost him his eyes.

EDMUND Thou hast spoken right, 'tis true.
The wheel is come full circle: I am here.

ALBANY Methought, thy very gait did prophesy
A royal nobleness. I must embrace thee:
Let sorrow split my heart, if ever I
Did hate thee, or thy father.

EDGAR Worthy prince, I know 't.

ALBANY Where have you hid yourself?
How have you known the miseries of your father?

EDGAR By nursing them, my lord. – List a brief tale;
And when 'tis told, O, that my heart would burst! –
The bloody proclamation to escape,
That follow'd me so near, (O, our lives' sweetness!
That we the pain of death would hourly die,
Rather than die at once!) taught me to shift
Into a madman's rags, to assume a semblance
That very dogs disdain'd: and in this habit
Met I my father with his bleeding rings,
Their precious stones new lost; became his guide,
Led him, begg'd for him, sav'd him from despair;
Never (O fault!) reveal'd myself unto him,
Until some half-hour past, when I was arm'd;
Not sure, though hoping, of this good success,
I ask'd his blessing, and from first to last
Told him my pilgrimage: but his flaw'd heart, –
Alack! too weak the conflict to support! –
'Twixt two extremes of passion, joy and grief,
Burst smilingly.

EDMUND This speech of yours hath mov'd me,
And shall, perchance, do good; but speak you on:
You look as you had something more to say.

ALBANY If there be more, more woeful, hold it in;
For I am almost ready to dissolve,
Hearing of this.

EDGAR This would have seem'd a period
To such as love not sorrow; but another,
To amplify too-much, would make much more,
And top extremity.
Whilst I was big in clamour, came there a man,
Who, having seen me in my worst estate,
Shunn'd my abhorr'd society; but then, finding
Who 'twas that so endur'd, with his strong arms
He fasten'd on my neck, and bellow'd out
As he'd burst heaven; threw him on my father;
Told the most piteous tale of Lear and him,
That ever ear receiv'd; which in recounting,
His grief grew puissant, and the strings of life
Began to crack: twice then the trumpets sounded,
And there I left him tranc'd.

ALBANY But who was this?

EDGAR Kent, sir, the banish'd Kent; who in disguise
Follow'd his enemy king, and did him service
Improper for a slave.

Enter a Gentleman, with a bloody knife.

GENTLEMAN Help, help! O, help!

EDGAR What kind of help?

ALBANY Speak, man.

EDGAR What means that bloody knife?

GENTLEMAN 'Tis hot, it smokes;
It came even from the heart of – O! she's dead.

ALBANY Who dead? speak, man.

GENTLEMAN Your lady, sir, your lady: and her sister
By her is poison'd; she confesses it.

EDMUND I was contracted to them both: all three
Now marry in an instant.

EDGAR Here comes Kent.

ALBANY Produce the bodies, be they alive or dead: –
This judgment of the heavens, that makes us tremble,
Touches us not with pity. *[Exit Gentleman.*

Enter Kent.

O, is this he?
The time will not allow the compliment,
Which very manners urges.

KENT I am come
To bid my king and master aye good night;
Is he not here?

ALBANY Great thing of us forgot! –
Speak, Edmund, where's the king? and where's Cordelia? –
Seest thou this object, Kent?

[The bodies of Goneril and Regan are brought in.

KENT Alack! why thus?

EDMUND Yet Edmund was belov'd:
The one the other poison'd for my sake,
And after slew herself.

ALBANY Even so. – Cover their faces.

EDMUND I pant for life: – some good I mean to do,
Despite of mine own nature. Quickly send –
Be brief in it – to the castle; for my writ

Is on the life of Lear, and on Cordelia. –
Nay, send in time.

ALBANY Run, run! O, run!

EDGAR To who, my lord? – Who has the office? send
Thy token of reprieve.

EDMUND Well thought on: take my sword,
Give it the captain.

ALBANY Haste thee, for thy life. *[Exit Edgar.*

EDMUND He hath commission from thy wife and me
To hang Cordelia in the prison, and
To lay the blame upon her own despair,
That she fordid herself.

ALBANY The gods defend her! – Bear him hence a while.
[Edmund is borne off.

Re-enter Lear, with Cordelia dead in his arms; Edgar, Officer, and others.

LEAR Howl, howl, howl, howl! – O! you are men of stones:
Had I your tongues and eyes, I'd use them so
That heaven's vault should crack. – She's gone for ever. –
I know when one is dead, and when one lives;
She's dead as earth. – Lend me a looking-glass;
If that her breath will mist or stain the stone,
Why, then she lives.

KENT Is this the promis'd end?

EDGAR Or image of that horror?

ALBANY Fall, and cease?

LEAR This feather stirs; she lives! if it be so,
It is a chance which does redeem all sorrows
That ever I have felt.

KENT O my good master! *[Kneeling.*

LEAR Pr'ythee, away.

EDGAR 'Tis noble Kent, your friend.

LEAR A plague upon you, murderers, traitors all!
I might have sav'd her; now, she's gone for ever! –
Cordelia, Cordelia! stay a little. Ha!
What is't thou say'st? – Her voice was ever soft,
Gentle, and low, – an excellent thing in woman. –
I kill'd the slave that was a-hanging thee.

OFFICER 'Tis true, my lords, he did.

LEAR Did I not, fellow?
I have seen the day, with my good biting falchion
I would have made them skip: I am old now,
And these same crosses spoil me. – Who are you?
Mine eyes are not o' the best: – I'll tell you straight.

KENT If fortune brag of two she lov'd and hated,
One of them we behold.

LEAR This is a dull sight. – Are you not Kent?

KENT The same;
Your servant Kent. Where is your servant Calus?

LEAR He's a good fellow, I can tell you that;
He'll strike, and quickly too. – He's dead and rotten.

KENT No, my good lord; I am the very man; –

LEAR I'll see that straight.

KENT That from your first of difference and decay
Have follow'd your sad steps –

LEAR You are welcome hither.

KENT Nor no man else. – All 's cheerless, dark, and deadly:
Your eldest daughters have fordone themselves,
And desperately are dead.

LEAR Ay, so I think.

ALBANY He knows not what he says, and vain is it,
That we present us to him.

EDGAR Very bootless.

Enter an Officer.

OFFICER Edmund is dead, my lord.

ALBANY That's but a trifle here. –
You lords, and noble friends, know our intent.
What comfort to this great decay may come,
Shall be applied: for us, we will resign,
During the life of this old majesty.
To him our absolute power. – *[To Edgar and Kent]* You, to your rights,
With boot, and such addition, as your honours
Have more than merited. – All friends shall taste
The wages of their virtue, and all foes
The cup of their deservings. – O! see, see!

LEAR And my poor fool is hang'd! No, no, no life!
Why should a dog, a horse, a rat, have life,
And thou no breath at all? Thou'lt come no more,
Never, never, never, never, never! –
Pray you, undo this button: thank you, sir. –
Do you see this? Look on her, – look, – her lips, –
Look there, look there! – *[Dies.*

EDGAR He faints! – My Lord, my lord! –

KENT Break, heart; I pr'ythee, break!

EDGAR Look up, my lord.

KENT Vex not his ghost: O, let him pass! he hates him,
That would upon the rack of this tough world
Stretch him out longer.

EDGAR He is gone, indeed.

KENT The wonder is, he hath endur'd so long:
He but usurp'd his life.

ALBANY Bear them from hence. – Our present business
Is general woe. – *[To Kent and Edgar.]* Friends of my soul, you twain
Rule in this realm, and the gor'd state sustain.

KENT I have a journey, sir, shortly to go:
My master calls me; I must not say, no.

EDGAR The weight of this sad time we must obey:
Speak what we feel, not what we ought to say.
The oldest hath borne most: we, that are young.
Shall never see so much, nor live so long.

[Exeunt, with a dead march.

OTHELLO
THE MOOR OF VENICE

DRAMATIS PERSONAE

Duke of Venice
Brabantio – *a Senator*
Other Senators
Gratiano – *Brother to Brabantio*
Lodovico – *Kinsman to Brabantio*
Othello – *a noble Moor in the service of the Venetian state*
Cassio – *his Lieutenant*
Iago – *his Ancient*
Roderigo – *a Venetian Gentleman*
Montano – *Governor of Cyprus*
Clown – *Servant to Othello*
Desdemona – *Daughter to Brabantio, and Wife to Othello*
Emilia – *Wife to Iago*
Bianca – *Mistress to Cassio*
Sailor, Messengers, Herald, Officers, Gentlemen, Musicians, and Attendants

SCENE

FOR THE FIRST ACT, IN VENICE; DURING THE REST OF THE PLAY, AT A SEA-PORT IN CYPRUS

ACT ONE

SCENE I – VENICE. A STREET.

Enter Roderigo and Iago.

RODERIGO Tush! never tell me; I take it much unkindly,
That thou, Iago, who hast had my purse,
As if the strings were thine, shouldst know of this.
IAGO 'Sblood, but you will not hear me:
If ever I did dream of such a matter,
Abhor me.
RODERIGO Thou toldst me, thou didst hold him in thy hate.
IAGO Despise me, if I do not. Three great ones of the city,
In personal suit to make me his lieutenant,
Off-capp'd to him; and, by the faith of man,
I know my price: I am worth no worse a place;
But he, as loving his own pride and purposes,
Evades them, with a bombast circumstance,
Horribly stuff'd with epithets of war;
And, in conclusion,
Nonsuits my mediators; for, 'Certes,' says he,
'I have already chose my officer.'
And what was he?
Forsooth, a great arithmetician,
One Michael Cassio, a Florentine,
A fellow almost damn'd in a fair wife;
That never set a squadron in the field,

Nor the division of a battle knows
More than a spinster; unless the bookish theoric,
Wherein the tongued consults can propose
As masterly as he: mere prattle, without practice,
Is all his soldiership. But he, sir, had the election:
And I, – of whom his eyes had seen the proof
At Rhodes, at Cyprus, and on other grounds
Christen'd and heathen, – must be be-lee'd and calm'd
By debitor-and-creditor; this counter-caster,
He, in good time, must his lieutenant be,
And I (God bless the mark!) his Moorship's ancient.

RODERIGO By Heaven, I rather would have been his hangman.

IAGO But there's no remedy: 'tis the curse of service,
Preferment goes by letter, and affection,
And not by old gradation, where each second
Stood heir to the first. Now, sir, be judge yourself,
Whether I in any just term am affin'd
To love the Moor.

RODERIGO I would not follow him then.

IAGO O, sir, content you:
I follow him to serve my turn upon him:
We cannot all be masters, nor all masters
Cannot be truly follow'd. You shall mark
Many a duteous and knee-crooking knave,
That, doting on his own obsequious bondage,
Wears out his time, much like his master's ass,
For nought but provender; and when he's old, cashier'd:
Whip me such honest knaves. Others there are,
Who, trimm'd in forms and visages of duty,
Keep yet their hearts attending on themselves,
And, throwing but shows of service on their lords,

Do well thrive by them, and, when they have lin'd their coats,
Do themselves homage: these fellows have some soul;
And such a one do I profess myself.
For, sir,
It is as sure as you are Roderigo,
Were I the Moor, I would not be Iago:
In following him, I follow but myself;
Heaven is my judge, not I for love and duty,
But seeming so, for my peculiar end:
For when my outward action doth demonstate
The native act and figure of my heart
In complement extern, 'tis not long after
But I will wear my heart upon my sleeve
For daws to peck at: I am not what I am.

RODERIGO What a full fortune does the thick-lips owe,
If he can carry 't thus!

IAGO Call up her father;
Rouse him: make after him, poison his delight,
Proclaim him in the streets: incense her kinsmen,
And, though he in a fertile climate dwell,
Plague him with flies: though that his joy be joy,
Yet throw such chances of vexation on 't,
As it may lose some colour.

RODERIGO Here is her father's house: I'll call aloud.

IAGO Do; with like timorous accent, and dire yell,
As when, by night and negligence, the fire
Is spied in populous cities.

RODERIGO What, ho! Brabantio! Signior Brabantio, ho!

IAGO Awake! what, ho! Brabantio! thieves! thieves! thieves!
Look to your house, your daughter, and your bags!
Thieves! thieves!

Enter Brabantio, above, at a window.

BRABANTIO What is the reason of this terrible summons?
What is the matter there?

RODERIGO Signior, is all your family within?

IAGO Are your doors lock'd?

BRABANTIO Why? wherefore ask you this?

IAGO 'Zounds, sir! you are robb'd; for shame, put on your gown;
Your heart is burst, you have lost half your soul:
Even now, now, very now, an old black ram
Is tupping your white ewe. Arise, arise!
Awake the snorting citizens with the bell,
Or else the devil will make a grandsire of you.
Arise, I say.

BRABANTIO What! have you lost your wits?

RODERIGO Most reverend signior, do you know my voice?

BRABANTIO Not I: what are you?

RODERIGO My name is Roderigo.

BRABANTIO The worser welcome:
I have charg'd thee not to haunt about my doors.
In honest plainness thou hast heard me say,
My daughter is not for thee; and now, in madness,
Being full of supper and distempering draughts,
Upon malicious knavery dost thou come
To start my quiet.

RODERIGO Sir, sir, sir, –

BRABANTIO But thou must needs be sure,
My spirit, and my place, have in them power
To make this bitter to thee.

RODERIGO Patience, good sir.

BRABANTIO What tell'st thou me of robbing? this is Venice;
My house is not a grange.

RODERIGO Most grave Brabantio,
In simple and pure soul I come to you.

IAGO 'Zounds, sir! you are one of those that will not serve God, if the devil bid you. Because we come to do you service, and you think we are ruffians, you'll have your daughter covered with a Barbary horse; you'll have your nephews neigh to you; you'll have coursers for cousins, and gennets for germans.

BRABANTIO What profane wretch art thou?

IAGO I am one, sir, that comes to tell you, your daughter and the Moor are now making the beast with two backs.

BRABANTIO Thou art a villain.

IAGO You are – a senator.

BRABANTIO This thou shalt answer: I know thee, Roderigo.

RODERIGO Sir, I will answer anything. But I beseech you,
If't be your pleasure, and most wise consent,
(As partly, I find, it is,) that your fair daughter,
At this odd-even and dull watch o' the night,
Transported with no worse nor better guard,
But with a knave of common hire, a gondolier,
To the gross clasps of a lascivious Moor, –
If this be known to you, and your allowance,
We then have done you bold and saucy wrongs;
But if you know not this, my manners tell me,
We have your wrong rebuke. Do not believe
That, from the sense of all civility,
I thus would play and trifle with your reverence:
Your daughter, if you have not given her leave,
I say again, hath made a gross revolt;
Tying her duty, beauty, wit, and fortunes,
In an extravagant and wheeling stranger,
Of here and everywhere. Straight satisfy yourself:

If she be in her chamber, or your house,
Let loose on me the justice of the state
For thus deluding you.

BRABANTIO Strike on the tinder, ho!
Give me a taper! – call up all my people! –
This accident is not unlike my dream;
Belief of it oppresses me already.–
Light, I say! light! *[Exit from above.*

IAGO Farewell; for I must leave you:
It seems not meet, nor wholesome to my place,
To be produc'd (as, if I stay, I shall)
Against the Moor: for, I do know, the state
(However this may gall him with some check)
Cannot with safety cast him; for he's embark'd
With such loud reason to the Cyprus wars
(Which even now stands in act), that, for their souls.
Another of his fathom they have none,
To lead their business: in which regard,
Though I do hate him as I do hell-pains,
Yet, for necessity of present life,
I must show out a flag and sign of love,
Which is indeed but sign. That you shall surely find him,
Lead to the Sagittary the raised search;
And there will I be with him. So, farewell. *[Exit.*

Enter, below, Brabantio and Servants with torches.

BRABANTIO It is too true an evil: gone she is;
And what's to come of my despised time,
Is nought but bitterness. – Now, Roderigo,
Where didst thou see her? – O unhappy girl! –
With the Moor say'st thou? – Who would be a father? –

How didst thou know 'twas she? – O! she deceives me
Past thought. – What said she to you? – Get more tapers!
Raise all my kindred! – Are they married, think you?

RODERIGO Truly, I think, they are.

BRABANTIO O Heaven! – How got she out? – O, treason of the blood! –
Fathers, from hence trust not your daughters' minds
By what you see them act. – Is there not charms,
By which the property of youth and maidhood
May be abus'd? Have you not read, Roderigo,
Of some such thing?

RODERIGO Yes, sir; I have, indeed.

BRABANTIO Call up my brother. – O, would you had had her! –
Some one way, some another. – Do you know
Where we may apprehend her and the Moor?

RODERIGO I think, I can discover him, if you please
To get good guard, and go along with me.

BRABANTIO Pray you, lead on. At every house I'll call;
I may command at most. – Get weapons, ho!
And raise some special officers of might. –
On, good Roderigo; – I'll deserve your pains. *Exeunt.*

SCENE II – THE SAME. ANOTHER STREET.

Enter Othello, Iago, and Attendants, with torches.

IAGO Though in the trade of war I have slain men,
Yet do I hold it very stuff' o' the conscience,
To do no contriv'd murder: I lack iniquity
Sometimes, to do me service. Nine or ten times
I had thought to have yerk'd him here, under the ribs.

OTHELLO 'Tis better as it is.

IAGO Nay, but he prated,
And spoke such scurvy and provoking terms
Against your honour,
That, with the little godliness I have,
I did full hard forbear him. But, I pray you, sir,
Are you fast married? Be assur'd of this,
That the magnifico is much beloved;
And hath, in his effect, a voice potential
As double as the duke's: he will divorce you;
Or put upon you what restraint, or grievance,
The law (with all his might to enforce it on)
Will give him cable.

OTHELLO Let him do his spite:
My services, which I have done the signiory,
Shall out-tongue his complaints. 'Tis yet to know,
(Which, when I know that boasting is an honour,
I shall promulgate,) I fetch my life and being
From men of royal siege; and my demerits
May speak, unbonneted, to as proud a fortune
As this that I have reach'd: for know, Iago,
But that I love the gentle Desdemona,
I would not my unhoused free condition
Put into circumscription and confine
For the sea's worth. But, look! what lights come yond?

IAGO Those are the raised father, and his friends:
You were best go in.

OTHELLO Not I; I must be found:
My parts, my title, and my perfect soul,
Shall manifest me rightly. Is it they?

IAGO By Janus, I think no.

Enter Cassio and certain Officers with torches.

OTHELLO The servants of the duke, and my liuetenant.
The goodness of the night upon you, friends!
What is the news?

CASSIO The duke does greet you, general;
And he requires your haste-post-haste appearance,
Even on the instant.

OTHELLO What is the matter, think you?

CASSIO Something from Cyprus, as I may divine.
It is a business of some heat: the galleys
Have sent a dozen sequent mesengers
This very night at one another's heels;
And many of the consuls, rais'd and met,
Are at the duke's already. You have been hotly call'd for;
When, being not at your lodging to be found,
The senate hath sent about three several quests,
To search you out.

OTHELLO 'Tis well I am found by you.
I will but spend a word here in the house,
And go with you. *[Exit.*

CASSIO Ancient, what makes he here?

IAGO 'Faith, he to-night hath boarded a land-carack:
If it prove lawful prize, he's made for ever.

CASSIO I do not understand.

IAGO He's married.

CASSIO To who?

Re-enter Othello.

IAGO Marry, to – Come, captain, will you go?

OTHELLO Have with you.

CASSIO Here comes another troop to seek for you.

IAGO It is Brabantio. – General, be advis'd:
He comes to bad intent.

Enter Brabantio, Roderigo, and Officers, with torches and weapons.

OTHELLO Holla! stand there!
RODERIGO Signior, it is the Moor.
BRABANTIO Down with him, thief!

[They draw on both sides.

IAGO You, Roderigo! come, sir, I am for you.
OTHELLO Keep up your bright swords, for the dew will rust them –
Good signior, you shall more command with years,
Than with your weapons.
BRABANTIO O thou foul thief! where hast thou stow'd my daughter? –
Damn'd as thou art, thou hast enchanted her;
For I'll refer me to all things of sense,
If she in chains of magic were not bound,
Whether a maid so tender, fair, and happy,
So opposite to marriage, that she shunn'd
The wealthy curled darlings of our nation,
Would ever have, to incur a general mock,
Run from her guardage to the sooty bosom
Of such a thing as thou; to fear, not to delight.
Judge me the world, if 'tis not gross in sense,
That thou hast practis'd on her with foul charms;
Abus'd her delicate youth with drugs, or minerals,
That weaken motion. – I'll have't disputed on;
'Tis probable, and palpable to thinking.
I therefore apprehend and do attach thee,
For an abuser of the world, a practiser

Of arts inhibited and out of warrant. –
Lay hold upon him! if he do resist,
Subdue him at his peril.

OTHELLO Hold your hands,
Both you of my inclining, and the rest:
Were it my cue to fight, I should have known it
Without a prompter. – Where will you that I go
To answer this your charge?

BRABANTIO To prison; till fit time
Of law, and course of direct session,
Call thee to answer.

OTHELLO What if I do obey?
How may the duke be therewith satisfied,
Whose messengers are here about my side,
Upon some present business of the state,
To bring me to him?

OFFICER 'Tis is true, most worthy signior:
The duke's in council, and your noble self,
I am sure, is sent for.

BRABANTIO How! the duke in council!
In this time of the night! – Bring him away.
Mine's not an idle cause: the duke himself,
Or any of my brothers of the state,
Cannot but feel this wrong as 'twere their own;
For if such actions may have passage free,
Bond-slaves and pagans shall our statesmen be. *[Exeunt.*

SCENE III – THE SAME. A COUNCIL CHAMBER.

The Duke, and Senators, sitting at a table; Officers attending.

DUKE There is no composition in these news,
That gives them credit.
1 SENATOR Indeed, they are disproportion'd:
My letters say, a hundred and seven galleys.
DUKE And mine, a hundred and forty.
2 SENATOR And mine, two hundred:
But though they jump not on a just account,
(As in these cases, where the aim reports,
'Tis oft with difference), yet do they all confirm
A Turkish fleet, and bearing up to Cyprus.
DUKE Nay, it is possible enough to judgment.
I do not so secure me in the error,
But the main article I do approve
In fearful sense.
SAILOR *[Within]* What, ho! what, ho! what, ho!
OFFICER A messenger from the galleys.

Enter a Sailor.

DUKE Now, what's the business?
SAILOR The Turkish preparation makes for Rhodes:
So was I bid report here to the state,
By Signior Angelo.
DUKE How say you by this change?
1 SENATOR This cannot be,
By no assay of reason: 'tis a pageant,
To keep us in false gaze. When we consider
The importancy of Cyprus to the Turk;

And let ourselves again but understand,
That, as it more concerns the Turk than Rhodes,
So may he with more facile question bear it
For that it stands not in such warlike brace,
But altogether lacks the abilities
That Rhodes is dress'd in: – if we make thought of this,
We must not think the Turk is so unskilful,
To leave that latest which concerns him first,
Neglecting an attempt of ease and gain,
To wake and wage a danger profitless.

DUKE Nay, in all confidence, he's not for Rhodes.

1 OFFICER Here is more news.

Enter a Messenger.

MESSENGER The Ottomites, reverend and gracious,
Steering with due course toward the isle of Rhodes,
Have there injointed them with an after fleet.

1 SENATOR Ay, so I thought. – How many, as you guess?

MESSENGER Of thirty sail; and now do they re-stem
Their backward course, bearing with frank appearance
Their purposes toward Cyprus. – Signior Montano,
Your trusty and most valiant servitor,
With his free duty, recommends you thus,
And prays you to believe him.

DUKE 'Tis certain then for Cyprus. –
Marcus Luccicos, is not he in town?

1 SENATOR He's now in Florence.

DUKE Write from us to him: post-post-haste despatch.

1 SENATOR Here comes Brabantio, and the valiant Moor.

Enter Brabantio, Othello, Iago, Roderigo, and Officers.

DUKE Valiant Othello, we must straight employ you
Against the general enemy Ottoman. –
[To Brabantio] I did not see you; welcome, gentle signior;
We lack'd your counsel and your help to-night.

BRABANTIO So did I yours. Good your grace, pardon me;
Neither my place, nor aught I heard of business,
Hath rais'd me from my bed; nor doth the general care
Take hold on me, for my particular grief
Is of so flood-gate and o'erbearing nature,
That it engluts and swallows other sorrows,
And it is still itself.

DUKE Why, what's the matter?

BRABANTIO My daughter! O, my daughter!

SENATOR Dead?

BRABANTIO Ay, to me:
She is abus'd, stol'n from me, and corrupted
By spells and medicines bought of mountebanks;
For nature so preposterously to err,
Being not deficient, blind, or lame of sense,
Sans witchcraft could not.

DUKE Whoe'er he be, that in this foul proceeding
Hath thus beguil'd your daughter of herself,
And you of her, the bloody book of law
You shall yourself read in the bitter letter,
After your own sense; yea, though our proper son
Stood in your action.

BRABANTIO Humbly I thank your grace.
Here is the man, this Moor; whom now, it seems,
Your special mandate, for the state affairs,
Hath hither brought.

DUKE AND SENATOR We are very sorry for it.
DUKE *[To Othello]* What, in your own part, can you say to this?
BRABANTIO Nothing, but this is so.
OTHELLO Most potent, grave, and reverend signiors,
My very noble and approv'd good masters,
That I have ta'en away this old man's daughter,
It is most true; true, I have married her:
The very head and front of my offending
Hath this extent, no more. Rude am I in my speech,
And little bless'd with the soft phrase of peace;
For since these arms of mine had seven years' pith,
Till now, some nine moons wasted, they have us'd
Their dearest action in the tented field;
And little of this great world can I speak,
More than pertains to feats of broil and battle;
And, therefore, little shall I grace my cause,
In speaking for myself. Yet, by your gracious patience,
I will a round unvarnish'd tale deliver
Of my whole course of love; what drugs, what charms,
What conjunction, and what mighty magic,
(For such proceeding I am charg'd withal,)
I won his daughter.
BRABANTIO A maiden never bold;
Of spirit so still and quiet, that her motion
Blush'd at herself; and she – in spite of nature,
Of years, of country, credit, everything –
To fall in love with what she fear'd to look on!
It is a judgment maim'd, and most imperfect,
That will confess, perfection so could err
Against all rules of nature; and must be driven
To find out practices of cunning hell,

Why this should be. I, therefore, vouch again,
That with some mixtures powerful o'er the blood,
Or with some dram conjur'd to this effect,
He wrought upon her.

DUKE To vouch this, is no proof:
Without more wider and more overt test,
Than these thin habits, and poor likelihoods
Of modern seeming, do prefer against him.

1 SENATOR But, Othello, speak:
Did you by indirect and forced courses
Subdue and poison this young maid's affections;
Or came it by request, and such fair question
As soul to soul affordeth?

OTHELLO I do beseech you,
Send for the lady to the Sagittary,
And let her speak of me before her father:
If you do find me foul in her report,
The trust, the office, I do hold of you,
Not only take away, but let your sentence
Even fall upon my life.

DUKE Fetch Desdemona hither.

OTHELLO Ancient, conduct them; you best know the place. –
[Exeunt Iago and Attendants
And, till she come, as truly as to Heaven
I do confess the vices of my blood,
So justly to your grave ears I'll present
How I did thrive in this fair lady's love,
And she in mine.

DUKE Say it, Othello.

OTHELLO Her father lov'd me; oft invited me;
Still question'd me the story of my life,

From year to year; the battles, sieges, fortunes,
That I have pass'd.
I ran it through, even from my boyish days,
To the very moment that he bade me tell it:
Wherein I spake of most disastrous chances,
Of moving accidents by flood and field;
Of hair-breadth scapes i' the imminent-deadly breach;
Of being taken by the insolent foe,
And sold to slavery; of my redemption thence,
And portance in my traveller's history;
Wherein of antres vast, and deserts idle,
Rough quarries, rocks, and hills whose heads touch heaven,
It was my hint to speak, – such was the process; –
And of the Cannibals that each other eat,
The Anthropophagi, and men whose heads
Do grow beneath their shoulders. This to hear,
Would Desdemona seriously incline:
But still the house-affairs would draw her hence;
Which ever as she could with haste despatch,
She'd come again, and with a greedy ear
Devour up my discourse. Which I observing,
Took once a pliant hour; and found good means
To draw from her a prayer of earnest heart,
That I would all my pilgrimage dilate,
Whereof by parcels she had something heard,
But not intentively; I did consent;
And often did beguile her of her tears,
When I did speak of some distressful stroke,
That my youth suffer'd. My story being done,
She gave me for my pains a world of sighs:
She swore, – in faith, 'twas strange, 'twas passing strange;

'Twas pitiful, 'twas wondrous pitiful;
She wish'd she had not heard it; yet she wish'd
That Heaven had made her such a man: she thank'd me;
And bade me, if I had a friend that lov'd her,
I should but teach him how to tell my story,
And that would woo her. Upon this hint I spake
She lov'd me for the dangers I had pass'd,
And I lov'd her, that she did pity them.
This only is the witchcraft I have us'd:
Here comes the lady; let her witness it.

Enter Desdemona, Iago, and Attendants.

DUKE I think, this tale would win my daughter too.
Good Brabantio,
Take up this mangled matter at the best:
Men do their broken weapons rather use,
Than their bare hands.

BRABANTIO I pray you, hear her speak;
If she confess that she was half the wooer,
Destruction on my head, if my bad blame
Light on the man! – Come hither, gentle mistress:
Do you perceive in all this noble company,
Where most you owe obedience?

DESDEMONA My noble father,
I do perceive here a divided duty:
To you I am bound for life and education;
My life and education, both do learn me
How to respect you; you are the lord of duty;
I am hitherto your daughter; but here's my husband;
And so much duty as my mother show'd
To you, preferring you before her father,

So much I challenge that I may profess
Due to the Moor, my lord.

BRABANTIO God be with you! – I have done. –
Please it your grace, on to the state affairs:
I had rather to adopt a child than get it. –
Come hither, Moor:
I here do give thee that with all my heart,
Which, but thou hast already, with all my heart
I would keep from thee. – For your sake, jewel,
I am glad at soul I have no other child;
For thy escape would teach me tyranny,
To hang clogs on them. – I have done, my lord.

DUKE Let me speak like yourself, and lay a sentence,
Which, as a grise, or step, may help these lovers
Into your favour.
When remedies are past, the griefs are ended
By seeing the worst, which late on hopes depended.
To mourn a mischief that is past and gone
Is the next way to draw new mischief on.
What cannot be preserv'd when fortune takes,
Patience her injury a mockery makes.
The robb'd, that smiles, steals something from the thief:
He robs himself, that spends a bootless grief.

BRABANTIO So let the Turk of Cyprus us beguile:
We lose it not, so long as we can smile.
He bears the sentence well, that nothing bears
But the free comfort which from thence he hears;
But he bears both the sentence and the sorrow,
That, to pay grief, must of poor patience borrow.
These sentences, to sugar, or to gall,
Being strong on both sides, are equivocal:

But words are words; I never yet did hear,
That the bruis'd heart was pierced through the ear.
I humbly beseech you, proceed to the affairs of state.

DUKE The Turk with a most mighty preparation makes for Cyprus. – Othello, the fortitude of the place is best known to you; and though we have there a substitute of most allowed sufficiency, yet opinion, a sovereign mistress of effects, throws a more safer voice on you: you must, therefore, be content to slubber the gloss of your new fortunes with this more stubborn and boisterous expedition.

OTHELLO The tyrant custom, most grave senators,
Hath made the flinty and steel couch of war
My thrice-driven bed of down: I do agnise
A natural and prompt alacrity,
I find in hardness; and do undertake
These present wars against the Ottomites.
Most humbly, therefore, bending to your state,
I crave fit disposition for my wife;
Due reference of place, and exhibition;
With such accommodation, and besort,
As levels with her breeding.

DUKE Why; at her father's.

BRABANTIO I'll not have it so.

OTHELLO Nor I.

DESDEMONA Nor I; I would not there reside,
To put my father in impatient thoughts,
By being in his eye. Most gracious duke,
To my unfolding lend your prosperous ear;
And let me find a charter in your voice,
To assist my simpleness.

DUKE What would you, Desdemona?

DESDEMONA That I did love the Moor to live with him,
My downright violence and storm of fortunes
May trumpet to the world: my heart's subdued
Even to the very quality of my lord:
I saw Othello's visage in his mind;
And to his honours, and his valiant parts,
Did I my soul and fortunes consecrate.
So that, dear lords, if I be left behind,
A moth of peace, and he go to the war,
The rites for why I love him are bereft me,
And I a heavy interim shall support
By his dear absence. Let me go with him.

OTHELLO Let her have your voice.
Vouch with me, Heaven, I therefore beg it not,
To please the palate of my appetite;
Nor to comply with heat, the young affects,
In my defunct and proper satisfaction;
But to be free and bounteous to her mind:
And Heaven defend your good souls, that you think
I will your serious and great business scant,
For she is with me. No, when light-wing'd toys
Of feather'd Cupid seel with wanton dulness
My speculative and offic'd instrument,
That my disports corrupt and taint my business,
Let housewives make a skillet of my helm,
And all indign and base adversities
Make head against my estimation.

DUKE Be it as you shall privately determine,
Either for her stay, or going. The affair cries haste,
And speed must answer it.

1 SENATOR You must away to-night.

OTHELLO With all my heart.
DUKE At nine i' the morning here we'll meet again.
Othello, leave some officer behind,
And he shall our commission bring to you;
With such things else of quality and respect,
As doth import you.
OTHELLO So please your grace, my ancient;
A man he is of honesty, and trust:
To his conveyance I assign my wife,
With what else needful your good grace shall think
To be sent after me.
DUKE Let it be so. –
Good night to every one. – *[To Brabantio]* And, noble signior,
If virtue no delighted beauty lack,
Your son-in-law is far more fair than black.
1 SENATOR Adieu, brave Moor! use Desdemona well.
BRABANTIO Look to her, Moor, if thou hast eyes to see:
She has deceiv'd her father, and may thee.
[Exeunt Duke, Senators, Officers, &c.
OTHELLO My life upon her faith! – Honest Iago,
My Desdemona must I leave to thee:
I pr'ythee, let thy wife attend on her;
And bring them after in the best advantage.
Come, Desdemona; I have but an hour
Of love, of worldly matters and direction,
To spend with thee: we must obey the time.
[Exeunt Othello and Desdemona.
RODERIGO Iago!
IAGO What say'st thou, noble heart?
RODERIGO What will I do, think'st thou?
IAGO Why, go to bed, and sleep.

RODERIGO I will incontinently drown myself.

IAGO Well, if thou dost, I shall never love thee after it. Why thou silly gentleman!

RODERIGO It is silliness to live, when to live is a torment; and then have we a prescription to die, when death is our physician.

IAGO O, villainous! I have looked upon the world for four times seven years, and since I could distinguish betwixt a benefit and an injury, I never found a man that knew how to love himself. Ere I would say, I would drown myself for the love of a Guinea-hen, I would change my humanity with a baboon.

RODERIGO What should I do? I confess, it is my shame to be so fond; but it is not in my virtue to amend it.

IAGO Virtue? a fig! 'tis in ourselves that we are thus, or thus. Our bodies are our gardens, to the which our wills are gardeners: so that if we will plant nettles, or sow lettuce; set hyssop, and weed up thyme; supply it with one gender of herbs, or distract it with many; either to have it steril with idleness, or manured with industry; why, the power and corrigible authority of this lies in our wills. If the balance of our lives had not one scale of reason to poise another of sensuality, the blood and baseness of our natures would conduct us to most preposterous conclusions: but we have reason to cool our raging motions, our carnal stings, our unbitted lusts; whereof I take this, that you call love, to be a sect, or scion.

RODERIGO It cannot be.

IAGO It is merely a lust of the blood, and a permission of the will. Come, be a man: drown thyself? drown cats, and blind puppies. I have profess'd me thy friend, and I confess me knit to thy deserving with cables of perdurable toughness: I could never better stead thee than now. Put money in thy purse;

follow these wars; defeat thy favour with an usurped beard; I say, put money in thy purse. It cannot be, that Desdemona should long continue her love to the Moor, – put money in thy purse, – nor he his to her: it was a violent commencement in her, and thou shalt see an answerable sequestration; – put but money in thy purse. – These Moors are changeable in their wills; – fill thy purse with money: – the food that to him now is as luscious as locusts, shall be to him shortly as bitter as coloquintida. She must change for youth: when she is sated with his body, she will find the error of her choice. – She must have change, she must: therefore, put money in thy purse. – If thou wilt needs damn thyself, do it a more delicate way than drowning. Make all the money thou canst. If sanctimony and a frail vow, betwixt an erring barbarian and a super-subtle Venetian, be not too hard for my wits, and all the tribe of hell, thou shalt enjoy her; therefore, make money. A pox of drowning thyself! it is clean out of the way: seek thou rather to be hanged in compassing thy joy, than to be drowned and go without her.

RODERIGO Wilt thou be fast to my hopes, if I depend on the issue?

IAGO Thou art sure of me. – Go, make money. – I have told thee often, and I re-tell thee again and again, I hate the Moor; my cause is hearted; thine hath no less reason. Let us be conjunctive in our revenge against him: if thou canst cuckold him, thou dost thyself a pleasure, me a sport. There are many events in the womb of time, which will be delivered. Traverse; go: provide thy money. We will have more of this to-morrow. Adieu.

RODERIGO Where shalll we meet i' the morning?

IAGO At my lodging.

RODERIGO I'll be with thee betimes.

IAGO Go to; farewell. Do you hear, Roderigo?

RODERIGO What say you?

IAGO No more of drowning, do you hear?

RODERIGO I am changed. I'll sell all my land.

IAGO Go to; farewell! put money enough in your purse.

[Exit Roderigo.

Thus do I ever make my fool my purse;
For I mine own gain'd knowledge should profane,
If I would time expend with such a snipe
But for my sport and profit. I hate the Moor;
And it is thought abroad, that 'twixt my sheets
He has done my office: I know not if 't be true;
Yet I, for mere suspicion in that kind,
Will do as if for surety. He holds me well;
The better shall my purpose work on him.
Cassio's a proper man: let me see now;
To get his place, and to plume up my will,
In double knavery, – How, how? – Let's see:–
After some time, to abuse Othello's ear,
That he is too familiar with his wife:
He hath a person, and a smooth dispose,
To be suspected; fram'd to make women false.
The Moor is of a free and open nature,
That thinks men honest, that but seem to be so,
And will as tenderly be led by the nose,
As asses are. –
I have 't; – it is engender'd: – hell and night
Must bring this monstrous birth to the world's light. *[Exit.*

~ ACT TWO ~

SCENE 1 – A SEA-PORT TOWN IN CYPRUS. A PLATFORM.

Enter Montano and two Gentlemen.

MONTANO What from the cape can you discern at sea?
1 GENTLEMAN Nothing at all: it is a highwrought flood:
I cannot, 'twixt the heaven and the main,
Descry a sail.
MONTANO Methinks, the wind hath spoke aloud at land;
A fuller blast ne'er shook our battlements;
If it hath ruffian'd so upon the sea,
What ribs of oak, when mountains melt on them,
Can hold the mortise? What shall we hear of this?
2 GENTLEMAN A segregation of the Turkish fleet:
For do but stand upon the foaming shore,
The chidden billow seems to pelt the clouds;
The wind-shak'd surge, with high and monstrous mane,
Seems to cast water on the burning bear,
And quench the guards of the ever-fixed pole:
I never did like molestation view
On the enchafed flood.
MONTANO If that the Turkish fleet
Be not enshelter'd and embay'd, they are drown'd;
It is impossible to bear it out.

Enter a third Gentleman.

3 GENTLEMAN News, lads! our wars are done.
The desperate tempest hath so bang'd the Turks,
That their designment halts: a noble ship of Venice.
Hath seen a grievous wrack and sufferance.
On most part of their fleet.

MONTANO How! is this true?

3 GENTLEMAN The ship is here put in,
A Veronessa; Michael Cassio,
Lieutenant to the warlike Moor, Othello,
Is come on shore: the Moor himself at sea,
And is in full commission here for Cyprus.

MONTANO I am glad on 't; 'tis a worthy governor.

3 GENTLEMAN But this same Cassio, though he speak of comfort,
Touching the Turkish loss, yet he looks sadly,
And prays the Moor be safe; for they were parted
With foul and violent tempest.

MONTANO 'Pray heavens he be;
For I have serv'd him, and the man commands
Like a full soldier. Let's to the sea-side, ho!
As well to see the vessel that's come in,
As to throw out our eyes for brave Othello,
Even till we make the main, and the aerial blue,
An indistinct regard.

3 GENTLEMAN Come, let's do so;
For every minute is expectancy
Of more arrivance.

Enter Cassio.

CASSIO Thanks, you the valiant of this warlike isle,

That so approve the Moor. – O! let the heavens
Give him defence against the elements,
For I have lost him on a dangerous sea.

MONTANO Is he well shipp'd?

CASSIO His bark is stoutly timber'd, and his pilot
Of very expert and approv'd allowance;
Therefore my hopes, not surfeited to death,
Stand in bold cure.

[Within] A sail, a sail, a sail!

Enter a Messenger.

CASSIO What noise?

MESSENGER The town is empty; on the brow o' the sea
Stand ranks of people, and they cry, 'A sail!'

CASSIO My hopes do shape him for the governor. *[Guns heard.*

2 GENTLEMAN They do discharge their shot of courtesy;
Our friends, at least.

CASSIO I pray you, sir, go forth,
And give us truth who 'tis that is arriv'd.

2 GENTLEMAN I shall. *[Exit.*

MONTANO But, good lieutenant, is your general wiv'd?

CASSIO Most fortunately: he hath achiev'd a maid
That paragons description and wild fame;
One that excels the quirks of blazoning pens,
And, in the essential vesture of creation,
Does tire the ingener.

Re-enter second Gentleman.

How now! who has put in?

2 GENTLEMAN 'Tis one Iago, ancient to the general.

CASSIO He has had most favourable and happy speed:
Tempests themselves, high seas, and howling winds,

The gutter'd rocks, and congregated sands,
Traitors ensteep'd to enclog the guiltless keel,
As having sense of beauty, do omit
Their mortal natures, letting go safely by
The divine Desdemona.

MONTANO What is she?

CASSIO She that I spake of, our great captain's captain,
Left in the conduct of the bold Iago;
Whose footing here anticipates our thoughts
A se'nnight's speed. – Great Jove! Othello guard,
And swell his sail with thine own powerful breath,
That he may bless this bay with his tall ship,
Make love's quick pants in Desdemona's arms,
Give renew'd fire to our extincted spirits,
And bring all Cyprus comfort!–

Enter Desdemona, Emilia, Iago, Roderigo, and Attendants.

O, behold,
The riches of the ship is come on shore!
Ye men of Cyrpus let her have your knees. –
Hail to thee, lady! and the grace of Heaven,
Before, behind thee, and on every hand,
Enwheel thee round!

DESDEMONA I thank you, valiant Cassio.
What tidings can you tell me of my lord?

CASSIO He is not yet arriv'd: nor know I aught
But that he's well, and will be shortly here.

DESDEMONA O! but I fear – How lost you company?

CASSIO The great contention of the sea and skies
Parted our fellowship. But, hark! a sail.

[Within] A sail, a sail! *[Guns heard.*

2 GENTLEMAN They give their greeting to the citadel:
This likewise is a friend.

CASSIO See for the news!–

[Exit Gentleman.

Good ancient, you are welcome – *[To Emilia]* Welcome, mistress. –
Let it not gall your patience, good Iago,
That I extend my manners: 'tis my breeding
That gives me this bold show of courtesy. *[Kissing her.*

IAGO Sir, would she give you so much of her lips,
As of her tongue she oft bestows on me,
You'd have enough.

DESDEMONA Alas! she has no speech.

IAGO In faith, too much;
I find it still, when I have list to sleep:
Marry, before your ladyship, I grant,
She puts her tongue a little in her heart,
And chides with thinking.

EMILIA You have little cause to say so.

IAGO Come on, come on; you are pictures out of doors,
Bells in your parlours, wild cats in your kitchens,
Saints in your injuries, devils being offended,
Players in your housewifery, and housewives in your beds.

DESDEMONA O, fie upon thee, slanderer!

IAGO Nay, it is true, or else I am a Turk:
You rise to play, and go to bed to work.

EMILIA You shall not write my praise.

IAGO No, let me not.

DESDEMONA What wouldst thou write of me, if thou shouldst praise me?

IAGO O gentle lady, do not put me to 't;

For I am nothing, if not critical.

DESDEMONA Come on; assay. – There's one gone to the harbour?

IAGO Ay, madman.

DESDEMONA I am not merry; but I do beguile
The thing I am, by seeming otherwise. –
Come, how wouldst thou praise me?

IAGO I am about it; but, indeed, my invention
Comes from my pate, as birdlime does from frize;
It plucks out brains and all: but my Muse labours,
And thus she is deliver'd,
If she be fair and wise, – fairness, and wit,
The one's for use, the other useth it.

DESDEMONA Well prais'd! How, if she be black and witty?

IAGO If she be black, and thereto have a wit,
She'll find a white that shall her blackness fit.

DESDEMONA Worse and worse.

EMILIA How, if fair and foolish?

IAGO She never yet was foolish that was fair;
For even her folly help'd her to an heir.

DESDEMONA These are old fond paradoxes, to make fools laugh i' the ale-house. What miserable praise hast thou for her that's foul and foolish?

IAGO There's none so foul, and foolish thereunto,
But does foul pranks which fair and wise ones do.

DESDEMONA O heavy ignorance! thou praisest the worst best. But what praise couldst thou bestow on a deserving woman indeed? one, that, in the authority of her merit, did justly put on the vouch of very malice itself?

IAGO She that was ever fair, and never proud;
Had tongue at will, and yet was never loud;

Never lack'd gold, and yet went never gay;
Fled from her wish, and yet said, 'Now I may;'
She that, being anger'd, her revenge being nigh,
Bade her wrong stay, and her displeasure fly;
She that in wisdom never was so frail,
To change the cod's head for the salmon's tail;
She that could think, and ne'er disclose her mind,
See suitors following, and not look behind:
She was a wight, – if ever such wights were, –

DESDEMONA To do what?

IAGO To suckle fools, and chronicle small beer.

DESDEMONA O most lame and impotent conclusion! – Do not learn of him, Emilia, though he be thy husband. – How say you, Cassio? is he not a most profane and liberal counsellor?

CASSIO He speaks home, madam: you may relish him more in the soldier, than in the scholar.

IAGO *[Aside]* He takes her by the palm: ay, well said, whisper: with as little a web as this will I ensnare as great a fly as Cassio. Ay, smile upon her, do; I will gyve thee in thine own courtship. You say true, 'tis so, indeed. If such tricks as these strip you out of your lieutenantry, it had been better you had not kissed your three fingers so oft, which now again you are most apt to play the sir in. Very good; well kissed, an excellent courtesy! 'tis so, indeed. Yet again your fingers to your lips? would, they were clyster-pipes for your sake! – *[A trumpet heard]* The Moor! I know his trumpet.

CASSIO 'Tis is truly so.

DESDEMONA Let's meet him, and receive him.

CASSIO Lo, where he comes!

Enter Othello and Attendants.

OTHELLO O my fair warrior!
DESDEMONA My dear Othello!
OTHELLO It gives me wonder great as my content,
To see you here before me. O my soul's joy!
If after every tempest comes such calms,
May the winds blow till they have waken'd death;
And let the labouring bark climb hills of seas,
Olympus-high, and duck again as low
As hell 's from heaven! If it were now to die,
'Twere now to be most happy; for, I fear,
My soul hath her content so absolute,
That not another comfort like to this
Succeeds in unknown fate.
DESDEMONA The heavens forbid,
But that our loves and comforts should increase,
Even as our days do grow!
OTHELLO Amen to that, sweet powers!
I cannot speak enough of this content;
It stops me here; it is too much of joy:
And this, and this, the greatest discords be, *[Kissing her*
That e'er our hearts shall make!
IAGO *[Aside]* O! you are well tun'd now;
But I'll set down the pegs that make this music,
As honest as I am.
OTHELLO Come, let us to the castle. –
News, friends: our wars are done, the Turks are drown'd.
How does my old acquaintance of this isle?
Honey, you shall be well-desir'd in Cyprus;
I have found great love amongst them. O my sweet,
I prattle out of fashion, and I dote

In mine own comforts. – I pr'ythee, good Iago,
Go to the bay, and disembark my coffers.
Bring thou the master to the citadel;
He is a good one, and his worthiness
Does challenge much respect. – Come, Desdemona,
Once more well met at Cyprus.

[Exeunt Othello, Desdemona, and Attendants.

IAGO Do thou meet me presently at the harbour. – Come hither. If thou be'st valiant, – as they say, base men being in love have then a nobility in their natures more than is native to them, – list me. The lieutenant to-night watches on the court of guard. – First, I must tell thee this, – Desdemona is directly in love with him.

RODERIGO With him! why, 'tis not possible.

IAGO Lay thy finger thus, and let thy soul be instructed. Mark me with what violence she first loved the Moor, but for bragging, and telling her fantastical lies; and will she love him still for prating? let not thy discreet heart think it. Her eye must be fed; and what delight shall she have to look on the devil? When the blood is made dull with the act of sport, there should be, again to inflame it, and to give satiety a fresh appetite, loveliness in favour, sympathy in years, manners, and beauties; all which the Moor is defective in. Now, for want of these required conveniences, her delicate tenderness will find itself abused, begin to heave the gorge, disrelish and abhor the Moor; very nature will instruct her in it, and compel her to some second choice. Now, sir, this granted (as it is a most pregnant and unforced position), who stands so eminent in the degree of this fortune, as Cassio does? a knave very voluble, no further conscionable than in putting on the mere form of civil and humane seeming, for the better compassing of his salt and most hidden-loose affection? why, none; why, none: a slipper and subtle knave; a finder-out of occasions; that has an eye can stamp and counterfeit advantages, though true advantage never present itself: a devilish knave! Besides, the knave is handsome, young, and hath all those requisites in him, that folly and green minds look after; a pestilent complete knave: and the woman hath found him already.

RODERIGO I cannot believe that in her: she is full of most blessed condition.

IAGO Blessed fig's end! the wine she drinks is made of grapes: if she had been blessed, she would never have loved the Moor: bless'd pudding! Didst thou not see her paddle with the palm of his hand? didst not mark that?

RODERIGO Yes, that I did; but that was but courtesy.

IAGO Lechery, by this hand! an index, and obscure prologue to the history of lust and foul thoughts. They met so near with their lips, that their breaths embraced together. Villainous thoughts, Roderigo! when these mutualities so marshal the way, hard at hand comes the master and main exercise, the incorporate conclusion. Pish! – But, sir, be you ruled by me: I have brought you from Venice. Watch you to-night; for the command, I'll lay 't upon you: Cassio knows you not: – I'll not be far from you: do you find some occasion to anger Cassio, either by speaking too loud, or tainting his discipline; or from what other course you please, which the time shall more favourably minister.

RODERIGO Well.

IAGO Sir, he is rash, and very sudden in choler, and, haply, may strike at you: provoke him, that he may; for even out of that will I cause these of Cyprus to mutiny, whose qualification shall come into no true taste again, but by the displanting of

Cassio. So shall you have a shorter journey to your desires, by the means I shall then have to prefer them; and the impediment most profitably removed, without the which there were no expectation of our prosperity.

RODERIGO I will do this, if you can bring it to any opportunity.

IAGO I warrant thee. Meet me by-and-by at the citadel: I must fetch his necessaries ashore. Farewell.

RODERIGO Adieu. *[Exit.*

IAGO That Cassio loves her, I do well believe it;
That she loves him, 'tis apt, and of great credit:
The Moor – howbeit that I endure him not –
Is of a constant, loving, noble nature;
And, I dare think, he'll prove to Desdemona
A most dear husband. Now, I do love her too;
Not out of absolute lust, (though, peradventure,
I stand accountant for as great a sin,)
But partly led to diet my revenge,
For that I do suspect the lusty Moor
Hath leap'd into my seat; the thought whereof
Doth like a poisonous mineral gnaw my inwards;
And nothing can, or shall, content my soul,
Till I am even'd with him, wife for wife;
Or, failing so, yet that I put the Moor
At least into a jealousy so strong
That judgment cannot cure. Which thing to do, –
If this poor trash of Venice, whom I trash
For his quick hunting, stand the putting-on, –
I 'll have our Michael Cassio on the hip;
Abuse him to the Moor in the rank garb; –
For I fear Cassio with my night-cap too; –
Make the Moor thank me, love me, and reward me,

For making him egregiously an ass,
And practising upon his peace and quiet,
Even to madness. 'Tis here, but yet confus'd:
Knavery's plain face is never seen, till us'd. *[Exit.*

SCENE II – A STREET.

Enter a Herald, with a proclamation; people following.

HERALD It is Othello's pleasure, our noble and valiant general, that, upon certain tidings now arrived, importing the mere perdition of the Turkish fleet, every man put himself into triumph; some to dance, some to make bonfires, each man to what sport and revels his addiction leads him; for, besides these beneficial news, it is the celebration of his nuptial. So much was his pleasure should be proclaimed. All offices are open; and there is full liberty of feasting, from this present hour of five, till the bell have told eleven. Heaven bless the isle of Cyprus, and our noble general, Othello! *[Exeunt.*

SCENE III – A HALL IN THE CASTLE.

Enter Othello, Desdemona, Cassio, and Attendants.

OTHELLO Good Michael, look you to the guard to-night:
Let's teach ourselves that honourable stop,
Not to out-sport discretion.
CASSIO Iago hath direction what to do;
But, notwithstanding, with my personal eye
Will I look to 't.

OTHELLO Iago is most honest.
Michael, good night: to-morrow, with your earliest,
Let me have speech with you. – *[To Desdemona]* Come, my dear love:
The purchase made, the fruits are to ensue;
That profit's yet to come 'twixt me and you. –
Good night.
[Exeunt Othello, Desdemona, and Attendants.

Enter Iago.

CASSIO Welcome, Iago: we must to the watch.

IAGO Not this hour, lieutenant; 'tis not yet ten o'clock. Our general cast us thus early for the love of his Desdemona, who let us not therefore blame: he hath not yet made wanton the night with her, and she is sport for Jove.

CASSIO She's a most exquisite lady.

IAGO And, I'll warrant her, full of game.

CASSIO Indeed, she is a most fresh and delicate creature.

IAGO What an eye she has! methinks! it sounds a parley to provocation.

CASSIO An inviting eye, and yet methinks right modest.

IAGO And, when she speaks, is it not an alarum to love?

CASSIO She is, indeed, perfection.

IAGO Well, happiness to their sheets! Come, lieutenant, I have a stoop of wine, and here without are a brace of Cyprus gallants, that would fain have a measure to the health of black Othello.

CASSIO Not to-night, good Iago. I have very poor and unhappy brains for drinking: I could well wish courtesy would invent some other custom of entertainment.

IAGO O! they are our friends; but one cup: I'll drink for you.

CASSIO I have drunk but one cup to-night, and that was craftily qualified too, and, behold, what innovation it makes here. I am unfortunate in the infirmity, and dare not task my weakness with any more.

IAGO What, man! 'tis a night of revels: the gallants desire it.

CASSIO Where are they?

IAGO Here at the door; I pray you, call them in.

CASSIO I'll do't; but it dislikes me. *[Exit.*

IAGO If I can fasten but one cup upon him,
With that which he hath drunk to-night already,
He'll be as full of quarrel and offence
As my young mistress' dog. Now, my sick fool, Roderigo,
Whom love has turn'd almost the wrong side out, –
To Desdemona hath to-night carous'd
Potations pottle-deep; and he's to watch.
Three lads of Cyprus – noble, swelling spirits,
That hold their honours in a wary distance,
The very elements of this warlike isle –
Have I to-night fluster'd with flowing cups,
And they watch too. Now, 'mongst this flock of drunkards,
Am I to put our Cassio in some action
That may offend the isle. – But here they come.
If consequence do but approve my dream,
My boat sails freely, both with wind and stream.

Re-enter Cassio, with him Montano, and Gentlemen.

CASSIO 'Fore Heaven, they have given me a rouse already.

MONTANO Good faith, a little one; not past a pint, as I am a soldier.

IAGO Some wine, ho!
[Sings] And let me the canakin clink, clink;

And let me the canakin clink:
A soldier's a man;
O, man's life's but a span;
Why then let a soldier drink.

Some wine, boys! *[Wine brought in.*

CASSIO 'Fore Heaven, an excellent song.

IAGO I learned it in England, where, indeed, they are most potent in potting; your Dane, your German, and your swag-bellied Hollander, – drink, ho! – are nothing to your English.

CASSIO Is your Englishman so expert in his drinking?

IAGO Why, he drinks you, with facility, your Dane dead drunk; he sweats not to overthrow your Almain; he gives your Hollander a vomit, ere the next pottle can be filled.

IAGO To the health of our general!

MONTANO I am for it, lieutenant; and I'll do you justice.

IAGO O sweet England!

King Stephen was a worthy peer,
His breeches cost him but a crown;
He held them sixpence all too dear,
With that he call'd the tailor – lown.
He was a wight of high renown,
And thou art but of low degree:
'T is pride that pulls the country down,
Then take thine auld cloak about thee.

Some wine, ho!

CASSIO Why, this is a more exquisite song than the other.

IAGO Will you hear 't again?

CASSIO No; for I hold him to be unworthy of his place, that does those things. – Well, Heaven's above all; and there be souls must be saved, and there be souls must not be saved.

IAGO It is true, good lieutenant.

CASSIO For mine own part, – no offence to the general, nor any man of quality, – I hope to be saved.

IAGO And so do I too, lieutenant.

CASSIO Ay; but, by your leave, not before me: the lieutenant is to be saved before the ancient. Let's have no more of this; let's to our affairs. – God forgive us our sins! – Gentlemen, let's look to our business. Do not think, gentlemen, I am drunk: this is my ancient; – this is my right hand, and this is my left hand. – I am not drunk now; I can stand well enough, and speak well enough.

ALL Excellent well.

CASSIO Why, very well then; you must not think then, that I am drunk. *[Exit.*

MONTANO To the platform, masters: come, let's set the watch.

IAGO You see this fellow, that is gone before:
He is a soldier, fit to stand by Caesar
And give direction; and do but see his vice.
'Tis to his virtue a just equinox,
The one as long as the other: 'tis pity of him.
I fear, the trust Othello puts him in,
On some odd time of his infirmity,
Will shake this island.

MONTANO But is he often thus?

IAGO 'Tis evermore the prologue to his sleep:
He'll watch the horologue a double set,
If drink rock not his cradle.

MONTANO It were well,
The general were put in mind of it.
Perhaps, he sees it not; or his good nature
Prizes the virtue that appears in Cassio,
And looks not on his evils. Is not this true?

Enter Roderigo.

IAGO [*Aside to him*] How now, Roderigo?
I pray you, after the lieutenant; go. [*Exit Roderigo.*
MONTANO And 'tis great pity, that the noble Moor
Should hazard such a place, as his own second,
With one of an ingraft infirmity:
It were an honest action to say
So to the Moor.
IAGO Not I, for this fair island:
I do love Cassio well, and would do much
To cure him of this evil. But hark! what noise?
[*Cry within: 'Help! help!'*

Re-enter Cassio, pursuing Roderigo.

CASSIO You rogue! you rascal!
MONTANO What's the matter, lieutenant?
CASSIO A knave teach me my duty!
I 'll beat the knave into a twiggen bottle.
RODERIGO Beat me!
CASSIO Dost thou prate, rogue?
[*Striking Roderigo.*
MONTANO Nay, good lieutenant;
[*Staying him.*
I pray you, sir, hold your hand.
CASSIO Let me go, sir,
Or I'll knock you o'er the mazzard.
MONTANO Come, come; you're drunk.
CASSIO Drunk! [*They fight.*
IAGO [*Aside to Roderigo*] Away, I say! go out, and cry – a mutiny.
[*Exit Roderigo.*
Nay! good lieutenant, – God's will, gentlemen! –

Help, ho! – Lieutenant, – sir, – Montano, – sir; –
Help, masters! – Here's a goodly watch, indeed! *[Bell rings.*
Who's that which rings the bell? – *Diablo*, ho!
The town will rise: God's will! lieutenant, hold!
You will be sham'd for ever.

Enter Othello and Attendants.

OTHELLO What is the matter here?
MONTANO I bleed still: I am hurt to the death. – He dies!
OTHELLO Hold, for your lives!
IAGO Hold, ho! Lieutenant, – sir, – Montano, – gentlemen! –
Have you forgot all sense of place and duty?
Hold! the general speaks to you: hold, for shame!
OTHELLO Why, how now, ho! from whence ariseth this?
Are we turn'd Turks, and to ourselves do that,
Which Heaven hath forbid the Ottomites?
For Christian shame, put by this barbarous brawl:
He that stirs next to carve for his own rage,
Holds his soul light; he dies upon his motion.
Silence that dreadful bell! it frights the isle
From her propriety. – What is the matter, masters? –
Honest Iago, that look'st dead with grieving,
Speak, who began this? on thy love, I charge thee.
IAGO I do not know: – friends all but now, even now,
In quarter, and in terms like bride and groom
Devesting them for bed; and then, but now,
(As if some planet had unwitted men,)
Swords out, and tilting one at other's breast,
In opposition bloody. I cannot speak
Any beginning to this peevish odds;
And would in action glorious I had lost

Those legs, that brought me to a part of it!
OTHELLO How came it, Michael, you are thus forgot?
CASSIO I pray you, pardon me; I cannot speak.
OTHELLO Worthy Montano, you were wont be civil;
The gravity and stillness of your youth
The world hath noted, and your name is great
In mouths of wisest censure: what's the matter,
That you unlace your reputation thus,
And spend your rich opinion, for the name
Of a night-brawler? give me answer to it.
MONTANO Worthy Othello, I am hurt to danger:
Your officer, Iago, can inform you –
While I spare speech, which something now offends me, –
Of all that I do know; nor know I aught
By me that's said or done amiss this night,
Unless self-charity be sometime a vice,
And to defend ourselves it be a sin,
When violence assails us.
OTHELLO Now, by Heaven,
My blood begins my safer guides to rule;
And passion, having my best judgment collied,
Assays to lead the way. If I once stir,
Or do but lift this arm, the best of you
Shall sink in my rebuke. Give me to know
How this foul rout began, who set it on;
And he that is approv'd in this offence,
Though he had twinn'd with me, both at a birth,
Shall lose me. – What! in a town of war,
Yet wild, the people's hearts brimful of fear,
To manage private and domestic quarrel,
In night, and on the court and guard of safety!

'Tis monstrous. – Iago, who began it?

MONTANO If partially affin'd, or leagu'd in office,
Thou dost deliver more or less than truth,
Thou art no soldier.

IAGO Touch me not so near:
I had rather have this tongue cut from my mouth,
Than it should do offence to Michael Cassio;
Yet, I persuade myself, to speak the truth
Shall nothing wrong him. – Thus it is, general.
Montano and myself being in speech,
There comes a fellow, crying out for help,
And Cassio following him with determin'd sword
To execute upon him. Sir, this gentleman
Steps in to Cassio, and entreats his pause:
Myself the crying fellow did pursue,
Lest by his clamour (as it so fell out)
The town might fall in fright: he, swift of foot,
Outran my purpose; and I return'd, the rather
For that I heard the clink and fall of swords,
And Cassio high in oath, which till to-night
I ne'er might say before. When I came back
(For this was brief), I found them close together,
At blow and thrust, even as again they were
When you yourself did part them.
More of this matter can I not report:–
But men are men; the best sometimes forget:
Though Cassio did some little wrong to him,
As men in rage strike those that wish them best,
Yet surely Cassio, I believe, received
From him that fled some strange indignity,
Which patience could not pass.

OTHELLO I know, Iago,
Thy honesty and love doth mince this matter,
Making it light to Cassio. – Cassio, I love thee;
But never more be officer of mine. –

Re-enter Desdemona, attended.

Look, if my gentle love be not rais'd up!–
I'll make thee an example.

DESDEMONA What's the matter?

OTHELLO All's well now, sweeting; come away to bed. –
Sir, for your hurts, myself will be your surgeon. –
Lead him off. – *[Montano is led off.*
Iago, look with care about the town,
And silence those whom this vile brawl distracted. –
Come, Desdemona; 'tis the soldiers' life,
To have their balmy slumbers wak'd with strife.

[Exeunt all but Iago and Cassio.

IAGO What, are you hurt, lieutenant?

CASSIO Ay; past all surgery.

IAGO Marry, Heaven forbid!

CASSIO Reputation, reputation reputation! O! I have lost my reputation. I have lost the immortal part of myself, and what remains is bestial. – My reputation, Iago, my reputation!

IAGO As I am an honest man, I thought you had received some bodily wound; there is more sense in that than in reputation. Reputation is an idle and most false imposition; oft got without merit, and lost without deserving: you have lost no reputation at all, unless you repute yourself such a loser. What, man! there are ways to recover the general again: you are but now cast in his mood, a punishment more in policy than in malice; even so as one would beat his offenceless dog, to affright an imperious lion. Sue to him again, and he's yours.

CASSIO I will rather sue to be despised, than to deceive so good a commander with so slight, so drunken, and so indiscreet an officer. Drunk? and speak parrot? and squabble? swagger? swear? and discourse fustian with one's own shadow? – O thou invisible spirit of wine! if thou hast no name to be known by, let us call thee devil.

IAGO What was he that you followed with your sword? What had he done to you?

CASSIO I know not.

IAGO Is 't possible?

CASSIO I remember a mass of things, but nothing distinctly; a quarrel, but nothing wherefore. – O God! that men should put an enemy in their mouths, to steal away their brains! that we should, with joy, pleasance, revel, and applause, transform ourselves into beasts!

IAGO Why, but you are now well enough: how came you thus recovered?

CASSIO It hath pleased the devil drunkenness, to give place to the devil wrath: one unperfectness shows me another, to make me frankly despise myself.

IAGO Come, you are too severe a moraler. As the time, the place, and the condition of this country stands, I could heartily wish this had not befallen; but since it is as it is, mend it for your own good.

CASSIO I will ask him for my place again: he shall tell me, I am a drunkard. Had I as many mouths as Hydra, such an answer would stop them all. To be now a sensible man, by-and-by a fool, and presently a beast! O, strange! – Every inordinate cup is unblessed, and the ingredient is a devil.

IAGO Come, come; good wine is a good familiar creature, if it be well used: exclaim no more against it. And, good lieutenant, I think you think I love you.

CASSIO I have well approved it, sir. – I drunk!

IAGO You, or any man living, may be drunk at some time, man. I'll tell you what you shall do. Our general's wife is now the general: – I may say so in this respect, for that he hath devoted and given up himself to the contemplation, mark, and denotement of her parts and graces: – confess yourself freely to her; importune her; she'll help to put you in your place again. She is of so free, so kind, so apt, so blessed a disposition, that she holds it a vice in her goodness, not to do more than she is requested. This broken joint, between you and her husband, entreat her to splinter; and my fortunes against any lay worth naming, this crack of your love shall grow stronger than it was before.

CASSIO You advise me well.

IAGO I protest, in the sincerity of love, and honest kindness.

CASSIO I think it freely; and, betimes in the morning, I will beseech the virtuous Desdemona to undertake for me. I am desperate of my fortunes, if they check me here.

IAGO You are in the right. Good night, lieutenant; I must to the watch.

CASSIO Good night, honest Iago. *[Exit.*

IAGO And what's he then, that says I play the villain?
When this advice is free, I give, and honest,
Probal to thinking, and, indeed, the course
To win the Moor again? For 't is most easy,
The inclining Desdemona to subdue
In any honest suit: she's fram'd as fruitful
As the free elements. And then for her
To win the Moor, – were 't to renounce his baptism,

All seals and symbols of redeemed sin,–
His soul is so enfetter'd to her love,
That she may make, unmake, do what she list,
Even as her appetite shall play the god
With his weak function. How am I then a villain,
To counsel Cassio to this parallel course,
Directly to his good? Divinity of hell!
When devils will their blackest sins put on,
They do suggest at first with heavenly shows,
As I do now; for whiles this honest fool
Plies Desdemona to repair his fortunes,
And she for him pleads strongly to the Moor,
I'll pour this pestilence into his ear,
That she repeals him for her body's lust;
And, by how much she strives to do him good,
She shall undo her credit with the Moor.
So will I turn her virtue into pitch,
And out of her own goodness make the net
That shall enmesh them all.

Re-enter Roderigo.

How now, Roderigo?

RODERIGO I do follow here in the chase, not like a hound that hunts, but one that fills up the cry. My money is almost spent: I have been to-night exceedingly well cudgelled; and, I think, the issue will be, I shall have so much experience for my pains; and so, with no money at all, and a little more wit, return again to Venice.

IAGO How poor are they, that have not patience!
What wound did ever heal, but by degrees?
Thou know'st, we work by wit, and not by witchcraft;

And wit depends on dilatory time.
Does 't not go well? Cassio hath beaten thee,
And thou, by that small hurt, hast cashier'd Cassio.
Though other things grow fair against the sun,
Yet fruits that blossom first will first be ripe:
Content thyself awhile. – By the mass, 'tis morning;
Pleasure and action make the hours seem short.
Retire thee; go where thou art billeted:
Away, I say; thou shalt know more hereafter:
Nay, get thee gone. *[Exit Roderigo.]* Two things are to be done,–
My wife must move for Cassio to her mistress;
I'll set her on;
Myself, the while, to draw the Moor apart,
And bring him jump when he may Cassio find
Soliciting his wife: – ay, that's the way:
Dull not device by coldness and delay. *[Exit.*

ACT THREE

SCENE I – BEFORE THE CASTLE.

Enter Cassio and some Musicians.

CASSIO Masters, play here; I will content your pains:
Something that's brief; and bid, 'Good morrow, general.'
[Music.

Enter Clown.

CLOWN Why, masters, have your instruments been in Naples, that they speak i' the nose thus?

1 MUSICIAN How, sir, how?

CLOWN Are these, I pray you, called wind-instruments?

1 MUSICIAN Ay, marry, are they, sir.

CLOWN O! thereby hangs a tail.

1 MUSICIAN Whereby hangs a tale, sir?

CLOWN Marry, sir, by many a wind-instrument that I know. But, masters, here's money for you; and the general so likes your music, that he desires you, for love's sake, to make no more noise with it.

1 MUSICIAN Well, sir, we will not.

CLOWN If you have any music that may not be heard, to't again; but, as they say, to hear music the general does not greatly care.

1 MUSICIAN We have none such, sir.

CLOWN Then put up your pipes in your bag, for I'll away. Go; vanish into air, away! *[Exeunt Musicians.*

CASSIO Dost thou hear, mine honest friend!

CLOWN No, I hear not your honest friend; I hear you.

CASSIO Pr'ythee, keep up thy quillets. There's a poor piece of gold for thee. If the gentlewoman that attends the general's wife be stirring, tell her there's one Cassio entreats her a little favour of speech: wilt thou do this?

CLOWN She is stirring, sir: if she will stir hither, I shall seem to notify unto her.

CASSIO Do, good my friend. *[Exit Clown.*

Enter Iago.

In happy time, Iago.

IAGO You have not been a-bed, then?

CASSIO Why, no; the day had broke
Before we parted. I have made bold, Iago,
To send in to your wife: my suit to her
Is, that she will to virtuous Desdemona
Procure me some access.

IAGO I'll send her to you presently;
And I'll devise a mean to draw the Moor
Out of the way, that your converse and business
May be more free.

CASSIO I humbly thank you for't. *[Exit Iago.]* I never knew
A Florentine more kind and honest.

Enter Emilia.

EMILIA Good morrow, good lieutenant: I am sorry
For your displeasure; but all will sure be well.
The general and his wife are talking of it,
And she speaks for you stoutly: the Moor replies,
That he you hurt is of great fame in Cyprus,
And great affinity, and that in wholesome wisdom

He might not but refuse you; but he protests he loves you,
And needs no other suitor but his likings,
To take the saf'st occasion by the front,
To bring you in again.

CASSIO Yet, I beseech you, –
If you think fit, or that it may be done,–
Give me advantage of some brief discourse
With Desdemona alone.

EMILIA Pray you, come in:
I will bestow you where you shall have time
To speak your bosom freely.

CASSIO I am much bound to you. *[Exeunt.*

SCENE II – A ROOM IN THE CASTLE.

Enter Othello, Iago, and Gentlemen.

OTHELLO These letters give, Iago, to the pilot,
And by him do my duties to the senate:
That done, I will be walking on the works;
Repair there to me.

IAGO Well, my good lord; I'll do't.

OTHELLO This fortification, gentlemen – shall we see't?

GENTLEMEN We'll wait upon your lordship. *[Exeunt.*

SCENE III – THE GARDEN OF THE CASTLE.

Enter Desdemona, Cassio, and Emilia.

DESDEMONA Be thou assur'd, good Cassio, I will do
All my abilities in thy behalf.

EMILIA Good madam, do: I warrant it grieves my husband,
As if the cause were his.
DESDEMONA O! that's an honest fellow. – Do not doubt, Cassio,
But I will have my lord and you again
As friendly as you were.
CASSIO Bounteous madam,
Whatever shall become of Michael Cassio,
He's never anything but your true servant.
DESDEMONA I know 't: I thank you. You do love my lord;
You have known him long: and be you well assur'd,
He shall in strangeness stand no further off
Than in a politic distance.
CASSIO Ay, but, lady,
That policy may either last so long,
Or feed upon such nice and waterish diet,
Or breed itself so out of circumstance,
That, I being absent, and my place supplied,
My general will forget my love and service.
DESDEMONA Do not doubt that: before Emilia here,
I give thee warrant of thy place. Assure thee,
If I do vow a friendship, I'll perform it
To the last article: my lord shall never rest;
I'll watch him tame, and talk him out of patience;
His bed shall seem a school, his board a shrift:
I'll intermingle everything he does
With Cassio's suit. Therefore, be merry, Cassio;
For thy solicitor shall rather die,
Than give thy cause away.

Enter Othello and Iago, at a distance.

EMILIA Madam, here comes my lord.

CASSIO Madam, I'll take my leave.

DESDEMONA Why, stay, and hear me speak.

CASSIO Madam, not now: I am very ill at ease,
Unfit for mine own purposes.

DESDEMONA Well, do your discretion. *[Exit Cassio.*

IAGO Ha! I like not that.

OTHELLO What dost thou say?

IAGO Nothing, my lord: or if – I know not what.

OTHELLO Was not that Cassio, parted from my wife?

IAGO Cassio, my lord? No, sure, I cannot think it,
That he would steal away so guilty-like,
Seeing you coming.

OTHELLO I do believe 'twas he.

DESDEMONA How now, my lord?
I have been talking with a suitor here,
A man that languishes in your displeasure.

OTHELLO Who is 't you mean?

DESDEMONA Why, your lieutenant Cassio. Good my lord,
If I have any grace, or power to move you,
His present reconciliation take;
For, if he be not one that truly loves you,
That errs in ignorance, and not in cunning,
I have no judgment in an honest face.
I pr'ythee, call him back.

OTHELLO Went he hence now?

DESDEMONA Ay, sooth; so humbled,
That he hath left part of his grief with me,
To suffer with him. Good love, call him back.

OTHELLO Not now, sweet Desdemona; some other time.

DESDEMONA But shall 't be shortly?

OTHELLO The sooner, sweet, for you.

DESDEMONA Shall 't be to-night at supper?
OTHELLO No, not to-night.
DESDEMONA To-morrow dinner then?
OTHELLO I shall not dine at home;
I meet the captains at the citadel.
DESDEMONA Why then, to-morrow night; or Tuesday morn;
On Tuesday noon, or night; on Wednesday morn:
I pr'ythee, name the time, but let it not
Exceed three days: in faith, he's penitent;
And yet his trespass, in our common reason,
(Save that, they say, the wars must make examples
Out of her best,) is not almost a fault
To incur a private check. When shall he come?
Tell me, Othello. I wonder in my soul,
What you could ask me that I should deny,
Or stand so mammering on. What! Michael Cassio,
That came a-wooing with you, and so many a time,
When I have spoke of you dispraisingly,
Hath ta'en your part; to have so much to do
To bring him in! Trust me, I could do much,–
OTHELLO Pr'ythee, no more: let him come when he will;
I will deny thee nothing.
DESDEMONA Why, this is not a boon;
'Tis as I should entreat you wear your gloves,
Or feed on nourishing dishes, or keep you warm,
Or sue to you to do a peculiar profit
To your own person: nay, when I have a suit
Wherein I mean to touch your love indeed,
It shall be full of poise and difficult weight,
And fearful to be granted.
OTHELLO I will deny thee nothing:

Whereon, I do beseech thee, grant me this,
To leave me but a little to myself.

DESDEMONA Shall I deny you? no. Farewell, my lord.

OTHELLO Farewell, my Desdemona: I'll come to thee straight.

DESDEMONA Emilia, come. – Be as your fancies teach you;
Whate'er you be, I am obedient. *[Exit, with Emilia.*

OTHELLO Excellent wretch! Perdition catch my soul,
But I do love thee! and when I love thee not,
Chaos is come again.

IAGO My noble lord, –

OTHELLO What dost thou say, Iago?

IAGO Did Michael Cassio, when you woo'd my lady,
Know of your love?

OTHELLO He did, from first to last: why dost thou ask?

IAGO But for a satisfaction of my thought;
No further harm.

OTHELLO Why of thy thought, Iago?

IAGO I did not think, he had been acquainted with her.

OTHELLO O, yes; and went between us very oft.

IAGO Indeed?

OTHELLO Indeed! ay, indeed: – discern'st thou aught in that?
Is he not honest?

IAGO Honest, my lord?

OTHELLO Honest! ay, honest.

IAGO My lord, for aught I know.

OTHELLO What dost thou think?

IAGO Think, my lord?

OTHELLO Think, my lord!
By Heaven, he echoes me,
As if there were some monster in his thought

Too hideous to be shown. – Thou dost mean something.
I heard thee say even now, – thou lik'dst not that,
When Cassio left my wife: what didst not like?
And, when I told thee, he was of my counsel
In my whole course of wooing, thou criedst, 'Indeed?'
And didst contract and purse thy brow together,
As if thou then hadst shut up in thy brain
Some horrible conceit. If thou dost love me,
Show me thy thought.

IAGO My lord, you know I love you.

OTHELLO I think, thou dost;
And, – for I know thou art full of love and honesty,
And weigh'st thy words before thou giv'st them breath,–
Therefore, these stops of thine fright me the more:
For such things, in a false disloyal knave,
Are tricks of custom; but in a man that's just,
They're close delations, working from the heart,
That passion cannot rule.

IAGO For Michael Cassio,–
I dare be sworn, I think that he is honest.

OTHELLO I think so too.

IAGO Men should be what they seem;
Or, those that be not, would they might seem none!

OTHELLO Certain, men should be what they seem.

IAGO Why then, I think Cassio's an honest man.

OTHELLO Nay, yet there's more in this.
I pray thee, speak to me as to thy thinkings,
As thou dost ruminate; and give thy worst of thoughts
The worst of words.

IAGO Good my lord, pardon me:
Though I am bound to every act of duty,

I am not bound to that all slaves are free to.
Utter my thoughts? Why, say, they are vile and false,–
As where's that palace, whereinto foul things
Sometimes intrude not? who has a breast so pure,
But some uncleanly apprehensions
Keep leets, and law-days, and in sessions sit
With meditations lawful?

OTHELLO Thou dost conspire against thy friend, Iago,
If thou but think'st him wrong'd, and mak'st his ear
A stranger to thy thoughts.

IAGO I do beseech you,–
Though I, perchance, am vicious in my guess,
(As, I confess, it is my nature's plague
To spy into abuses, and oft my jealousy
Shapes faults that are not,) – that your wisdom yet,
From one that so imperfectly conceits,
Would take no notice; nor build yourself a trouble
Out of his scattering and unsure observance.
It were not for your quiet, nor your good,
Nor for my manhood, honesty, and wisdom,
To let you know my thoughts.

OTHELLO What dost thou mean?

IAGO Good name in man and woman, dear my lord,
Is the immediate jewel of their souls:
Who steals my purse, steals trash; 'tis something, nothing;
'Twas mine, 'tis his, and has been slave to thousands;
But he that filches from me my good name,
Robs me of that which not enriches him,
And makes me poor indeed.

OTHELLO By Heaven, I'll know thy thoughts.

IAGO You cannot, if my heart were in your hand;

Nor shall not, whilst 'tis in my custody.

OTHELLO Ha!

IAGO O! beware, my lord, of jealousy;
It is the green-ey'd monster, which doth mock
The meat it feeds on: that cuckold lives in bliss,
Who, certain of his fate, loves not his wronger;
But, O! what damned minutes tells he o'er,
Who dotes, yet doubts; suspects, yet soundly loves!

OTHELLO O misery!

IAGO Poor, and content, is rich, and rich enough;
But riches, fineless, is as poor as winter,
To him that ever fears he shall be poor.–
Good Heaven, the souls of all my tribe defend
From jealousy!

OTHELLO Why? why is this?
Think'st thou, I'd make a life of jealousy,
To follow still the changes of the moon
With fresh suspicions? No: to be once in doubt,
Is once to be resolv'd. Exchange me for a goat,
When I shall turn the business of my soul
To such exsufflicate and blown surmises,
Matching thy inference. 'Tis not to make me jealous,
To say – my wife is fair, feeds well, loves company,
Is free of speech, sings, plays, and dances well;
Where virtue is, these are more virtuous:
Nor from mine own weak merits will I draw
The smallest fear, or doubt of her revolt;
For she had eyes, and chose me. No, Iago;
I'll see, before I doubt; when I doubt; prove;
And, on the proof, there is no more but this,–
Away at once with love, or jealousy.

IAGO I am glad of it: for now I shall have reason
To show the love and duty that I bear you
With franker spirit: therefore, as I am bound,
Receive it from me. I speak not yet of proof.
Look to your wife; observe her well with Cassio;
Wear your eye thus, not jealous, nor secure:
I would not have your free and noble nature,
Out of self-bounty, be abus'd; look to 't.
I know our country disposition well:
In Venice they do let Heaven see the pranks
They dare not show their husbands; their best conscience
Is, not to leave 't undone, but keep 't unknown.
OTHELLO Dost thou say so?
IAGO She did deceive her father, marrying you;
And, when she seem'd to shake and fear your looks,
She lov'd them most.
OTHELLO And so she did.
IAGO Why, go to, then;
She that so young could give out such a seeming,
To seel her father's eyes up, close as oak,–
He thought, 'twas witchcraft;– but I am much to blame;
I humbly do beseech you of your pardon,
For too much loving you.
OTHELLO I am bound to thee for ever.
IAGO I see, this hath a little dash'd your spirits.
OTHELLO Not a jot, not a jot.
IAGO Trust me, I fear it has.
I hope, you will consider what is spoke
Comes from my love. – But, I do see you're mov'd:
I am to pray you, not to strain my speech
To grosser issues, nor to larger reach,
Than to suspicion.

OTHELLO I will not.

IAGO Should you do so, my lord,
My speech should fall into such vile success
As my thoughts aim not at. Cassio's my worthy friend –
My lord, I see you're mov'd.

OTHELLO No, not much mov'd –
I do not think but Desdemona's honest.

IAGO Long live she so! and long live you to think so!

OTHELLO And yet, how nature erring from itself, –

IAGO Ay, there's the point: – as, – to be bold with you, –
Not to affect many proposed matches,
Of her own clime, complexion, and degree,
Whereto, we see, in all things nature tends:
Foh! one may smell, in such, a will most rank,
Foul disproportion, thoughts unnatural. –
But pardon me; I do not in position
Distinctly speak of her, though I may fear,
Her will, recoiling to her better judgment,
May fall to match you with her country forms,
And, happily, repent.

OTHELLO Farewell, farewell.
If more thou dost perceive, let me know more;
Set on thy wife to observe. Leave me, Iago.

IAGO My lord, I take my leave. *[Going.*

OTHELLO Why did I marry? – This honest creature, doubtless,
Sees and knows more, much more, than he unfolds.

IAGO *[Returning.]* My lord, I would I might entreat your honour
To scan this thing no further; leave it to time.
Although 'tis fit that Cassio have his place,
(For sure, he fills it up with great ability,)
Yet, if you please to hold him off a while,

You shall by that perceive him and his means:
Note, if your lady strain his entertainment
With any strong or vehement importunity;
Much will be seen in that. In the meantime,
Let me be thought too busy in my fears
(As worthy cause I have to fear I am),
And hold her free, I do beseech your honour.

OTHELLO Fear not my government.

IAGO I once more take my leave. *[Exit.*

OTHELLO This fellow's of exceeding honesty,
And knows all qualities, with a learned spirit,
Of human dealings; if I do prove her haggard,
Though that her jesses were my dear heart-strings,
I'd whistle her off, and let her down the wind,
To prey at fortune. Haply, for I am black,
And have not those soft parts of conversation
That chamberers have; or, for I am declin'd
Into the vale of years; – yet that's not much:
She's gone, I am abus'd; and my relief
Must be to loathe her. O curse of marriage!
That we can call these delicate creatures ours,
And not their appetites. I had rather be a toad,
And live upon the vapour of a dungeon,
Than keep a corner in the thing I love
For others' uses. Yet, 'tis the plague of great ones;
Prerogativ'd are they less than the base;
'T is destiny unshunnable, like death:
Even then this forked plague is fated to us,
When we do quicken. Look, where she comes.
If she be false, O! then Heaven mocks itself.
I'll not believe it.

Re-enter Desdemona and Emilia.

DESDEMONA How now, my dear Othello?
Your dinner and the generous islanders,
By you invited, do attend your presence.
OTHELLO I am to blame.
DESDEMONA Why do you speak so faintly?
Are you not well?
OTHELLO I have a pain upon my forehead here.
DESDEMONA 'Faith, that's with watching; t'will away again:
Let me but bind it hard, within this hour
It will be well.
OTHELLO Your napkin is too little;
Let it alone. Come, I'll go in with you.
DESDEMONA I am very sorry that you are not well.
[Exeunt Othello and Desdemona.
EMILIA I am glad I have found this napkin.
This was her first remembrance from the Moor:
My wayward husband hath a hundred times
Woo'd me to steal it; but she so loves the token,
(For he conjur'd her she should ever keep it,)
That she reserves it evermore about her,
To kiss, and talk to. I'll have the work ta'en out,
And give 't Iago:
What he will do with it, Heaven knows, not I;
I nothing, but to please his fantasy.

Re-enter Iago

IAGO How now! what do you here alone?
EMILIA Do not you chide; I have a thing for you.
IAGO A thing for me? – it is a common thing –
EMILIA Ha?

IAGO To have a foolish wife.

EMILIA O! is that all? What will you give me now
For that same handkerchief?

IAGO What handkerchief?

EMILIA What handkerchief!
Why, that the Moor first gave to Desdemona;
That which so often you did bid me steal.

IAGO Hast stol'n it from her?

EMILIA No, 'faith: she let it drop by negligence;
And, to the advantage, I, being here, took 't up.
Look, here it is.

IAGO A good wench; give it me.

EMILIA What will you do with 't, that you have been so earnest
To have me filch it?

IAGO Why, what's that to you?
[Snatching it.

EMILIA If it be not for some purpose of import,
Give 't me again: poor lady! she'll run mad,
When she shall lack it.

IAGO Be not acknown on 't; I have use for it.
Go, leave me. *[Exit Emilia.*
I will in Cassio's lodging lose this napkin,
And let him find it: trifles, light as air,
Are, to the jealous, confirmations strong
As proofs of holy writ. This may do something.
The Moor already changes with my poison:
Dangerous conceits are in their natures poisons,
Which at the first are scarce found to distaste;
But, with a little act upon the blood,
Burn like the mines of sulphur. – I did say so:–
Look, where he comes!

Re-enter Othello.

Not poppy, nor mandragora,
Nor all the drowsy syrups of the world,
Shall ever medicine thee to that sweet sleep
Which thou ow'dst yesterday.

OTHELLO Ha! ha! false to me?

IAGO Why, how now, general? no more of that.

OTHELLO Avaunt! be gone! thou hast set me on the rack. –
I swear, 'tis better to be much abus'd,
Than but to know't a little.

IAGO How now, my lord?

OTHELLO What sense had I of her stol'n hours of lust?
I saw it not, thought it not, it harm'd not me:
I slept the next night well, fed well, was free and merry;
I found not Cassio's kisses on her lips:
He that is robb'd, not wanting what is stolen,
Let them not know't, and he's not robb'd at all.

IAGO I am sorry to hear this.

OTHELLO I had been happy, if the general camp,
Pioners and all, had tasted her sweet body,
So I had nothing known. O now, for ever,
Farewell the tranquil mind! farewell content!
Farewell the plumed troops, and the big wars,
That make ambition virtue! O, farewell!
Farewell the neighing steed, and the shrill trump,
The spirit-stirring drum, the ear-piercing fife,
The royal banner, and all quality,
Pride, pomp, and circumstance of glorious war!
And O you mortal engines, whose rude throats
The immortal Jove's dread clamours counterfeit,
Farewell! Othello's occupation's gone!

IAGO Is it possible? – My lord, –
OTHELLO Villain, be sure thou prove my love a whore;
Be sure of it: give me the ocular proof;
Or, by the worth of mine eternal soul,
Thou hadst been better have been born a dog,
Than answer my wak'd wrath.
IAGO Is it come to this?
OTHELLO Make me to see 't; or, at the least, so prove it.
That the probatioan bear no hinge, nor loop,
To hang a doubt on: or woe upon thy life!
IAGO My noble lord,–
OTHELLO If thou dost slander her, and torture me,
Never pray more; abandon all remorse;
On horror's head horrors accumulate;
Do deeds to make heaven weep, all earth amaz'd:
For nothing canst thou to damnation add,
Greater than that.
IAGO O grace! O Heaven forgive me!
Are you a man? Have you a soul, or sense? –
God be wi' you; take mine office. – O wretched fool,
That liv'st to make thine honesty a vice! –
O monstrous world! Take note, take note, O world!
To be direct and honest is not safe. –
I thank you for this profit; and, from hence,
I'll love no friend, sith love breeds such offence.
OTHELLO Nay, stay. – Thou shouldst be honest.
IAGO I should be wise; for honesty's a fool,
And loses that it works for.
OTHELLO By the world,
I think my wife be honest, and think she is not;
I think that thou art just, and think thou art not.

I'll have some proof. Her name, that was as fresh
As Dian's visage, is now begrim'd and black
As mine own face. – If there be cords, or knives,
Poison, or fire, or suffocating streams,
I'll not endure it. – Would I were satisfied!

IAGO I see, sir, you are eaten up with passion.
I do repent me that I put it to you.
You would be satisfied?

OTHELLO Would! nay, I will.

IAGO And may; but how? how satisfied, my lord?
Would you, the supervisor, grossly gape on, –
Behold her tupp'd?

OTHELLO Death and damnation! O!

IAGO It were a tedious difficulty, I think,
To bring them to that prospect. Damn them then,
If ever mortal eyes do see them bolster,
More than their own! What then? how then?
What shall I say? Where's satisfaction?
It is impossible you should see this,
Were they as prime as goats, as hot as monkeys,
As salt as wolves in pride, and fools as gross
As ignorance made drunk; but yet, I say,
If imputation, and strong circumstances,
Which lead directly to the door of truth,
Will give you satisfaction, you might have it.

OTHELLO Give me a living reason she's disloyal.

IAGO I do not like the office;
But, sith I am enter'd in this cause so far,
Prick'd to 't by foolish honesty and love,
I will go on. I lay with Cassio lately;
And, being troubled with a raging tooth,

I could not sleep.
There are a kind of men so loose of soul,
That in their sleeps will mutter their affairs:
One of this kind is Cassio.
In sleep I heard him say, – 'Sweet Desdemona;
Let us be wary, let us hide our loves!'
And then, sir, would he gripe, and wring my hand,
Cry, – 'O sweet creature!' and then kiss me hard,
As if he pluck'd up kisses by the roots,
That grew upon my lips; then laid his leg
Over my thigh, and sigh'd, and kiss'd; and then
Cried, – 'Cursed fate, that gave thee to the Moor!'

OTHELLO O monstrous! monstrous!

IAGO Nay, this was but his dream.

OTHELLO But this denoted a foregone conclusion:
'Tis a shrewd doubt, though it be but a dream.

IAGO And this may help to thicken other proofs,
That do demonstrate thinly.

OTHELLO I'll tear her all to pieces.

IAGO Nay, but be wise; yet we see nothing done;
She may be honest yet. Tell me but this;
Have you not sometimes seen a handkerchief,
Spotted with strawberries, in your wife's hand?

OTHELLO I gave her such a one: 'twas my first gift.

IAGO I know not that: but such a handkerchief
(I am sure it was your wife's) did I to-day
See Cassio wipe his beard with.

OTHELLO If it be that, –

IAGO If it be that, or any that was hers,
It speaks against her, with the other proofs.

OTHELLO O, that the slave had forty thousand lives!

One is too poor, too weak for my revenge.
Now do I see 'tis true – Look here, Iago;
All my fond love thus do I blow to heaven:
'Tis gone. –
Arise, black vengeance, from the hollow hell!
Yield up, O love, thy crown and hearted throne
To tyrannous hate! Swell, bosom, with thy fraught,
For 'tis of aspics' tongues!

IAGO Yet be content.

OTHELLO O, blood, blood, blood!

IAGO Patience, I say; your mind perhaps may change.

OTHELLO Never, Iago. Like to the Pontic sea,
Whose icy current and compulsive course
Ne'er feels retiring ebb, but keeps due on
To the Propontic and the Hellespont:
Even so my bloody thoughts, with violent pace,
Shall ne'er look back, ne'er ebb to humble love,
Till that a capable and wide revenge
Swallow them up. – *[Kneeling]* Now, by yond marble heaven,
In the due reverence of a sacred vow
I here engage my words.

IAGO Do not rise yet. – *[Kneeling.*
Witness, you ever-burning lights above!
You elements that clip us round about!
Witness, that here Iago doth give up
The execution of his wit, hands, heart,
To wrong'd Othello's service! Let him command,
And to obey shall be in me remorse,
What bloody business ever.

OTHELLO I greet thy love,
Not with vain thanks, but with acceptance bounteous,

And will upon the instant put thee to 't:
Within these three days let me hear thee say,
That Cassio's not alive.

IAGO My friend is dead; 'tis done at your request:
But let her live.

OTHELLO Damn her, lewd minx! O, damn her!
Come, go with me apart; I will withdraw,
To furnish me with some swift means of death
For the fair devil. Now art thou my lieutenant.

IAGO I am your own for ever. *[Exeunt.*

SCENE IV – BEFORE THE CASTLE.

Enter Desdemona, Emilia and Clown.

DESDEMONA Do you know, sirrah, where Lieutenant Cassio lies?

CLOWN I dare not say he lies anywhere.

DESDEMONA Why, man?

CLOWN He is a soldier; and for one to say a soldier lies, is stabbing.

DESDEMONA Go to. Where lodges he?

CLOWN To tell you where he lodges, is to tell you where I lie.

DESDEMONA Can anything be made of this?

CLOWN I know not where he lodges; and for me to devise a lodging, and say, he lies here, or he lies there, were to lie in mine own throat.

DESDEMONA Can you inquire him out, and be edified by report?

CLOWN I will catechise the world for him; that is, make questions, and by them answer.

DESDEMONA Seek him; bid him come hither; tell him, I have

moved my lord in his behalf, and hope, all will be well.

CLOWN To do this is within the compass of man's wit; and therefore I will attempt the doing it. *[Exit.*

DESDEMONA Where should I lose that handkerchief, Emilia?

EMILIA I know not, madam.

DESDEMONA Believe me, I had rather have lost my purse
Full of cruzadoes; and but my noble Moor
Is true of mind, and made of no such baseness
As jealous creatures are, it were enough
To put him to ill thinking.

EMILIA Is he not jealous?

DESDEMONA Who? he! I think the sun, where he was born,
Drew all such humours from him.

EMILIA Look, where he comes.

DESDEMONA I will not leave him now, till Cassio
Be call'd to him. –

Enter Othello.

OTHELLO Well, my good lady. – *[Aside]* O, hardness to dissemble! –
How do you, Desdemona?

DESDEMONA Well, my good lord.

OTHELLO Give me your hand. This hand is moist, my lady.

DESDEMONA It yet has felt no age, nor known no sorrow.

OTHELLO This argues fruitfulness, and liberal heart:
Hot, hot, and moist: this hand of yours requires
A sequester from liberty, fasting and prayer,
Much castigation, exercise devout;
For here's a young and sweating devil here,
That commonly rebels. 'Tis a good hand,
A frank one.

DESDEMONA You may, indeed say so;
For 'twas that hand that gave away my heart.
OTHELLO A liberal hand: the hearts of old gave hands;
But our heraldy is – hands, not hearts.
DESDEMONA I cannot speak of this. Come now, your promise.
OTHELLO What promise, chuck?
DESDEMONA I have sent to bid Cassio come speak with you.
OTHELLO I have a salt and sorry rheum offends me.
Lend me thy handkerchief.
DESDEMONA Here, my lord.
OTHELLO That which I gave you.
DESDEMONA I have it not about me.
OTHELLO Not?
DESDEMONA No, indeed, my lord.
OTHELLO That's a fault. That handkerchief
Did an Egyptian to my mother give;
She was a charmer, and could almost read
The thoughts of people: she told her, while she kept it,
'Twould make her amiable, and subdue my father
Entirely to her love; but if she lost it,
Or made a gift of it, my father's eye
Should hold her loathed, and his spirits should hunt
After new fancies. She, dying, gave it me;
And bid me, when my fate would have me wived,
To give it her. I did so: and take heed on 't;
Make it a darling like your precious eye;
To lost 't or give 't away, were such perdition,
As nothing else could match.
DESDEMONA Is 't possible?
OTHELLO 'Tis true: there's magic in the web of it.
A sibyl, that had number'd in the world

The sun to course two hundred compasses,
In her prophetic fury sew'd the work;
The worms were hallow'd that did breed the silk,
And it was dy'd in mummy, which the skilful
Conserv'd of maidens' hearts.

DESDEMONA Indeed! is 't true?

OTHELLO Most veritable; therefore look to 't well.

DESDEMONA Then would to Heaven that I had never seen it.

OTHELLO Ha! wherefore?

DESDEMONA Why do you speak so startingly and rash?

OTHELLO Is 't lost? Is 't gone? speak, is it out o' the way?

DESDEMONA Heaven bless us!

OTHELLO Say you?

DESDEMONA It is not lost; but what an if it were?

OTHELLO How?

DESDEMONA I say, it is not lost.

OTHELLO Fetch 't, let me see 't.

DESDEMONA Why, so I can, sir; but I will not now.
This is a trick, to put me from my suit:
I pray, let Cassio be receiv'd again.

OTHELLO Fetch me that handkerchief: my mind misgives.

DESDEMONA Come, come;
You'll never meet a more sufficient man.

OTHELLO The handkerchief!

DESDEMONA I pray, talk me of Cassio.

OTHELLO The handkerchief!

DESDEMONA A man that, all his time,
Hath founded his good fortunes on your love;
Shar'd dangers with you;–

OTHELLO The handkerchief!

DESDEMONA In sooth, you are to blame.

OTHELLO Away! [*Exit.*

EMILIA Is not this man jealous?

DESDEMONA I ne'er saw this before.
Sure, there's some wonder in this handkerchief:
I am most unhappy in the loss of it.

EMILIA 'Tis not a year or two shows us a man;
They are all but stomachs, and we all but food;
They eat us hungerly, and when they are full,
They belch us. – Look you! Cassio, and my husband.

Enter Iago and Cassio

IAGO There is no other way; 'tis she must do 't:
And, lo, the happiness! go, and importune her.

DESDEMONA How now, good Cassio? what's the news with you?

CASSIO Madam, my former suit. I do beseech you,
That by your virtuous means I may again
Exist, and be a member of his love,
Whom I, with all the office of my heart,
Entirely honour: I would not be delay'd.
If my offence be of such mortal kind,
That nor my service past, nor present sorrows,
Nor purpos'd merit in futurity,
Can ransom me into his love again,
But to know so must be my benefit;
So shall I clothe me in a forc'd content,
And shut myself up in some other course,
To fortune's alms.

DESDEMONA Alas! thrice-gentle Cassio,
My advocation is not now in tune;
My lord is not my lord; nor should I know him,

Were he in favour, as in humour, alter'd.
So help me every spirit sanctified,
As I have spoken for you all my best,
And stood within the blank of his displeasure,
For my free speech. You must awhile be patient:
What I can do, I will; and more I will,
Than for myself I dare; let that suffice you.

IAGO Is my lord angry?

EMILIA He went hence but now,
And, certainly, in strange unquietness.

IAGO Can he be angry? I have seen the cannon,
When it hath blown his ranks into the air,
And, like the devil, from his very arm
Puff'd his own brother;– and can he be angry?
Something of moment, then: I will go meet him.
There's matter in 't, indeed, if he be angry.

DESDEMONA I pr'ythee, do so. *[Exit Iago.]* – Something, sure, of state –
Either from Venice, or some unhatch'd practice,
Made demonstrable here in Cyprus to him –
Hath puddled his clear spirit; and, in such cases,
Men's natures wrangle with inferior things,
Though great ones are their object. 'Tis even so;
For let our finger ache, and it indues
Our other healthful members ev'n to that sense
Of pain. Nay, we must think, men are not gods;
Nor of them look for such observancy
As fits the bridal. – Beshrew me much, Emilia,
I was (unhandsome warrior as I am)
Arraigning his unkindness with my soul:
But now I find, I had suborn'd the witness,

And he's indited falsely.

EMILIA Pray Heaven it be state-matters, as you think,
And no conception, nor no jealous toy,
Concerning you.

DESDEMONA Alas the day! I never gave him cause.

EMILIA But jealous souls will not be answer'd so;
They are not ever jealous for the cause,
But jealous for they are jealous: 'tis a monster
Begot upon itself, born on itself.

DESDEMONA Heaven keep that monster from Othello's mind!

EMILIA Lady, Amen.

DESDEMONA I will go seek him. – Cassio, walk hereabout:
If I do find him fit, I'll move your suit,
And seek to effect it to my uttermost.

CASSIO I humbly thank your ladyship.

[Exeunt Desdemona and Emilia.

Enter Bianca.

BIANCA Save you, friend Cassio!

CASSIO What make you from home?
How is it with you, my most fair Bianca?
I' faith, sweet love, I was coming to your house.

BIANCA And I was going to your lodging, Cassio.
What! keep a week away? seven days and nights?
Eight score eight hours? and lovers' absent hours,
More tedious than the dial eight score times?
O weary reckoning!

CASSIO Pardon me, Bianca;
I have this while with leaden thoughts been press'd;
But I shall, in a more continuate time,
Strike off this score of absence. Sweet Bianca,

[Giving her Desdemona's handkerchief.

Take me this work out.

BIANCA O Cassio, whence came this?
This is some token from a newer friend.
To the felt absence now I feel a cause.
It is come to this? Well, well.

CASSIO Go to, woman!
Throw your vile guesses in the devil's teeth,
From whence you have them. You are jealous now,
That is from some mistress, some remembrance:
No, in good troth, Bianca.

BIANCA Why, whose is it?

CASSIO I know not neither: I found it in my chamber.
I like the work well: ere it be demanded
(As like enough it will), I'd have it copied:
Take it, and do 't; and leave me for this time.

BIANCA Leave you! wherefore?

CASSIO I do attend here on the general,
And think it no addition, nor my wish,
To have him see me woman'd.

BIANCA Why, I pray you?

CASSIO Not that I love you not.

BIANCA But that you do not love me.
I pray you, bring me on the way a little;
And say, if I shall see you soon at night.

CASSIO 'Tis but a little way, that I can bring you,
For I attend here; but I'll see you soon.

BIANCA 'Tis very good: I must be circumstanc'd. *[Exeunt.*

ACT FOUR

SCENE I – BEFORE THE CASTLE.

Enter Othello and Iago.

IAGO Will you think so?
OTHELLO Think so, Iago?
IAGO What!
To kiss in private?
OTHELLO An unauthoris'd kiss.
IAGO Or to be naked with her friend a-bed,
An hour, or more, not meaning any harm?
OTHELLO Naked a-bed, Iago, and not mean harm?
It is hypocrisy against the devil:
They that mean virtuously, and yet do so,
The devil their virtue tempts, and they tempt Heaven.
IAGO If they do nothing, 'tis a venial slip:
But if I give my wife a handkerchief,–
OTHELLO What then?
IAGO Why, then 'tis hers, my lord; and, being hers,
She may, I think, bestow 't on any man.
OTHELLO She is protectress of her honour too:
May she give that?
IAGO Her honour is an essence that's not seen;
They have it very oft, they have it not:
But, for the handkerchief,–
OTHELLO By Heaven, I would most gladly have forgot it.
Thou saidst, – O! it comes o'er my memory,

As doth the raven o'er the infectious house,
Boding to all, – he had my handkerchief.

IAGO Ay, what of that?

OTHELLO That's not so good, now.

IAGO What, if I had said, I had seen him do you wrong?
Or heard him say, – as knaves be such abroad,
Who, having, by their own importunate suit,
Or voluntary dotage of some mistress,
Convinced or supplied them, cannot choose
But they must blab.

OTHELLO Hath he said anything?

IAGO He hath, my lord; but, be you well assur'd,
No more than he'll unswear.

OTHELLO What hath he said?

IAGO 'Faith, that he did – I know not what he did.

OTHELLO What? what?

IAGO Lie –

OTHELLO With her?

IAGO With her, on her; what you will.

OTHELLO Lie with her! lie on her! – We say, lie on her, when they belie her. Lie with her! that's fulsome. – Handkerchief, – confessions, handkerchief. – To confess, and be hanged for his labour. – First, to be hanged, and then to confess:– I tremble at it. Nature would not invest herself in such shadowing passion, without some instruction. It is not words, that shakes me thus. – Pish! – Noses, ears, and lips. – Is it possible? – Confess! – Handkerchief! – O devil! – *[Falls in a trance.*

IAGO Work on,
My medicine, work! Thus credulous fools are caught;
And many worthy and chaste dames, even thus,
All guiltless, meet reproach. – What, ho! my lord!

My lord, I say! Othello! –

Enter Cassio.

How now, Cassio?

CASSIO What's the matter?

IAGO My lord is fall'n into an epilepsy:
This is his second fit; he had one yesterday.

CASSIO Rub him about the temples.

IAGO No, forbear.
The lethargy must have his quiet course;
If not, he foams at mouth; and, by-and-by,
Breaks out to savage madness, Look, he stirs:
Do you withdraw yourself a little while,
He will recover straight: when he is gone,
I would on great occasion speak with you. –

[Exit Cassio.

How is it, general? have you hurt your head?

OTHELLO Dost thou mock me?

IAGO I mock you! no, by Heaven.
'Would you would bear your fortune like a man.

OTHELLO A horned man's a monster, and a beast.

IAGO There's many a beast then in a populous city,
And many a civil monster.

OTHELLO Did he confess it?

IAGO Good sir, be a man;
Think, every bearded fellow, that's but yok'd,
May draw with you: there's millions now alive,
That nightly lie in those unproper beds,
Which they dare swear peculiar: your case is better.
O! 't is the spite of hell, the fiend's arch-mock,
To lip a wanton in a secure couch,

And to suppose her chaste. No, let me know;
And, knowing what I am, I know what she shall be.

OTHELLO O! thou art wise; 'tis certain.

IAGO Stand you awhile apart;
Confine yourself but in a patient list.
Whilst you were here, o'erwhelmed with your grief
(A passion most unsuiting such a man),
Cassio came hither: I shifted him away,
And laid good 'scuse upon your ecstasy;
Bade him anon return, and here speak with me;
The which he promis'd. Do but encave yourself,
And mark the fleers, the gibes, and notable scorns,
That dwell in every region of his face;
For I will make him tell the tale anew,
Where, how, how oft, how long ago, and when
He hath, and is again to cope your wife:
I say, but mark his gesture. – Marry, patience;
Or I shall say, you are all in spleen,
And nothing of a man.

OTHELLO Dost thou hear, Iago?
I will be found most cunning in my patience;
But (dost thou hear?) most bloody.

IAGO That's not amiss;
But yet keep time in all. Will you withdraw?

[Othello withdraws.

Now will I question Cassio of Bianca,
A housewife, that by selling her desires
Buys herself bread and clothes: it is a creature,
That dotes on Cassio, as 'tis the strumpets' plague,
To beguile many, and be beguil'd by one.
He, when he hears of her, cannot refrain

From the excess of laughter. – Here he comes. –

Re-enter Cassio.

As he shall smile, Othello shall go mad;
And his unbookish jealousy must construe
Poor Cassio's smiles, gestures, and light behaviour
Quite in the wrong. – How do you now, lieutenant?

CASSIO The worser, that you give me the addition,
Whose want even kills me.

IAGO Ply Desdemona well, and you are sure on 't.
[Speaking lower] Now, if this suit lay in Bianca's dower,
How quickly should you speed!

CASSIO Alas, poor caitiff!

OTHELLO *[Aside.]* Look, how he laughs already!

IAGO I never knew woman love man so.

CASSIO Alas, poor rogue! I think, i' faith, she loves me.

OTHELLO *[Aside.]* Now he denies it faintly, and laughs it out.

IAGO Do you hear, Cassio?

OTHELLO *[Aside]* Now he importunes him
To tell it o'er. Go to; well said, well said.

IAGO She gives it out, that you shall marry her:
Do you intend it?

CASSIO Ha, ha, ha!

OTHELLO *[Aside.]* Do you triumph, Roman! do you triumph?

CASSIO I marry her! – what! a customer? I pr'ythee, bear some charity to my wit; do not think it so unwholesome. Ha, ha, ha!

OTHELLO *[Aside.]* So, so, so, so. They laugh that win.

IAGO 'Faith, the cry goes, that you shall marry her. –

CASSIO Pr'ythee, say true.

IAGO I am a very villain else.

OTHELLO *[Aside.]* Have you scored me? Well.

CASSIO This is the monkey's own giving out: she is persuaded I will marry her, out of her own love and flattery, not out of my promise.

OTHELLO *[Aside.]* Iago beckons me: now he begins the story.

CASSIO She was here even now; she haunts me in every place. I was, the other day, talking on the sea-bank with certain Venetians, and thither comes the bauble; and, by this hand, she falls me thus about my neck;–

OTHELLO *[Aside.]* Crying, O dear Cassio! as it were: his gesture imports it.

CASSIO So hangs, and lolls, and weeps upon me; so hales and pulls me: ha, ha, ha! –

OTHELLO *[Aside.]* Now he tells, how she plucked him to my chamber. O! I see that nose of yours, but not that dog I shall throw it to.

CASSIO Well, I must leave her company.

IAGO Before me! look, where she comes.

CASSIO 'Tis such another fitchew! marry, a perfumed one.

Enter Bianca.

What do you mean by this haunting of me?

BIANCA Let the devil and his dam haunt you! What did you mean by that same handkerchief, you gave me even now? I was a fine fool to take it. I must take out the work! – A likely piece of work, that you should find it in your chamber, and know not who left it there! This is some minx's token, and I must take out the work! There, give it your hobby-horse: wheresoever you had it, I'll take out no work on 't.

CASSIO How now, my sweet Bianca! how now, how now!

OTHELLO *[Aside.]* By Heaven, that should be my handkerchief!

BIANCA An you 'll come to supper to-night, you may; an you

will not, come when you are next prepared for. *[Exit.*

IAGO After her, after her.

CASSIO 'Faith, I must; she'll rail in the street else.

IAGO Will you sup there?

CASSIO 'Faith, I intend so.

IAGO Well, I may chance to see you, for I would very fain speak with you.

CASSIO Pr'ythee, come; will you?

IAGO Go to; say no more. *[Exit Cassio.*

OTHELLO *[Advancing.]* How shall I murder him, Iago?

IAGO Did you perceive how he laughed at his vice?

OTHELLO O, Iago!

IAGO And did you see the handkerchief?

OTHELLO Was that mine?

IAGO Yours, by this hand: and to see how he prizes the foolish woman, your wife! she gave it him, and he hath given it his whore.

OTHELLO I would have him nine years a-killing. – A fine woman! a fair woman! a sweet woman!

IAGO Nay, you must forget that.

OTHELLO Ay, let her rot, and perish, and be damned to-night; for she shall not live. No, my heart is turned to stone; I strike it, and it hurts my hand. O! the world hath not a sweeter creature; she might lie by an emperor's side, and command him tasks.

IAGO Nay, that's not your way.

OTHELLO Hang her! I do but say what she is. – So delicate with her needle! – An admirable musician! O! she will sing the savageness out of a bear. – Of so high and plenteous wit and invention! –

IAGO She's the worse for all this.

OTHELLO O! a thousand, a thousand times. And then, of so gentle a condition!

IAGO Ay, too gentle.

OTHELLO Nay, that's certain; – but yet the pity of it, Iago! – O, Iago! the pity of it, Iago!

IAGO If you are so fond over her iniquity, give her patent to offend: for, if it touch not you, it comes near nobody.

OTHELLO I will chop her into messes. – Cuckold me!

IAGO O! 'tis foul in her.

OTHELLO With mine officer!

IAGO That's fouler.

OTHELLO Get me some poison, Iago; this night:– I'll not expostulate with her, lest her body and beauty unprovide my mind again. – This night, Iago.

IAGO Do it not with poison, strangle her in her bed, even the bed she hath contaminated.

OTHELLO Good, good: the justice of it pleases; very good.

IAGO And for Cassio, let me be his undertaker: you shall hear more by midnight. *[A trumpet within.*

OTHELLO Excellent good. – What trumpet is that same?

IAGO Something from Venice, sure. 'Tis Lodovico,
Come from the duke; and see, your wife is with him.

Enter Lodovico, Desdemona and Attendants.

LODOVICO God save the worthy general!

OTHELLO With all my heart, sir.

LODOVICO The duke and senators of Venice greet you.
[Giving him a packet.

OTHELLO I kiss the instrument of their pleasures.
[Opens the packet, and reads.

DESDEMONA And what's the news, good cousin Lodovico?

IAGO I am very glad to see you, signior:
Welcome to Cyprus.
LODOVICO I thank you. How does Lieutenant Cassio?
IAGO Lives, sir.
DESDEMONA Cousin, there 's fall'n between him and my lord
An unkind breach, but you shall make all well.
OTHELLO Are you sure of that?
DESDEMONA My lord?
OTHELLO *[Reading.]* 'This fail you not to do, as you will' –
LODOVICO He did not call; he's busy in the paper.
Is there division 'twixt my lord and Cassio?
DESDEMONA A most unhappy one: I would do much
To atone them, for the love I bear to Cassio.
OTHELLO Fire and brimstone!
DESDEMONA My lord?
OTHELLO Are you wise?
DESDEMONA What! is he angry?
LODOVICO May be, the letter mov'd him;
For, as I think, they do command him home,
Deputing Cassio in his government.
DESDEMONA Trust me I am glad on't.
OTHELLO Indeed?
DESDEMONA My lord?
OTHELLO I am glad to see you mad.
DESDEMONA How, sweet Othello?
OTHELLO Devil! *[Striking her.*
DESDEMONA I have not deserv'd this.
LODOVICO My lord, this would not be believ'd in Venice,
Though I should swear I saw it. 'Tis very much:
Make her amends, she weeps.
OTHELLO O devil, devil!

If that earth could teem with woman's tears,
Each drop she falls would prove a crocodile –
Out of my sight!

DESDEMONA I will not stay to offend you. *[Going.*

LODOVICO Truly, an obedient lady. –
I do beseech your lordship, call her back.

OTHELLO Mistress!

DESDEMONA My lord?

OTHELLO What would you with her, sir?

LODOVICO Who, I, my lord?

OTHELLO Ay; you did wish, that I would make her turn:
Sir, she can turn, and turn, and yet go on,
And turn again; and she can weep, sir, weep;
And she's obedient, as you say – obedient, –
Very obedient. – Proceed you in your tears. –
Concerning this, sir, – O well-painted passion! –
I am commanded home. – Get you away;
I'll send for you anon. – Sir, I obey the mandate,
And will return to Venice. – Hence! avaunt! –
[Exit Desdemona.
Cassio shall have my place. And, – sir, to-night,
I do entreat that we may sup together:
You are welcome, sir, to Cyprus. – Goats and monkeys! *[Exit.*

LODOVICO Is this the noble Moor whom our full senate
Call all-in-all sufficient? – Is this the nature
Whom passion could not shake? whose solid virtue
The shot of accident, nor dart of chance,
Could neither graze nor pierce?

IAGO He is much chang'd.

LODOVICO Are his wits safe? is he not light of brain?

IAGO He 's that he is: I may not breathe my censure.

What he might be, – if, what he might, he is not, –
I would to Heaven, he were!

LODOVICO What! strike his wife!

IAGO 'Faith, that was not so well; yet 'would I knew,
That stroke would prove the worst.

LODOVICO Is it his use?
Or did the letters work upon his blood,
And new create his fault?

IAGO Alas, alas!
It is not honesty in me, to speak
What I have seen and known. You shall observe him,
And his own courses will denote him so,
That I may save my speech. Do but go after,
And mark how he continues.

LODOVICO I am sorry, that I am deceiv'd in him. *[Exeunt.*

SCENE II – A ROOM IN THE CASTLE.

Enter Othello and Emilia.

OTHELLO You have seen nothing then?

EMILIA Nor ever heard; nor ever did suspect.

OTHELLO Yes, you have seen Cassio and she together.

EMILIA But then I saw no harm; and then I heard
Each syllable that breath made up between them.

OTHELLO What, did they never whisper?

EMILIA Never, my lord.

OTHELLO Nor send you out o' the way?

EMILIA Never.

OTHELLO To fetch her fan, her gloves, her mask, nor nothing?

EMILIA Never, my lord.
OTHELLO That's strange.
EMILIA I durst, my lord, to wager she is honest,
Lay down my soul at stake: if you think other,
Remove your thought; it doth abuse your bosom.
If any wretch have put this in your head,
Let Heaven requite it with the serpent's curse!
For, if she be not honest, chaste, and true,
There's no man happy; the purest of their wives
Is foul as slander.
OTHELLO Bid her come hither:– go. – *[Exit Emilia.*
She says enough;– yet she's a simple bawd,
That cannot say as much. This is a subtle whore,
A closet-lock-and-key of villainous secrets:
And yet she'll kneel, and pray; I have seen her do't.

Re-enter Emilia, with Desdemona.

DESDEMONA My lord, what is your will?
OTHELLO Pray, chuck, come hither.
DESDEMONA What is your pleasure?
OTHELLO Let me see your eyes:
Look in my face.
DESDEMONA What horrible fancy 's this?
OTHELLO *[To Emilia.]* Some of your function, mistress;
Leave procreants alone, and shut the door;
Cough, or cry hem, if anybody come:
Your mystery, your mystery;– nay, despatch. *[Exit Emilia.*
DESDEMONA Upon my knees, what doth your speech import?
I understand a fury in your words,
But not the words.
OTHELLO Why, what art thou?

DESDEMONA Your wife, my lord; your true and loyal wife.

OTHELLO Come, swear it, damn thyself;
Lest, being like one of heaven, the devils themselves
Should fear to seize thee: therefore, be double-damn'd;
Swear thou art honest.

DESDEMONA Heaven doth truly know it.

OTHELLO Heaven truly knows, that thou art false as hell.

DESDEMONA To whom, my lord? with whom? how am I false?

OTHELLO Ah, Desdemon! – away, away, away!

DESDEMONA Alas, the heavy day! – Why do you weep?
Am I the motive of these tears, my lord?
If, haply, you my father do suspect
An instrument of this your calling back,
Lay not your blame on me; if you have lost him,
Why, I have lost him too.

OTHELLO Had it pleas'd Heaven
To try me with affliction; had they rain'd
All kinds of sores, and shames, on my bare head;
Steep'd me in poverty to the very lips;
Given to captivity me and my utmost hopes;
I should have found in some place of my soul
A drop of patience; but, alas! to make me
The fixed figure, for the time of scorn
To point his slow and moving finger at, –
Yet could I bear that too; well, very well;
But there, where I have garner'd up my heart,
Where either I must live, or bear no life,
The fountain from the which my current runs,
Or else dries up; to be discarded thence,
Or keep it as a cistern, for foul toads
To knot and gender in! – turn thy complexion there,

Patience, thou young and rose-lipp'd cherubin;
Ay, there, look grim as hell!
DESDEMONA I hope, my noble lord esteems me honest.
OTHELLO O! ay; as summer flies are in the shambles,
That quicken even with blowing. O thou weed?
Who art so lovely fair, and smell'st so sweet
That the sense aches at thee, – 'would thou
hadst ne'er been born!
DESDEMONA Alas! What ignorant sin have I committed?
OTHELLO Was this fair paper, this most goodly book,
Made to write whore upon? What committed?
Committed! – O thou public commoner!
I should make very forges of my cheeks,
That would to cinders burn up modesty,
Did I but speak thy deeds. – What committed?
Heaven stops the nose at it, and the moon winks;
The bawdy wind, that kisses all it meets,
Is hush'd within the hollow mine of earth,
And will not hear it. What committed? –
Impudent strumpet!
DESDEMONA By Heaven, you do me wrong.
OTHELLO Are you not a strumpet?
DESDEMONA No, as I am a Christian.
If to preserve this vessel for my lord,
From any other foul unlawful touch,
Be not to be a strumpet, I am none.
OTHELLO What, not a whore?
DESDEMONA No, as I shall be saved.
OTHELLO Is it possible?
DESDEMONA O, Heaven forgive us!
OTHELLO I cry you mercy then:

I took you for that cunning whore of Venice,
That married with Othello. – You, mistress,
That have the office opposite to Saint Peter,
And keep the gate of hell!

Re-enter Emilia.

You, you, ay, you:
We have done our course; there's no money for your pains.
I pray you, turn the key, and keep your counsel. *[Exit.*

EMILIA Alas! what does this gentleman conceive? –
How do you, madam? how do you, my good lady?

DESDEMONA 'Faith, half asleep.

EMILIA Good madam, what's the matter with my lord?

DESDEMONA With who?

EMILIA Why, with my lord, madam.

DESDEMONA Who is thy lord?

EMILIA He that is yours, sweet lady.

DESDEMONA I have none: do not talk to me, Emilia:
I cannot weep; nor answer have I none,
But what should go by water. Pr'ythee, to-night
Lay on my bed my wedding sheets, – remember; –
And call thy husband hither.

EMILIA Here's a change, indeed! *[Exit.*

DESDEMONA 'Tis meet I should be us'd so, very meet.
How have I been behav'd, that he might stick
The small'st opinion on my least misuse?

Re-enter Emilia, with Iago.

IAGO What is your pleasure, madam? How is 't with you?

DESDEMONA I cannot tell. Those, that do teach young babes,
Do it with gentle means and easy tasks:

He might have chid me so; for, in good faith,
I am a child to chiding.

IAGO What's the matter, lady?

EMILIA Alas, Iago, my lord hath so bewhor'd her,
Thrown such despite and heavy terms upon her,
As true hearts cannot bear.

DESDEMONA Am I that name, Iago?

IAGO What name, fair lady?

DESDEMONA Such as she says my lord did say I was.

EMILIA He call'd her whore: a beggar in his drink
Could not have laid such terms upon his callat.

IAGO Why did he so?

DESDEMONA I do not know; I am sure, I am none such.

IAGO Do not weep, do not weep. Alas the day!

EMILIA Hath she forsook so many noble matches,
Her father, and her country, and her friends,
To be call'd whore? would it not make one weep?

DESDEMONA It is my wretched fortune.

IAGO Beshrew him for't!
How comes this trick upon him?

DESDEMONA Nay, Heaven doth know.

EMILIA I will be hang'd, if some eternal villain,
Some busy and insinuating rogue,
Some cogging cozening slave, to get some office,
Have not devis'd this slander; I'll be hang'd else.

IAGO Fie! there is no such man: it is impossible.

DESDEMONA If any such there be, Heaven pardon him!

EMILIA A halter pardon him, and hell gnaw his bones!
Why should he call her whore? who keeps her company?
What place? what time? what form? what likelihood?
The Moor's abus'd by some most villainous knave,

Some base notorious knave, some scurvy fellow. –
O Heaven! that such companions thou'dst unfold,
And put in every honest hand a whip,
To lash the rascals naked through the world,
Even from the east to the west!

IAGO Speak within door.

EMILIA O, fie upon them! Some such squire he was,
That turn'd your wit the seamy side without,
And made you to suspect me with the Moor.

IAGO You are a fool; go to.

DESDEMONA O good Iago!
What shall I do to win my lord again?
Good friend, go to him; for, by this light of heaven,
I know not how I lost him. Here I kneel:–
If e'er my will did trespass 'gainst his love,
Either in discourse of thought, or actual deed;
Or that mine eyes, mine ears, or any sense,
Delighted them in any other form;
Or that I do not yet, and ever did,
And ever will, – though he do shake me off
To beggarly divorcement, – love him dearly,
Comfort forswear me! Unkindness may do much;
And his unkindness may defeat my life,
But never taint my love. I cannot say whore:
It does abhor me, now I speak the word;
To do the act that might the addition earn,
Not the world's mass of vanity could make me.

IAGO I pray you, be content; 'tis but his humour:
The business of the state does him offence,
And he does chide with you.

DESDEMONA If 't were no other, –

IAGO 'Tis but sc, I warrant.

[Trumpets.

Hark, how these intruments summon to supper!
The messengers of Venice stay the meat.
Go in, and weep not; all things shall be well.

[Exeunt Desdemona and Emilia.

Enter Roderigo

How now, Rogerigo?

RODERIGO I do not find that thou deal'st justly with me.

IAGO What in the contrary?

RODERIGO Every day thou daff'st me with some device, Iago; and rather, as it seems to me now, keep'st from me all conveniency, than suppliest me with the least advantage of hope. I will, indeed, no longer endure it; nor am I yet persuaded, to put up in peace what already I have foolishly suffered.

IAGO Will you hear me, Roderigo?

RODERIGO 'Faith, I have heard too much; for your words, and performances, are no kin together.

IAGO You charge me most unjustly.

RODERIGO With nought but truth. I have wasted myself out of my means. The jewels you have had from me, to deliver to Desdemona, would half have corrupted a votarist: you have told me, she hath received them, and returned me expectations and comforts of sudden respect and acquaintance; but I find none.

IAGO Well; go to; very well.

RODERIGO Very well! go to! I cannot go to, man: nor 'tis not very well: by this hand, I say, it is very scurvy; and begin to find myself fopped in it.

IAGO Very well.

RODERIGO I tell you, 'tis not very well. I will make myself known to Desdemona: if she will return me my jewels, I will give over my suit, and repent my unlawful solicitation; if not, assure yourself, I will seek satisfaction of you.

IAGO You have said now.

RODERIGO Ay, and I have said nothing, but what I protest intendment of doing.

IAGO Why, now I see there's mettle in thee; and even, from this instant, do build on thee a better opinion than ever before. Give me thy hand, Roderigo: thou hast taken against me a most just exception; but yet, I protest I have dealt most directly in thy affair.

RODERIGO It hath not appeared.

IAGO I grant, indeed, it hath not appeared, and your suspicion is not without wit and judgment. But, Roderigo, if thou hast that within thee indeed, which I have greater reason to believe now than ever, – I mean, purpose, courage, and valour, – this night show it: if thou the next night following enjoyest not Desdemona, take me from this world with treachery, and devise engines for my life.

RODERIGO Well, what is it? Is it within reason and compass?

IAGO Sir, there is especial commission come from Venice, to depute Cassio in Othello's place.

RODERIGO Is that true? why, then Othello and Desdemona return again to Venice.

IAGO O, no! he goes into Mauritania, and takes away with him the fair Desdemona, unless his abode be lingered here by some accident; wherein none can be so determinate, as the removing of Cassio.

RODERIGO How do you mean, removing him?

IAGO Why, by making him uncapable of Othello's place; knocking out his brains.

RODERIGO And that you would have me do?

IAGO Ay; if you dare do yourself a profit, and a right. He sups to-night with a harlotry, and thither will I go to him: he knows not yet of his honourable fortune. If you will watch his going thence (which I will fashion to fall out between twelve and one), you may take him at your pleasure: I will be near to second your attempt, and he shall fall between us. Come, stand not amazed at it, but go along with me; I will show you such a necessity in his death, that you shall think yourself bound to put it on him. It is now high supper-time, and the night grows to waste: about it.

RODERIGO I will hear further reason for this.

IAGO And you shall be satisfied. *[Exeunt.*

SCENE III – ANOTHER ROOM IN THE CASTLE.

Enter Othello, Lodovico, Desdemona, Emilia, and Attendants.

LODOVICO I do beseech you, sir, trouble yourself no further.

OTHELLO O! pardon me; 'twill do me good to walk.

LODOVICO Madam, good night; I humbly thank your ladyship.

DESDEMONA Your honour is most welcome.

OTHELLO Will you walk, sir? –
O! – Desdemona, –

DESDEMONA My lord?

OTHELLO Get you to bed on the instant; I will be returned forthwith: dismiss your attendant there: look it be done.

DESDEMONA I will, my lord.

[Exeunt Othello, Lodovico, and Attendants.

EMILIA How goes it now? he looks gentler than he did.

DESDEMONA He says, he will return incontinent;
He hath commanded me to go to bed,
And bade me to dismiss you.

EMILIA Dismiss me!

DESDEMONA It was his bidding; therefore, good Emilia,
Give me my nightly wearing, and adieu:
We must not now displease him.

EMILIA I would you had never seen him.

DESDEMONA So would not I: my love doth so approve him, That even his stubbornness, his checks, and frowns, – Pr'ythee, unpin me, – have grace and favour in them.

EMILIA I have laid those sheets you bade me on the bed.

DESDEMONA All's one. – Good father! how foolish are our minds! –
If I do die before thee, pr'ythee, shroud me
In one of those same sheets.

EMILIA Come, come, you talk.

DESDEMONA My mother had a maid call'd Barbara;
She was in love; and he she lov'd prov'd mad,
And did forsake her: she had a song of – willow;
An old thing 'twas, but it express'd her fortune,
And she died singing it: that song, to-night,
Will not go from my mind; I have much to do,
But to go hang my head all at one side,
And sing it like poor Barbara. Pr'ythee, despatch.

EMILIA Shall I go fetch your night-gown?

DESDEMONA No, unpin me here. –
This Lodovico is a proper man.

EMILIA A very handsome man.

DESDEMONA He speaks well.

EMILIA I know a lady in Venice would have walked barefoot to Palestine, for a touch of his nether lip.

DESDEMONA *[Singing.] The poor soul sat sighing by a sycamore tree;*
Sing all a green willow;
Her hand on her bosom, her head on her knee;
Sing willow, willow, willow:
The fresh streams ran by her, and murmur'd her moans;
Sing willow, willow, willow;
Her salt tears fell from her, and soften'd the stones;
Lay by these. –
Sing willow, willow, willow.
Pr'ythee, hie thee: he'll come anon. –
Sing all a green willow must be my garland.
Let nobody blame him, his scorn I approve, –
Nay, that's not next. – Hark! who is it that knocks?

EMILIA It is the wind.

DESDEMONA *I call'd my love, false love; but what said he then?*
Sing willow, willow, willow;
If I court moe women, you'll couch with moe men.
So, get thee gone; good night. Mine eyes do itch;
Doth that bode weeping?

EMILIA 'Tis neither here nor there.

DESDEMONA I have heard it said so. – O, these men, these men! –
Dost thou in conscience think, – tell me, Emilia, –
That there be women do abuse their husbands
In such gross kind?

EMILIA There be some such, no question.

DESDEMONA Wouldst thou do such a deed for all the world?

EMILIA Why, would not you?

DESDEMONA No, by this heavenly light!

EMILIA Nor I neither by this heavenly light: I might do 't as well i' the dark.

DESDEMONA Wouldst thou do such a deed for all the world?

EMILIA The world is a huge thing: 'tis a great price
For a small vice.

DESDEMONA In troth, I think thou wouldst not.

EMILIA In troth, I think I should, and undo 't when I had done. Marry, I would not do such a thing for a joint-ring, nor for measures of lawn, nor for gowns, petticoats, nor caps, nor any petty exhibition; but, for the whole world, – why, who would not make her husband a cuckold, to make him a monarch? I should venture purgatory for 't.

DESDEMONA Beshrew me, if I would do such a wrong
For the whole world.

EMILIA Why, the wrong is but a wrong i' the world; and, having the world for your labour, 'tis a wrong in your own world, and you might quickly make it right.

DESDEMONA I do not think there is any such woman.

EMILIA Yes, a dozen; and as many to the vantage,
As would store the world they played for.
But, I do think, it is their husbands' faults,
If wives do fall. Say, that they slack their duties,
And pour our treasures into foreign laps;
Or else break out in peevish jealousies,
Throwing restraint upon us; or, say, they strike us,
Or scant our former having in despite:
Why, we have galls; and, though we have some grace,
Yet have we some revenge. Let husbands know,
Their wives have sense like them: they see, and smell,
And have their palates, both for sweet and sour,
As husbands have. What is it that they do,
When they change us for others? Is it sport?
I think, it is. And doth affection breed it?

I think, it doth. Is 't frailty, that thus errs?
It is too. And have not we affections,
Desires for sport, and frailty, as men have?
Then, let them use us well; else let them know,
The ills we do, their ills instruct us so.

DESDEMONA Good night, good night: Heaven me such uses send,
Not to pick bad from bad, but by bad mend! *[Exeunt.*

ACT FIVE

SCENE I – A STREET

Enter Iago and Roderigo

IAGO Here, stand behind this bulk; straight will he come:
Wear thy good rapier bare, and put it home.
Quick, quick; fear nothing; I'll be at thy elbow.
It makes us, or it mars us; think on that,
And fix most firm thy resolution.

RODERIGO Be near at hand; I may miscarry in 't.

IAGO Here, at thy hand; be bold, and take thy stand. *[Retires.*

RODERIGO I have no great devotion to the deed;
And yet he has given me satisfying reasons. –
'Tis but a man gone: – forth, my sword; he dies.

IAGO I have rubb'd this young quat almost to the sense,
And he grows angry. Now, whether he kill Cassio,
Or Cassio him, or each do kill the other,
Every way makes my gain: live Rodgerigo,
He calls me to a restitution large
Of gold, and jewels, that I bobb'd from him,
As gifts to Desdemona;
It must not be: if Cassio do remain,
He hath a daily beauty in his life,
That makes me ugly; and, besides, the Moor
May unfold me to him: there stand I in much peril.
No, he must die: – but, so I hear him coming.

Enter Cassio.

RODERIGO I know his gait; 'tis he. – Villain, thou diest.
[Rushing out, and making a pass at Cassio.

CASSIO That thrust had been mine enemy indeed,
But that my coat is better than thou know'st:
I will make proof of thine.
[Draws, and wounds Roderigo.

RODERIGO O, I am slain!
[Iago rushes from his post, cuts Cassio behind in the leg, and exit.

CASSIO I am maim'd for ever. – Help, ho! murder! murder!
[Falls.

Enter Othello, at a distance.

OTHELLO The voice of Cassio:– Iago keeps his word.

RODERIGO O, villain that I am!

OTHELLO It is even so.

CASSIO O, help! ho! light! a surgeon!

OTHELLO 'Tis he. – O brave Iago, honest, and just,
That hast such noble sense of thy friend's wrong!
Thou teachest me, – Minion, your dear lies dead,
And your unblest fate hies:– strumpet, I come!
Forth of my heart those charms, thine eyes, are blotted;
Thy bed, lust-stain'd, shall with lust's blood be spotted.
[Exit.

Enter Lodovico and Gratiano, at a distance.

CASSIO What, ho! no watch? no passage? murder! murder!

GRATIANO 'Tis some mischance; the cry is very direful.

CASSIO O, help!

LODOVICO Hark!

RODERIGO O wretched villain!

LODOVICO Two or three groan. – It is a heavy night!
These may be counterfeits; let's think 't unsafe
To come in to the cry without more help.

RODERIGO Nobody come? then shall I bleed to death.

LODOVICO Hark!

Re-enter Iago, with a light.

GRATIANO Here's one comes in his shirt, with light and weapons.

IAGO Who's there? whose noise is this, that cries on murder?

LODERIGO We do not know.

IAGO Did not you hear a cry?

CASSIO Here, here! for Heaven's sake, help me!

IAGO What's the matter?

GRATIANO This is Othello's ancient, as I take it.

LODOVICO The same, indeed; a very valiant fellow.

IAGO What are you here, that cry so grievously?

CASSIO Iago? O! I am spoil'd, undone by villains:
Give me some help.

IAGO O me, lieutenant! what villains have done this?

CASSIO I think that one of them is hereabout,
And cannot make away.

IAGO O treacherous villains! –
[To Lodovico and Gratiano.] What are you there? come in, and give some help.

RODERIGO O, help me here!

CASSIO That's one of them.

IAGO O murderous slave! O villain!
[Stabs Roderigo.

RODERIGO O damn'd Iago! O inhuman dog!

IAGO Kill men i' the dark! – Where be these bloody thieves? –

How silent is this town! – Ho! murder! murder!
What may you be? are you of good, or evil?

LODOVICO As you shall prove us, praise us.

IAGO Signior Lodovico?

LODOVICO He, sir.

IAGO I cry you mercy. Here's Cassio hurt by villains.

GRATIANO Cassio?

IAGO How is 't, brother?

CASSIO My leg is cut in two.

IAGO Marry, Heaven forbid! –
Light, gentlemen; I'll bind it with my shirt.

Enter Bianca.

BIANCA What is the matter, ho? who is 't that cried?

IAGO Who is 't that cried?

BIANCA O my dear Cassio! my sweet Cassio!
O Cassio, Cassio, Cassio!

IAGO O notable strumpet! – Cassio, may you suspect
Who they should be, that have thus mangled you?

CASSIO No.

GRATIANO I am sorry to find you thus: I have been to seek you.

IAGO Lend me a garter: – so. – O, for a chair,
To bear him easily hence!

BIANCA Alas! he faints. – O Cassio, Cassio, Cassio!

IAGO Gentlemen all, I do suspect this trash
To be a party in this injury. –
Patience awhile, good Cassio. – Come, come.
Lend me a light. – Know we this face, or no?
Alas! my friend, and my dear countryman,
Roderigo? no:– yes, sure. O Heaven! Roderigo.

GRATIANO What, of Venice?

IAGO Even he, sir; did you know him?

GRATIANO Know him? ay.

IAGO Signor Gratiano? I cry you gentle pardon:
These bloody accidents must excuse my manners,
That so neglected you.

GRATIANO I am glad to see you.

IAGO How do you, Cassio? – O, a chair, a chair!

GRATIANO Roderigo?

IAGO He, he, 'tis he. – *[A chair brought in.]* O! that's well said;– the chair.–
Some good man bear him carefully from hence;
I'll fetch the general's surgeon. – *[To Bianca.]* For you, mistress,
Save you your labour. – He that lies slain here, Cassio,
Was my dear friend. What malice was between you?

CASSIO None in the world; nor do I know the man.

IAGO *[To Bianca.]* What, look you pale? – O, bear him out o' the air.–

[Cassio and Roderigo are borne off.

Stay you, good gentlemen. – Look you pale, mistress? –
Do you perceive the ghastness of her eye? –
Nay, if you stare, we shall hear more anon. –
Behold her well; I pray you, look upon her:
Do you see, gentlemen? nay, guiltiness will speak,
Though tongues were out of use.

Enter Emilia.

EMILIA 'Las! what's the matter! what's the matter, husband?

IAGO Cassio hath here been set on in the dark
By Roderigo, and fellows that are 'scap'd.
He's almost slain, and Roderigo dead.

EMILIA Alas, good gentleman! alas, good Cassio!

IAGO This is the fruits of whoring. – Pr'ythee, Emilia,
Go know of Cassio where he supp'd to-night. –
What! do you shake at that?

BIANCA He supp'd at my house; but I therefore shake not.

IAGO O, did he so? I charge you, go with me.

EMILIA Fie, fie upon thee, strumpet!

BIANCA I am no strumpet; but of life as honest,
As you that thus abuse me.

EMILIA As I? foh! fie upon thee!

IAGO Kind gentlemen, let's go and see poor Cassio dress'd.–
Come, mistress, you must tell 's another tale. –
Emilia, run you to the citadel,
And tell my lord and lady what hath happ'd. –
Will you go on afore? – *[Aside.]* This is the night,
That either makes me, or fordoes me quite. *[Exeunt.*

SCENE II – A BEDCHAMBER.

Desdemona in bed asleep. A light burning. Enter Othello.

OTHELLO It is the cause, it is the cause, my soul, –
Let me not name it to you, you chaste stars! –
It is the cause. – Yet I'll not shed her blood;
Nor scar that whiter skin of hers than snow,
And smooth as monumental alabaster.
Yet she must die, else she'll betray more men.
Put out the light, and then put out the light:
If I quench thee, thou flaming minister,
I can again in thy former light restore,
Should I repent me; but once put out thy light,
Thou cunning'st pattern of excelling nature,

I know not where is that Promethean heat
That can thy light relume. When I have pluck'd thy rose,
I cannot give it vital growth again,
It needs must wither: – I'll smell it on the tree. – *[Kissing her.*
O balmy breath, that dost almost persuade
Justice to break her sword! – One more, one more. –
Be thus when thou art dead, and I will kill thee,
And love thee after. – One more, and this the last:
So sweet was ne'er so fatal. I must weep,
But they are cruel tears: this sorrow's heavenly;
It strikes where it doth love. – She wakes.

DESDEMONA Who's there? Othello?

OTHELLO Ay, Desdemona.

DESDEMONA Will you come to bed, my lord?

OTHELLO Have you pray'd to-night, Desdemon?

DESDEMONA Ay, my lord.

OTHELLO If you bethink yourself of any crime,
Unreconcil'd as yet to Heaven and grace,
Solicit for it straight.

DESDEMONA Alas, my lord! what may you mean by that?

OTHELLO Well, do it, and be brief; I will walk by:
I would not kill thy unprepared spirit;
No, – Heaven forfend! – I would not kill thy soul.

DESDEMONA Talk you of killing?

OTHELLO Ay, I do.

DESDEMONA Then, Heaven
Have mercy on me!

OTHELLO Amen, with all my heart!

DESDEMONA If you say so, I hope you will not kill me.

OTHELLO Hum!

DESDEMONA And yet I fear you; for you are fatal then,

When your eyes roll so. Why I should fear, I know not,
Since guiltiness I know not; but yet, I feel I fear.

OTHELLO Think on thy sins.

DESDEMONA They are loves I bear to you.

OTHELLO Ay, and for that thou diest.

DESDEMONA That death's unnatural, that kills for loving. –
Alas! why gnaw you so your nether lip?
Some bloody passion shakes your very frame:
These are portents; but yet I hope, I hope,
They do not point on me.

OTHELLO Peace, and be still!

DESDEMONA I will so. What's the matter?

OTHELLO That handkerchief, which I so lov'd and gave thee,
Thou gav'st to Cassio.

DESDEMONA No, by my life and soul!
Send for the man, and ask him.

OTHELLO Sweet soul, take heed,
Take heed of perjury: thou art on thy death-bed.

DESDEMONA Ay, but not yet to die.

OTHELLO Yes, presently:
Therefore, confess thee freely of thy sin;
For to deny each article with oath
Cannot remove, nor choke, the strong conception,
That I do groan withal. Thou art to die.

DESDEMONA Then Lord have mercy on me!

OTHELLO I say, Amen.

DESDEMONA And have you mercy too! – I never did
Offend you in my life: never lov'd Cassio,
But with such general warranty of Heaven
As I might love: I never gave him token.

OTHELLO By Heaven, I saw my handkerchief in 's hand.

O perjur'd woman! thou dost stone my heart,
And mak'st me call what I intend to do,
A murder, which I thought a sacrifice:
I saw the handkerchief.

DESDEMONA He found it then;
I never gave it him. – Send for him hither;
Let him confess a truth.

OTHELLO He hath confess'd.

DESDEMONA What, my lord?

OTHELLO That he hath us'd thee.

DESDEMONA How? unlawfully?

OTHELLO Ay.

DESDEMONA He will not say so.

OTHELLO No; his mouth is stopp'd:
Honest Iago hath ta'en order for 't.

DESDEMONA O, my fear interprets. – What, is he dead?

OTHELLO Had all his hairs been lives, my great revenge
Had stomach for them all.

DESDEMONA Alas! he is betray'd, and I undone.

OTHELLO Out, strumpet! Weep'st thou for him to my face?

DESDEMONA O! banish me, my lord, but kill me not.

OTHELLO Down, strumpet!

DESDEMONA Kill me to-morrow; let me live to-night.

OTHELLO Nay, if you strive, –

DESDEMONA But half an hour!

OTHELLO Being done, there is no pause.

DESDEMONA But while I say one prayer.

OTHELLO It is too late. *[He smothers her*

EMILIA *[Within.]* My lord, my lord! what, ho! my lord my lord!

OTHELLO What noise is this? – Not dead? not yet quite dead?
I, that am cruel, am yet merciful;

I would not have thee linger in thy pain. –
So, so.

EMILIA *[Within.]* What, ho! my lord, my lord!

OTHELLO Who's there!

EMILIA *[Within.]* O, good my lord! I would speak a word with you.

OTHELLO Yes; – 'tis Emilia: – by-and-by. – She 's dead. –
'Tis like she comes to speak of Cassio's death;
The noise was high. – Ha! no more moving?
Still as the grave. – Shall she come in? Were 't good: –
I think she stirs again: – no. – What's best to do?
If she come in, she'll sure speak to my wife:
My wife! my wife! what wife? – I have no wife:
O, insupportable! O heavy hour!
Methinks it should be now a huge eclipse
Of sun and moon, and that the affrighted globe
Should yawn at alteration.

EMILIA *[Within.]* I do beseech you, I may speak with you.
O, good my lord!

OTHELLO I had forgot thee. O! come in, Emilia. –
Soft, – by-and-by: – let me the curtains draw. –
Where art thou? What's the matter with thee now?
[Unlocks the door.

Enter Emilia.

EMILIA O, my good lord! yonder's foul murder done.

OTHELLO What! now?

EMILIA But now, my lord.

OTHELLO It is the very error of the moon;
She comes more nearer earth than she was wont,
And makes men mad.

EMILIA Cassio, my lord, has kill'd a young Venetian,
Call'd Roderigo.
OTHELLO Roderigo kill'd!
And Cassio kill'd!
EMILIA No; Cassio is not kill'd.
OTHELLO Not Cassio kill'd? Then murder's out of tune,
And sweet revenge grows harsh.
DESDEMONA O, falsely, falsely murder'd!
EMILIA Alas! what cry is that?
OTHELLO That! what?
EMILIA Out, and alas! that was my lady's voice: –
Help! help, ho! help! – O lady, speak again!
Sweet Desdemona! O, sweet mistress, speak!
DESDEMONA A guiltless death I die.
EMILIA O, who hath done this deed?
DESDEMONA Nobody; I myself: farewell:
Commend me to my kind lord. O, farewell! *[Dies.*
OTHELLO Why, how should she be murder'd?
EMILIA Alas, who knows?
OTHELLO You heard her say herself, it was not I.
EMILIA She said so: I must needs report the truth.
OTHELLO She's like a liar gone to burning hell:
'Twas I that kill'd her.
EMILIA O! the more angel she,
And you the blacker devil!
OTHELLO She turn'd to folly, and she was a whore.
EMILIA Thou dost belie her, and thou art a devil.
OTHELLO She was false as water.
EMILIA Thou art rash as fire, to say
That she was false: O! she was heavenly true.
OTHELLO Cassio did tup her; ask thy husband else.

O! I were damn'd beneath all depth in hell,
But that I did proceed upon just grounds
To this extremity. Thy husband knew it all.

EMILIA My husband?

OTHELLO Thy husband.

EMILIA That she was false to wedlock?

OTHELLO Ay, with Cassio. Nay, had she been true,
If Heaven would make me such another world
Of one entire and perfect chrysolite,
I'd not have sold her for it.

EMILIA My husband?

OTHELLO Ay, 'twas he that told me first:
An honest man he is, and hates the slime
That sticks on filthy deeds.

EMILIA My husband?

OTHELLO What needs this iterance, woman? I say, thy husband.

EMILIA O mistress! villainy hath made mocks with love. –
My husband say, that she was false?

OTHELLO He, woman;
I say, thy husband: dost understand the word?
My friend, thy husband, honest, honest Iago.

EMILIA If he say so, may his pernicious soul
Rot half a grain a day! he lies to the heart:
She was too fond of her most filthy bargain.

OTHELLO Ha!

EMILIA Do thy worst:
This deed of thine is no more worthy heaven,
Than thou wast worthy her.

OTHELLO Peace! you were best.

EMILIA Thou hast not half that power to do me harm,.
As I have to be hurt. O gull! O dolt!

As ignorant as dirt! thou hast done a deed, –
I care not for thy sword; I'll make thee known,
Though I lost twenty lives. – Help! help, ho! help!
The Moor has kill'd my mistress! Murder! murder!

Enter Montano, Gratiano, and Iago.

MONTANO What is the matter? – How now, general?
EMILIA O! are you come, Iago? you have done well,
That men must lay their murders on your neck.
GRATIANO What is the matter?
EMILIA Disprove this villain, if thou be'st a man:
He says, thou told'st him that his wife was false.
I know, thou didst not, thou'rt not such a villain.
Speak, for my heart is full.
IAGO I told him what I thought; and told no more
Than what he found himself was apt and true.
EMILIA But did you ever tell him, she was false?
IAGO I did.
EMILIA You told a lie; an odious, damned lie;
Upon my soul, a lie; a wicked lie. –
She false with Cassio! – Did you say with Cassio?
IAGO With Cassio, mistress. Go to, charm your tongue.
EMILIA I will not charm my tongue; I am bound to speak.
My mistress here lies murder'd in her bed.
ALL O heavens forfend!
EMILIA And your reports have set the murder on.
OTHELLO Nay, stare not, masters: it is true, indeed.
GRATIANO 'Tis a strange truth.
MONTANO O monstrous act!
EMILIA Villainy! villainy! villainy!
I think upon 't, – I think, – I smell 't: – O villainy!

I thought so then: – I'll kill myself for grief. –
O villainy, villainy!

IAGO What! are you mad? I charge you, get you home.

EMILIA Good gentlemen, let me have leave to speak:
'Tis proper I obey him, but not now. –
Perchance, Iago, I will ne'er go home.

OTHELLO O! O! O! *[Falling on the bed.*

EMILIA Nay, lay thee down, and roar;
For thou hast kill'd the sweetest innocent,
That e'er did lift up eye.

OTHELLO *[Rising.]* O! she was foul. –
I scarce did know you, uncle. There lies your niece,
Whose breath, indeed, these hands have newly stopp'd.
I know, this act shows horrible and grim.

GRATIANO Poor Desdemon! I am glad thy father's dead.
Thy match was mortal to him, and pure grief
Shore his old thread in twain: did he live now,
This sight would make him do a desperate turn,
Yea, curse his better angel from his side,
And fall to reprobance.

OTHELLO 'Tis pitiful; but yet Iago knows,
That she with Cassio hath the act of shame
A thousand times committed: Cassio confess'd it;
And she did gratify his amorous works
With that recognisance and pledge of love
Which I first gave her. I saw it in his hand;
It was a handkerchief, an antique token
My father gave my mother.

EMILIA O Heaven! O heavenly powers!

IAGO Come, hold your peace.

EMILIA 'Twill out, 'twill out: I hold my peace, sir? no;

No, I will speak as liberal as the north;
Let Heaven, and men, and devils, let them all,
All, all, cry shame against me, yet I'll speak.

IAGO Be wise, and get you home.

EMILIA I will not.

[Iago offers to stab his wife.

GRATIANO Fie!
Your sword upon a woman!

EMILIA O thou dull Moor! that handkerchief thou speak'st of,
I found by fortune, and did give my husband;
For often, with a solemn earnestness,
(More than, indeed, belong'd to such a trifle,)
He begg'd of me to steal it.

IAGO Villainous whore!

EMILIA She give it Cassio! no, alas! I found it,
And I did give 't my husband.

IAGO Filth, thou liest!

EMILIA By Heaven, I do not; I do not, gentlemen. –
O murderous coxcomb! what should such a fool
Do with so good a wife?

[Iago stabs Emilia, then runs out.

OTHELLO Are there no stones in heaven,
But what serve for the thunder? – Precious villain!

GRATIANO The woman falls: sure he hath kill'd his wife.

EMILIA Ay, ay. O, lay me by my mistress' side!

GRATIANO He 's gone, but his wife 's kill'd.

MONTANO 'Tis a notorious villain. Take you this weapon,
Which I have here recover'd from the Moor.
Come, guard the door without: let him not pass,
But kill him rather. I'll after that same villain,
For 'tis a damned slave. *[Exit.*

OTHELLO I am not valiant neither,
But every puny whisper gets my sword.
But why should honour outlive honesty?
Let it go all.

EMILIA What did thy song bode, lady?
Hark, canst thou hear me? I will play the swan,
And die in music. – *[Singing.] Willow, willow, willow.* –
Moor, she was chaste; she lov'd thee, cruel Moor:
So come my soul to bliss, as I speak true;
So speaking as I think, I die, – I die. *[Dies.*

OTHELLO I have another weapon in this chamber;
It is a sword of Spain, the ice-brook's temper.
O! here it is. – Uncle, I must come forth.

GRATIANO If thou attempt it, it will cost thee dear:
Thou hast no weapon, and perforce must suffer.

OTHELLO Look in upon me then, and speak with me,
Or, naked as I am, I will assault thee.

GRATIANO What is the matter?

OTHELLO Behold! I have a weapon;
A better never did itself sustain
Upon a soldier's thigh: I have seen the day,
That with this little arm, and this good sword,
I have made my way through more impediments
Than twenty times your stop. – But, O vain boast!
Who can control his fate? 'tis not so now. –
Be not afraid, though you do see me weapon'd:
Here is my journey's end, here is my butt,
And very sea-mark of my utmost sail.
Do you go back dismay'd? 'tis a lost fear;
Man but a rush against Othello's breast,
And he retires. – Where should Othello go? –

Now, how dost thou look now? O ill-starr'd wench!
Pale as thy smock! when we shall meet at compt,
This look of thine will hurl my soul from heaven,
And fiends will snatch at it. Cold, cold, my girl!
Even like thy chastity.
O, cursed, cursed slave! – Whip me, ye devils,
From the possession of this heavenly sight!
Blow me about in winds! roast me in sulphur!
Wash me in steep-down gulfs of liquid fire!
O Desdemon! dead, Desdemon! dead! O!

Enter Lodovico, Montano, Cassio, carried in a chair, and Officers, with Iago, prisoner.

LODOVICO Where is this rash and most unfortunate man?
OTHELLO That's he that was Othello; – here I am.
LODOVICO Where is that viper? bring the villain forth.
OTHELLO I look down towards his feet; – but that's a fable:
If that thou be'st a devil, I cannot kill thee.
[Wounds Iago.
LODOVICO Wrench his sword from him.
IAGO I bleed, sir; but not kill'd.
OTHELLO I am not sorry neither: I'd have thee live;
For, in my sense, 'tis happiness to die.
LODOVICO O thou Othello! that wert once so good,
Fall'n in the practice of a damned slave,
What shall be said to thee?
OTHELLO Why, anything:
An honourable murderer, if you will;
For nought did I in hate, but all in honour.
LODOVICO This wretch hath part confessed his villainy;
Did you and he consent in Cassio's death?

OTHELLO Ay.
CASSIO Dear general, I never gave you cause.
OTHELLO I do believe it, and I ask you pardon.
Will you, I pray, demand that demi-devil,
Why he hath thus ensnar'd my soul and body?
IAGO Demand me nothing: what you know, you know:
From this time forth I never will speak word.
LODOVICO What! not to pray?
GRATIANO Torments will ope your lips.
OTHELLO Well, thou dost best.
LODOVICO Sir, you shall understand what hath befall'n.
Which, as I think, you know not. Here is a letter,
Found in the pocket of the slain Roderigo;
And here another: the one of them imports
The death of Cassio to be undertook
By Roderigo.
OTHELLO O villain!
CASSIO Most heathenish, and most gross!
LODOVICO Now, here's another discontented paper,
Found in his pocket too; and this, it seems,
Roderigo meant to have sent this damned villain;
But that, belike, Iago in the interim
Came in and satisfied him.
OTHELLO O thou pernicious caitiff! –
How came you, Cassio, by that handkerchief,
That was my wife's?
CASSIO I found it in my chamber:
And he himself confess'd, but even now,
That there he dropp'd it, for a special purpose,
Which wrought to his desire.
OTHELLO O fool! fool! fool!

CASSIO There is, besides, in Roderigo's letter,
How he upbraids Iago, that he made him
Brave me upon the watch; whereupon it came
That I was cast: and even but now he spake,
After long seeming dead, – Iago hurt him,
Iago set him on.

LODOVICO You must forsake this room, and go with us:
Your power and your command is taken off,
And Cassio rules in Cyprus. For this slave, –
If there be any cunning cruelty,
That can torment him much, and hold him long,
It shall be his. You shall close prisoner rest,
Till that the nature of your fault be known
To the Venetian state. – Come, bring him away.

OTHELLO Soft, you; a word or two, before you go.
I have done the state some service, and they know
No more of that. – I pray you, in your letters,
When you shall these unlucky deeds relate,
Speak of me as I am; nothing extenuate,
Nor set down aught in malice: then must you speak
Of one that lov'd not wisely, but too well;
Of one not easily jealous, but, being wrought,
Perplex'd in the extreme; of one, whose hand,
Like the base Indian, threw a pearl away,
Richer than all his tribe; of one, whose subdu'd eyes,
Albeit unused to the melting mood,
Drop tears as fast as the Arabian trees
Their medicinable gum. Set you down this;
And say, besides, that in Aleppo once,
Where a malignant and a turban'd Turk
Beat a Venetian, and traduc'd the state,

I took by the throat the circumcised dog,
And smote him – thus. *[Stabs himself.*

LODOVICO O bloody period!

GRATIANO All that's spoke is marr'd.

OTHELLO I kiss'd thee, ere I kill'd thee: – no way but this,
[Falling upon Desdemona.
Killing myself to die upon a kiss. *[Dies.*

CASSIO This did I fear, but thought he had no weapon;
For he was great of heart.

LODOVICO *[To Iago.]* O Spartan dog!
More fell than anguish, hunger, or the sea!
Look on the tragic loading of this bed;
This is thy work: the object poisons sight;
Let it be hid. – Gratiano, keep the house,
And seize upon the fortunes of the Moor,
For they succeed on you. – To you, lord governor,
Remains the censure of this hellish villain;
The time, the place, the torture: – O, enforce it!
Myself will straight aboard, and to the state
This heavy act with heavy heart relate. *[Exeunt.*